Dreams by Starlight

Published by:
Spirit Light Publishing

Printed in the United States of America

Cover Design by KDJ Outsourcing
design@kdjoutsourcing.com

Library of Congress Cataloging-in-Publication Data is available upon request

ISBN

978-0-6151-5326-1

Publisher's Note: This is a work of fiction. Names, places, characters, and incidents either are the product of the author's imagination or are used fictitiously, and any resemblance to actual persons, living or dead, events, or locales is entirely coincidental.

Dreams by Starlight

Staci Stallings

To anyone who has a dream, given by God,
Entwined within your heart.
Never let anyone talk you out of it. It is a gift given,
A destiny inscribed by God
Written in the stars
Embodied in you.

"Any suggestions?" Jaylon asked, tilting his head to the side to look at her.

"Umm, I don't know. Classes?" Camille asked, feeling the pained look cross her face as her hand tugged at the heel of her shoe.

"Okay." He paused a beat. "Umm, you have to look at me, remember?"

"Oh, y-yeah." She stumbled over the words as she forced her gaze back to his.

Looking back at her, his gaze held only sincere interest. "So, what's your favorite class?"

She smiled as her entire body instantly relaxed. "Math."

"Math?" he asked in surprise.

"Yeah. Why? Is that so hard to believe?"

"Well, no. I guess not, but I hate math." He ran his fingers through his hair to push it back out of his face. "I'm just surprised anybody likes it."

"You hate it?" she asked, forgetting this was supposed to be hard. "But it's so fascinating."

"Fascinating? I can think of another word for it," he said, wrinkling his nose.

"Oh, yeah? What's that?"

"Torture."

She laughed and shook her head. "No, now you're talking about drama."

"Huh?" he asked, and her gaze dropped from his to her shoestrings.

With a shove she forced her gaze back up although this time it didn't lock on his. Instead it wandered around the stage and the auditorium at the other partners.

"How can you not like drama?" he asked in genuine confusion. "Drama is awesome."

Her eyebrows raised as she looked back at him in open-eyed mortification. "Not when you're me. It isn't."

<u>Chapter 1</u>

Grateful for the minimal shield her wire-rimmed copper and gold glasses afforded, Camille Wright sat in the counselor's office digging her fingernails into her palms and praying that things could get no worse.

"I have to be honest, Camille," Gerald Marsh said as he shook his head, streaked with gray and silver. "I am looking at this, and I'm saying to myself, 'Okay, she's got the grades, but I want somebody with something other than just academic abilities." He held up her transcript. "I see nothing here that leads me to believe you would do well with anything other than books."

Camille let the long, limp strands of her dead-weed, dull hair fall into her face as her shoulders shrank over her chest. "I thought that was a good thing."

"It is, but so are other things—like speaking and sports and music," Mr. Marsh said. "I'm just saying if you'd take a class that's not purely academic, it'd sure help your chances of getting into Princeton."

She didn't say anything—she couldn't. Her stomach was wound around the air in her lungs so tightly that even breathing was asking too much of her system.

Mr. Marsh held the class schedule across the desk so she could see it. "I was thinking you could choose between debate and drama."

"How about Journalism?" Camille asked, her voice squeaking on the word.

He shook his head. "You're not hearing me. You need something where you have to get up in front of people."

"Band," she said quietly as her finger pushed back her hair and then let if fall back exactly where it had been.

"The marching band has already been on the field working for three weeks, and the symphonic band is your only other option." His narrowed eyes surveyed her. "But if I'm not mistaken you don't even play an instrument."

"I could play the tambourine or something. That can't be too hard."

Slowly he looked at the transcript on his desk and then back up at her. "Drama or debate?"

It sounded like a death sentence. She didn't want to do either. She wanted to take another math class or computers, anything other than the two classes staring at her from that class schedule.

Her gaze finally dropped back to her fingernails. "Drama."

"Good." Mr. Marsh wrote the course choice on her schedule. "Now, about your SAT scores."

"Hey, it's J.P. and Ariana, back from summer vacation," Seth Taylor said, ambling up to his locker with his black and gold backpack slung over his shoulder.

"It's the S man," Jaylon Patrick Quinn said, raising his hand, which Seth immediately hit in greeting. "Senior year. Can you believe we finally made it?"

"Are you kidding? I was born for senior year." Seth's arm stuck out from under his off-white-and-red plaid, button-down shirt as he opened his locker and shoved his belongings into it. "How about you, Ari? You excited about this new adventure?"

Putting a long, slender hand to her mouth, Ariana Vandivere yawned as if she had never been so bored.

Jaylon laughed. He laid one arm across her shoulders and shifted his books to his other hip. "So what do you have first thing?"

"Chemistry," Seth said as an annoyed smirk crossed his freckled features. "You?"

He hadn't even been yet, and Jaylon was already tired of it. "English."

"English?" Seth raised his red-blonde eyebrows. "Yikes."

Jaylon shrugged. "You have English sometime, too. Don't you?"

"I wouldn't know. I haven't looked that far down my schedule yet."

Jaylon shook his head, causing his feathery brown locks to fall across his eye. Retrieving his hand from her shoulders, he swooped his hair back as the tall, leggy brunette by his side yawned again.

Seth laughed. "You know, Ari, if I didn't know better, I'd think you didn't get enough sleep last night." He slammed his locker just as the bell sounded above them.

With a kick, Jaylon pushed away from the lockers. "Let the agony begin."

"Maybe I could go to the nurse's station and tell them I'm sick," Camille said, actually feeling more sick than well at the moment.

"For the whole year?" Lexie Everson, Camille's best friend, asked with a shake of her head. "I don't think that'll work."

Camille's slender shoulders sank even lower until they almost touched the table. "There has to be some way out of this. I mean, drama? Ugh."

After a slow survey of her friend, Lexie shook her head and laughed.

Camille narrowed her eyes in frustration at her friend. "What?"

"You act like you're being sent to the gas chamber."

"I am," Camille said pitifully as the table pulled her head all the way down.

"It could be worse." Lexie's cocoa-colored hand brought another bite to her mouth, and she ate that bite while Camille's mind searched through its files trying to find anything that could conceivably be worse. "Marsh could've signed you up for debate."

Camille lifted her head only inches from the table. "Ha. Ha."

Lexie's almond eyes gazed back at her friend playfully and then caught on movement by the cafeteria doors. Her shoulders did a slow seductive relaxation at the sight. "Besides any class where you can look at Jaylon Quinn all period is okay in my books."

Camille glanced over her shoulder at the strong face, framed by the wispy, brown hair that seemed disheveled and perfect at the same time, and she shook her head. Still watching him cross the cafeteria, a flicker of hope slipped through her. "The only good thing is, with Ariana around, I don't have a prayer of getting anything more than a line or two."

"True," Lexie said, and then she looked at her friend and shrugged. "So don't worry about it. They'll probably put you on make-up detail or something."

Her mind said she should be offended by the comment, but Camille's heart hoped that the universe would be so kind. "From your mouth to God's ears."

"Class," Mrs. Allen called from the stage as students milled about the auditorium. She clapped twice in a vain attempt to get their attention. "Please, come on up and take your seats."

With an exasperated shake of her head, Camille pushed away from the shadow she was hoping to hide in for the next year. Keeping her gaze on her feet, which were swathed in darkness somewhere beneath her, she walked down the center aisle and slipped into a fourth row seat. The majority of the class sat in the first three rows until it was clear that she and two other similarly be-speckled and reluctant thespians would be the only ones in the fourth row.

"Good." Mrs. Allen, a forty-ish ex-dancer with cinnamon-colored skin and a voice that seemed to come from her toes, moved like grace personified from the edge of the auditorium to the center. "I'd like to welcome you all to Theatre Production. I'm sure we are going to have a wonderful year together. First, I'd like to go over the ground rules."

Camille studied the chipped peach paint on her fingernails. No matter how hard she tried, she could never keep polish on them. She forced her attention back to the stage.

"...and no matter what, remember that every person is here to learn. There will be no making fun of anyone. Is that understood?" Mrs. Allen's gaze swept across her audience.

In front of Camille, heads nodded, and although she was in the back, it felt like every gaze in the auditorium was on her. With her around, the others would have plenty of laugh material. She closed her eyes, slid further down into the seat, and pursed her lips together trying to remember why it was she was here.

"Good. Now, I'd like you all to come up onto the stage," Mrs. Allen said, pulling them forward with welcoming arms that looked like a willow trees branches blowing in the wind.

Students stood, filed out of the rows, up the steps, and onto the stage. They stood in various spots around the stage shifting their feet and their gazes nervously even though there wasn't a soul left in the audience.

"Okay, we're going to start with breathing exercises." Mrs. Allen pulled her body and shoulders up a full inch.

Camille swallowed and pushed up her glasses. Breathing. That couldn't be too hard.

An hour later when Camille walked out of the auditorium after stuffing her new drama book into her backpack along with the others, she fought to stay invisible in the middle of a crush of students. The air flowing into her lungs stung.

"So, how was it?" Lexie asked as Camille grabbed most of her books out of her locker.

"Awful."

"Really? What did you do?" Lexie asked with concern.

Making as much noise as possible, Camille slammed two books back into the locker. "We breathed for a whole hour."

Lexie raised her jet-black eyebrows. "Yeah, that sounds like real torture."

"I know how to breathe." Camille swung her backpack to her shoulder angrily. "I've been doing it for 17 years now."

"So, great, an easy A then."

"Yeah, real easy," Camille said just as Lexie grabbed her arm in a death grip. "Hey. That hurts."

"It's him." Lexie's eyes widened into two full moons as she gazed down the hallway.

Camille looked in the direction Lexie was staring and shook her head. Jaylon Quinn. He was good-looking but really, he wasn't a god or anything. "Come on."

"Where are we going?" Lexie asked in surprise.

"Single dipped cones on me. To celebrate making it through our first day of senior year."

"I'd like everyone to get a partner," Mrs. Allen said the next afternoon as Camille and the rest of the class stood on stage. Very few were even brave enough to make eye contact. "We're going to practice mirroring."

A collective groan went up from the group, and Camille looked around wondering what mirroring was and knowing at the same time it would be far worse than breathing.

"Want to partner?" a nice looking blonde-headed guy, who suddenly stood at her elbow, asked.

Camille pushed at her hair with her finger and shrugged. "Whatever."

"Okay." Mrs. Allen walked among her charges. "The object of this exercise is to create a perfect mirror for your partner. Choose which of you will go first, and the other person is to match their partner's body language and facial expression as perfectly as you can. Basically, you are to be your partner's mirror. You may begin."

The blonde-headed guy who was at least six inches taller than Camille glanced at her shyly. "Umm, you want to go first, or should I?"

"I don't care. You can—if you want," Camille said, looking around at their fellow-students who were already well into the exercise.

"Okay," her partner said with a small smile. He struck an innocent pose with his head slightly tilted to the side.

Camille cocked her own head and watched him for his next cue. Slowly he raised his arms in a stretch and then bent to one side, which she followed to perfection. It felt strange to be only inches from someone she didn't know but even more strange was watching that person without being able to look away. They both came back to the center, and her arms followed his down.

Her entire concentration was focused on him—not as a person but as her own reflection. He put his arms out at his sides and twisted, an action that baffled her for a moment as she started to turn in the same direction he did and then realized that a mirror would turn the other way. Immediately she reversed her course, just as he reversed his. Her body jerked from the fluidity of the previous moment, and the concentration dropped from her grasp.

She squeezed her eyes closed trying to get it back, but when she opened them again, her partner was doing a cross-body toe-touch that she had somehow missed. Quickly she tried to imitate him just as he straightened back up meeting the top of her forehead on the way down.

The crack of her skull sent tiny white pulses spiraling through it. "Oww!" she yelped, backing away from her partner but her heel snagged on the student behind her and before she realized what was happening the hardwood stage floor was rushing toward her. "Ahh!"

In less than a heartbeat she hit the wooden slats with a thud. For a minute she didn't know what part of her body hurt worse—her head or her tailbone. In the next breath, however, she realized that every other person on the stage was staring at her.

Like a displeased drill sergeant Mrs. Allen walked up as several students around the stage snickered. "What's going on over here?"

"I'm sorry," Camille's partner said, clutching his own head as he offered Camille a hand up. "I didn't see her coming down."

Mrs. Allen regarded them with a look that could've cut glass. "You see, class, this is a perfect example of what happens when you break concentration on stage for even a second." She planted both hands on her hips and shook her head in annoyance. "Learn from this people."

She walked away from the disaster as Camille scrambled to her feet and resumed her place in front of her partner. Once there, however, she had to blink twice to get her head to stop spinning.

Her partner leaned in to her. "Sorry about that."

"Don't worry about it," she whispered back, brushing her jeans off and readjusting her glasses as she willed the heat pulsing through her ears to subside. "It was my fault."

"Okay," Mrs. Allen said with a clap of her hands. "I see that mirroring is a little advanced for the second day, so we're just going to try to do some more breathing exercises. Maybe we'll try this again next week."

Oh, good, Camille thought. *Something to look forward to.*

"Hey." The blonde-headed guy sprinted up the aisle to Camille's side as she tried to make a quick exit. "I didn't catch your name."

Her spirit surrendered to the mortification. "Why would you want it?"

"That was an accident," he said, mirroring her steps through the hallway. "Besides, somebody had to break up the monotony."

"I hear you there," Camille said still walking but no longer trying to get away from him.

"So?" he asked after they had walked several steps. "I still didn't catch your name."

"Camille." She swung her braid to the other shoulder and put out a falsely positive hand. "Camille Wright."

He smiled a toothy white smile. "Well, Camille Wright. It's nice to meet you. I'm Nick. Nick McGee."

"It's nice to meet you, Nick," Camille said, wishing he hadn't just been witness to her most embarrassing moment ever.

"Well, Cami," Lexie said, apparently not realizing Camille's shadow was actually walking with her. "So, how bad was drama today?"

Heat seared over Camille's ears. "Lexie." She cleared her throat, and swung her braid in the other direction. "I'd like you to meet Nick McGee."

Camille watched as Nick stopped in the same breath that Lexie's face fell in utter shock.

"Hi," Lexie breathed as Nick took her hand and smiled.

"Hi." Their gazes locked, and for a full second Camille felt totally invisible.

"Well, I'd better get going," Nick said, finally dropping Lexie's hand but not her gaze. "I guess I'll see you tomorrow, Camille."

"Sure," Camille said, knowing neither one of them heard the word.

Nick turned and disappeared into the crowd, but Lexie never moved.

"Oh, man." Camille turned to her locker in exasperation. "That's got to be the most embarrassing thing that's ever happened to me, and for me, that's saying a lot." She looked over at Lexie who hadn't moved. "Lexie, hey!" Frustrated at having no one listening to her plight, Camille waved her hand in front of her friend's face. "You still in there?"

"Sure," Lexie said, but Camille knew Lexie hadn't even heard her own voice.

"They really should have two separate drama classes—at least." Ariana clicked her tongue in annoyance as they sat in a small booth at Sal's Place, the local kids' hangout, Friday night. "I mean really, are they kidding me, putting someone like her in a class with us? Jeez. It's the most ridiculous thing I've ever heard of."

"It was that bad?" Seth asked over his cheese fries.

"Worse," Ariana said, shaking her head.

Jaylon nodded, trying to be more diplomatic about the situation than his girlfriend but not really succeeding. "We started with breathing yesterday. Breathing. That's like preschool drama, and you should see these kids. They couldn't breathe right if someone did it for them. Does not bode well for the Spring Production from what I can see."

"Ugh! If I don't get into Julliard, my life will be over," Ariana said like the drama queen Jaylon had so gotten used to appeasing over the past three years.

"Don't worry, honey." Jaylon rested his arm over her side of the booth.

"We're going—just like we planned. Even Mrs. Allen can't mess that up."

Chapter 2

"So, are you still seeing stars?" Nick asked Camille with a laugh on Monday afternoon.

She looked up from her seat mid-way from the front of the auditorium and closed her Physics II book. "No, they left sometime Sunday night."

"You're lucky," he said with a smirk as he leaned against the chair back in front of her. "I woke up with them again this morning."

"Class!" Mrs. Allen said as she pulled a blackboard onto the stage. "Let's get started. Take out your notebooks and pens, please."

"Joy for joy," Nick said under his breath as he straightened. "Come on."

Camille stumbled to her feet and followed Nick wishing there was some way to run the other direction. He went all the way down the aisle where he turned into the third row, right. She didn't want to follow him that far forward as the fiasco from Friday continued to replay itself in her mind, but he had been so nice to her, she didn't see any other option. Carefully she wound her way into the row of seats and sat down next to him.

He laid his books on his lap as she quickly pulled her own notebook from her backpack and pulled one of the pens from behind her ear.

"Today we're going to talk about your other assignments for this class besides actual acting," Mrs. Allen said not even waiting for the class to get quiet. "First of all we're going to discuss play analysis. When you're presented with a new character to play, you take your first cues from the script. That way you don't approach a character from different angles in each scene.

"The point of playing any character—no matter how small or large the part—is to understand the motivations of that character and to convey them to the audience whether you're speaking or not." Mrs. Allen turned toward the blackboard. "Every character has a story arc that has a beginning, a middle, and an end, and each character must come to some conclusion by the end of the play, most if not all characters are changed somehow by the action of the play."

She turned back from the blackboard and began pacing the stage in front of them as all gazes followed her. "You, the actor, are responsible for making that happen in a believable, realistic fashion. One way to divine a character's motivation is to read and analyze the stage directions for that character."

Once again at the blackboard she rolled the chalk in her hands for a moment and then began copying in very small letters the words on the sheet clipped onto the board she held in the other hand. "For example, if you have these stage directions for a character: indulgent, jovial, hoarsely, fury, crying, rising, emphatic, exasperated, very annoyed, morosely, hoarsely, heavily, glare, morosely, awkward, roars, irately, very courtly, gallantly, marches off, hastily, stares, cannot hold it back, stomps, roaring, marches, hardly notice, nonplussed, uncertainly, very annoyed, outraged, astonished, endeavors to control voice, in a wrath, snatches, in a sputter of ire, with dignity, toss, marches, very angry, reluctantly, with patience, vexedly, dourly, exploding, nonplussed, frowning, red-faced, stares hard, teeth in cigar, stares, heavily, irate surrender, shakes the cigar, marches out and slams the door, grasps his wrist, twisting him half to his knees, angrily, throws him away, with contempt, stands motionless, gently, harshly, heavily, indulgent, gently, curiously, consenting, gently, smiles, offers an arm, serving, not noticing, embarrassed, gently, reasonably, testily, tolerant, angrily, glares, stare is unbelieving, even a little fascinated, gruff, mildly, goes to his knees . . . What can you tell me about this character without ever reading a single line of dialogue?"

"He's a control freak," Jaylon Quinn said from the other side of the auditorium, and immediately Camille's attention snapped to him.

"Interesting," Mrs. Allen said with a nod. "And how do you know the character is a he?"

Jaylon shrugged. "Cigar? Twisting an opponent to his knees? Offered an arm? Women don't do that kind of thing, and at the end he went to *his* knees."

"Very observant. Okay, so how do you know he's a control freak?"

"Well." Jaylon shifted in his seat and scratched the bridge of his nose. "He's alternately angry then gentle, then angry again, then gentle. And then when things really get out of his control, he sputters with ire and explodes. I think that he thinks he's really in control, but he's not."

"How can someone believe he's in control if he's really not?" Mrs. Allen asked as though she had never considered this question.

Jaylon shook his head as his gaze narrowed in concentration. "He's trying to put on this gallant, dignified front, but for some reason he feels out of control so he does everything he can to get control again."

Camille couldn't tear her gaze from Jaylon's profile across the room—

not because of the straight jaw line or the feathers of hair—but because of the depth of his words and the certainty with which he spoke them.

"Would anyone else like to add anything to that observation?" Mrs. Allen asked, looking at the rest of the class.

"I think at the end he comes to some realization," Nick said in full voice right in Camille's ear causing her to jump back to reality.

"Why do you say that?" Mrs. Allen asked.

Nick pointed his pen at the blackboard. "He goes to his knees. Someone who's a control freak doesn't go to his knees. That shows weakness, vulnerability. Control freaks refuse to be vulnerable."

"Well," Mrs. Allen said with a nod, "I'm impressed. The character the two of you just described is from a play called, *The Miracle Worker*. Has anybody heard of it?"

Most of the heads in the room nodded.

"Could someone tell me what the play is about?"

"Helen Keller," someone offered from in front of Camille.

"Good, Kara, and what was remarkable about Helen Keller?"

"She was born blind and deaf," someone else from the other side of the auditorium said.

Mrs. Allen nodded and gestured to the small letters on the blackboard. "So, is this describing Helen Keller?"

"No," several students said at once.

"Then who is it describing?" Mrs. Allen asked, and the auditorium fell silent for a beat.

"Her father," Jaylon said with a conviction that yanked Camille's gaze back to his face.

Instantly Mrs. Allen smiled. "Very good, Jaylon. Mind telling me how you came to that conclusion?"

"Well, we've already said that it's a he, so that rules out the mother. And we've said he feels out of control. I think having a blind and deaf daughter—especially if you're used to being in control of things—would make you feel out of control. It follows that it's the father."

Mrs. Allen's head fell in respect. "You see. You haven't read a single line of the play, and yet look how much you know about this character." She laid the chalk in the tray and rubbed her hands together. "That will be your first assignment. In your books, the first play is *The Glass Menagerie* by Tennessee Williams. Your assignment is to choose one character and read through only the stage directions for that character, picking out words that describe motivation. Then I want you to write a 400-word paper describing that character based solely on his or her stage cues."

Camille wrote the assignment in her notebook.

"This is due Friday when you walk into class," Mrs. Allen said, and

Camille transferred that information to her notebook as well just as the bell rang.

In surprise she looked at her watch, having not realized so much time had evaporated. She closed her notebook, shoved it into her backpack, and stood.

Nick swung his own backpack to his shoulder and stood. "You going to your locker?"

"Uh, yeah," Camille said as she pulled the backpack to her shoulder.

"Mind if I tag along?" Nick asked, following her out of the row.

She shrugged not really seeing a good reason to tell him no, and together they walked out of the auditorium. In the hallway, students rushed in a myriad of directions around them.

"That was some class," Nick finally said after they were halfway down the hall.

"Yeah. I never realized you could get so much information from the stage directions. I thought they were just like there. You know?"

Nick nodded just as they reached her locker.

"Hey, Lex," Camille said to her friend who turned and immediately froze. "I missed you at lunch."

"Yeah," Lexie said never so much as glancing at her friend.

Camille looked back from her locker and raised a concerned eyebrow. The two of them looked like they'd just been transported to an alternate universe where other students weren't jostling them like a liquid in a blender. She shook her head. "So, are we going to my place or not?"

"Umm, yeah, of course," Lexie said, and Camille was sure Lexie had no idea what she'd just agreed to.

"Great." Camille yanked her backpack from the floor and pulled three more books out of her locker. "Then let's go." She took hold of Lexie's arm and turned her toward the door. "We'll see you later, Nick."

"Okay," he said as if he was talking to a ghost. "See ya."

Camille was nearly at the bus stop before she let Lexie's arm go. However, she knew with only one look at her friend that if she let her out of her sight, Lexie might end up at the far ends of the earth and never be found again.

Wordlessly, they walked to the city bus stop, mounted the steps, and rode to Camille's stop. Every so often Camille would look over at Lexie and shake her head. She had never seen Lexie like this—not in ten years, and although she would never have admitted it to anyone, it scared her. With one look at some mildly good-looking boy, her friend had completely forgotten she even existed. Her gaze found the back of the bus seat and then the floorboard.

Reflexively she pulled her books down to look over her homework for the evening. The first book her glance chanced on was *Experiments in Drama*, and she smiled. If everyday could be like today, she could almost envision herself enjoying the class. If they just didn't have to get on stage. She pushed that thought away and grabbed her Chemistry II book. Important things first.

Camille managed to stay out of Mrs. Allen's sights the whole week, and on Friday she laid her paper on the stack of others being sent to the center aisle. She shrank back into the darkness of the seats, praying they wouldn't have to go on stage today. Out here, in the darkness was where she belonged—more than that, it was the only place in the auditorium where her body knew what to do.

On stage it was as if everyone in the whole world was looking at her, waiting for her to fall on her face again. It frazzled her nerves to the point that crashing off the stage into the front row was not an improbability.

"I thought we'd take a little break today and play wink murder," Mrs. Allen said from her perch on the center of the stage.

Camille shifted in her seat. 'Wink' sounded okay, but 'murder' could be a problem.

"I want you all to come up here." Mrs. Allen pushed her hands under her and vaulted to her feet as her students filed slowly up onto the stage. "Now, I want you all to sit in a circle facing each other."

"I bet they don't do this at Julliard," the tall reed-thin girl with the blunt-cut, barely shoulder length, just-lighter-than-ebony hair that Camille recognized as Ariana Vandivere said as she folded herself onto the floor theatrically. Her creamy white skin coupled with the severe straight skirt told Camille with one look that Ariana hadn't sat on many floors. Right next to drama queen, Jaylon Quinn knelt and then sat without so much as a word of complaint, and it occurred to Camille that he could make planting petunias on Neptune look perfectly realistic.

Giggles sounded around Camille as she forced her gaze away from Ariana and Jaylon. A picture of him shrouded in a dim auditorium expounding on the intricacies of a fearful father flooded her mind. Quickly she pushed that thought away too and straightened her jeans that were a bit too tight for sitting on floors.

"The object of this game is for the murderer to kill everyone in the circle before someone else guesses who the murderer is." Mrs. Allen handed out regular playing cards around the assembled circle, her voice taking on the air of a Masterpiece Theatre narrator. "The murderer kills people by winking at them, but he or she does it in such a way so as to not get caught by anyone else. When you get winked at, you must die—in whatever manner you choose. All I ask is that when you die you don't hurt yourself or anyone else."

Nervous laughter flitted across the group as they sat looking at each other.

"If you catch the murderer, you get a bonus five points on your analysis paper. If you are the murderer, and you do not get caught, you receive ten points. If you die, you're out of luck."

Camille sat up straighter with the raising of the stakes.

"Now, I want you to look at your card, but don't show it to anyone else. If you have the ace of spades, you are the murderer. Good luck everyone. You may begin."

Uneasy gazes flitted from face-to-face as Camille surveyed each face in the group. Most were merely average, a few more striking, and one of them was now a murderer. A shriek erupted right next to her, and Camille turned just in time to watch Nick fall over—dead from a wink.

She steeled her nerves, swallowed the ridiculous trepidation that jumped into her chest, and looked back at the group. After several heart-stopping moments a gasp sounded across the room, and immediately another student slumped forward. Camille's attention was locked on the fallen girl just long enough for another student at her left to clutch his chest and wheeze his final breath. Her mind fought to remind her nerves that this was just a game, but her nerves weren't getting the message.

"AAHHHH!" one student yelled, jumping to his feet and running for the stairs where he stumbled forward, then backward two steps before falling dead on the top step.

More nervous laughter surrounded her as Camille looked over the "dead" bodies into the eyes of each of the remaining students. A scream yanked her attention to the girl sitting right next to her and then another sounded across the room, and she watched Jaylon fall forward, where he twitched for a moment before falling still.

"It's Mark," a girl from her right shrieked.

"Shoot!" Mark slapped his hands on the stage as everyone laughed.

"Good job, Tessa." Mrs. Allen stood and beckoned to the boy still draped over the top stair. "Keane, you can come back now." She dealt out another round of cards, and the game began again.

Tony, Jill, Darrin, Cathy, Stephanie. One-by-one they were each unmasked before they could fell more than a few victims. However, by the end of class they were facing the craftiest murderer yet. Fourteen students lay dead on the floor already—only five remained, four potential victims, and one killer. The bell rang, but not a single student in the auditorium moved.

Camille's nerves jumped to the surface as she felt Nick's shoulder brush hers. The two of them were locked in a deadly hunt. She could feel it.

She fought to keep her gaze on the faces in the circle.

"That's the bell," Mrs. Allen said, standing when it seemed no one else had heard it.

"No," Nick said instantly. "We want to finish this."

Without taking her gaze off her adversaries, Camille nodded. One at a time, she scrutinized the remaining male faces—Nick, the blonde hair, the blue eyes; Mark, buzz-cut red hair and freckles framing the hazel eyes; Jaylon, the high cheekbones rising beneath the steel hard eyes; and Keane, the ash blonde hair moused to attention above playful mischievous green eyes. Just then as she watched him, Keane's face contorted in horror.

"Oh! OH! OH!" Keane screamed in a voice that would've shattered the eardrums of a person in the back row had there been one.

Camille's gaze locked for a single moment on Jaylon's profile—it was the direction Keane had been looking just before his demise. His eye fell closed—killing Mark just as Camille and Nick jumped up simultaneously.

"It's Jaylon!" they both shouted, pointing at him from across the circle and pulling all gazes to them.

Jaylon's gaze snapped to them as Camille shrank behind Nick for shelter from the searing look.

"Very good." Mrs. Allen came toward the circle clapping. "But I guess the two of you'll have to split the five points."

Nick shrugged and put his hand up for Camille. "We win! Good job."

"Thanks." Awkwardness leaped over her as she reached up to slap his hand but barely touched it instead.

"Have a good weekend, everyone," Mrs. Allen called as the students filed off the stage and out of the auditorium.

"Good job." Jaylon extended his hand to Nick without bothering to address Camille.

"Thanks," Nick said as he descended the stairs. "I was starting to think we had a master killer on our hands."

Jaylon nodded respectfully. "But you brought me down anyway."

Nick grabbed his books from the seats. "Yeah. Better luck next time."

At the door Ariana joined them, and Jaylon draped a casual arm over her shoulder. "So, you want to join us for some after-school beverages at Sal's?"

Camille shrank even farther back, cowering behind her books. She knew the invitation did not include her.

"No can do," Nick said with a shake of his head. "Camille and I already have plans. Isn't that right, Camille?"

In utter shock Camille looked at him and then readjusted her glasses. "Oh, umm, sure. We're going... to the... umm, library." It was all she could think of, but once it was out of her mouth, she knew how lame that sounded.

"Oh, well." Ariana fanned out her long, straight hair and smiled the fakest smile Camille had ever seen. "That's too bad."

"Yeah," Jaylon said, looking at Camille as though she had just appeared there out of thin air. "Too bad."

Camille's gaze searched the near-empty hallway for anything resembling shelter as the tips of her ears went red-hot.

"Well, we'd better get." Nick took hold of Camille's arm and steered her in the other direction. "We'll see you guys Monday."

Jaylon shrugged once and then turned in the other direction.

Her mind was in turmoil. "Do you mind telling to me what just happened?"

Nick sighed. His face went hard as he dropped her arm. "They're jerks." Dismissively he shook his head. "They think they own the whole darn place and everybody in it. It just gets to me sometimes."

Camille nodded her complete understanding of that fact. Then she scratched her braid. "Mind if I ask you something else?"

"Sure," he said, glancing at her as they walked.

"How did you know I wasn't the killer?"

"Oh, that's easy." A smile broke over his face. "You were sitting too close to me for it to have been you."

Her gaze dropped to the floor in embarrassment as she thought back to the stage and realized that they had been shoulder-to-shoulder although the stage was big enough to get thirty people between them if need be. Instantly the fire seared across her ears.

"Besides, Jaylon's the only one I know that could kill that many people without getting caught," Nick said as they approached Camille's locker.

"What's that supposed to mean?" Camille asked.

Nick shrugged. "I just know how he operates." Then he turned his attention to Lexie who was already leaning against the lockers watching them. "Hey, Lexie. How was your day?"

"Other than I'll never get all of this homework done, pretty good," Lexie said with a shy smile.

Camille threw her stuff into her locker and pulled out everything she needed for the weekend. With a swing she mounted the backpack on her shoulder and grabbed her other books. The only thing left in her locker was her drama book.

"Jeez, Camille," Nick said just as she slammed her locker closed. "Do you always take all your books home?"

She looked down at the books in her hands as her shoulders slumped over them. "I'm a little behind."

Nick raised an eyebrow at that and shook his head before shrugging. "Well, take care, you two. I'll see you Monday."

"'K. See ya," Camille said, wishing she could wave but not daring to even try it.

They stood in the middle of the empty hallway and watched him walk away.

"He's nice," Camille finally said as she turned for the door.

"Ugh," Lexie said as though Camille didn't have a clue. "He's more than nice. He's dreamy. So what do you know about him anyway? Is he going with anybody?"

"I don't know. We just kind of ended up together in drama. I know he's a senior, and he's been in drama since freshman year. That's about it."

Lexie wrinkled her face in annoyance as they mounted the bus steps. "You've spent two weeks with the dreamiest guy in school, and you didn't even bother to find out if he's going with anyone? What kind of moron are you anyway?"

"The kind who's not going to ask for you if you don't start being nice to me," Camille said with a smirk.

"Oh, would you?" Lexie actually bounced in her seat. "And find out about his family, too."

"Well, what do you want me to do, run a background check on the guy?"

Lexie's eyes widened. "Could you?"

Camille looked at her friend and laughed. "I'll find out as much as I can."

The Community Center was jammed with kids when Jaylon strode through the door Saturday morning. So far his plan was working to perfection. Ariana's idea of fun Saturday entertainment was walking though the mall until your feet fell off, and he had long-since begged off of that scene. Seth was usually busy with either his car or someone else's, and Seth had decided long ago that having Jaylon around anything mechanical meant several extra hours spent fixing everything Jaylon broke, so Seth no longer even asked.

In fact, although he and Seth had become friends in third grade, when they hit high school, that friendship had changed. Each of them had found their own paths, and their friendship transformed from spending every, single waking moment together to just spending time together when the opportunity presented itself, which didn't seem nearly as often anymore.

That void had been filled by Ariana, and to Jaylon, that was just fine. He had a friend who never demanded anything and a girlfriend who demanded everything. They were a perfect fit.

"Jaylon," Mrs. Dixon, his direct supervisor, said with a glint in her eye. "The kids are so excited about this."

"They're ready?" he asked, trying not to sound like his heart might burst out of his chest at any moment.

"Yeah, they're already on the stage. You've got about 18 of them signed up. Are you sure you'll be able to handle that many?"

"Piece of cake," he said with a confident smile.

"Great." Mrs. Dixon handed him the list. "I'm here if you need anything."

Jaylon nodded and walked casually to the auditorium. Dressed in black pants, suspenders, and a gray-and-white striped shirt topped with a burgundy tie not to mention towering over the elementary kids, he looked every bit the part of the new teacher in town although he had never taught a class in his life.

"Please have a seat on the stage." His stage voice boomed through the auditorium. He looked over the kids who would be his charges for the next semester if all went well as they found a seat and got quiet. Jaylon had to fight not to laugh at how serious and awestruck they all looked. "I have a list of your names, but instead of reading it, I'd like for each of you to stand, say your name, and tell us your favorite thing to do." He surveyed the circle. "Let's start over here."

With heads ducked and gazes glued to the floor, the students stood one by one and introduced themselves. As they did, Jaylon checked the name they gave against the list, listened for their favorite things, and then matched the two pieces of information with the face. Once all of the children were finished, Jaylon walked around the circle, and the gazes followed him.

"And my name is Jaylon Patrick Quinn." When he reached the opposite side of the circle, he sat down. "My favorite thing to do is to get up on stage and make audiences happy. Who can tell me what an audience is?"

Several hands went up.

"Katelyn?" Jaylon asked a small round-faced kid with a huge pink bow in her hair.

"It's the people who aren't on stage," Katelyn said.

"Very good. And can someone tell me what the people on the stage are called?"

Hands went up all around him.

"Cory?"

"Actors."

"Very good," Jaylon said. "Boy, I have a smart class."

Soft giggles wafted around him.

"Today we're going to practice being actors who can't talk," Jaylon said. "It's called pantomime. I'll show you how to do it first, and then I'll let you try."

Two hours later Jaylon was having the time of his life working to get out of an imaginary box when the parents started to show up to retrieve their kids. He heard the kids talking non-stop about the morning as their parents led them out, and he smiled. Volunteering had been a good idea.

When the last child had been collected, he walked back out to the office and told Mrs. Dixon he was leaving. On his way out of the building, he checked his watch. 12:25. He had more than two hours before he had to be at Ariana's. That was plenty of time to make his other stop of the day.

His metallic navy Camaro Z28 flashed through the streets of Ridgecrest, New York, as he crossed town to the Hollybrook Care Center where he whipped into a parking spot with the precision of hundreds of practice runs. He grabbed the book on the passenger's seat, hopped out, and strode across the parking lot and into the building where he greeted the receptionist.

"Elana will be happy to see you," the receptionist said as he signed the guest book.

With a smile he stepped over to the elevator and punched the button. The elevator dinged, and the doors slid open. He stepped on and punched the button for the basement. When the doors opened again, the smell of a place too sterile invaded his nostrils.

The pace of his steps increased on the white tile until they brought him right up to a set of heavy double doors. He punched in the code and then pushed through the doors. He had rounded still another corner before he met anyone.

"Good afternoon, Mr. Gosa," Jaylon said to the man bent over a walker taking steps so tiny it seemed that he wasn't moving at all. "How are you today?"

"Humph," the old man said, peering for a moment into Jaylon's eyes.

"Yeah. I'm here to see Grandma. Have you seen her lately?"

"Humph," Mr. Gosa said again.

"Oh, well, I'll be sure to tell her you said that." Jaylon laid a gentle hand on the old man's shoulder. "You take care of yourself. Okay?"

"Humph."

Jaylon walked past the man and into Hollybrook's Alzheimer's Wing.

"Hey." He leaned on the nurse's station desk with both elbows. "How's everything?"

"Elana's in the sitting room," Ms. Lawson, the ebony-black head nurse, said with a smile.

"Got it." Jaylon pushed away from the desktop and ambled through the unit to the little room that overlooked the garden outside. There, in a wheelchair wrapped in her worn pink and yellow afghan, sat his grandmother. "Good afternoon, Beautiful."

He bent and kissed her cheek, and she looked up at him with unseeing eyes.

"Mr. Gosa said to say, 'Hi' when I came in." Jaylon leaned in closer to her ear. "I think he has a thing for you."

His grandmother just stared at him.

"Look what I brought." He held up a thin volume of Shakespeare's sonnets with a wink. "Just for you." Carefully he sat down on one of the vacant chairs and opened the book. "I think we left off with number 71."

Chapter 3

"Three sisters?" Camille asked Nick with an interested nod. "Wow. That must be tough to get bathroom time in the morning."

Nick shrugged next to her in the dim theatre seats. "My two older sisters are already gone, so it's not too bad."

"And your mom and dad?" Camille plowed through her list of carefully constructed questions.

"Dad's an architect. Mom stays home and takes care of us."

"Huh," Camille said with a smirk. "Tough gig."

"Hey." Nick frowned. "I'm easy to take care of. I make my own bed, wash my own clothes—when they get piled up too high on my floor, and I even cook once in awhile."

"Impressive," Camille said, thinking of the million meals she had cooked for her mom and her little sister, Daria, over the years. "I bet your girlfriend is thrilled."

Nick laughed and shook his head.

"No?" Camille asked in horror. "What is she insane?"

"Non-existent would be a better word for it," Nick said. "Drama and choir take up too much time to have a girlfriend."

"So you're not looking?"

"I'm not not looking. I'm just not looking."

"Okay," Camille said with a confused shake of her head. "So, what you're saying is if a girl like drops out of the sky onto your lap, then maybe you'd consider it?"

He laughed. "Yeah. Something like that."

"Good afternoon class," Mrs. Allen said, rolling the chalkboard out. "If you'll all gather down here, we'll go ahead and get started."

After class Lexie was waiting for them at the lockers, and the second they walked up, Camille thought again about the girl dropping from the sky. Nick might not have realized it yet, but one had done exactly that.

"Hi, Lexie," he said with a soft smile.

"Hi," she said as her almond gaze turned down. "How was drama?"

"Good," Nick said, but his voice faded out midway through the word.

Camille transferred her books in her locker as she fought to keep from laughing. Romeo and Juliet couldn't have been more love-struck. When she unburied her head from her locker, they were still standing there, neither saying anything but clearly that wasn't a problem.

"Well, Nick," Camille said, only semi-successful in her attempt to get his attention away from her friend. "I'll see you in class tomorrow?"

"Sure," Nick said, never even glancing at Camille. Then he shook his head and looked right at her. "Sure. Umm, I'd better go." He turned and quickly strode away from the lockers.

He was out of sight before Lexie turned to Camille. "Tell me everything."

"Just as each character has a beginning, middle, and end," Mrs. Allen said, tapping her chalk on her opposite hand. "So does the play itself. First the conflict is established, complications arise from that conflict—sometimes called rising action—followed by a climax, and then the denouement, or resolution. Each part is important to the action. Would someone like to take us through these steps using Jack and the Beanstalk?"

"The conflict is that Jack finds some magic beans that make a beanstalk, and he climbs it," Nick said without bothering to raise his hand.

"It's complicated by the fact that at the top, he finds a giant who wants to eat him," Mark said from in front of Camille. "The rising action would be the giant chasing Jack through the sky kingdom to the beanstalk. The climax would be him following Jack down."

"And the resolution," Camille said, somehow finding her voice, "would be when Jack chops the beanstalk down and kills the giant."

"Exactly," Mrs. Allen said. "Most of literature follows this pattern, and this is the pattern I want you to begin to see. Your next written assignment is to take the play *Ghosts* by Henrick Ibsen and map the conflict, the rising action, the climax, and the resolution. 500 words. The paper is due Friday."

Camille wrote the assignment and the date down in her notebook carefully as Mrs. Allen rolled the blackboard away.

"Today we're going to work on establishing a voice. Come on up."

With great effort and trepidation Camille got to her feet and followed Nick up the stairs.

"I want you to choose a partner and have a seat on the floor."

Nick looked at Camille with a smile, and she smiled back, amazed that he hadn't gone running from the auditorium the first day when she'd almost cracked his head open.

"Now, I want you to choose a nursery rhyme, any one that you remember the entire thing." Mrs. Allen positioned herself in the middle of the stage and looked around at her students. "You got it? Good. I want you to tell your partner what it is."

"Little Boy Blue," Nick said without hesitation.

"Humpty Dumpty," Camille said not quite meeting Nick's steady gaze.

"Okay," Mrs. Allen said. "I want you to choose three types of voices—like angry, sad, fearful, indifferent, joyous, pleading. Got them?"

Camille nodded as she shifted her weight first one way and then the other trying to find a comfortable position on the hardwood floor.

"I want one partner to choose a voice," Mrs. Allen said.

Nick looked at Camille as a silent conversation passed between them. 'I'll take it,' his gaze finally said. "Sad."

"Now," Mrs. Allen said, "I want the other partner to say the rhyme that you chose in the voice your partner has chosen for you."

Instantly Camille's fear shield flew up, and she wished someone would yell fire so she didn't have to do this.

"You may begin," Mrs. Allen said.

With one, small shift Nick focused his complete attention on Camille, a move, which sent her gaze careening for a safe place to rest. She looked at him and attempted a smile, which never quite made it to her face, and then she relocated her gaze to the hardwood floor.

"Umm, Humpty Dumpty sat on a wall," she said softly. "Humpty Dumpty had a great fall. All the king's horses and all the king's men couldn't put Humpty Dumpty back together again."

After a moment the murmurs of nursery rhymes around her stopped.

"Now, partners, I want you to give your partner feedback. How could they improve on their performance?"

Camille sighed and closed her eyes against the humiliation already rising in her chest. That was without a doubt the worst performance of Humpty Dumpty ever uttered. After several moments when Nick had said nothing, she opened her eyes and found him smiling at her.

"I think you can do better," he said, and his eyes were soft and gentle. "Why don't you try it again?"

"Okay," Camille squeaked out. "Sad, right?"

Nick nodded, and she forced herself to concentrate on the rhyme as she started over. It took three times before Nick finally decided her version was sad enough. With a sigh of relief, she chose a voice for him and watched in fascination as Little Boy Blue suddenly became a raging, angry storm at her command and then a gentle, lilting lullaby in the next breath. After two more renditions, she attempted Humpty Dumpty again, first in a fearful voice and then in a happy one, and both were better than the sad one had been earlier.

When the bell rang, Nick vaulted to his feet and offered her a hand up, which she accepted. Once on her feet she readjusted her glasses, twisted her hair over her shoulder, and then made her way off the stage thanking anyone listening for the blessing of having Nick by her side.

"Don't forget to read *Ghosts*," Mrs. Allen called from the stage.

They were all the way to the door before Camille remembered her mission for Lexie. "So, Nick, how's choir?"

"Great," he said, obviously happy that she remembered. "We're working on Beethoven's Choral Fantasia right now."

"Oh?" Camille said, genuinely interested. "What part do you sing?"

"Baritone."

"How long have you been into singing and performing?"

"Since I was little. I've been in a few community plays. Nothing major."

"And you've been in all the plays here at school. Right?"

"Yeah, but that's just one a year." He shrugged. "And I've never had more than a few lines in anything."

Camille nodded as they approached the lockers. "Did you know that Lexie used to take ballet?"

"Ballet?" Nick said just as they got in earshot of Lexie. "Really?"

Lexie's eyes widened to U.F.O. size as she stared at Camille in horror.

"Yeah, she was good, too," Camille said, nodding.

"So, why'd you quit?" Nick asked Lexie, and Camille knew she had ceased to be visible again.

It was kind of fun in an odd sort of way. She could watch them dance around each other, and neither one ever noticed she was watching. It was unusual to see Lexie so totally bowled over. Tongue-tied had never been a word to describe Lexie—she had an opinion about everything. But although her opinion of Nick was obvious, she couldn't seem to get three words strung together to save her life.

"Don't know," Lexie said, leaning against the lockers. "I guess I outgrew it."

"She took tap for awhile, too," Camille said from the depths of her locker, and when she turned, the U.F.O.s had developed knives. "You'll have to see her tap sometime. She's really good."

"Yeah." Nick's soft smile returned. "I'll have to."

Camille pulled her over-stuffed backpack out of the locker and then grabbed her books. "Well..."

Nick looked at Camille and seemed to remember where he was again. "Umm, I'd better let you two go. I'll see you tomorrow?"

"Sure," Camille said.

He turned and walked away down the hall.

"Are you completely insane?" Lexie asked when he had disappeared around a corner.

With an exasperated sigh, Camille shook her head and walked away from the lockers.

"What did that mean?" Lexie asked angrily as she followed her friend down the hall.

"It means, why don't you just talk to him?" Camille pushed through the double doors. "You like him. So talk to him. Why is that so hard?"

"I talked to him," Lexie said as she hugged her books to her chest.

"'I don't know' is not talking," Camille said as they walked down to the bus stop.

"Well, you're not helping matters." One side of Lexie's face dropped into a frown. "Why would you go and tell him about ballet—and tap? That was like a million years ago."

"He's in the choir and drama. I figured it could give you something in common."

"Yeah? Well, he probably thinks I'm an idiot now."

"He doesn't think you're an idiot," Camille said with a laugh as they climbed onto the bus.

"Well, just do me a favor, and stay out of it."

"Stay out of it? What happened to 'I want you to find out everything you can about him'?"

"About *him*. Not about me! Jeez, Cami, sometimes you can be so dumb."

Camille's gaze narrowed at the seat in front of her as her heart turned over inside her chest. She was just trying to help. It wasn't her fault they were both acting like deer caught in headlights. "Fine."

Immediately Lexie slumped in the seat next to her. "I'm sorry."

"No," Camille said, and the anger had switched sides of the seat. "It's okay. I mean if you want me to butt out, I will."

"I don't want you to butt out," Lexie said, and her tone was now more pleading than angry.

"Well, it certainly sounded like you do," Camille said as the bus rolled to her stop, and she stood.

"I'll see you tomorrow?" Lexie asked, but Camille just dismounted the stairs and walked away.

You're so dumb, Cami. You never understand anything. Jeez. You should've just kept your nose out of it. Her anger at getting stepped on for trying to help bubbled to the surface as she unlocked the door to her apartment, and immediately she saw the disaster area her sister had created.

"What am I, the maid?" Camille yelled to the back bedroom as she threw her own backpack to the floor. With a swipe she picked up a handful of debris from the floor. "Daria! Hey! Get out here! I'm not your maid!"

After a long moment Daria appeared, sleep-tousled in her nightshirt and slippers. "Why are you yelling?"

Camille stopped in mid-rant. "What happened to you?"

"I got sick this morning at school." Daria plopped her slender frame on the couch between the box of Kleenex and the abandoned pillow, which she promptly fell over on.

"Have you been here by yourself all day?" Camille said, softening as she knelt to examine the pixy-headed ten-year-old.

"Uh-huh," Daria said, and even that small amount of movement clearly sapped her remaining energy.

Camille put a gentle hand on the little forehead and shook her head. "Fever. Have you taken your temperature?"

The little mouth turned down in a frown.

"'Course not. Just a second." Camille pushed up from the couch, went down the hall to the bathroom, and grabbed the thermometer. "What time did you come home?"

"About ten." Daria accepted the thermometer. "The teacher called Mom."

"That's okay. Don't talk," Camille said, smoothing out the waves of hair. She waited a minute, then pulled the thermometer out, and looked at it in the sunshine. "102. Yep. You're sick." She moved the Kleenex box and pulled Daria's feet onto the couch. "Can I get you something? How about some Sprite?"

The little head went up and down slowly.

Camille went into the kitchen. "Have you eaten anything today?"

"A peanut butter sandwich, but I threw that up."

With the Sprite in hand, Camille returned and sat on the little couch. "Here. Does chicken noodle soup sound good?"

Daria took a small drink and shrugged. Camille put her head down in frustration. *Mom should've called me. What is she thinking leaving Daria home by herself like that?*

It was nearly seven o'clock when Brenda Cordell trudged through the door and found her two daughters huddled on the couch. Her eldest was busy fee-fie-foeing her way through Jack in the Beanstalk.

"How's my baby girl?" Brenda asked, kneeling in front of them to check on Daria.

"Fine, Mommy," Daria said, and the happiness barely tinged the sick sound in her voice.

"Well, I'm glad to hear that." Brenda gave her daughter a quick hug before she stood. "Something smells wonderful."

"Camille made me chicken soup," Daria said.

"I'll bet that was good on a sour tummy."

Daria nodded as her mother walked off down the hallway. Camille sat for one more second and then resumed the story.

"You should've called me," Camille hissed across the table so Daria wouldn't hear from her room.

"You were in school," her mother said as she looked through the classified ads. "Besides she wasn't that sick."

Camille grimaced and fought to keep her voice under control. "She had a 102 fever when I got home. I call that sick."

"Look, I'm doing the best I can. What do you want from me?"

On solid legs Camille stood from the table. "Nothing. I don't want anything from you."

Chapter 4

"So, where were you yesterday?" Nick asked as he slid into his seat next to Camille in the auditorium on Wednesday.

"I was sick," Camille lied just as she had done to the school secretary when she had called in the day before.

"Well, I'm glad it wasn't fatal."

"Nope, just a 48-hour bug," Camille said with a shrug. "No big deal."

"48? But . . ." Nick began as he looked at Camille in confusion.

"That's the bell, people," Mrs. Allen said from the front as she sat down center stage. "Today we're going to talk about an on-going assignment for the semester. You will be using your knowledge of the stage to critique plays that are performed in the area. There are performances of *Oklahoma* on Friday, Saturday and Sunday at the Mance Theatre. I've got the information here."

She handed a stack of bright yellow paper to Keane in the front row. "There will of course be performances by other groups throughout the semester, and I'll try to let you know about them. But it's up to you to get to at least two of them. I want a 500-word paper critiquing each play based on what we have learned thus far in class. Are there any questions?"

No hands went up.

"Good." Mrs. Allen pulled herself up off the stage. "Today we're going to talk a little bit about how intuitive acting is. By that I mean how much you already know about how a character or characters would relate in a given scenario. I'd like—let's see—Ariana and Nick to come up here."

Camille cowered farther in her seat as Nick crossed in front of her. She was sure to her core that the teacher would never call on her to come up in front of the class, but she did not want to take any chances.

"Okay." Mrs. Allen pulled her two actors to the center so they faced each other. "Nick, I want you to play Ariana's father. She has been dating someone that you do not approve of, and you have come to confront her about it. You are in her bedroom in your house." She narrowed her eyes at

Nick. "You got it?"

With one motion he nodded as his face went hard, and Mrs. Allen backed away.

"I said, 'Answer me'!" Nick shouted, jolting Camille out of her seat and riveting her eyes to the stage. "Were you out with him last night or not?"

Ariana's porcelain jaw line shifted as she crossed her arms. "I'm sixteen years old. I don't have to listen to you."

"Well, I'm your father, and you're going to listen to me!"

"Why? You never listen to me," Ariana said, standing toe-to-toe with Nick, facing him down even though she was several inches shorter than he. "I love him, and if you can't see that, then maybe it would be better if I just left."

"Great," Mrs. Allen said with a clap. "You see. Instant conflict from the simplest of directions." She swung two chairs onto the stage and positioned them facing each other. "Now, I want you to do the same scene only this time you are in the middle of a fancy restaurant."

Nick and Ariana sat down and put their stage faces on as Camille watched in fascination.

"You may begin," Mrs. Allen said.

"I forbid you to see him," Nick whispered over the invisible menu that he held, his voice carrying effortlessly to the back row.

"I'm sixteen," Ariana hissed back as she leaned across the non-existent table that suddenly appeared very real. "I can see whomever I want."

"Well, I'm your father." Nick laid the menu in front of him, obviously straining to control his voice. "And you will do as I say."

Ariana's face widened in disbelief and then narrowed in utter hate. "Make me."

"Very, very good." Mrs. Allen resumed her place on the stage. "You may take your seats again."

Camille's gaze was glued to Nick as he stood, smoothed out his jeans, and descended the stairs.

"When you look at a character, you will know how to play that part," Mrs. Allen said as Nick sat back down by Camille. "You will know it down here." She laid both hands on her stomach. "After you do all your background work, then you have to simply trust your gut. That's what being a good actor is about."

"That was unbelievable," Camille said quickly gathering her things and following Nick out of the auditorium.

"You thought so?" he asked as he pushed the door open and held it for her.

"Are you kidding me? I'd never be able to do that. Just get up there—no lines, no rehearsal and make it sound that good?"

"Sometimes it's easier with no lines. You get to play it the way you feel it instead of trying to play somebody else's vision of how it should be."

She let that statement wind through her. "I never thought of it like that." She pushed her feet down the hall still contemplating his words. "You know you should write plays yourself. I mean you really seem to understand it."

Nick shrugged. "I've written a few—mostly for class and stuff, but they're not very good."

"Really? I'd love to read one sometime." Camille walked up to her locker, and her easy conversation suddenly hardened. "Hey, Lex."

Camille had done her level best to avoid her friend all day long—going so far as to carry her entire backpack around the whole day, but now there was no where to hide.

"Hey, Lexie," Nick said, leaning a shoulder against Lexie's locker.

Lexie's gaze went from Nick to Camille and back again. Camille on the other hand was doing everything she could to make herself truly invisible.

"So, how's Economics?" Nick nodded at Lexie's book.

"Fine," Lexie said before she smiled the most normal smile Camille had seen from her in Nick's presence. "It's a lot of reading though."

"You don't like to read?"

"Oh, no," Lexie said in mortification. "I like to. I just don't read very fast. I get kind of behind sometimes."

"Oh, like Camille," Nick said, indicating the three-ton backpack and full stack of books Camille pulled out of her locker.

"I wish." Lexie sighed. "She could read every one of those books tonight if she wanted."

A confused look crossed Nick's face, and then he focused his attention back on Lexie and smiled. "Well, if you ever need any help reading, I'm not too bad at it."

There's an understatement. Camille slammed her locker and turned down the hallway. "I'll see you two tomorrow."

Instantly Lexie peeled her gaze from Nick's face. "Wait. I'm coming with you. I'll see you later, Nick."

"Yeah," he said with a small wave. "See ya."

They walked down the hall, out the door, and all the way onto the bus stop without a word.

"So, are you going to talk to me or not?" Lexie finally asked.

"I thought you were mad at me," Camille said in her best stage voice.

"I'm not mad at you. I just..."

"Just what? Wanted me to butt out? Well, I did." Camille stomped up the bus steps. "You should be happy."

"Come on, Cami. When I said that, I didn't mean I didn't want you in my life."

"Yeah, well, that's what it sounded like to me."

Lexie exhaled in frustration. "Look, I appreciate you trying to find out about him for me—I just wasn't expecting you to inform him about me. That's all."

"All I told him was that you used to dance. I don't think that's a crime."

"It's not," Lexie said. "It's just that when he's around... I don't know. I feel all tingly, and it's like everything about me is all wrong, and I want it to be right, but I don't know how to do that."

"Just relax," Camille said as though she'd had years of practice in the guy department. "He's a nice guy, and he likes you."

Lexie's eyes widened. "You think so?"

"Hello. Where've you been?" Camille said with a laugh.

The bus rolled up to Camille's stop.

"So, can I come home with you tonight?" Lexie asked, her gaze following Camille out of the seat.

Instantly Camille shook her head. "Daria's been sick. I'd hate for you to catch anything."

"Is that where you were yesterday?"

"Yep." Camille hoisted her backpack to her shoulder. "Playing Mommy again as usual. See ya."

"Come on, Lex, it'll be fun," Camille said, giving Lexie her best puppy dog eyes. "Please."

"A musical?" Lexie wrinkled her nose over the manager's surprise on her cafeteria tray. "I don't know."

"Nick might be there," Camille said, hoping that would tip the scales and her friend would agree to go; however, she immediately regretted it when Lexie's eyes widened in fear. "But he might not, too."

Lexie twirled the corn with her fork. "He might?"

"I could ask him," Camille said and then reversed course at the look of sheer terror on Lexie's face. "Or not."

"Okay, I'll go," Lexie finally said slowly, "but do *not* ask him if he's going. You got that? I don't want to look like I'm chasing him or anything."

"Even though you are."

Defensive petulance etched on Lexie's face. "I am not."

Camille shook her head. One thing was for sure—she would never understand Lexie's complete aversion to the topic of Nick McGee. "Fine. I won't ask him."

"So, Camille," Nick said as he slid into the auditorium seat next to hers, "are you going to the play this weekend?"

"Yeah, I'll probably go tomorrow night," Camille said as she dug in her backpack, trying to sound as if she hadn't been rehearsing this conversation for the past two hours.

"Really? Cool. I was thinking about going then, too." The toothy smile was back. "So, do you want to meet there or something? I mean if you want to..."

"That sounds like fun," Camille said with a hidden smile. "What time do you want to meet?"

"In the lobby at seven?"

"I'll be there."

"Hey, Camille!" Nick called through the crush of the crowd.

She waved at him and grabbed Lexie's arm before her friend had a chance to run.

"What did you do?" Lexie hissed in Camille's ear as she was dragged through the crowd. "I told you not to ask him."

"I didn't," Camille said smoothly. "He asked me."

"Cami!"

"Hi, Nick," Camille said and saw his eyes widen in surprise when he caught sight of her shadow.

Nick's gaze went placid. "Hey, Lexie."

"Hey," Lexie said, and Camille sighed. This was going to be a very long night.

They found their seats in the mid-sized theatre, and Camille expertly slipped past Lexie into the row, leaving Nick to follow Lexie in.

"So, Lexie, I didn't know you liked musicals," Nick said after they had gotten situated.

"I don't," Lexie said and looked at Camille with knives in her eyes. "I came for moral support."

Nick looked past Lexie to Camille. "Oh?"

"Yeah," Lexie said, her courage returning only because she was focused solely on Camille. "As freaked out as she was about being in drama, I was afraid she might rent the tape or something just to get out of getting near a stage."

Embarrassment flooded over her as Camille sank into her seat, avoiding both gazes. Why hadn't she thought of simply renting the tape?

"She was freaked out about drama?" Nick asked in confusion. "Why?"

"Are you kidding? It's Camille," Lexie said with a laugh. "She'd much rather have her nose in a book than actually have to talk to someone."

"Huh," Nick said, taking that information in. "So, I guess you two have been friends a long time then?"

"Since second grade," Lexie said, still determinedly focusing on Camille. "And she's just as hopeless now as she was back then."

Camille wanted to protest, but it stopped at the top of her throat.

"Hopeless, huh? Like what?"

And then, much to Camille's horror, Lexie launched into a detailed account of every embarrassing thing that Camille had ever done. A list which she was sure could have continued well past midnight except that the lights dimmed and the curtain went up cutting into the litany.

Deftly she put her notebook on her lap and pulled the pen from her ear. If she could just concentrate on taking notes and the fact that this was an assignment from school, she might be able to outrun the fact that in every situation she was nothing more than a temporary humorous diversion for everyone else.

Camille wasn't at all sure how it had happened, but sometime in the middle of the three-hour performance, Lexie and Nick had made a genuine connection. By the time the three of them walked out, he was holding Lexie's hand, and no one would ever have guessed they hadn't been able to say four intelligent words to each other in the last three weeks.

"How about we stop somewhere for a soda?" Nick asked as they pushed through the theatre doors into the city-lit darkness outside.

"Sure," Lexie said, accepting for both of them before Camille had a chance to complain about the headache that was pounding through her brain.

Realizing that arguing would take too much energy, she shrugged.

"Great," Nick said, and his smile lit his eyes. He led them through the darkening streets to his not-new-but-nice car. With a flourish he opened the passenger door, and Camille waited by the back door until Lexie unlocked it. At least in the back, she could truly be invisible.

Somehow she had stumbled into the middle of a date she didn't know was happening until she was there. It was like someone had turned a light bulb on in both of her companions' brains at the same time. They were both talking—most of the time simultaneously—laughing like old friends and generally having the times of their lives. Camille was content to listen, so long as the conversation had nothing to do with her.

It didn't matter though because neither of the other two participants noticed she was there either. They talked; she listened until well past 11:30 when Nick finally looked at his watch and sighed.

"I hate to say this, but I'd really better be getting home." He stood and offered Lexie a hand up. "Would you like a ride home?"

She smiled, seeing nothing other than him. "Sure."

Lexie guided Nick to Camille's house first and then waved as they left

Camille out at the curb to her apartment. As Camille unlocked her door and then watched them drive off, she knew that life with Lexie would never be the same again.

"I didn't say it was a great performance," Jaylon said as he and Ariana sat on either side of the booth at Sal's place on Saturday night after *Oklahoma*.

"Are you kidding? Tara was so flat, you could've run a truck over her tone." Ariana took a small sip of her soda and set the glass down a bit harder than need be. "I mean who in their right mind would cast *her* as the lead in anything?"

"Tara's okay," Jaylon said with a shrug. Their castmate from two years before hadn't 'made it big,' but Jaylon knew she was happy where she was. "She's still learning."

Ariana shook her head in annoyance. "Always the optimist."

Defensiveness sprang to his chest, but he beat it back. "What's wrong with that?"

"In this business?" she asked with a snort. "You'll get killed. That's what. So, have you sent your application for Julliard in yet?"

His gaze dropped to the table as he dropped the French fry in his hand. "I'll get to it."

"Get to it?" She narrowed her dark eyes in disbelief. "We're not talking about taking out the garbage, Jaylon. We're talking about Julliard."

"I know what we're talking about," he said as the heat rose in him. "I said, 'I'll get to it.'"

After a moment she backed off. "Well, you better get to it soon, or I may just have to go without you."

Jaylon's jaw locked unconsciously. *Maybe you will.*

"Cartoons again?" Camille asked as she walked out into the living room and saw Daria sprawled in front of the television on Saturday morning.

"Mom said I could," Daria said with only the slightest glance over her shoulder.

"Of course she did," Camille said under her breath. She went into the kitchen and rummaged for a bowl and some cereal. "You eat breakfast yet?"

"Yeah, I had a Twinkie."

"A Twinkie?" Camille asked, looking back out into the living room.

"Yeah, Mom..."

"...said I could," Camille finished for her and then shook her head and replaced the cereal. "How about I make us some eggs?"

"'K," Daria said.

Jaylon steeled his nerves as he sat at the formal dining table, forking through the brunch his stepmother had prepared Sunday afternoon.

"I got the stuff from Julliard," he said as non-threateningly as possible, but without looking, he saw his father's fork drop a full inch.

"I thought we'd already discussed this," Russ Quinn said, his voice like stone.

"No." Jaylon looked up into the steel blue eyes but instantly lost his courage. "You discussed it. *We* never have."

Russ looked over at his wife, which sent her into a panic.

"Do we really have to talk about this now?" Marianne Quinn asked as the crystal glass fell from her perfectly applied lipstick. "I thought maybe just once we could enjoy a nice, quiet meal together."

But Jaylon had come this far, and he had let it go too many times in the past. "And when are we supposed to talk about it? When they stop accepting applications? When I've missed my chance?"

"Don't talk to your mother like that," Russ said as the vein over his pressed shirt collar pulsated. "We can talk about this later."

"Later," Jaylon said, the anger and frustration crashed through his voice even though his decibel level remained fixed. "A nice way of saying never."

His father's fork clattered to the table, jolting the other two table occupants. "I can't eat like this. It gives me indigestion." He stood and threw his napkin to the table.

"Where are you going?" Marianne asked, her gaze following him to the doorway.

"Out."

Neither Jaylon nor his stepmother moved until the door slammed behind his father, and his footsteps faded out.

"Why do you have to do that?" Marianne asked with a click of her tongue. Her perfectly hair-sprayed red helmet hair followed the turning of her head. "You know that's going to upset him."

Jaylon exhaled, fighting not to shift his anger with his father onto her. "I'm eighteen. He can't tell me what to do anymore."

"He loves you, and he wants what's best for you."

"No, he wants what's best for him. He wants me to be like him, but I'm not. I'm not like him. I never have been, and I never will be." Jaylon stood from the table.

"Where are you going?"

"Out."

The Z28 streaked through the streets until the buildings disappeared in Jaylon's rearview mirror. He knew exactly where he was going. He had been there many times just like today—running to get away from his father. *If he could just be reasonable for two seconds, I could explain how hard I've worked for this, but he's never listened, and he never will.*

The houses had turned to fields and trees and then to rolling cliffs by the time his attention shifted from the history of fights back into the car. He slowed the car and turned off the main highway onto a side road. He drove a few minutes before he saw the single tree towering in the distance. Drawn to it, he drove as close as he could get and then parked, got out, and walked to the edge of the slope that had been cut many years before by the small creek running somewhere below the trees and brush that surrounded it.

He flopped to the grass at the base of the sprawling oak tree and squeezed his eyes closed against the pain in his chest. Somehow he had to find a way to follow his dream. Life without it seemed too bleak to even contemplate.

"Lord," he said, opening his eyes and gazing through the branches above him to the sunlight beyond, "please, I'm asking You. Help me find a way to make him understand."

Chapter 5

"So, Cami are you going to the play on Friday?" Lexie asked over her chalupa.

"I don't know." Camille's attention never wavered from the grasp of the formulas she was memorizing for her physics test the next period. "I hadn't really thought about it. Why?"

"Well, Nick and I are going," Lexie said. It had been more than a month since they had connected at the *Oklahoma* play, and even though they had spent practically every free moment together, Lexie still had that wispy quality in her voice when she talked about him. "I just thought you might want to go with us."

The formulas slipped from Camille's mind as she looked at Lexie, fighting not to let the hurt find her voice. Being a third wheel was getting old. "I'm sure you guys would have more fun without me."

Instantly Lexie's eyes narrowed in confusion. "No we wouldn't. We want you to come." She looked up past Camille's shoulder and smiled like the dawn. "Don't we, honey?"

"Don't we what?" Nick straddled the table bench next to Lexie and planted a kiss on her forehead as she leaned into him.

"Want Camille to come with us on Friday," Lexie said with the tiniest of giggles.

"Oh, sure." Nick looked across the table as though he hadn't yet noticed that Camille was sitting there. "There's always room for one more."

One more. Great.

Although Camille had grown accustomed to the written assignments that Mrs. Allen came up with every other week, they had done nothing to make her feel better about being on stage. She stood stage left shifting from foot-to-foot as Mrs. Allen pushed the chalkboard away in anticipation of the current day's torture session.

"Now, in the past week, I've noticed that when I ask for pairs, most of you tend to pair with the same person over and over again. I understand that, but I think it's time to move out of your comfort zone a little and start learning about the other people in the class."

Camille's fear shield flew up. *No, comfort is good. Please. Comfort is fine.*

"Rather than try to pair people myself, I've cut up numbers in this hat. You are to take a number and then find the other person with that number, and for today the two of you will be partners."

For one brief second Camille thought she might be sick on her shoes, and at the moment that looked like a really good idea. It would solve so many problems. Mrs. Allen approached her with the hat, and with a short sigh, Camille reached in and pulled out a number. It really didn't matter what the number was. If it was anything other than Nick's number, it meant trouble.

"What'd you get?" Nick asked, holding his number out for her inspection. 7.

She unfolded her own. 3.

"Rats," Nick said. "Well, see ya." And he walked off to find his match.

Camille looked around as the trepidation rose in her chest. She didn't want to be number 3. She didn't want to be number anything. She wanted to leave. Now.

"Are you number 3?" a voice asked behind her.

"Yeah." Camille turned and found herself gazing into a face framed by wispy brown hair and sporting perfectly gorgeous cheekbones. Jaylon. Instantly her gaze dropped to her clothes as her hand flew to her glasses and then to her hair. "Umm, yeah. I am."

He smiled at her although she saw only the beginning of that smile as her eyes wanted nothing more than to force her feet to run.

"Okay," Mrs. Allen said when the class had paired off. "Your exercise today is eye-to-eye contact."

Camille squeezed her eyes closed and fought to make herself disappear. She should've paid more attention at that magic show she'd seen when she was five.

"I want you to face each other and count to fifty very slowly—looking directly into your partner's eyes the entire time."

Camille's gaze was fixed on his shoes, and for the life of her she couldn't figure out how she was ever going to get it to move again.

"It's okay." Jaylon tilted his head as if he were talking to a frightened animal. "I don't bite."

For a brief second her gaze traveled up to his as she laughed, but immediately it dropped back down again. Trying not to think about what she was about to do, she swallowed once and then forced her gaze back up to his as she pushed her glasses up on her nose.

"Go," Mrs. Allen said.

Camille bit her bottom lip as she stared into his eyes—unable to look away even though she wanted to. The blue eyes, the high cheekbones, the wisps of hair—all met in perfect unison.

"Eight, nine, ten," Jaylon counted as his mouth moved in slow methodical motion.

She shifted her shoulders struggling to break the spell his gaze cast over her, but there was no breaking this spell.

"Fifteen, sixteen," he said as she forced the air into her lungs.

Never in her life had she looked into anyone's eyes for a full minute. Most of the time she did everything she could not to get caught in someone else's sights. Just keep moving, keep your head down, and they won't notice you're there. That was her motto. For most of the last ten years, they were the words she had lived by. Until this moment.

"Twenty-seven, twenty-eight."

It was then that her thoughts shifted from her own thoughts to those staring back at her from his eyes. She wasn't sure what she had expected to find in his eyes exactly—arrogance, cruelty, superiority—but not one of that was hidden anywhere in the pools of blue. Staring back from the depths of his eyes was the same fear and uneasiness her own spirit felt.

"Forty-two, forty-three," he said, and her ears caught on the softness of his voice.

It sounded like a breeze brushing past her, and she wondered how she had ever lived before hearing his voice in this way.

"Forty-nine, fifty," he said, and their gazes held for one more moment.

"Good," Mrs. Allen said, breaking the spell between them and jerking both gazes across the stage.

Camille ran a damp palm down the front of her jeans and readjusted her glasses.

"Now I want the partners to find a place in the auditorium. Not necessarily on stage. I'm going to give you five minutes. I want you to find a topic and discuss it, but I want you to do it looking into each other's eyes as much as possible."

Camille's toe made an arc around her other foot. She still hadn't recovered from the first exercise, and five minutes was far different than one.

"How about if we go over here?" Jaylon asked, pointing to the stairs as he reached out and touched her elbow.

His touch carried a jolt of electricity with it, and she had to force herself to shrug and walk to the stage steps nonchalantly. She sat on the third step from the bottom, but when he followed her down, her knee tensed so as not to touch his.

"You may begin," Mrs. Allen said.

"Any suggestions?" he asked, tilting his head to the side to look at her.

"Umm, I don't know. Classes?" she asked, feeling the pained look cross her face as her hand tugged at the heel of her shoe.

"Okay," he said and paused a beat. "Umm, you have to look at me, remember?"

"Oh, y-yeah." She stumbled over the words as she forced her gaze back to his.

Looking back at her was sincere interest. "So, what's your favorite class?"

She smiled as her entire body instantly relaxed. "Math."

"Math?" he asked in surprise.

"Yeah. Why? Is that so hard to believe?"

"Well, no. I guess not, but I hate math." He ran his fingers through his hair to push it back out of his face. "I'm just surprised anybody likes it."

"You hate it?" she asked, forgetting this was supposed to be hard. "But it's so fascinating."

"Fascinating? I can think of another word for it," he said, wrinkling his nose.

"Oh, yeah? What's that?"

"Torture."

She laughed and shook her head. "No, now you're talking about drama."

"Huh?" he asked, and her gaze dropped from his to her shoestrings.

With a shove she forced her gaze back up although this time it didn't lock on his. Instead it wandered around the stage and the auditorium at the other partners.

"How can you not like drama?" he asked in genuine confusion. "Drama is awesome."

Her eyebrows raised as she looked back at him in open-eyed mortification. "Not when you're me. It isn't."

His gaze immediately reflected concern. "Why not when you're you?"

Mrs. Allen clapped her hands, which almost sent Camille tumbling backward off the steps.

"I'd like everyone to come back over to the seats again," Mrs. Allen said.

Camille scrambled up from the steps and swiped at the dirt she was sure was on the back of her jeans. She turned and walked down past the front of the stage feeling him right behind her. Quickly she walked to her normal seat in the third row, and it wasn't until she sat down and realized Jaylon had taken his usual spot on the other side of the auditorium that she began to breathe again.

"Good," Mrs. Allen said as she sat down on the center of the stage. "Could someone tell me what you learned from that exercise?"

"That looking at anyone for five minutes is asking way too much," Mark said, and several students laughed.

Mrs. Allen smiled. "Try 25 years."

"No, thanks," Mark said seriously.

"Okay," Mrs. Allen said. "Anyone else?"

"That we hide who we really are by not looking people in the eye," Jaylon said, and Camille's gaze snapped to his profile.

"How so?" Mrs. Allen asked.

Jaylon sat for one moment during which Camille's heart felt like it might actually leap from her chest. "Well, when you really look into someone's eyes, it's like there's nowhere to hide. It's like letting them look into who you really are. It's pretty intimidating."

"Hmm. Intimidating?" Mrs. Allen asked. "Interesting word choice. Anyone else?"

Several other students spoke, but Camille didn't hear any of them. Jaylon Quinn thought she was intimidating? He must be joking. There wasn't an intimidating bone in her entire body.

When the bell rang, she grabbed her things and walked next to Nick out the door.

"So, you're coming with Lex and me to the play then?" Nick asked, pushing the door open for her as the crush of students spun around them on the other side.

"Yeah, I guess so." Camille shrugged. "I might as well get it over with."

Nick leaned away surveying her. "Well, don't get all excited on my account."

Camille laughed softly. "It's not that. I just feel... unwanted when I'm around you two. Not that you're doing it on purpose. I mean if I had my soulmate with me, I probably wouldn't pay much attention to anyone else either."

"Are we that bad?"

She raised her eyebrows at him, and he grinned.

"Okay. We are."

"It's okay," Camille said. "I understand."

They walked to the lockers where Lexie was waiting, and Nick gave her a peck on the cheek.

"How was drama?" Lexie asked.

"It was drama." Nick leaned on the lockers next to Lexie. "So, what are you doing now?"

"Going home, I guess," Lexie said, peeking through the fringe of her eyelashes. "Why?"

"I don't know. I was just wondering if you wanted to go over to Sal's with me."

"Sal's?" Lexie asked as her eyes widened. "Now?"

"Yes, now," Nick said, laughing.

Camille busied herself digging into the depths of her locker. Her mind traced over all of her assignments for the evening.

"Well, yeah, it sounds like fun," Lexie said, and Camille heard the lilt in her voice.

"Great," Nick said.

With a heave Camille pulled her backpack to her shoulder. "I'll see you guys tomorrow."

"What? Aren't you coming with us?" Nick asked obviously pulled up short by his lack of foresight.

"No, somebody's got to cook," Camille said with a brave smile. "You two have fun." Without another word, she turned down the hallway and trudged off.

As she climbed onto the bus alone, she pictured them at Sal's—a place she had seen only from the outside. Girls like her never got invited to Sal's; girls like her never got invited anywhere. It wasn't that she was jealous. She was happy for Lexie and for Nick. It just hurt that no one wanted her like that.

She closed her eyes and leaned back against the headrest. Immediately Jaylon's eyes were there, staring back at her. Even in her imagination she couldn't tear her gaze from his. Intense. That was a good word to describe his eyes. Like piercing laser beams cutting right into her soul.

Annoyed with herself she shook her head and opened her eyes, realizing with a start that the next stop was hers. Daydreaming had never gotten her anywhere, and it certainly wouldn't now—especially about something as impossible as Jaylon Quinn being even vaguely interested in her. There was a reason he was Jaylon Quinn and she was Camille Wright and it had nothing to do with them ever getting together.

With determination she pushed all the thoughts of his eyes out of her mind and descended the bus steps. It was an exercise, and it was over. There was no more to the story.

Jaylon was casually draped over Ariana in a booth at Sal's listening to Seth expound on the torment of Chemistry when he saw Nick come in. His arm slipped from Ariana's shoulders as his protective nature jumped to the surface. He and Nick McGee had never gotten along—ever since middle school when he had won the lead in a community play he no longer even remembered the name of, but he'd never really had a reason to hate the guy until now.

The instant he saw the darkened skin and deep brown eyes of the girl Nick was obviously with, Jaylon's claws came out.

What man in his right mind would cheat on his girlfriend? Even if that girlfriend wore funny glasses and had her head stuck in a book most of the time. That didn't give him the right to flaunt someone else in her face. That was just plain cruel.

"I thought so too," Ariana said and then punched Jaylon. "Didn't you?"

"Oh, yeah," Jaylon said with a shake of his head. "Of course I did."

The rest of the week Camille continued to remind herself that she and Jaylon might as well be from different planets. Every time she sat in drama and caught herself watching him without realizing she was. Every time she closed her eyes and his were right there. Every time her gaze traveled to his profile as they discussed plays. Every time she reminded herself again, and every time, she would somehow forget and find herself right back in that place she'd promised herself she wouldn't go.

"So, you're coming tonight, right?" Nick asked as he followed her out of the auditorium on Friday.

She sighed. "Yeah, I'm coming."

Nick walked a few steps without saying anything. "Look, I wanted to tell you I'm really sorry about the other day."

She looked at him in confusion.

"When I didn't invite you... I mean I meant to... it was a general invitation."

Her gaze fell to her feet. "Don't worry about it. Sal's really isn't my kind of place anyway."

"Oh, really?" he asked. "So what is?"

She thought about that for a moment. "Home." She transferred her attention from her shoelaces to her locker. "Hey, Lex."

"Hey," Lexie said, beaming at Nick. "So, you want us to come get you tonight, Cami?"

"Oh, no," Camille said instantly. "I'll just catch the bus."

"It's really no trouble," Nick said, leaning a shoulder against the lockers.

"No, that's okay." Camille forced a smile onto her face. "I'll just meet you there at... seven?"

"You sure?" Lexie asked, and the pity in her eyes stung the backs of Camille's.

"Yeah." She slammed her locker door. "I'll see you there tonight."

Without a backward glance she walked away as slowly as her pride would let her. They were just being nice. That was part of it. Be nice to the best friend. But reality was they didn't want her around, and one way or another she was determined to make herself as scarce as possible.

By the time she arrived at the theatre it was almost 7:30, and the place was wall-to-wall people. Of course she was late. That's what happened when the babysitter didn't show up on time. Carefully she scanned the crowd searching for them. She couldn't remember if they were each getting tickets or if they were going to get hers. After several minutes of searching, however, she gave up. If she didn't get into the theatre soon, she would miss the opening. Quickly she went up to the window and purchased one of the few remaining tickets.

Clutching her notebook to her, she took one more look through the crowd in the lobby and then gave up for good. Ticket in hand she went to the door and then carefully descended the rose-colored carpet berating herself for not pulling her hair back. It was always such a mess when she let it down because she spent most of her time pushing it out of her eyes anyway.

One day with it down convinced her to pull it back the rest of the year. She pulled her ticket closer and squinted in the growing darkness. G7. "G... G." Carefully she descended the steps and then turned right into row G and found seat seven, which was three seats from the side curtain. "Excuse me. Excuse me." In annoyance she pushed her hair over her ear again as she struggled to get past the other people already seated. "Sorry."

The lights faded to black just as she slipped into her seat. Quietly she opened her notebook and pulled the pen from behind her ear as a hazy blue light illuminated the stage. She glanced down at the playbill resting on her notebook. *My Fair Lady.*

Huh, must be something about musicals. With a shake of her head, she focused her attention on the stage.

Two rows back Jaylon watched her. He had seen her the second she descended the aisle step next to his seat. He was sure it was her although she looked totally different with her hair down around her face like that. Unconsciously he sat forward to get a better look at her as the memory of her eyes filled his mind. They were eyes he wanted nothing more than to look into again.

He surveyed the seats on either side of her. One was full. One was not. He wondered where her Romeo was. Had Nick stood her up? If she was his date, he would never stand her up. It occurred to him that he should be watching the play, but every time he tried, his attention fell back to the curve of her shoulders under the fall of light brown whisper soft hair.

Math? Tonight she didn't look like a math ace. Far from it. She looked like the quintessential theatre patron—all creative new age. The flowing print skirt, the non-fitted top, not one thing about her was harsh or even awkward tonight. The audience around him laughed, and it pulled his attention back to the stage just as the lights went up. Intermission already? The people next to him stood, and he moved his knees. After they were gone, he watched to see if she too would leave, but besides allowing the people next to her out, she remained.

He wanted to go talk to her—just to say hi, but something in his stomach said that would be presumptuous. Nick was probably meeting her at intermission anyway.

But she didn't move, didn't even look around. It looked like she was deeply engrossed in something. It was then that he realized she was writing. Without him telling them to, his legs stood, and he slid out of his row, descended two steps, and slipped into hers. Fighting to appear casual as he got to the seat next to her, he leaned on the seat in front of him and almost toppled over it when it leaned forward.

"Oh, excuse me." Camille glanced up, swiping at her belongings on the ground to get them out of his way. Then in mid-swipe she stopped, and ever-so-slowly her gaze traveled up his legs, past his chest, to his eyes, a move which sent his heart racing.

"Hi," he said totally unsure of how she would take this intrusion.

"Oh." Her gaze jumped from his eyes past him into oblivion and then dropped. "Hi. Umm. I didn't... umm, where..." She looked around like an animal trapped in a cage. "Hi."

Careful not to throw her into more confusion, he smiled again. "Umm, I saw you sitting down here, and I thought I should at least come and say hello."

"Oh, okay. Hello." She pushed her glasses up as her translucent locks fell over her face. Quickly she pushed them behind her ear. "Umm, what are you doing here?"

"Watching the play," he lied, flicking his head backward toward the stage.

"Oh, yeah, of course." She pushed her glasses up again.

The people from her row returned, and Jaylon suddenly found himself trapped as well.

"Mind if I sit down?" he asked, pointing at the empty seat next to hers.

"Yeah," she said instantly and then shook her head. "I mean no. I mean, yes, you may."

"Cool." In one motion he slipped past her and into the seat. The other people crossed in front of them and took their seats. "So, what's that? Notes?"

"Umm, yeah." She looked down at her notes, and then she looked around behind them to the back of the theatre. "Where's Ariana?"

"Ari... oh," he said, realizing he hadn't even thought about his girlfriend for more than an hour. "She had a family thing. So where's Nick?"

"Oh, I don't know. We were supposed to meet, but we kind of had a mix up with the tickets or the time or something. I couldn't find him when I got here."

"So you decided to see the play by yourself?"

She shrugged, and his thoughts went to the light reflecting off the fall of hair on her shoulders. "I figured since I was here, I might as well."

The lights began to dim again, and with one more smile at her, Jaylon settled back into the seat to watch the second act.

Camille hadn't breathed a single breath for more than an hour. Her brain could handle nothing other than screaming, "Jaylon Quinn is sitting right next to you!" She was more than sure that her notes would make no sense at all when she got home, but she kept writing for fear that he would suspect she was having as much trouble comprehending anything as she was.

In utter frustration she nailed her gaze to the stage. If she didn't pay attention, she was going to have to come back again tomorrow night to even have a chance at writing a paper about this play. However, the only thing her attention could focus on was the heat of his arm two inches from hers. Balancing her notebook, keeping her attention on stage and away from him was making her head swim. She put her head down and pushed her glasses up, swinging her annoying hair out of her face when she straightened.

Nothing about the play or life was making any sense. If she didn't get out of this auditorium and away from him, she was quite sure the coroner could simply come pick her up right there.

Applause erupted around her, and her thoughts crashed back into the auditorium. She picked up her hands to clap, a move, which sent her notebook sliding off her knee. "Oh." She grabbed for it, which sent it flying into the seat back in front of her and then crashing to the floor. She bent down to retrieve it, but before finding the notebook, her hand met up with Jaylon's. The applause around them froze as their gazes met. She wanted to move, to say something, anything, but nothing other than his eyes was getting through to her nervous system.

"I'm sorry," he finally said as he reached down between them and pulled her notebook off the floor. Carefully he wiped it off and handed it to her.

"It wasn't your fault," she said utterly mesmerized. Then her attention caught on the people standing behind him, waiting to get out. "Oh."

His gaze followed hers up, and he scrambled to his feet. "Sorry."

"No problem," the well-dressed lady said as she and the man with her slipped past them.

Once on his feet, Jaylon leaned against the chair facing Camille's as his gaze flitted across the auditorium. When Camille looked up at him, he was running his fingers through the feathers of his hair, and her heart told her that looking at him was a very bad idea.

"So," he said in a voice that sounded like he was being strangled, "are you... doing anything now?"

"Now?" she asked, standing and pushing the pen behind her ear. "Umm, no, I mean, yes. I mean I was going home."

"Home?" Jaylon looked over her shoulder at the dwindling crowd. "Oh, well, I was wondering if maybe you'd like to go get some ice cream or something."

"Me?" she asked, trying to shake herself awake knowing this must be a dream.

"Of course you," he said with the most amazingly soft smile she'd ever seen. "I know a place just down the block. Come on."

As though it was the most normal thing in the world, he took hold of her elbow and guided her out of the row. Once in the aisle he took her hand and helped her up the stairs. It was an act of gallantry she was supremely grateful for because without it, she would probably have tumbled right back down the aisle and into the orchestra pit.

On soft wings, he steered her through the lobby and out into the neon lit night.

"My car's over here," he said as he routed her path through the departing theatre patrons.

When she reached the car, her heart which was already well into cardiac arrest, stopped completely. "Oh, you really don't have to do this. I mean I really need to get home."

But he opened the passenger door as though she hadn't spoken a word. Without saying anything, he took her hand and helped her into the car. The soft gray leather seat wrapped around her as a feeling of safety that she had never known wound over her heart.

Like a rock star sliding into his limo, he climbed in on his side and smiled at her for one brief second before starting the car.

"So, what else do you do besides math and detective work?" Jaylon asked, resting an arm over his side of the booth in a hopeless attempt to look casual.

Camille shot him a confused look and then laughed. "Oh, wink murder."

"Yeah," he said as his heart lit up with a smile.

"That was fun." She ducked her head. "I thought we were all done for."

"Yeah, but I wasn't counting on who I was up against," he said, and then his face fell as the memory of Nick standing in the line leaving the theatre streaked through his mind. Hand-in-hand with the other girl, Nick hadn't even looked like he was trying to hide it. With a shove Jaylon pushed that image out of his mind and focused on Camille again. "So are you planning on going to college next year?"

Her fingers drummed on the table. "Yeah. If I can get in."

"In where?"

"Princeton."

"Princeton?" he asked as his arm slid from the booth back. "Impressive, and you're going to study..."

As if she had just floated away from the table, she laid her chin in her hand. "Aerospace engineering."

Jaylon's eyes widened in surprise. "Aerospace engin...? Wow. That's... that's... wow."

Camille shrugged, the dream crashing out of her eyes. "If I can get in."

He regarded her for a moment. "And you think that's going to be a problem?"

"I don't know. I've got the grades and everything, but..."

"But?"

She glanced up and readjusted her glasses before digging her spoon into her ice cream without taking even a single bite of it. "I'm going to have to get a lot of scholarships and stuff. That's why I really like Princeton. They have this no-loan/grants only program for financially challenged students, which is a lot better than the other schools."

"Like?"

"Cornell for one. Or Yale. Or Columbia."

Jaylon lowered his head and stared at her. "Jeez, you don't aim low. Do you?"

At that she seemed to shrink over the bowl of ice cream. "As far as finances, Princeton's my best bet. But then there's the problem of actually getting accepted there. I mean I'm not really the most well-rounded person in the world, and Mr. Marsh seems to think that's going to hurt my chances."

"But if your grades are good..."

"Yeah, but they look at a lot more stuff than just grades these days, and in those categories, well..."

Jaylon's gaze dropped to his own rapidly melting soft serve as the fights over Julliard played through his mind.

"So, what about you?" she asked, glancing at him. "I'm sure you've got colleges falling all over you."

He laughed. "I wish. UCLA seems interested, but I don't know. That's a long way to go for school. Besides, I really want to go to Julliard."

"Talk about shooting for the stars."

Ache screeched through him as he shrugged. "Not that it'll ever happen."

Her confident face fell in puzzlement. "Why not?"

"Oh, I don't know, a lot of reasons. I guess."

"Name one."

His thoughts contorted around the screaming matches in his brain. "My dad mostly. He doesn't want me to go."

"Are you kidding? Julliard is an incredible school. There are people who would kill to go there."

"Yeah, well, it may kill him if I go there."

"Why's that?"

"Oh, he basically thinks it's a disgrace to have an actor for a son," Jaylon said, immediately regretting the statement. He had never told anyone about his father's harsh words.

Camille shook her head as though that made no sense. "But he has to know how good you are—up there on the stage."

His gaze slid across the table and plummeted to the floor beyond. "He's never even been to a performance."

"He's never...? You're kidding me?" she asked in consternation. "Why not?"

"I don't know. He's busy, I guess." Jaylon half-shrugged. "It's no big deal really."

She swirled her ice cream around in the bowl. "I can't imagine someone saying that I couldn't do math anymore. They might as well cut out my heart."

"What with the sharp tip of a compass?" he asked with a wry smile.

With a glance up, she laughed. "Yeah. Something like that."

"How was your 'scream?" he asked, pointing at her bowl with the tip of his spoon.

"Oh, good," she said, looking down at it. "Thanks. I really didn't expect this."

"Well, it seemed kind of pointless to waste a perfectly good Friday alone." He gazed at her, liking the view. "It's nice to have a friend to share it with."

She shook her head, and locks of hair cascaded down around her face. Off-handedly she pushed them behind her ear. "Yeah, friends seem to be in short supply these days."

His thoughts returned to Nick and his "other" date, and his gaze fell to the table. "Well, anytime you need a friend..." He looked up and caught the disbelieving look in her eyes. "What?"

"I don't know." She fidgeted with the zipper on her jacket. "You're just being so nice to me."

"And that's a bad thing?" he asked, not really sure where his misstep had come but seeing it in her eyes just the same.

"No," she said softly. "It's just that... well, we're not exactly from the same crowd."

"But we're both in drama."

"No, you're in drama. I'm in a class I was forced into."

His forehead furrowed, and then he understood. "Marsh."

She nodded. "He said Princeton won't even look at me if I don't have something other than academics on my record. Not to mention the scholarships I'm going to miss out on." Her hair glinted over her shoulder as she shrugged. "If I can just make it to the end of the semester, I think I can drop out and take another computer class or something."

That thought whacked into him. "Drop out? But the production isn't until spring."

She smiled in self-deprecation. "Trust me, no one wants me in the Spring Production—least of all Mrs. Allen."

"Mrs. Allen's cool."

"She hates me."

"No she doesn't," he said incredulously.

"Yes, she does. Ever since that falling on my face incident the first week. Believe me, I know when I'm out of my league with something."

"Just because something's new, doesn't mean you won't get it," he said, wishing his gaze could find something other than her hair or the soft curve of her chin to concentrate on. "When I feel like I'm out of my league with something, I always think about that saying about God putting a light at your feet. He didn't say on your head so you can see everything. Just at your feet so you can see the next step."

"Yeah? Well, I'm liable to trip on every step there is."

He frowned. "You don't mess up everything you try."

"Ha, you don't know me very well, do you?"

No, but I'd like to. "What does that mean?"

Abruptly she looked at her watch. "I've got to go."

She stood, and he followed her up, throwing a few bucks onto the table as he hurried to the door to push it open for her.

"I asked you a question," he said as his steps quickened beside her.

"Thanks for the ice cream," she said, walking right past his car. "I'd better get home."

"Where are you going?" he asked, stopping by his car for a second too long.

"Don't worry. I'll just take the bus," she said over her shoulder.

"The bus?" He forced his confused feet to turn and follow her down the sidewalk. "But I can take you home."

"No," she said without slowing her steps. "I'm fine, but thanks."

The air brakes of the bus exhaled at the curb as without even checking the bus number on the city map, she climbed aboard, leaving Jaylon standing on the curb, hands in the air, and confusion coursing through every brain cell.

Even after the bus had disappeared around the corner, he stood for another long moment before turning as he replayed their conversation in his head. She loved math. She hated drama, but she was willing to do something she hated to be able to do something she loved. It made sense in a way. He opened his car door, climbed behind the wheel, and sat, staring after the long gone bus before he reached down to start the car. It was then that he saw the notebook in the passenger seat. Her notebook.

As though it might explode if he even touched it, he picked it up and flipped on the interior light. Something told him he shouldn't open it, but his hand wasn't listening to his head. He turned the top page over.

"Fragile Glass"

It was the beginning of the rough draft of her analysis of Laura from *The Glass Menagerie*.

"In a world of glass houses, it may take only one, small stone to bring a life down, to crumble it to the core, to shatter the hopes and the dreams of someone with only hopes and dreams to live on. It may be a simple laugh, hurled at someone at her most vulnerable moment. It may be a comment, a thoughtless aside, meant to be funny but actually so devastating that the object of it never really recovers. Or it could be a parent's expectations set so high that no mere mortal could ever reach them, and then hurled with every opportunity at the fragile glass the child has constructed. Whatever it is, the stone seldom matters to the person hurling it, but to the person on the receiving end, it could be all it takes to destroy a house, painstakingly constructed, and meant only to shelter a lost, hurting soul from a cold, cruel world of stone throwers."

With tear-blurred vision, Jaylon looked up into the neon-lit street, and his eyes fell closed against her pain.

"It was so amazing," Lexie said, flopping on Camille's bed the next evening. "Nick is just so great. We sat together the whole play, and he held my hand, and then after it was over, he took me to Sal's, and he sat on my side of the booth and put his arm around me—like we were a real couple."

"You are a real couple." Camille sat at her vanity table pulling a hairbrush through her hair slowly as she examined her reflection in the mirror. Dork. It was etched on every fiber of her. She was a dork, a geek. Even sitting with Jaylon Quinn could never change that.

"No, I mean a real couple," Lexie breathed on the bed. "And then when he dropped me off at my house, he didn't get out of the car like he usually does. He sat there for like a real long time, and for a minute I thought maybe he was going to break up with me, but then he asked me if I'd be his girlfriend. Just like that, 'Will you be my girlfriend?' It was so romantic."

The hairbrush clattered to the vanity table as Camille stood and walked over to the desk absently. "You were already his girlfriend. Big deal."

"Yeah, but it wasn't official until last night," Lexie said.

Camille shuffled through her books looking for her notebook so she could get started on the assignment. However, she shook her head as she reached the bottom of the stack and still hadn't found it. Slowly she restacked her books to the other side of the desk in confusion. Her notebook had to be here somewhere. It wasn't like it could've gotten lost... and then she remembered, and her heart jumped into her throat. Jaylon's car. She hadn't gone back there after the whole ice cream fiasco. Jaylon Quinn had her notebook.

The chair caught her as her knees buckled. No, surely she couldn't have been that stupid. With increasing urgency, she dug back through her books.

"He asked me out to the Homecoming dance next weekend," Lexie said never losing the wispiness of her voice. "I'm going to go downtown to get me a dress... What's wrong?"

Camille slammed her bottom drawer, opened the next one up, and then slammed it closed too. "I forgot a notebook."

"So, you'll get it on Monday. Big deal," Lexie said with a shrug.

But it was a big deal. It was a very big deal.

Chapter 6

From the moment she got to school, Camille looked for him, rehearsing her speech until she had it memorized. But she never saw him, not even once. However, in reality, she knew that even if she did, she would never have the nerve to go up and ask him for the notebook.

By the time she got to Drama, her nerves were frazzled, and her head was pounding. Somehow she had to get that notebook without humiliating herself in front of Jaylon or Ariana or Nick.

"Hey, you're early," Nick said, sliding into the seat to her left, causing her heart to skip a beat.

"Yeah." She shifted in her own seat and tried to look like she was thoroughly engrossed in her physics homework. "I wanted to get some work done on my drama paper."

Nick pointed to her notebook scrawled with formulas. "That's not drama."

"Oh, no, it's not." She shifted in her seat again just as her attention snagged on the black jeans gliding down the center aisle. In frustration her eyes fell closed, and then she forced them opened again in resignation. "I couldn't think of where to start, so I gave up." She smiled at Nick helplessly. "So, I figured I might as well make some headway with this."

"So you won't have to lug everything home tonight," he said with a knowing nod.

"Something like that," she said, forcing herself not to glance into the front row.

Nick dug into his jacket pocket for his pen. "The play was good."

"Yeah, it was." She wished she remembered more about it. Writing the paper without her notes was not going to be easy. "Lexie liked it, too."

Immediately Nick's face flushed.

"She told me you're a couple now," Camille said, temporarily forgetting the notebook problem. "Congratulations."

He ducked in embarrassment. "Yeah, well."

"Yeah, well." Camille leaned into him with a laugh. "Seems like girlfriends must just be dropping from the sky these days."

With a shake of his head, he laughed. "What can I say?"

For one, single second she glanced past Nick and found herself gazing right into Jaylon's steel hard gaze. Her heart dropped like a rock as the smile slid from her face. Jaylon turned back around to answer Ariana, who had obviously just asked him something. Camille watched them for a moment and then yanked her gaze back to her Physics book.

Concentrate on something you can do—not on the impossible.

For most of class the only thing Jaylon could concentrate on for more than a second or two was the two lovebirds across the room. If he had only slightly less self-control he might actually have walked up and knocked Nick's head off his shoulders; however, explaining that to Ariana much less to Mrs. Allen would not be pleasant.

So he was resigned to watching them from across the room, wishing the entire time that he had the guts to tell Camille what a scum her boyfriend was.

He was supposed to be critiquing Ariana's monologue, but sitting on the stage only inches from her what he really wanted to do was hear the monologue Camille was reading for Nick on the steps. She smiled at something Nick said and ducked her head. Her braid swung gently over her shoulder, and he remembered the way her hair fell over the sides of her face the night of their ice cream social. The thought sent his heart racing.

"Hey," Ariana suddenly said in front of him. "I said, 'What do you think?'"

"What do I think?" he asked, struggling to come back from his journey to the steps.

"About the monologue?"

"Oh, yeah." He yanked his attention back to her. "It was great."

"Great?" Ariana asked in horror. "What kind of critique is that?"

Jaylon shook his head to clear it. "I'm sorry. Umm, it could use some work."

Ariana's eyes went hard as he squirmed under her scrutiny. "That attitude's never going to get you into Julliard."

"I'm sorry." He shifted again. "I zoned out for a minute." His gaze caught Camille's hand as it pushed up the edge of her glasses and then fell to the other one holding the page of script. "It won't happen again."

Just then the bell rang, and he watched Nick offer Camille a hand up off the stairs.

"Play critiques are due Wednesday," Mrs. Allen called over the clattering of departing students. "We'll continue this tomorrow."

Jaylon scrambled up to his feet.

"I finished my essay for the Julliard application in history today," Ariana said over her shoulder as Jaylon followed her off the stage, his attention focused squarely on the braid already swaying up the center aisle. "I thought you might like to read it... you know, to get some ideas for yours."

"Okay," Jaylon said, trying to map out a plan to get the notebook to Camille without Nick or Ariana as an audience. He couldn't very well call her name out as that would attract the attention of more than just Nick and Ariana. Quickly he reached down and grabbed his things just as Camille walked out the auditorium door.

"I can help you with yours if you want," Ariana said, following him up the aisle. "I mean if you need some inspiration."

He never heard the implication in her voice. His hopes for getting the notebook to Camille today evaporated as Ariana stuck right to his side.

"...Seth's dad's house Halloween weekend," Ariana said. "He's going to Vegas, so Seth has the house all to himself."

"Cool," Jaylon said, hoping that was an appropriate answer.

When they crossed out into the hallway, the braid was long gone.

It was an act of utter desperation. Camille knew her notebook had gone down a permanent black hole that she didn't want to focus on too much or her head might explode. The only other logical explanation was to rent the video. It wasn't a totally bad idea, except that she had no idea how many little details could've been done differently in the real, live version.

More than that, she felt like she was cheating on the assignment. They were supposed to go watch a play—not rent a movie. But then again, she reasoned as she paid for the movie, she had gone to the play. Watching it again on television was doing more work than was required.

However, not even she was buying that. She hadn't seen anything past the second act, and she knew it. At home she popped the video in and grabbed another notebook. This one she wouldn't let out of her sight.

Although she basically remembered the first part, for the sake of her note taking, she watched the whole thing. The cockney accents on the video were much harsher than the ones the actors had used in the theatre, and it took awhile for her ears to adjust to the new language.

As she watched, her options of what to focus on for her paper widened. The voices, the characters, the storyline. They were all possibilities. However, by the time Higgins and Pickering were congratulating themselves on their great accomplishment, Camille's stomach had formed a hard ball of disgust for the two. Eliza, who had made it through the ball without falling on her face once, was cowering in a dark corner as her benefactors reveled in how preposterous the whole ordeal had been.

Camille's face grew hot with the implication of their presumptuousness. She watched Eliza, listening to them, and Camille's heart went out to her. She knew all too well about being someone's charity project, and it really didn't matter how well-intentioned the benefactor was. It was still the deepest form of insult.

She watched the lady the common ignorant flower girl had become, and somewhere, deep down, she wished that she too could be turned into a perfect lady. However, her heart plummeted to the depths of her soul when behind Higgins, Eliza offered no protest to his final demand for his slippers. As the credits rolled, Camille wanted to take Eliza and shake her. Didn't she see, even after coming into herself, how beautiful she was, how it no longer mattered what everyone else thought, how she didn't have to be a doormat for Higgins to step on?

Higgins and his stupid bet. He was above Eliza. He believed it, and so did she, and no amount of coaching and teaching could ever change that. She was who she was, he was who he was, and no matter what she did, in his eyes, she would never be anything more than a common, ignorant flower girl.

As the tape hit the end and whirred into rewind mode, Camille's thoughts turned to Jaylon. He was no different than Higgins. His place in the hierarchy of the school was set, and so was hers. Just because he talked to her, took her out for ice cream, drove her around in his car. It changed nothing. In his eyes, she would always be the klutz with the funny glasses. That hurt, but that was reality, and allowing herself to believe anything else was an invitation to getting her heart shattered.

"All I have to do is get through this semester, and then I'll never have to worry about being Jaylon Quinn's charity case again."

Jaylon looked for her all day on Tuesday as the notebook burned holes through his backpack and his brain. "In a world of glass houses, it takes only one, small stone..."

He had read and reread that paragraph over and over until it was a part of him. More than once his thoughts carried him back to the day when she had fallen on the stage, and he knew he was as guilty as anyone else on that stage for hurling a stone at her. That stone stung his own spirit now as he recalled that the one person who didn't laugh was not him, but Nick.

In a haze of her words, he made his way through the day, now seeing even the smallest encounter with his fellow students in a different light. Without bothering to go to his locker after sixth period, he raced down the hallway to the auditorium. Maybe he could catch her there before Ariana or Nick had a chance to change out their books. He yanked the heavy door open and stepped into the cool, darkness of the auditorium. That room had a way of wrapping around him like a favorite, old blanket.

Carefully he searched the seats as he strode down the aisle. Then just off to the right, he caught her movement, and he smiled. So she was here. His steps quickened as he walked down the slight incline to where she sat. However, when he reached her chair, she didn't look up like he'd expected. Noise pulled his attention to the door, and he knew he had only a few seconds.

"Camille," he said, laying a soft hand on the chair arm beside her and sitting on his heels in the aisle by her seat.

Her pencil streaked across the page at the first sound of his voice, and he laughed as his heart raced out ahead of him.

"Oh, my gosh." She laid a hand over her chest before she flipped the pencil over and erased the errant mark. "You scared me to death."

"Sorry," he said, liking how close his hand was to the heat of her arm. The clattering of students entering the auditorium brought his attention back to his mission. Quickly he dug in his backpack and pulled out the notebook. "I... umm, you left this... in my car... the other night." Fighting to keep his hand from shaking as he held the notebook out to her, he glanced at her only once as she accepted it. "Sorry, I didn't get it back to you sooner."

"Oh, that's okay." She pushed up her glasses as she laid the notebook on top of her other work. "Umm, thanks for returning it."

"No problem," he said just as he looked up and saw Ariana breeze in through the door. In the next breath he realized Nick was already halfway down her row on the other side of her seat. "I'll see ya later." On unsteady legs he stood as Ariana met him in the center of the aisle. "Hey, babe."

Guilt or something very much like it caused him to reach out to Ariana and wind his arm through hers. Without another glance at Camille, he guided Ariana the rest of the way down the aisle to the front row although he could feel her fury in the ice of the glance she shot back in Camille's direction.

"What were you doing talking to super freak?" she asked in what sounded to him like a stage whisper—loud enough for the back row to hear.

"She just said, 'Hi,'" he said with a shrug. "I couldn't very well just walk past her." The stone was out of his hand before he realized it was there, and immediately his spirit regretted it.

"Huh," Ariana said, shaking her head in annoyance. "I would have."

Jaylon watched her take her seat, and then he fell into the seat next to her before busying himself with pulling out his things. "That doesn't surprise me."

"What did Jaylon want?" Nick asked, the anger just underneath his tone as they exited the auditorium in perfect lockstep with each other.

"Oh, nothing, he dropped a book by my chair," Camille said. "I was just giving it back to him." The heat in her ears made them pound. Just thinking about Jaylon's mesmerizing presence was enough to send her sanity flitting away from her.

"How's your paper coming?" Nick asked, shifting to a new topic while Camille's mind was left stuck on the old one.

"Paper?"

"The critique," Nick said with a puzzled look furrowing across his forehead. "*My Fair Lady*?"

"Oh, that paper," she said as though the wheels of her brain had just unlocked. "Pretty good. How's yours?"

"Great. I'm doing it on 'enry 'iggins," Nick said perfectly replicating the cockney accent of Eliza Dolittle.

"What about him?" Camille asked as her brain finally moved from the auditorium seat and Jaylon's gaze to her present conversation with Nick.

"About how his character evolved—you know, rising action, falling action."

"Evolved?" Camille's eyebrows raised in disbelief. "He didn't evolve. At the end he was still as condescending as he was at the beginning."

"No, he wasn't."

"Yes, he was. He expected Eliza to go get his slippers like a good, little puppy dog. He never even considered her feelings. Not once."

"But he helped her. He was glad she was there."

"No, he wasn't," Camille said, her thoughts crashing into Jaylon's eyes again. "He wasn't helping her for her. He was helping her for himself."

Nick shook his head. "What difference does that make? He still helped her."

Camille swung her head to the side in annoyance. "Maybe she didn't want his help."

"Of course she did. She agreed."

"Oh, yeah, like she had a choice."

They walked several more paces in stony silence.

"Well, what are you doing your paper on?" Nick finally asked again.

"Eliza, and how she put way too much emphasis on what everyone else thought."

"What does that mean?"

"It means, she was just fine before Higgins came along, and she would've been just fine without him. Better probably."

"But she would've stayed a flower girl forever if he hadn't offered to help her," Nick protested. "She needed someone to get her out of the gutter, to show her what she could do."

"You don't pick someone out of the gutter as an experiment."

"Higgins was just trying to prove his point."

"And he used Eliza to do it."

They walked up to the lockers, and Camille yanked hers open. "People have feelings, Nick. It doesn't matter if they're rich people and can speak correctly or if they think they come from the gutter. They still have feelings."

"What's up?" Lexie asked, looking from one to the other as Nick planted a kiss on her cheek.

"Nick's doing his paper on how wonderful Higgins was," Camille said not trying to hide the contempt in her voice.

"I didn't say he was wonderful," Nick protested. "I said he evolved."

"Well, apparently you need to look up the word 'evolved.'" Camille yanked her books out and then swung her backpack to her shoulder.

Lexie looked from Nick to Camille as Camille started down the hall and then turned. "Are you coming or not?"

With one helpless look at Nick, Lexie took off after her friend.

"What was that about?" Lexie asked as they walked outside and rounded the corner to the bus stop.

"He doesn't get how condescending and elitist Higgins was," Camille said, anger searing through her voice.

"Nick?" Lexie asked in disbelief. "Nick is the most kind-hearted person I know."

"Yeah, kind-hearted enough to make sure no one is left out," Camille said as the humiliation she felt at being Jaylon's charity case transferred itself to Nick. "Got to be sure everyone is included."

"What's wrong with that?" Lexie asked.

"Nothing," Camille said with a vehement shake of her head. "Nothing's wrong with that, unless that person would rather not be helped."

As she lay in bed with the light on later, the humiliation ran over her again like rainwater. Her paper was far from complete. It hurt too much to write. Eliza was a spineless, helpless guttersnipe just like Higgins said. If Camille could just write about that without all of her own feelings coming out, she would be fine. However, every time she thought about Eliza, she saw herself—hanging back, hoping no one would notice that she wasn't participating, wishing that it all didn't feel like it was ripping her soul to shreds.

Of course, there had always been those teachers who thought they were helping by pulling her into the middle of whatever was going on. They weren't helping. How could they be helping if every time she tried, she fell on her face? It was she who had to deal with the cruel comments in the dressing rooms. It was she who had to endure the annoyance of her classmates when she was reluctantly chosen last for every team. It was she who had to live with knowing she would never aspire to be even average in any field that didn't somehow incorporate numbers.

No, it was she, not they who had to live her life, and all she wanted to do was stay as far away from anything bearing humiliation as possible. They didn't understand. They thought anyone could do it. But they were wrong, and she knew it. No amount of coaching could raise a flower girl up if that flower girl was meant to stay a flower girl.

By the time Camille got to drama Wednesday, she was in knots. Her paper still wasn't finished, and writing even a sentence was hopeless. Everything she wrote made far too much sense, and every word felt like admitting her own failure in life.

Nick slid into the seat next to her. "Where were you at lunch?"

"Trying to get my homework done," Camille said. It wasn't a total lie. She had been working on her paper, but it didn't come close to the real reason she had chosen not to go to the cafeteria with him and Lexie.

"We missed you." He sat, staring at her for a long moment. "Listen, I wanted to say I was sorry about yesterday. I went back last night and looked over my notes, and I guess I kind of see what you mean."

"No," she said, thankful for the darkened theatre. "I shouldn't have jumped all over you about it. I was just stressing out about my paper, and I kind of took it out on you. I shouldn't have. I'm sorry."

"I understand." He smiled and extended his hand. "Truce?"

"Truce."

When the papers were passed down the aisle, Camille made sure Nick wasn't watching as she handed them on. For some reason explaining why she hadn't written the paper seemed even worse than not writing it.

"Today we're going to work on voice expression," Mrs. Allen said as she accepted the papers from the student in the front row. "This it?" She held up the papers, and Camille nodded as though the question was meant explicitly for her. "Remember you need two by semester's end. Some of you need to get on the ball."

Mrs. Allen laid the papers on the stage. "Now, what I want you to do is open in your books to page 72. There are three different mini-scripts to choose from. I want you to choose one, and then with a partner, you are to sit back-to-back and act out the script using only your voice for expression. Okay, that's the assignment, spread out."

Without questioning their partnership, Camille and Nick stood.

"Want to go on stage?" he asked.

Camille shrugged her acceptance. Together they climbed the steps and sat down side-by-side to decide what reading they were going to tackle.

"I like this third one," Nick said, pointing to the last reading after a few minutes.

Without bothering to read through it, Camille agreed. Slowly they slid around each other until she felt the light touch of his back on hers. It was a strange sensation. She slipped her book into her lap and closed her eyes to get herself together. However, when she opened them again, she found herself staring right at Jaylon who sat just across the stage from her. Instantly she ducked her head and shifted uncomfortably. *Don't think about him, just read.*

"You're first," Nick said when the silence behind him had stretched on too long.

"Oh, sorry." She swallowed and focused her attention on the book. "Umm, I didn't ask you to do it *for* me, I asked you to help."

"I was helping," Nick said from behind her.

Her jaw set unconsciously. "No, you weren't. You weren't helping. You were doing. There's a difference."

"There's not a difference. Here, hold this. Now, we just need to glue this down." He paused two beats. "Hold it still."

"I am holding it still."

"No, you're not."

"Yes, I am,'" Camille said vehemently. "I'm doing the best I can."

"Well, that's not good enough," Nick said totally into the scripted fight.

Camille opened her mouth to deliver the next line, but the tears in her throat drowned out the words. She fought to read the words, but the blur in her eyes made that impossible. Desperately she blinked them back, struggling to remember that this was only a script.

"Camille?" Nick finally asked, turning slightly. "It's your line."

"You're right." She sniffled softly. "It's not good enough, and it never will be."

Jaylon watched her face crumple behind her glasses. He knew about readings that hit too close to the truth. It was always a threat on a cold read. As he continued to read his own script, he wondered which one they were doing and what made the tears come to her eyes.

"I just want to make sure we understand each other," Ariana said from behind him.

His gaze reached across the stage to Camille. "Yeah, we understand each other perfectly."

"Sorry about before," Nick said, laying a gentle hand on Camille's back as they started back up the center aisle after the bell had rung. "I was just play-acting. You know?"

"I know," she said from behind the mask she had clamped down over the tears. "It's okay. I should've read the dumb thing before we started."

"Well, next time I'm opting for the love scene instead."

They made their way out into the brightly lit hallway as Camille laughed. "I think we'd better warn Lexie before we start doing any love scenes together."

"You've got a point there," Nick said with a laugh. "By the way, you know Lexie's birthday's next month. I was wondering if you're planning on doing anything for it."

"Anything? Like what? Make a cake?"

"No, I was thinking more along the lines of a party…or maybe a double date."

"Oh, I don't know," Camille said, trying to make it sound light and cheerful although the suggestion sounded more like a death sentence. "Lexie's not much on parties, and I don't know of anyone who'd want to take me out."

Nick took a half-step back and looked at her. "You know, I think we're going to have to find somebody for you."

"Oh, no," Camille said in horror. "Don't you go getting any ideas."

"What? You think you're the only one who can play matchmaker?"

"Matchmaker?" Lexie asked as they walked up. "For Camille? Good luck."

Camille knew the comment was a joke, but somehow it didn't feel like one.

"Why not?" Nick asked. "She can't be any harder to fix up than Eliza was."

"Oh, brother," Camille said in exasperation. "Let's not go there."

"What do you think, Lex? How about Zac?"

"No," Lexie said, appraising Camille. "Better go a little slower than that."

"Slower. Okay. How about Oren?"

"I said slow, not dead."

"Point taken," Nick said. "What about Landon?"

"I don't know," Lexie said, surveying Camille carefully.

"How about nobody." Camille slammed her locker for punctuation. "Look, I'm not interested. Okay? I'm not looking, and I do not want to be set up. Now, I'm going home because I have a very important date with a Calculus book." She slapped her hand on the side of the book. "So if you'll excuse me."

They watched her walk down the hallway.

Nick shook his head. "She needs a date."

Chapter 7

The last thing Camille needed was a date at this point in her life. What she needed was to focus on her schoolwork and heaven forbid getting through drama in one piece.

"Daria!" Camille called when she walked through the door and noticed the pillows stacked next to the television that was blabbering something about detergent. "Hey!"

Daria emerged from her room. Her steps slowed the closer she got to Camille.

"What are you doing home so soon?" Camille asked as she shifted into mother mode.

"I was sick," Daria said, her voice stretching for pathetic.

"Again?" Camille strode over and placed a hand on the child's forehead. "You don't feel hot."

"My head hurt."

"Did you take some aspirin?"

"I can't take aspirin. They're way up in the cabinet."

Camille leveled a skeptical gaze at her sister. "Did the nurse call Mom?"

"Uh-huh."

"And Mom came and got you?"

"And brought me home."

"Uh-huh. And this sickness, how did it start?"

"Right before recess. My tummy started hurting."

"I thought you said you had a headache."

"Yeah, and then my head started hurting, so I went to the nurse."

Camille shook her head. It was the fourth time in two weeks she had come home to this story, and although she wasn't actually the mother, she realized that if she didn't do something about it, no one would.

"Go get cleaned up, and you can help me make supper," Camille said, fighting not to let the exasperation sound in her voice. She picked up the pillows and threw them back on the couch as she watched her little sister's shoulders slink down the hallway. There was something wrong all right, but it wasn't a headache.

"I was thinking about Daria," Camille said as she and her mother sat at the dinner table, the remnants of chicken kiev between them. Daria had been sent to take her bath, and now was as good a time as any to broach the subject.

"Oh, what about her?"

"Well, she's been having trouble in school."

"Trouble?" her mother asked with instant concern. "What kind of trouble?"

"I don't think she fits in too well." Camille chose her words carefully. The last thing Daria needed was to referee a fight. "She's been getting sick a lot lately. She's missed more than a week this month."

"She's still recovering from that flu she had."

"Yeah," Camille said with a laugh. "That was some flu." She stood and slowly put the dishes in the dishwasher as she gathered her courage. "I was thinking I might take her down to the Community Center on Saturday. They've got lots of stuff for kids her age. It might be good for her to make some new friends—get her out of the apartment for awhile."

The shrug was barely there. "All right, but this is your responsibility. I'm not taking her down there. I don't have time to be chauffeuring you kids around."

"I'll take care of it, Mom. Don't worry about it."

"It's okay, Dar," Camille said as the little girl clutched her hand on Saturday morning. "I promise I won't leave."

"Why can't I just watch cartoons?" Daria asked in sheer panic. "Why do I have to come here?"

"Because there are a lot of neat things you can learn here that you can't learn watching cartoons."

"I don't want to learn anything new. I want to watch cartoons."

Camille heaved a sigh of resignation. "I'll tell you what. You try it for a couple of weeks, and if you still don't want to come, you don't have to."

"I don't want to come."

"I said in a couple of weeks," Camille said. The little girl fell into a pouting silence at her side as Camille pulled her to the front counter. "Good morning."

"Hello," a nicely dressed woman behind the counter said with a kind smile. "May I help you?"

"Yes. At least I hope so. My name is Camille, and this is my little sister, Daria."

"Nice to meet you. I'm Mrs. Dixon."

Camille exchanged handshakes with the lady and then pressed on. "Daria would like to take one of your classes."

"Oh." Mrs. Dixon laid down her clipboard and smiled down at Daria. "Which one are you interested in?"

"Well, we're not really sure. What do you have open?"

"Let's see." Mrs. Dixon pulled another notebook out of the stack on the counter. "We've got a couple of spots in the soccer class."

"How about that, Dar? Soccer?" The look on Daria's face told Camille that suggestion was out.

"No?" the lady asked. "Well, we have an opening in the pottery class, but I'm afraid the teacher isn't coming in today. We also have one spot left in the Theatre Arts class."

"Theatre Arts?" Camille asked as her attention piqued. "What do they do in there?"

"Mostly they just do little exercises to get them over shyness and get them more comfortable with being on stage."

Somehow she felt exactly like Mr. Marsh must have when she bent down and looked into her little sister's eyes. "That sounds like fun. Don't you think? You'll get to do like I'm doing at school." The night Camille had come home and announced that she was taking drama, Daria had asked her every question in the book and then some. However, that enthusiasm had now turned to utter fear. "What do you think, Dar? Doesn't that sound like fun?"

The little head moved first to one side and then to the other as the tiny waves fell into the little girl's face. "I want to go home."

Camille stood and looked at Mrs. Dixon. "We'll take Theatre Arts."

After the appropriate papers were filled out, Camille followed Mrs. Dixon down the little hallway with Daria's hand clutching her own until her fingers felt like they might turn purple. She, of all people, understood the fear behind Daria's eyes, but she also knew that hiding in a tiny apartment watching cartoons was not the way to overcome that fear. Just because she had turned into an Eliza didn't mean Daria had to.

"They're right in here," Mrs. Dixon said. "We're really lucky that Mr. Quinn offered to get this class started. It's so hard to find good volunteers these days."

Camille nodded politely as they entered the small auditorium, which surrounded a stage filled with giggling, squirming children.

"Okay," the young man with suspenders standing with his back to the audience at center stage said. "It's time to get started."

"Mr. Quinn," Mrs. Dixon said at Camille's side as they approached the stage.

By the time she made the connection, it was too late to run. In one breath Camille found herself at the base of a stage, staring up into the laser-hot intensity of his unfathomable blue eyes, wondering how in the world she had gotten there.

"Oh, hi," Jaylon said, and his voice registered almost as much surprise as her heart felt.

"Hi," she said as the rest of the room dropped away.

"This is Daria," Mrs. Dixon said, indicating the child. "She's going to be joining your class."

"Oh," Jaylon said as his gaze fell from Camille's face to the little girl cowering behind her. "That's great."

Camille's entire body had gone numb the second he had turned around, and although she knew she should be saying something, nothing would come out.

"Why don't you come on up?" Jaylon asked, offering his hand to Daria.

The fingernails digging into her hand brought Camille back from la-la land. "It's okay, Dar." She turned and knelt next to her sister. "You'll be fine."

"No," Daria said in a voice strangled by fear. "I don't want to!"

"Hey, listen," Camille said, hugging her little sister. "It's okay. I can stay for awhile if you want me to." The tears in her sister's eyes ripped her heart out. It was like looking into the fear that lurked in her own soul. "It's all right. I'll stay."

Fighting not to look across the stage at him, Camille walked up the steps with Daria, found a spot in the group, and sat down. Daria sat on her lap and huddled into her as far as the limits of her body would allow.

"We're so glad we've got some more friends to join us today," Jaylon said, sitting down on a chair that was far too small for him. But Camille noticed how he didn't look at all uncomfortable or out of place on it. In fact, he looked like this was his favorite chair in the whole world. "But we need our new friends to introduce themselves so we can get to know them."

Immediately every set of eyes on the stage shifted to them, and Camille felt Daria's panic.

"We just need to know your name and one thing that you like to do," Jaylon said to Daria, effortlessly creating a safe place for her to venture into.

The little girl shifted slightly on Camille's lap as she looked at her new teacher.

"My name is Daria Marek," the little girl said softly, "and I like to watch cartoons."

"Cartoons?" Jaylon asked as though she was the first kid he'd ever met who liked cartoons. "What kind of cartoons do you like?"

"Mickey Mouse," Daria said with a small giggle.

"Oh, yeah, Mickey. He's great," Jaylon said, nodding seriously. "My favorite is Daffy Duck. 'Wwhath's that you thay?'"

The children around him laughed, and Camille laughed with them as she felt Daria relax.

"Okay," Jaylon said as he looked at Camille, "and now our other new friend."

The blood drained from Camille's face as the gazes came back on her. "Me? Oh, well, umm, my name is Camille Wright, and I like math."

"Eeww!" the children said, and Jaylon joined in good-naturedly. "Math? Eeww!"

Camille laughed in spite of her lightheadedness.

"Cool," Jaylon said with a smile as he stood. "Now, last week we talked about space substances. Remember how we played with my favorite toy?" He held up a perfectly formed, perfectly invisible ball. "Remember how we played with my favorite toy? Katelyn?"

"We threw it to each other and didn't let it drop."

"Good girl," Jaylon said. "Well, today, I brought a whole bunch of my favorite toys. You want to see what they are?"

"Yeah!" the children chorused.

"Okay, let's see what I've got." Jaylon laid the ball on the floor, stood, and walked over to the side of the stage that was utterly empty. He stopped two feet from the curtain and bent over what Camille would've sworn was a cardboard box had her eyes not told her that there was absolutely nothing there. "Let's see."

Slowly he reached in and pulled up a long string. "Does anyone know what this is?"

"A jump rope," one of the children said.

"That's right, Katelyn. Here, why don't you come hold this jump rope?" One-by-one he pulled things out of his magical box until three children held the magical items—a jump rope, a Frisbee, and a set of marbles. "Now we need a Magic Chooser." He looked around at the remaining children. "Daria, why don't you come choose for us?"

Camille felt her sister shrink back as Jaylon stood a moment and then approached slowly holding his hand out to her.

"It's okay. I'll help you." He stopped a foot from them and gazed down at Daria as though she had just appeared there by real magic. "Come on. It'll be fun."

Little by little Daria's hand went up, and when their hands were together, she let go of Camille, and he led her across the stage. Camille couldn't tell if her heart was racing for Daria or from being able to look into his eyes again.

"Okay, this is really simple," Jaylon said, bending down to Daria's height and putting his hands on her shoulders, "but it's really important."

Daria nodded as if the world might end if she didn't get it just right.

"Now, what I need you to do is to make our teams for us. First, you go choose somebody out there." He pointed to the children still seated on the stage. "And you bring them over here, and choose which team they are supposed to be on."

Daria nodded again solemnly and turned to get her first match.

"Oh, no wait!" Jaylon leaped to his feet. "You need your magic matchmaking wand." He went over to his infamous magic box and started digging through it. "No, not my rock." With effort he heaved the invisible boulder over his shoulder, and several students ducked out of the way to avoid being crushed. "No, not the map to my house."

Giggles rang out around her as Camille, too, sat mesmerized by his performance.

"Ah, here it is." He pulled a long wand out of the box and ceremoniously handed it to Daria. "Now, Magic Chooser. You may begin."

In fascination, Camille looked at the little girl who only moments before had cringed at the thought of being left alone with these people, and she smiled. Daria's face glowed with the unquestioned belief that she was important. She was the Magic Chooser.

Thoughtfully she made her way around the room, matching children to their rightful team, and no one who just happened into the room would've been able to guess that this was anything other than a very solemn ceremony of the highest importance.

When the last child had been matched, Daria looked back at Camille.

"Oh, no, I'm not playing," Camille said quickly.

"On this stage everybody plays," Jaylon said, looking at her with a seriousness that melted her protest.

Camille's gaze snapped from Daria to his, and it was difficult to remember that he wasn't some master wizard. Staring into his eyes, she could see the magic all the way through him.

"Okay," she said softly.

Daria paired her up with the jump rope team and then put the magic wand back into Jaylon's box before joining Camille, but the magic aura still seemed to surround the little girl.

"Great," Jaylon said with a smile. "Now, remember, your space object is not imaginary. It is real. It has a shape and a substance all it's own. You must respect that."

All the children nodded right along with Camille.

"You may begin."

Camille looked at the children for direction as to what to do next.

"I'll take this side," Katelyn said, taking charge of her group. "Here,

Jomei, you take this side."

The small Japanese child took the other side of the rope, and after only a moment's worth of confusion, the two were swinging the rope for someone to jump in.

"Daria, you go first," Katelyn called, and Daria hesitated for only one second before running into the middle of the rope.

And for all the information of her eyes, Camille would've sworn there was actually a rope there to be jumped.

"That was so great!" Daria said as Camille watched Jaylon talking with the other parents.

She wanted to say something to him. Thank you or you're amazing or something. Suddenly his little chat session disintegrated, and he walked up the three stage steps, grabbed his coat, and turned, looking every bit the polished actor she now knew he was.

If Julliard didn't accept him, they were crazy.

"Hey, there," he said when he descended the steps and caught sight of them still standing off to the side. In one motion he threw the coat over his shoulder.

"Hi," Camille said suddenly wishing they had just ducked out when they had the chance. "I just wanted to say thanks."

His face broke into a smile as he ran his fingers through his hair. "So, you had fun?" Then he remembered the real reason she was there. "Daria?"

"It was so cool!" Daria said, bouncing between them as Camille smiled down at her.

"I'm glad you liked it." His smile emphasized the words. Then he redirected his focus on Camille. "So, you liked jumping rope?"

"I haven't jumped rope since I was Daria's age," Camille said with a laugh as they turned to exit the auditorium. "But I have to say, it's much easier with an invisible rope."

He looked at her questioningly.

"Oh, I'm sorry, a space-substance rope," she corrected herself. "So, where'd you learn that anyway?"

"Theatre Camp when I was 10," he said with a smirk. "Only we played with water balloons."

Camille nodded in mock fear. "I'm glad we got the jump rope."

They walked outside being met instantly with an overhang of clouds and the first few droplets of rain.

"Great day," Jaylon said, throwing his coat on and stuffing his hands in his pockets.

"Yeah, fabulous," Camille said with a laugh, matching his steps perfectly as she held on to Daria's hand.

"You want a ride?" he asked, suddenly stopping on the sidewalk by his car.

"A ride? Oh, no. No," Camille said. "But thanks anyway. I guess I'll see you Monday."

"I'm looking forward to it," he said with a casual wave.

"Oh, okay." Her hand went up in something resembling a wave. "'Bye."

"'Bye," he said, watching every step she took backward. "'Bye, Daria. See you next week."

"'Bye, Mr. Quinn," Daria said at Camille's side.

With one final wave they turned and ran to the bus.

He stood on the sidewalk watching them go long after they'd climbed the bus steps. Camille Wright. Something about her made him question every word that came out of his mouth. The thought of playing Magical Box with her or anyone else he knew made his head spin.

That was such a kid's game. Guys who were cool didn't play Magical Box. In fact, as he climbed into his car and felt it roar to life beneath him, he thought about what Ariana would say if she ever found out.

"Magical Box?" he said in perfect mimic of her. "I bet they don't do that at Julliard."

He steered into traffic and punched a CD into the player. Ariana was right. The dream of Julliard was slipping away while he was busy playing Magic Jump Rope with a bunch of kids. But then a picture of Camille sitting on the stage, watching him in fascination, slipped across his mind.

Somehow he knew that she didn't think it was silly of him to be there. Somehow she felt the same magic he did. He could see it in her eyes.

The car rolled into Hollybrook only a few short minutes later, and still his thoughts were on Camille. Slowly he climbed out of the car, walked in, and in no time he was sitting with Grandma Elana in the Garden Room watching the rain slide down the picture windows in various patterns.

After three sonnets about love, his heart could take no more. "Grandma Lani? Mind if I ask you a question?"

She just stared straight ahead with unseeing eyes.

"See, it's like this... there's this girl at school, and she and I could be really good friends I think. 'Cept she's not really my type. I mean, she likes math, and who likes math?" He shook his head as though it was the most absurd idea in the world. In exasperation, he ran one set of fingers through his hair. "Anyway, she really seems nice, and I'd really like to get to know her better, but she has this boyfriend, and they seem really happy together... except I think he's seeing someone else too... and then there's Ari... and I don't know."

He looked at his grandmother. Wishing she could really answer him, he laid a soft palm on her wrist. "You know, sometimes I wish I could be five-years-old again, and we could just go out and swing. Remember that?"

For one brief second he saw the recognition in her eyes, and then it was gone again. "Yeah," he said softly as he hugged the bony shoulders to him. "I miss that, too."

For the rest of the weekend Camille thought about him. There wasn't all that much else to do. Lexie went to Homecoming with Nick—an event she and Lexie had spent the last three years sitting at Camille's house together ridiculing. But things had changed drastically since then, for Lexie anyway.

By Monday afternoon Camille wasn't exactly sure what she expected to happen when she saw Jaylon, but whatever it was, it didn't. He walked right past her seat as though Saturday was actually just the dream she'd convinced herself it was.

"Class!" Mrs. Allen clapped at center stage. "Last week we worked on voice expression. Today we're going to work on the level below voice expression—a much more difficult ability to learn. They say that when communicating, only 7 percent of our meaning is conveyed with the words we use. Thirteen percent is conveyed by the tone of our voices, but 80 is conveyed by our body language."

Camille shifted in her chair, not liking where this exercise was headed at all.

"Now, of that 80 percent, you can break it down into hand gestures, body stance, facial expression, and eye expression. I'm sure you've seen people who could tell you more with one look than they could say in a volume of text."

The laser-intensity of his steel-blue eyes stared down at her from the Community Center stage as Camille sank into her seat.

"In the interest of broadening our horizons, I think today we will work in two circles."

Camille's stomach roiled. It was bad enough to have to do these exercises with Nick. She didn't want to broaden her horizons. She wanted to stay right where she knew she was perfectly safe.

"Come on up," Mrs. Allen said, motioning with her arms.

The students began filing onto the stage, and one clump at a time, Camille followed them up the steps as though she was headed directly to the gas chamber.

"Please form two circles facing each other."

Camille stood on the inside circle, hoping that Nick would be there when she opened her eyes again, but when she looked up it was Mark, not Nick she was looking at. Shyly she smiled as Mrs. Allen continued.

"Let me explain how this works. I want you to stand together with the person who is now your partner—much like you did when we did the last eye contact exercise, but this time you are to put your hands up to each other's—just barely touching. In a way this is a combination of the mirroring exercise and the eye contact exercise, only this time, you must actually communicate with your eyes.

"Your goal is to move your hands as one while maintaining eye contact. Ultimately you should be able to do this in complete silence, but for this exercise I'll help you out with some music. Call this shadow dancing." Mrs. Allen went over to the curtain and pulled out a CD player. "Remember that you must always be in the experience. That is the number one goal in acting. Become your character, and follow the give and take of your fellow actors on more than just a script level.

"We'll start with one hand only. Remember, there is to be no talking at all," Mrs. Allen said as the soft rock song filled the stage area. "Okay. You may begin."

In slow motion, Camille's gaze traveled up to Mark's eyes and locked. Wordlessly her right palm mirrored his left. She tried to breathe as his hand slid to one side and then back. Touching only at the fingertips, she followed his lead until after only moments, they were moving in perfect unison.

"Good," Mrs. Allen said as she walked around the circle, arms crossed. "Now, I want the inner circle to shift one person to your left, and start over."

Camille's palm dropped from Mark's, and her feet pulled her to the left where she met up with Stephanie's eyes. Stephanie was barely an inch shorter than Camille and looked about as comfortable with all of this as Camille felt. They smiled just before Camille's gaze dropped. With a breath she looked up, and blocking out an overwhelming desire to crumple into a pit of self-consciousness, she held up her palm and met Stephanie's.

It took a minute before they determined a leader, but once Stephanie took the lead, the exercise became effortless.

"Okay, inner circle, left again," Mrs. Allen said.

Camille's brain went on revolt. It seemed that just when she became accustomed to one partner, it was time to change. However, with relief she realized her feet had pulled her in front of Nick. Their eyes and smiles said, "Hi" for them as their palms went up with no pretense.

Before Mrs. Allen even had the chance to commence the exercise, they were moving in perfect sync. It occurred to Camille as she looked into his perfectly kind eyes that she wished he and she had been the ones to fall for each other. However, although their friendship was rock-solid, that was all either of them would ever want from the other. Looking into his eyes, she knew that completely.

"Okay, change," Mrs. Allen said.

With a smile, they said, "Good-bye," and Camille shifted left, coming face-to-face with Ariana. In annoyance Ariana put up her palm, and Camille was sure she felt the shiver of revulsion run through her partner the second their hands touched.

It was amazing how condescending a single look could be. Camille's spirit withered under the hot, blinding sun of Ariana's gaze. She tried to follow Ariana's movement, but her brain was concentrating so hard on finding ways not to screw up, that it couldn't follow a thing.

When Ariana moved left, Camille invariably moved right. When Ariana went up, Camille's hand went down. Contempt coursed through Ariana's eyes with each mistake Camille made until it felt that her partner was a full foot taller than she.

Finally, mercifully, Mrs. Allen called, "Change."

With one shift of her feet, Camille found herself looking into the steel hard blue gaze she had been fighting so hard to forget for three days. Immediately her gaze fled, searching for safety. However, when she looked back at him, it was only kindness not contempt that she saw.

Struggling not to release her fear from the Ariana-partnership, she put her palm up to meet his. The first touch sent an electric shock right down to her toes, and she felt herself falling into the trance of his eyes.

Without her noticing, the music stopped.

"Before we begin this next song, I want to take this a little farther. Instead of just one palm, I want you to try two," Mrs. Allen said as Camille and Jaylon continued to stare at each other.

Ever-so-slowly his other palm came up in invitation to hers. Without glancing at it, Camille's hand came up to meet it. In one breath her entire being was charged with his touch.

"You may begin," Mrs. Allen said as the music started.

As one they began to move, first one hand and then the other—never so much as questioning which they would move next. After a few moments, Camille realized that it wasn't simply a matter of her falling in and following his actions. Alternately he would take the lead and then as though he had made a sweeping gesture allowing her permission to take the lead, she would step in front of him, and his hand would follow hers.

Hand-to-hand their souls moved as though they were spinning around a dance floor in perfect arcs.

"Great. Great," Mrs. Allen said with a clap that didn't phase either one of them.

Their dance ended although their gazes held for two more breaths.

"Please, have a seat," Mrs. Allen said, motioning to the stage.

Camille turned and folded her legs underneath her without really realizing she had moved. She didn't have to look; she could feel him right there behind her.

"Tell me what you learned by this exercise," Mrs. Allen said, looking around the circle.

"That some people are more clumsy than they first appear," Ariana said in undisguised disgust, and immediately Camille remembered where she was and more to the point who she was.

Her confidence collapsed in on itself and plummeted through the stage floor like a rock. She wished again for the safety of the darkened walls. Suddenly the stage seemed bathed in searing, white, hot light, and there was no where to run from that light.

"Acting is about give and take, Ariana," Mrs. Allen said, folding her arms across her chest. "It's not about proving how wonderful you are at someone else's expense."

Ariana's gaze rolled heavenward. "Well, sometimes that just can't be helped."

With a shake of her head Mrs. Allen turned to the rest of the class. "Anyone else?"

"It's harder to read someone's thoughts than it looks," Keane said.

"It certainly can be," Mrs. Allen said with a nod. "It becomes even more difficult when you're talking about connecting with several different actors in a scene rather than just one."

"But it's magic when you get it right," Jaylon said from behind Camille, and her pulse began racing until she realized there was no way he could be talking about her.

"Yes, it is," Mrs. Allen said just as the bell rang. "Well, that's it for today. We'll start here tomorrow."

Camille was fighting to make sense of what just happened when suddenly she realized Jaylon was standing over her with his hand out-stretched. With a smile of genuine gratitude, she laid her hand in his as the now-familiar electricity raced up her arm. Once she was on her feet, they stood for one more moment simply lost in the unbelievable magic of the other's eyes.

"Jaylon?" Ariana asked derisively.

"Yeah," he said as one corner of his mouth went up in a silent apology to Camille. "I'm coming."

Then he stepped past her and took Ariana's hand, leaving Camille stranded dead center stage.

"Hey, Camille," Nick called from the base of the stage. "You coming?"

Her gaze dropped from Jaylon's departing back as her spirit and heart dropped with it. "Yeah."

Chapter 8

It is utterly stupidity to let yourself fall for someone so totally out of your reach. Over and over Camille told herself that, and over and over throughout the rest of the week she forgot. During class when she was supposed to be concentrating on the day's exercise, she would catch herself staring in his direction. The magic seemed to follow him at every step. It would seep through her soul so that it felt like she, too, could do anything. But then Ariana's comments would come back to her, and the magic would vanish again.

Her heart wanted nothing more than to go up and tell him exactly what she was feeling, but her brain knew better than to let her feet have that much freedom. An actual, "Get lost" from him would kill her. No, it was far better to hang back in the darkness of the theatre walls and watch him from there.

On Saturday morning when she opened the Community Center door with Daria's hand in hers, it was all she could do to keep her feet on the ground. They walked down the hallway to the auditorium, but as soon as they walked through the door, her spirit took flight again.

In khaki pants, a white pinstriped shirt, and suspenders, he looked totally ready to take on the whole world, and all she wanted to do was take a seat and watch.

"Daria," Jaylon said happily as he looked down from the stage. Then a smile spread across his face and right into Camille's heart. "And you brought your big sister again."

Camille's gaze couldn't hold his. She was sure he could see every feeling rushing through her. "I'm not staying. Umm, I think Daria will be fine without me."

"Not staying?" he asked as though that was terrible news. "Oh, man, I was hoping I could get you to help me."

"Help?" she asked, looking up and getting caught in the swirling excitement of his eyes. "Me?"

"Yeah," he said quickly repositioning himself on the stage. "I could use a couple of extra hands. That is, if you're not doing anything else."

"Oh," she said taken aback by the offer. "No, I just didn't think you would want me around."

He checked her with an odd look before that amazing smile spread across his face again. "Of course I want you around."

Her gaze fell to the floor as her heart took off around a racetrack.

"So, will you stay?" he finally asked, tilting his head so he could get a better look at her.

"Yeah," she said even as she warned her heart not to read too much into the offer, but it was too late. With one look in his eyes, it was speed-racing around the track.

Jaylon could feel her watching him, following him around the stage, and he had to keep reminding himself how professional he was supposed to act. She was just someone who brought her kid sister to his class. If he held onto that, he would make it through this. Somehow.

He had watched her all week, jealousy burning in his stomach every time Nick touched her or made her laugh. And the only way he had made it through the week was by focusing on Saturday when they could be together—no Ariana, no Nick—just the two of them and a room full of kids.

"Okay, everybody have a seat, and we'll get started," he said, wishing his voice would stop squeaking.

The kids sat down, and slowly the chattering subsided.

"We're going to play a game today called Dr. Mix-up." He sat down on his little chair and prayed that it wouldn't dump him in the floor. "Now, I'm going to choose somebody to be it."

Instantly 19 hands went in the air.

"Not yet," he laughed. "Let me explain the rest of the game." The hands sank as he glanced at Camille for one second and then thought better of that move. "First, I'm going to split you into two groups to make it easier the first couple of times. One group will go with Camille, and one group will stay with me. Let's see..."

Quickly he split them into groups before continuing the instructions. "We're going to choose someone to be Dr. Mix-up." He looked at Camille who immediately fell into her role as teacher. Two Dr. Mix-ups were chosen and sent into the hallway. "Okay in your group, everyone link hands. Good. Now, I want you to mix yourselves up. Like this."

He took hold of Cory's shoulders and pushed him under the hands of two other children around to one side and through the arms of two other children. "Get as mixed-up as you possibly can, but don't let go. Okay?"

The children nodded as did Camille.

"Great. Then mix up."

Gradually and then faster the children began to crumple the circles.

"Don't let go," he called over the growing confusion. "Don't break your hold."

Screams and shouts in the midst of the increasing chaos erupted as Camille's whole group struggled to stay on their feet.

"Okay, great! Now, when you think you're as mixed up as you can get. You yell, 'Doctor Mix-up!'" Instantly the children mimicked his call for help as their laughter mounted.

The two Dr. Mix-ups walked back in and looked skeptically at the groups.

"Come on! Come on!" Jaylon waved them up onto the stage. "Your job is to get this untwisted without breaking anyone's hold."

"Help!" the twisted children chorused.

"Go for it," Jaylon said, smiling at the wide-eyed skepticism of the two doctors.

They went to work on their respective groups as Jaylon and Camille called out helpful hints. Slowly the two sets of tangled students disentangled and became perfect circles once again.

"Good job!" Jaylon said, laughing and clapping. "We need new doctors."

"Me! Me!" the children chorused.

"Let's see, Katelyn and Daria."

The two girls raced off the stage, and as soon as the door closed behind them, he looked back at the remaining children. "Okay, go."

They had played for more than an hour before Jaylon suggested that they combine the groups. Camille was slightly disappointed at the suggestion. It meant that her usefulness for the day was over. But she never moved from the stage as she watched the kids tangle and untangle several times. Finally just before it was time to leave Jomei came up with a brilliant suggestion.

"We want you to play," Jomei said to Jaylon.

"Me?" Jaylon asked as though he had never considered such a thing. "Oh, I don't think so."

"Come on! Please!" the children called. "One time!"

"Okay," he finally said with a mischievous grin, "I'll play if Camille will."

Her shields didn't have time to come up before she was hit double barrel with his smile and his eyes.

"Oh, I don't think so," she said instantly backing off the stage. "I'm not very good at this kind of thing."

"Please! Please!" the children yelled. "Please, Camille!"

She looked across their heads at him and shook her head, knowing she couldn't run. "Fine."

"Yeah!"

Jaylon joined the group on one side, and Camille joined on the other.

Cory was chosen to be Doctor Mix-up, and the second he left the room, with glee the children set about snarling themselves into one big, tangled mess. In no time Camille's arms felt like they should be made of spaghetti. One was wrapped completely around her back as she knelt on the floor. The other was stretched out between two little legs in the other direction. At the first cry for help, she joined right in. "Dr. Mix-up! Help!"

Once Dr. Mix-up was back, it took an eternity of untangling and giggles to sort out the mess.

"Could you please hurry?" Camille asked, trying to be polite and teacher-like although her arms were about to snap off. "Please?"

"Here," Cory said, pulling one leg over her arm making a little more air at the bottom of the pile.

She took a breath of fresher air just as she looked across the mess and caught Jaylon laughing at her. Suddenly trapped in the hilarity of the situation, a small laugh escaped her throat. The more she laughed, the wider his smile became. She was caught, and she was helpless, but she was having the time of her life.

"Okay, Jason," Cory said from somewhere far above her. "You step over here."

At that moment the pile on top of her shifted dangerously as she felt a small foot wedge itself securely in the crook of her elbow. "Be careful." With one glance at the sudden fear in Jaylon's eyes she knew the whole thing was falling.

Without questioning the move, she let go of her hold on the two hands on either side of her and landed on her back flat on the stage just as small bodies began pummeling hers. They bounced off of her as her own body cushioned their landings. In less than a heartbeat she was at the bottom of an entire stack of children.

"Here," she heard Jaylon saying from somewhere above her. Daylight seemed a million miles away. Second by second the stack seemed to get lighter until finally she was once again free, and Jaylon was looking down at her with concern. "You okay?"

She rubbed the back of her head gently as she sat up. "Yeah. I'm fine."

"Here." He held out a hand to her, which she accepted and pulled herself to her feet, still smoothing her hair.

When she looked around, she was met by 19 sets of fearful eyes. With a quick brush of her jeans, she laughed. "Just do me a favor, and don't let Cory operate on me anymore."

The children laughed as the first parent walked through the doorway. Jaylon went off to match children with parents, and Camille found Daria and smiled. "That was fun, huh?"

"Yeah," Daria said enthusiastically. "Did you see when I had my hand behind my back like this..."

Just as Camille turned to lead Daria off the stage, she saw Cory standing off to the side, his gaze glued to his shoelaces.

"Stay here. Okay?" Camille said to Daria. She walked over to the little boy with his hands stuffed in his pockets. "Hey."

He didn't look up, so she sat down beside him.

"It's okay," she said, watching him. Her heart could hear the derisive words flowing through his little head.

"I didn't mean to make it fall," he said softly.

"I know you didn't. I was just trying to make a joke," she said, feeling the sadness pour out of his soul into hers. "Hey, it wasn't your fault. Those things happen sometimes."

"But you got hurt."

"No, I didn't. I'm fine. See." She held out her hands for his inspection. "Besides we can't learn if we don't make a few mistakes. Right?"

Slowly he looked up at her, and tears shimmered on his lashes. "I'm sorry."

"No, hey." She folded him into her embrace. "You didn't do it on purpose. You were trying your best. That's what counts. Okay?"

After a moment, he nodded.

"Good. Now, I'll see you next week, and maybe we can play jump rope again. Does that sound fun?"

The little boy's eyes shone with only the smallest hint of sadness as he nodded and then skipped off to join his mother at the bottom of the stage steps. Camille stood and descended the steps herself. She glanced over at Jaylon who was talking to a parent. He was busy, best not to disturb him.

However, just as she was about to gather her coat and head out the door, Jaylon held up his hand to stop her even as he continued his conference. Reluctantly she stopped and shifted feet.

It would've been better if she could've made a clean break. But that wouldn't be happening today. When the parent finally nodded and steered her child in the other direction, Jaylon walked over to Camille, a concerned look etched on his face.

"Are you sure you're okay?" he asked.

"Yeah, few little elbow-sized bruises, no biggy."

"What was wrong with Cory?"

Camille's gaze dropped from his as the guilt over her earlier comment hit her hard. "He thought he was the reason I got hurt. I just told him I was okay, and that I was looking forward to seeing him next week."

A soft smile crossed Jaylon's face. "I'm glad you worked everything out."

"Yep, all better." Camille looked down at Daria so she would have somewhere other than his face to look. "Well, we'd better be going."

Quickly Jaylon headed for the stairs. "Just a second. I'll walk you out."

Foiled again. Why couldn't she just get away from him—and stay away from him? It was a vexing question; however, with him so close, her brain had no hope of tackling it.

"Ready?" he asked, descending the stairs with three clumps.

Camille shrugged. "I guess so."

With Daria between them, they left the auditorium, told Mrs. Dixon good-bye, and walked out into the sunshine.

"Well, I guess this is it," Camille said, hugging her coat to her more as protection against him than because she was cold.

"It doesn't have to be." His eyes called hers to look up. "We could go down the block here and get some burgers."

"We really should be getting home," Camille said, gauging how far it was to the bus stop and how quickly she could make it there with Daria in tow.

"Oh, come on. You've got to eat. Don't you?"

The heat traveled up Camille's ears. "I... didn't really bring any money to..."

"My treat," he said instantly.

Her gaze snapped up from the concrete to his face. "You don't have to do that."

"You didn't have to stay and help either."

"But I wanted to do that," she said, and then she saw a strange look flash through his eyes, and she regretted that statement.

"I just want to take you and Daria for a burger. Come on. That's not asking all that much. Is it?"

Movement at Camille's elbow pulled her gaze down to Daria's upturned face.

"Please, Cami" Daria said, the pleading in her face and her tone. "Please."

"Yeah, please, Cami," Jaylon said, and when she looked up at him again, there was something close to a smirk playing at his mouth.

Finally she shook her head, knowing she was out numbered. "Fine. But we can't stay long."

"One extra-speedy burger coming up."

Camille was careful to keep Daria between them. There was something about the possibility that their elbows might touch that threw her mind into chaos. Once they were in the little burger joint, they sat down, and she made a point to survey the menu carefully. Anything to keep her gaze off of his face and his eyes.

A waitress came and took their order, and then there was nothing left to escape into.

"So, did you have fun today?" Jaylon asked Daria who bounced in the booth three times, jarring Camille's already worn-out nervous system.

"I liked Dr. Mix-up. That was fun. That one time I had one hand behind me and my foot was like between two people, and I was twisted like this." Daria contorted herself into a pretzel and then giggled. "It was great."

Jaylon laughed. "We played that with a hundred people in camp when I was about your age. Talk about crazy. We had four doctors, and they were supposed to get us all untangled. Turned out this one girl would've had to do a back flip to get back in the circle. I still don't know how that happened."

The waitress arrived with their drinks, and Jaylon took a small sip of his. "So Daria, what are you going to be for Halloween?"

Camille watched Daria shrink back into her seat a little bit, and she knew the source of her sister's discomfort.

"We really don't have the money for a costume," Camille said, feeling the need to protect Daria from having to tell Jaylon that herself.

"You don't need money," Jaylon said taken aback. "The best costumes are the ones you come up with on your own anyway."

"We're not very creative around our house," Camille said, wishing he would just drop the subject.

However, Jaylon had already zeroed in on the idea. "Let's think about this. Hmm. You could be a ghost. All you've got to do is get an old sheet for that."

Daria's face scrunched in revulsion. "Boring."

"Okay. How about a card like the king and queen of hearts from Alice in Wonderland? You get a cardboard box and color it like a card. Then you wear black underneath it."

"We're really not very artistic," Camille said, trying again to throw him off this ridiculous idea.

"I had this friend one time who showed up as a sheet of music. She drew notes on a sheet like it was real music. That was pretty cool."

Daria considered that and then shook her head.

"Not that either?" he asked as though he was stymied. "Well, how about this? Why don't you tell me something you really like?"

Knowing she was the center of attention, Daria milked the moment for all it was worth. She cocked her head to one side, presumably going through every experience of her life in search of what she really liked.

"Computers," she finally said with a nod. "We get to play on them at school. They're fun."

"Computers," Jaylon said as the waitress set their plates in front of them. He picked up the ketchup and shook it hard. "Let's see. We could get a big box, and some markers." He put ketchup on his plate and then held it up as an offering to the two of them.

With concern Camille accepted the ketchup wondering when this discussion had gone from you to we.

"I've got an old keyboard at home I could loan you. Actually the thing is pretty useless to me, so you could basically have it. And we could draw a screen on the box or maybe cut the screen out of the box, and we could string cords and wires around you."

Daria was mesmerized by the idea. "That sounds like fun."

"It's just Halloween," Camille said suddenly seeing the stakes of his offer getting much too high. "We can just throw a sheet over her and go around our building."

But Daria was having none of that simple stuff anymore. "No, I want to be a computer."

"We really don't have time to do that," Camille said, hating the fact that she had to be the one to live on ground earth. "Besides, where would we find a box that big?"

"I bet they have something here we can use," Jaylon said between bites. Then before Camille could protest, he summoned the waitress. "You wouldn't happen to have a box about this big would you?"

"A take out box?" the waitress asked in confusion.

"No, for a Halloween costume."

"Oh. I don't know. I could go check."

"Would you mind?"

"No. I'll be right back."

Camille felt like prison bars had just assembled themselves all around her. "You really don't have to do this. I mean we won't be able to get the thing on the bus anyway."

"That's okay." He shrugged as he bit into his hamburger. "I can take you home."

This was getting out of hand.

"I don't know if that's such a good idea," Camille said in trepidation. "I'm sure you've got other things to do."

"Nope. I'm free all afternoon."

The waitress came back carrying a large box. "Is this what you're looking for?"

"Perfect," Jaylon said with a smile.

"Terrific," Camille said under her breath. "Just what we need."

Jaylon found a way to defeat every protest Camille could come up with. In fact, he and Daria seemed to not even be listening to her anymore. They were on a mission to make the best Halloween costume ever, and somehow Camille was just along for the ride. His car pulled up in front of his house, and he jumped out of it with a quick, "Be right back."

Although she told herself not to, Camille sat in the front seat looking in not very well disguised awe at the enormous house beyond. It was huge. Trees shrouded some of it, but she could see enough to push her soul further away from him. What was she doing here? This was Jaylon Quinn, not some geeky freshman with a protractor strapped to his wrist.

As though to remind her of that fact, Jaylon stepped out of his front door at that moment. The promised keyboard was tucked casually under one arm and a brown briefcase-type thing swung from the other hand. He looked like he had just stepped off some men's wear catalog page.

"Sorry," he said when he slid back into the car. "I had to dislodge the keyboard from a mountain of computer stuff."

Camille nodded, wishing her brain could stay on the same track. Maybe if she just didn't look at him, she would be better off. Gazing out her side window, she whipped her thoughts into one straight line. "I didn't know you were into computers."

"Oh, I play around with them some when I get bored."

"So you have your own computer?" Camille glanced over at him and then quickly reversed course to look out the window again.

"Two of them that work, but one of them is basically junk."

He had two working computers? That said volumes about Jaylon Quinn and the world he lived in—far, far removed from her own dank, dark existence.

"You know, I just realized something," Jaylon said as the car slowed.

"What's that?"

"I have no idea where we're going."

For one split second Camille thought he was joking, and then she realized she didn't know where they were going either.

"Oh, I... guess we could go to... my house," she said, wanting that less than anything.

Jaylon drove several more feet. "That doesn't help me much."

"Oh. Yeah. Umm..." And then despite every screaming protest in her head, she directed him through the traffic to their apartment. Every other part of her was trying to find a way out of the situation, but inexplicably her mouth kept giving him the directions until in the blink of an eye, they were sitting at the curb in front of her apartment. The juxtaposition with his house wasn't at all lost on Camille.

They got out, and Jaylon went to the trunk to extricate the box from its depths. When he came around to them again, Daria held the keyboard, and Camille the brown case.

"What's this for anyway?" Camille asked, raising the case slightly.

"Set design," Jaylon said as they followed Daria up the walk to the apartment.

"We're not designing a set."

"Okay. Costume design," he said with a laugh.

Camille surveyed him with a skeptical look.

"Trust me," he said teasingly. "I really can do more than act."

That's what she was afraid of.

They entered the darkened apartment, and Camille's critical eye danced over the room seeing everything that was out of place or a sad replica of the items that she was sure were in his house.

"Let's see what we can do," Jaylon said, sitting down on the couch that Camille was quite sure still smelled like the thrift shop they had gotten it from. However, he seemed not even to notice as he set the box on the coffee table and reached for the case.

She handed it to him and glanced back into the kitchen. "Umm, you want something to drink or something?"

Bolts of steel blue met her gaze when it returned to the living room.

"You have any tea?"

"Yeah... umm, I think so." Her eyes wanted to run, but they couldn't tear themselves from his. Math. His eyes always reminded her of their conversation at the bottom of the stage steps. Vehemently she shook her head to get it to clear. "I'll just get us some."

With wings on her feet, she fled into the kitchen and busied herself with the glasses. If she could just stay in here long enough, he would leave. That would be more than she could ask for at this moment.

"You want sugar?" she called, breaking into the strategizing going on in the living room.

"No, thanks," he called back, and even the sound of his voice was enough to send her heart galloping.

Her shaking fingers managed to get the two glasses of tea and one of orange juice together. When she stepped back into the living room, neither of them noticed her, and for one moment she stood there and simply took in the picture. Jaylon sat, mapping the project out as Daria carefully fingered the contents of the mystery case.

As Camille got closer, she could see its contents—art supplies really, paints in half-a-hundred colors, scissors in various sizes and shapes, pencils and pens arrayed in a rainbow of colors.

"Be careful, Dar," Camille said a little too harshly as she set the glasses on the side table.

"It's okay," Jaylon said off-handedly. "She can't do too much damage." He picked up the box. "Here, stand up. Let's see how we want to do this."

Daria stood, and carefully he set the box over her head. It dropped and covered her all the way past her shoulders.

"I think we can cut our screen out of right here, and then we can make little shoulder straps for the inside so it won't be resting on her head the whole night." Deftly he lifted the box up, and Daria stepped out. "I'm going to need the long scissors." He pointed into the box but didn't grab the scissors, which were easily within his reach.

Very carefully Daria lifted them out and handed them to him like a nurse in the emergency room. With remarkable precision he punctured the box and sent the scissors around the side.

"Cool," he said when he was finished. He positioned the box over Daria again, and then went to work on the shoulder straps. "Here, why don't you two decorate the outside of it?"

Wide-eyed Daria surveyed the case of paints.

"It's okay. Use anything you want," he said with a nod.

Quickly Camille slid to Daria's side before the child had time to destroy the contents of the case. "Here, let me help."

Without question or complaint, Daria settled in between the two of them, and together they worked to fashion the best computer costume ever.

An hour later the paint was drying on the box that sat on the coffee table. Like it or not, Daria would have a costume for the first time in four years. As Camille stood with Jaylon at the door, she tried to push the last time they had gone out trick-or-treating away from her consciousness. It was pointless to go back to that time. All that accomplished was making the pit of her stomach hurt, and to her way of thinking, it had hurt enough.

"Thanks for your help," Camille said deliberately putting a small note of displeasure in her voice. She didn't want to give him the idea that she had enjoyed the afternoon. That seemed far too desperate.

"I had fun," Jaylon said with a soft smile. "If you ever need a great costume, I'm your man."

His words danced through her head. "I'll see you Monday?"

"Count on it."

When he left, she quickly shut the door, but then her heart couldn't take not seeing him one more time. She walked over to the blinds on the window and pushed them aside. Jaylon Quinn. Even if she could actually tell anyone, she knew they would never believe her. She didn't believe it herself. Reluctance and determination struggled to make her heart drop the blind.

"It must be some geek out reach program," she finally said, yanking the anger to her. "Forget about him, Wright."

If only it were that easy.

Chapter 9

By Monday afternoon Camille believed she had succeeded in convincing herself that the whole Saturday thing was a mirage—some trick of magic that made her believe in illusions. That was simply the only explanation for it.

Shrouded in the relative obscurity of the darkened auditorium, she sat crouched over her Physics II book. According to her nervous system, she was concentrating solely on her homework; however, the second her ears picked up Jaylon's voice from behind her, every piece of her body jumped to attention.

Fighting to look casual, she glanced over her shoulder, and her hand went unconsciously to lift her glasses. Like the perfect couple they were, Jaylon and Ariana strode down the center aisle side-by-side. They seemed to be locked in a riveting conversation.

"I got everything we need," Ariana said as she reached up and feathered her fingers through his hair, "my Marc Antony."

"I'm sure Cleopatra herself would be jealous," Jaylon said, wrapping an arm around Ariana's waist, and Camille's gaze fell back to her book.

So it was a mirage. Okay. Now you know. Forget about them. Forget about him. To him you're air. Vapor. Just get some studying done, and get on with your life.

"Good afternoon," Nick said jovially as he slid into the seat next to Camille.

Her pencil continued to make unintelligible marks on her paper. "Whatever."

His eyes narrowed with concern. "What's wrong with you?"

"You have to ask?" She nailed him with a stone-hard gaze that caused him to back up several inches.

"Jeez. You're pleasant this afternoon."

"I've just been hiding my true nature for two months. Be thankful it lasted this long."

Mrs. Allen walked onto the stage, and with an annoyed sigh Camille stuffed her Physics II book into her backpack. Why did her whole life have to be one long drawn out torture session? Avoiding Nick's gaze, she focused on the stage and folded her hands in front of her. One part of her said she shouldn't be mean, but then she glanced across the auditorium where Cleopatra and Marc Antony sat, and every raw nerve in her body throbbed.

"Today we're going to try some improvisation," Mrs. Allen said, and instinctively Camille sunk deeper in her chair. "Please count off starting over here."

Slowly the count worked its way over to Camille who wished she could just crawl under the auditorium seat and stay there forever. However, when the count got to her, she dutifully said, "18."

"Good," Mrs. Allen said when everyone had counted off. "I want all the even numbers on this side of the stage, and all the odd numbers on that side."

Reluctantly Camille followed Nick up the steps and took her place on the opposite side of the stage. She looked around at her fellow "evens," realizing with a sinking feeling that Ariana was in her group. That had to be trouble.

"Okay. I want one player from each side to come to the center of the stage," Mrs. Allen said, waving Keane and Mark forward. "There are two hats filled with character suggestions. Please choose a character." She waited a moment for them to have their characters in hand. "Your task is to become the character you chose and act that out at this door. Keane you are the visitor. Mark you are the house occupant. The rest of you are to watch carefully and decide what they are supposed to be. Whomever gets their character guessed first and the person who guesses correctly win a candy bar for Halloween."

Camille slunk into the stage curtains. Nothing this degrading was worth a candy bar.

"Go," Mrs. Allen said.

Instantly Mark's shoulders hunched over, and Keane dropped to his knees and knocked on the imaginary door. Slowly Mark opened it.

"The hunchback of Notre Dame," someone yelled out, and Mark shook his head in annoyance.

"Santa's elf," someone else yelled.

"Yes?" Mark asked in a squeaky voice as his hand rested on a cane made only of thin air. "May I help you?"

"Hello," Keane said in a high-pitched falsetto. "I'm with Troop 76..."

"A girl scout selling cookies," Jill called out.

"Very good," Mrs. Allen said and doled out candy bars to both Keane and Jill. "Next?"

Two more willing volunteers stepped up, drew out characters, and went through the process again. It wasn't until there were only six people left on the stage that Camille realized she wasn't going to get out of this. Stupidly she had let Nick slide through the door with someone else, so now she was on her own.

She looked across the stage at the three remaining partners—Jaylon, Tessa, and Stephanie.

"Next," Mrs. Allen said, and when no one moved, the moment of doom had arrived. "Stephanie, why don't you come try it?"

If there had been a trap door leading to the fires of hell, Camille would have gratefully jumped down it. But it didn't appear, so with her eyes closed, she stepped forward toward the door.

The lights felt like they were a million degrees, and Camille's heart was thudding with such ferocity that she could barely hear Mrs. Allen's instructions. Trying not to think about the ramifications of the action, she reached into the hat and pulled out a slip of paper. 'A small child left home alone.'

Camille pushed the fact that there were 20 other people watching her away, and slowly sank to her knees. She willed Daria's best terrified look onto her face as she took her place next to what she decided would be her window. In her arm she "held" a teddy bear, thanking providence above for the extra credit work with Jaylon's Magic Box. She peeked out the window as Stephanie, hunched over and holding something in her hand, knocked on the other side. Camille looked over at the door, and her face crumpled.

A single inch at a time, she crossed the stage to the door, and by the time she made it to the door, she was a tiny bucket of water works. The entire frame of her body had become no more than three feet tall. Wiping the tears from her eyes, she examined the door. "Who is it?"

"Hello?" Stephanie said in a shaky old woman's voice. "Buy an apple from an old woman..."

The menacing evil sound in Stephanie's voice forced Camille's true fear to jump to the surface.

Just as she reached up to stick her thumb in her mouth, someone called out, "She's the wicked witch from Snow White!"

"Very good," Mrs. Allen said, clapping. "We didn't even have to open the door for that one."

Camille got to her feet and stepped past the make-believe door, grateful only that today's torture was over. She didn't even pause at the bottom of the steps before she retook her seat next to Nick.

"Nice job," he said, offering her a hand, which she slapped awkwardly. "A little kid, right?"

She nodded and settled back to watch Jaylon become the most annoying, pushy salesman she had ever seen. Tony, on the other side of the door, never had a prayer. As soon as he opened the door, Jaylon hauled his "product," which resembled an enormous vacuum cleaner into the house without so much as a thank you for asking me in.

"Let me explain how wonderful this machine is," Jaylon said, setting up the pieces of the machine as Tony stood blinking in shock. "It's got seven. Count them seven additional attachments... six of which you can only get if you live in Ohio, but that's okay for a small upgrade fee, we can order the attachments for... where am I again?"

"A salesman," several people shouted, laughing.

Jaylon smiled and nodded in satisfaction.

"Very realistic, Mr. Quinn," Mrs. Allen said as she tossed him a candy bar.

He took a quick bow as he departed the stage, and Camille's nausea machine turned on full-blast. How could she possibly have thought he was anything other than an arrogant jerk? Nick was right. Jaylon Quinn thought he owned the school, and his lady vampire, who was at the moment vamping all over the stage, was just as bad or worse.

Liking him was such a joke. It wasn't that he was out of her league. It was more that she wanted nothing to do with the league he was in. The bell rang even as Ariana continued her over-dramatic scene. Without pause, everyone in the audience stood and started talking right over the top of her.

Wanting only to escape, Camille stood and started gathering her things. However, students on their way out bumped into her like foosball men. Fighting to stay on her feet, she reached down and swung her backpack to her shoulder just as someone bumped squarely into her other shoulder.

"The teddy bear was a nice touch," the person said right in her ear.

Instantly Camille spun around and caught Jaylon's gaze as he stepped past her. For half a moment, she thought she must have imagined he'd said anything because he just kept walking. But then he turned and winked at her, and although she knew she shouldn't, she couldn't stop the smile.

"Jerk," Nick said from behind her, and Camille looked back at him. "He ought to learn that the world doesn't revolve around him."

She couldn't agree, and she couldn't disagree, so she changed the subject. "So what are you and Lexie doing for Halloween?"

"I've got a paper for English to finish."

"No trick-or-treating?"

"Nope, not this year," Nick said as they crossed over into the hallway.

"That's too bad."

Nick shrugged. "Halloween was never one of my favorite holidays anyway."

"Oh, yeah, what is?"

"Thanksgiving."

Camille checked him with a questioning look.

"Turkey," Nick said, rubbing his stomach. "Lots and lots of turkey."

"Who's a turkey?" Lexie asked, linking her arm through Nick's.

Camille ducked into her locker quickly. "I didn't say anything."

"Bad news," Nick said, chagrinned.

"You didn't get it finished?" Lexie asked.

"'Fraid not. You're going to have to go be a spook without me." Nick laid his head on the top of Lexie's. "But maybe Camille will take you out trick or treating."

"Yeah," Camille said, wondering when she and Lexie had been out alone together last. Long before Nick, that was for sure. "I'm going to take Dar out later. You're welcome to tag along if you want."

Lexie looked at Nick as though her petulant face might change his mind. "Okay. Fine. I guess since I'm dating Scrooge, I'll have to go with you."

"Hey, Scrooge doesn't like Christmas," Nick said, picking his head up in protest.

"And you don't like Halloween." Lexie said as she punched him softly in the stomach. "Yes, Camille, I'd love to go with you and Daria."

It was such a resounding yes, how could Camille possibly say no?

The plates of false gold draped over Jaylon's Egyptian loincloth did little to ward off the late-October chill.

"Man, it's freezing out here," he said as he hurried his steps next to Ariana's Cleopatra sweeping entrance walk. "Could we hurry it up a little?"

"Cleopatra doesn't *hurry anywhere*," Ariana said regally.

"Oh, yeah, forgive me." He stepped in front of her to open the door to Seth's house. With Seth's parents safely in Las Vegas, it was a foregone conclusion that tonight's party would be a blow out. The only damper was the fact that tomorrow was a school day, but by the looks of the turnout, not many students were overly concerned about that.

As they made their way through the crowd, Jaylon had to remember not only to keep from crashing into anyone, but also not to get too close to Ariana's train. At the refreshment table Seth stood, ripping bags of chips and cans of dip open.

"Hey!" Seth said happily when the two of them sauntered up. "Great costumes."

Ariana bowed gallantly. "As always."

"Where'd you pick her up?" Seth asked. "Egyptians R Us?"

"You should be careful of whom you speak," Ariana said, never breaking character. "My army is poised to defend my throne."

Seth raised an eyebrow and looked over at Jaylon. "Good luck."

"Thanks," Jaylon said dramatically. Taking Seth's hint, Jaylon turned Ariana away from the refreshments and back out to the dancers. "How about it? You want to dance?"

"Is that any way to address your queen?"

Jaylon bowed although what he really wanted to do was throw up. "A thousand pardons your majesty. Wouldst thou endeavor to partake in some rhythmic movement with thy humble servant?"

"Your words are my guide." Ariana outstretched her hand, and Jaylon accepted it.

Not one particle of him wanted to be here. As he took Ariana in his arms for a slow dance, his mind searched for the place on the earth that he really wanted to be. Then the thought of a tiny body, sporting a giant computer head, flashed through his mind, and he had to physically stifle the laugh.

Without question that's where he wanted to be.

"Hey, check out Cleopatra," someone called over the music, and Jaylon felt a roomful of gazes travel past him to his queen.

As though he was merely a decoration, Ariana released herself from him and bowed to her audience. He was sure that had there been roses in the room, they would now be raining down around them. Around her. This impromptu adulation had nothing to do with him, and as he stood in her shadow, he wondered if it ever had.

"One more, and that's enough," Camille said in annoyance.

"Ahh, come on," Daria and Lexie begged simultaneously. "It's early, and I'm not even tired yet. We can do the next block..."

"No. We've got enough candy to rot six people's teeth right out of their heads. Now we'll do this last porch light, and then we're going home."

"But I don't want to quit," Daria said petulantly.

"Too bad," Camille said, hating the harshness in her voice. "Now, go get your candy, and let's go home."

Sullenly Daria turned her feet up the walk, and Camille thought of a small child, clutching a teddy bear, peering out an imaginary window. With a shake she banished that thought.

In its place floated another memory of the two of them sitting in the car in thrift shop costumes waiting for their mother to come out of the house she had disappeared into an eternity before. Vehemently Camille shook her head. The less she thought about anything, the better off she was.

As Daria made her way up the last sidewalk, Camille and Lexie stood at the curb.

"You're awful quiet tonight," Lexie said.

Camille shrugged. "I just want to get this over with. I've got history to read."

"Dar's costume is great," Lexie said, glancing at her friend. "I didn't know you were so talented."

"Yeah," Camille said with the fakest laugh she'd ever heard. "Neither did I."

"Drama must not be too bad if you're learning to come up with costumes like that."

"Oh, don't let it fool you. It's torture from minute one on. I hate it," Camille said as Daria skipped back down the sidewalk. "I'm going to quit at semester."

"Quit? But I thought you needed a year of it."

"College applications go out in January, so they won't have my last semester's class schedule on them anyway." They turned down the walk and started home. "I'm just not cut out for drama. I knew that when I started, and it's becoming more obvious every class."

"I like drama," Daria said sweetly.

"Oh?" Lexie asked with amusement, and Camille's chest filled with air it refused to release.

"Yeah, Mr. Quinn is nice," Daria said through the computer box on her head.

"Mr. Quinn?" Lexie asked in confusion.

"He's Daria's drama teacher," Camille said quickly. The more pieces she could fill in, the fewer there would be for Daria to add. "She's started going down to The Community Center on Saturdays. I thought it would be good for her to get out of the apartment for a change."

"So, do you like drama?" Lexie asked.

"It's great. We play magic box, and I even got to be the Magic Chooser."

"Impressive," Lexie said with a serious nod. "You'll have to show me how to play magic box sometime."

At her front door, Camille unlocked it and let them in. "Dar, why don't you go get out of your costume? We've only got a few minutes before it's bedtime."

"Okay," Daria said, reluctantly dragging her feet down the hallway.

Camille threw her keys on the table and stalked into the kitchen. "You want something?"

"Oh, no thanks." Lexie slid up onto the counter and watched her friend fill a glass of water from the refrigerator. "Where's your mom?"

Off-handedly Camille shrugged. "Some party."

Lexie sat for a moment, watching her friend take a drink, and then she shook her head. "Daria's lucky to have you."

Wordlessly Camille scrounged around the kitchen for something to eat, praying that Lexie would quit being so sentimental. Life wasn't great, but as long she kept moving and didn't think about it too much, it was at least bearable. "You sure you don't want something?"

Slowly Lexie shook her head. "No, I don't want anything."

The fake-gold armor clinked in the quiet of the night as Jaylon escorted Ariana to her front door.

"I had fun tonight," Jaylon said, knowing that was what he was supposed to say.

"Yeah, it was okay for a high school party."

Ariana was still using that sweeping walk that annoyed Jaylon to no end, but he focused on her front door and fought to pretend that nothing between them had changed.

"I'm sure the parties at Julliard will be ten times better though." At her door she turned to him and reached up to run both sets of fingers through his hair. "We're going to have so much fun there. I can't wait."

Her gaze fell back to his, and he forced a smile onto his face. "Yeah, I can't either."

Chapter 10

"First thing today," Mrs. Allen said on Tuesday afternoon as she sat on the edge of the stage, "I've gotten the play choices in for the Spring Production."

A ripple of excitement rolled through the auditorium.

"I want each of you to read all three by next Friday. You don't have to do any analyzing, just read them, get a feel for each one, and we will take a vote about which one we want to do. You need to remember that I will choose the one we ultimately do, but I want you all to have some say as well."

She pulled herself up and dusted her hands off. "Okay. We're going to work on some more improv today."

Camille sank deeper into her seat. Why couldn't the semester just be over already?

"The object of this exercise is to catch and hold the audiences' attention with a pitch for some kind of product. It might be a household cleaner or a garden tool or any one of a number of other products. You will be competing against another salesperson who will be pitching his or her product simultaneously.

"We'll do one test run to show you what I mean, and then the audience will be asked to judge which salesman stays and which one is sent packing." Mrs. Allen stopped and looked out across her students. "Tony, why don't you and Keane come on up?"

The two boys stood and made their way up the stage steps. Mrs. Allen positioned them about midway back on the stage and then backed away. "Okay. You've got 30 seconds. Go."

"This is the best chainsaw on the market today," Keane said.

"Hate those nasty orange stains on your shower? Want them gone? Here's Stain-B-Gone, the newest most remarkable shower cleaner ever."

"Filling up a gas can and trying to fill a chainsaw is messy and dangerous. This new chainsaw operates not on gasoline, but on electricity. It has a fully rechargeable battery which will run for..."

"Time," Mrs. Allen called, and instantly both boys deflated. She looked out into the audience. "Got the idea?"

Several students nodded.

She looked back at her guinea pigs on stage. "Okay. You may choose a new product, or you may keep the same one and try again. Ready?" Both contestants nodded as though they were standing in the starting blocks. "Go."

"I'll bet every student has done this... gone to your locker, opened it up, and wham, books, papers, pens, supplies everywhere," Keane said, and this time his voice was a notch louder.

"Don't waste another moment sitting in class," Tony said. "Now, the makers of Clone-a-Kid have just what you need. Yes, a perfect replica of you, fashioned right down to your smelly gym shoes. Teachers won't be able to tell the difference."

"Now to the rescue comes the unbelievable Locker Genie..."

"In fact, the Clone-a-Kid can be used for many other purposes as well... holiday with the family? Let your Clone-a-Kid go. Awful blind date? Clone-a-Kid will get you right out of it..."

"Stop." Mrs. Allen held up her hands. "Which one was more convincing?"

Tony's name rang out, and Mrs. Allen smiled at Keane. "Nice try. Who's next?"

"I'll do it," Nick said, vaulting out of the seat next to Camille even as she disappeared farther into the darkness. Jauntily Nick stepped to center stage.

"Ready?" Mrs. Allen asked, and both of them nodded. "Go."

"Dances will never be the same again after you try the all-new Wavy Wax," Nick said. "Yes, that's right. One coat and you will be spinning like an expert."

"...tree branches in your way? Try Branch-B-Gone..."

In amazement Camille watched as Nick spun into a break dance rendition that would've left the Solid Gold Dancers breathless. Then once again he was standing.

"Wavy Wax can make even the most inept dancer become John Travolta on a good day."

"Stop," Mrs. Allen said, holding up her hands.

"Nick," most of the audience yelled. Tony shrugged and departed the stage.

"Next? How about you Mark?"

Three challengers went down to Nick who successfully sold soap that cleans without water, a computer that writes English papers, and a swing that swings itself—so you don't have to waste your energy. When Mrs.

Allen called for another challenger, Jaylon stood and swaggered to the stage.

In her seat, Camille's breath caught. How was it possible that anyone could be that gorgeous? It just wasn't fair to the rest of the population.

"Go," Mrs. Allen said.

"Stop wasting time searching for your remote control," Nick started as he frantically pulled cushions off an imaginary couch. "The Remote Magnet is the answer to all your troubles..."

Next to Nick, Jaylon shrugged out of his black leather jacket and struck a model's pose wordlessly. Two camera clicks and he shifted the coat to the other shoulder and struck a different pose even as Nick continued to expound on the benefits of the Remote Magnet.

Camille's gaze was firmly locked on Jaylon. He could be a model in her magazine any day.

"Stop," Mrs. Allen said.

"Jaylon," several students called.

With a confused look, Mrs. Allen gazed at the students. "What was he selling?"

"Who cares?" one of the girls next to Camille asked, and Camille laughed softly.

"His leather jacket," someone else said.

"Is that right?" Mrs. Allen asked, and Jaylon laid his head to the side demurely. "Okay. Well, nice run, Nick."

In a huff Nick exited the stage as Jill was called up to challenge Jaylon. Nick sat down next to Camille in a heap.

"Good job," she said as the battle of products started on the stage again.

"I hate him."

Camille looked at Nick with sympathy. "I know."

"Stop," Mrs. Allen said, and once again the audience chose Jaylon. It was hard not to. He had a way of capturing and holding your attention without you even realizing he had it. "Ari, why don't you be our next challenger?"

With a dramatic yawn, Ariana stood from her seat and every step she took across the front row and up the stage was measured to attract the most attention possible. She strode to center stage, overtaking even Jaylon's place. Camille watched as he slid to the side so that Ariana had two-thirds of the stage, and he was left with the remainder.

"Go."

"Make-up. Make-up, everywhere," Ariana said in her best, practiced stage voice. "Have you ever wished you could just carry it all with you? Out on a date? Into class..."

"You know them—those people, annoying and obnoxious," Jaylon said from his portion of the stage as though he and the audience were having their own private conversation. "All you want to do is get rid of them. Erase them from your life. Well, now you can! With this." He held up an invisible can that looked very much like Raid. "Just spray it on."

Camille couldn't stop her laughter as he stepped over to Ariana and began spraying her with the contents of his product.

"...it's an all-in-one," Ariana continued, but her sales pitch had been thrown off track by Jaylon's theatrics around her coupled with the raucous laughter from the audience. "Would you stop it? ... Yes, ladies, you will never again have to... Quit it!"

"Stop," Mrs. Allen called.

"Jaylon!" the whole audience roared.

"That's one way to get rid of her," Nick said under his breath as Ariana exited the stage in a huff. "Now if we could just get a bottle for him, we'd be all set."

Camille choked back her remaining laughs as she tried to regain her composure.

"Let's see. Who do we lack?" Mrs. Allen asked from the stage. "Camille. How about you come try it?"

In one breath all her laughter was gone.

"Go get him, Tiger," Nick said, but Camille could tell that he knew she was dead meat just by the tone in his voice.

She stood and walked to the stage as anger and defiance replaced her fear. She was tired of being humiliated by this whole process. Once on center stage, she reached up and repositioned her glasses without so much as glancing at Jaylon. Although it wanted to, she wouldn't let her gaze travel over the waiting faces of her audience. Instead she focused on the very empty back row.

"Go."

"I hold in my hand the answer to every math question you've ever had," Camille said, surveying the invisible palm-sized gadget in her hand. "Yes, you heard me right, friends—the answer to every math question ever. And I'm not just talking about a calculator...oh, no. This little beauty is better."

"...tennis shoes are state-of-the-art..."

"How much better you ask? Normal everyday calculators only give you the answer if you know the right way to work a problem."

"...here's our spokesman, Michael Jordan..."

"With this Answer Wizard, all you do is type the actual problem into it, and it will give you not only the answer, but it gives you every step along the way to solve it."

"...can be used for basketball, track..."

"Even algebraic letters are no problem for the Answer Wizard. $2a \times 3 =$

42?" She punched the buttons on the gadget. "A equals seven. Just like magic..."

"Stop."

"Camille!" Her name sounded out through the auditorium just as the bell rang. Immediately her gaze fell from the back row to the amazed faces fanned out in front of her.

"Good job, everyone!" Mrs. Allen called over the departing students. "Oh, don't forget to grab a play book!"

"So, how can I get one of those Answer Wizards?" Jaylon asked, sliding up beside her as he pulled his jacket back on, and Camille's face went hot.

"I'll trade you for some of your Obnoxious Person Spray."

"Oh, yeah? Got anyone in mind to use it on?"

Together they walked to the edge of the stage. He bent down, picked up two scripts, and handed her one.

"Oh, you know. There's always somebody I'd like to make disappear," Camille said, thinking the number one person was herself.

"So, how was Daria's costume?" he asked as he followed her down the stage steps.

"Great," Camille said with a sincere smile. "We've got enough candy for a small army, but she had fun."

Jaylon nodded. "That's good. I really had..."

"Jaylon, are you coming or not?" Ariana asked from the front row, and the anger in her voice and her stance was not lost on Camille.

Camille's gaze fell to the carpet. "I'd better let you go."

"Yeah," he said reluctantly. "I'll catch you later."

"Later," Camille said with the slightest of waves, and she watched as he put his arm around Ariana and disappeared with her up the aisle.

"Way to go, Wright," Nick said, holding a hand up for her to slap. "Dethroning the king. Impressive."

She shook her head. "It was a fluke."

"Fluke or not, you were great."

"Well, don't get too excited. I'll probably be back on my face tomorrow," she said, but the fact that she had actually not choked while on the stage carried her right out of the auditorium and through the rest of the night. It was a great feeling.

The moment they fell in step with one another, Jaylon knew he was in serious trouble. He couldn't remember a time when Ariana had shrugged him off, but it felt like having his arm around a solid block of wood. As they walked down the hall, the people bumping into him going the other direction kept yanking his arm from her shoulders, and he had to fight to keep up with her.

"Jeez. What's up with you?" he asked, and he pushed the script into his pocket as they turned the corner and started for their lockers.

"Me?" In a blink Ariana turned on him. "You humiliate me—on stage, and you have the nerve to ask me what's wrong with me?"

She was practically shrieking, and Jaylon glanced around him wishing they could do this somewhere else. A fight with Ariana was bad enough, but right in the middle of the school's hallway was far worse.

"I'm sorry," he said, pushing his own anger down. "I thought it was funny."

"Well, it wasn't." On her heel she turned and stalked down the hallway. He stood for one more heartbeat and then followed her, knowing he had to but not really wanting to all the same.

He came abreast of her again just as she got to her locker. "I really am sorry. I wasn't trying to make you mad."

"Yeah? Well, you did." With a clang she opened her locker, slamming it into the one next to it. "So, is that really what you think? That I'm obnoxious?"

"It was a joke," he said. "A joke."

"Ha. Ha," she said like the grim reaper. She slammed her locker closed, causing him to jump. "Don't worry... I'll find my own way home."

And with that he was left standing at the lockers for the first time in three years.

The blue sports car streaked through the streets. All Jaylon wanted was to get away. Away from the anger in Ari's voice, away from the tension he felt every time he stepped through the door of his house, away from the wreck his life had become.

He turned onto the little dirt road and stopped just yards from the slope. Somehow he had to find a way to get his head screwed back onto his shoulders again. It wasn't really clear how, but some time in the last month or so it had somehow come loose. That was the only rational explanation for the reckless act of spraying Obnoxious Person Spray on Ariana in front of an entire audience of their peers.

Hearing the swish of the tall yellow weeds brush across his pant leg, he walked right to the slope edge and sat down. The water below whispered up to him, and he pulled in a slow breath. Ariana. She had been at his side since their first cold reading freshman year.

Even then she was beautiful. Her near-black hair falling in continuous motion down her shoulders and all the way to the small waist she prided herself on. It was the hair as well as her body that had first attracted him. That and the unwavering determination that followed her like a cloud. She was so sure of herself, it was hard not to get caught up in that confidence when you stood in her presence.

At least that's how it used to be. Until this year. This year her confidence had become more like conceit. Slowly he leaned onto the roots of the huge oak tree. His thought waves slipped from Ariana to his own actions, and conceit and arrogance stared him squarely in the face.

In truth, he didn't feel like he was better than his classmates. Truth be told, he felt like he was constantly playing catch-up. Ariana had Julliard. Seth had cars. And all he had was a few kids down at the youth center and an ego the size of New York City. Suddenly the question in his mind was not why he was going with Ariana, but why she would want to be with him.

He wouldn't want to be with him. His gaze fell to the brush-covered bank below. Unconsciously he put his hand into his pocket where it met up with the script. With a sigh he pulled it out and scanned it. *Don't Listen to the Fates.*

It was easier than thinking. Pushing everything else from his mind, he stood, went to the tree, sat down, huddled next it and disappeared into the fantasy world of the playwright's mind.

"Have you heard?" Lexie asked conspiratorially as she slid her tray across the cafeteria table the next afternoon.

"Heard what?" Camille asked even as her gaze continued to scan the formulas she would need for the physics test the next period.

"Jaylon and Ariana broke up yesterday."

The news crashed onto the table in front of Camille like a guided missile. "What?"

"Yeah, they had this huge fight in the middle of the hall after school yesterday, and she dumped him."

Camille's skeptical side jumped to the forefront. "Why would she do something like that?"

Lexie shrugged. "I don't know. I guess she got tired of hanging out with a gorgeous, perfect guy."

"Why thank you," Nick said, sliding into the seat next to Lexie.

She smiled at him. "In your dreams."

"No, in yours," he said, snuggling in next to her.

At another time, Camille would've been wishing for the ground to swallow her and take her out of her misery, but at the moment, nothing other than the bomb blast that had just hit was getting through. They broke up. They broke up. How could they have broken up? What could Ariana possibly be thinking? She couldn't be. That was more than clear. To break up with Jaylon Quinn was nothing short of certifiable insanity.

"So, Camille, have you read the play yet?" Nick asked, forking through his meatloaf.

"I read the mystery last night," Camille said, still struggling through the news. "It's okay." She shrugged. "But I don't really know a whole lot about choosing plays."

"Well, I read the farce. It wasn't as great as I thought it was going to be. It's kind of corny."

"Isn't a farce supposed to be corny?" Camille asked.

Nick leveled his fork at her. "You've got a point there. I don't know. I just can't see us worrying about a villain that wouldn't know his head from a hole in the ground. Although, you know, I think we have the perfect person to play that part."

Camille glanced up, and just past Nick's shoulder, she caught sight of Jaylon who had just stepped into the cafeteria. He looked tired—like the light inside him had been extinguished. Without willing it to, her heart slowed in her chest. It was obvious he was in pain, and as she looked around the cafeteria at the whisperings of the other students, she knew why. The pieces of his glass house were scattered around him, and the core that was left was exposed, wounded, and bleeding.

"Maybe the other one is better," she said, wishing her gaze could tear itself away from his face. Finally she forced it down onto her tray although truthfully his face was still right behind her eyelids every time she blinked. "There's nowhere to go from here but up."

"It's such a cliché," Ariana said obviously in one of her more bitter moods as Jaylon took his seat in the front row, being careful to leave two empty seats between them. Just because they were no longer together didn't mean he had to give up the place where he had sat since freshman year.

"I thought it was kind of cute. Very 'She's All That,'" Tessa who sat on the other side of Ariana said.

Briefly Jaylon wondered when Tessa and Ari had become such good friends. He couldn't recall ever even talking to Tessa. More to the point, he couldn't recall Ariana ever saying more than a word or two to the girl. But it was difficult to challenge what was right in front of his eyes. They were locked in a conversation like friends from preschool.

"But it's been done a thousand times," Ariana continued to complain. "Why can't we do something bigger—more theatre?"

"Like what? Dr. Zhivago?"

"Oh, I'd make such a good Laura. Don't you think?" In a heartbeat Ariana was spinning plans to recreate winter land Russia across the expanse of their high school stage.

"I don't think our set designers could pull something like that off," Tessa said skeptically.

"Yeah, but it's a challenge. Nobody around here understands what it's like to want to be challenged in a role. This stuff is all just so high school."

'What's wrong with that?' Jaylon wanted to scream at her. 'We're in high school. Remember?'

But Ariana had already graduated to costume designing her fantasy play. He slunk down in his seat. How many times had he sounded just like that? It was humiliating. He had never been so grateful to see Mrs. Allen in his life. Breathing wouldn't be such a bad thing to practice today.

"Good afternoon," she said cheerfully. Mumbles circulated through the auditorium. "I wanted to remind you of a couple of on-going assignments, lest you get too involved in all of our other excitement and forget. First, there's the play choice. We will be taking a vote on the play choice next Friday, so you will need to have read each selection before then."

"Can we choose none of the above?" Ariana said softly, causing Tessa to laugh and Jaylon to slide further into his seat.

"The other assignment is the analysis of two community plays. There is a performance of *True North* at the Ashcroft Theatre next weekend. Some of you haven't turned in even one of these assignments, and I don't want to alarm you, but you're beginning to run out of time."

Jaylon's thoughts slipped from the auditorium to a theatre row two seats back from a fall of soft, light brown hair. He hadn't seen enough of *My Fair Lady* to write anything resembling a descent review of it. Mentally he checked through his schedule. It had suddenly become very free. On his mental notebook he penciled in *True North* for the next weekend.

"We're going to work on concentration today," Mrs. Allen said, pulling the students forward with her arms. "Come on up."

Without waiting for Ariana like he usually did, Jaylon stood and walked over to the stage steps. He couldn't remember a time when he'd hated being on stage, but today the lights seemed brighter and hotter, and he could feel his fellow students' gazes fall on him and then turn away as they had all day.

Here, there was no shield from those gazes, no shelter, and instinctively he pushed the pockets of his jacket around him tighter, trying to deflect the insinuation of those glances.

"Please, have a seat in a circle," Mrs. Allen said.

In a heap Jaylon sat down and trained his gaze to the small boards that formed the stage. He felt like a piece of meat hung in the butcher's window for inspection. Conspicuous. That was a good word for it. His mind traced back through his lifetime, and with the one exception of being at home, he couldn't remember ever not wanting people to take notice of him. However, he'd had enough practice blending into the woodwork at home that becoming invisible here should be easy.

"The object of this exercise is relatively simple," Mrs. Allen said. "You are to tell a story in one continuous string. However, you only get to tell one piece of that story. We'll start over here with Nick, and when I say, 'Change,' the next person in the circle is to pick up the story on the word the person before left off.

"Please concentrate." Mrs. Allen pulled a stool over to one edge of the circle. "Okay, Nick. Start us out."

"Last night I went to the store where I saw..."

"Change."

For a split second no one said anything, and Jaylon's gaze went to Nick's side. In the space of the remainder of that second his heart lifted.

"...a purple and green monster with white flecks," Camille said conspiratorially, and Jaylon laughed at the serious look that was scrunched on her face. She could have easily been explaining a space-time continuum to an entire group of scientists. "He stepped around the corner, looked at me and said, '..."

"Change."

"'Take me to your leader,'" Mark said menacingly.

"Change."

"I didn't know what to do," Stephanie said in a petrified voice. "So, I turned around and..."

"Change."

"Hit him with a round kick right to his stomach," Keane said.

"Change."

Tony exhaled. "Let me tell you, that big ol' purple monster with green and white spots doubled over like a folded pastry. He started..."

"Change."

"Choking and coughing. And he said, '..."

"Change."

Instead of saying something, bug-eyed, Jaylon clutched his throat and made strangling noises.

"Change."

"Are you choking?" Cathy asked Jaylon.

"Change."

On the other side of Cathy, Darrin nodded desperately.

"Change."

"Now I ask you, have you ever done the Heimlich maneuver on a seven-foot green and purple monster?" Tessa asked dramatically. "Let me tell you it's..."

"Change."

"Lame," Ariana said in annoyance. "Lame. Lame. Lame."

"Change."

"But it's not as easy as it looks," Garrett said, taking up where Tessa left off. "I couldn't very well leave him like that, so I..."

"Change."

"...wrapped my arms around his slimy midsection..."

"Change."

"...and I pulled both hands toward me..."

"Change."

"Ugh. This pukey yellow slime stuff came up out of that monster's mouth..."

"Change."

" ...and you've never seen such a mess."

"Change."

"I spent all night cleaning the yellow slime off of my Air Jordans."

"Change."

"So, you see, Teacher, that's why I'm late this morning."

"Change."

"Now that will count as an excused absence. Won't it?" Nick asked as the group started laughing around him.

"Very nice," Mrs. Allen said, standing. "Except for the yellow slime part. That's just gross."

Jaylon laughed along with everyone else and slowly slid his jacket off and onto the floor.

"Okay, let's start over with Jaylon this time," Mrs. Allen said, and incredibly when the gazes found him, he sat up straighter not beaten down by them at all.

"Have you ever walked through a forest by yourself at night?" he asked, effortlessly setting an instant picture in the minds of every student there with his tone.

When class ended, Jaylon collected his jacket, stood, and followed his fellow students off the stage. Everyone else was talking and laughing together about their latest creation, and although he was smack in the middle of them, he felt all-but invisible.

"You going to get a different play?" Nick asked Camille two steps in front of Jaylon, and he wished he could be up there asking her that question himself.

"Yeah," she said. "Or maybe we could just switch. That'd be easier than fighting the mob."

"Now, there's a good idea," Nick said. They turned toward up the center aisle, and together they disappeared into the dimness of the auditorium.

With a sigh, Jaylon walked to his own seat in the front row and gathered his books. He too needed to get a different play. Unfortunately, he no longer had anyone to "just switch with." In no great hurry to get out, he waited for the crowd around the scripts to dissipate before he ventured up to the stage.

"Jaylon," Mrs. Allen said when she caught sight of him, "just the person I've been meaning to talk to."

Nonchalantly, Jaylon threw one script into the sea of them on the stage. "Oh, yeah? What about?"

"Well, Ariana came by and picked up her recommendation last week, I was wondering when you'd be by to get yours."

"Oh." He slid the new script in with his other books. "I'm not so sure I need it anymore."

"You don't need it?" Mrs. Allen asked with concern. "Why not?"

He shrugged, fighting not to let the overwhelming depression catch up with him. "I'm kind of having second thoughts about Julliard."

Mrs. Allen shook her head. "You're not getting cold feet are you?"

"More like frozen ones."

"Want to talk about it?"

For a long moment he considered her offer, but he had no idea what to tell her. It was all just one jumbled, confusing mess as far as he could tell. "It's stupid."

"Stupid's a pretty broad assessment. Mind if I ask for something more specific."

Jaylon exhaled. "Ari and I are just in different places with this thing. She wants to be the lead on some Broadway stage."

"And you?"

"I don't know." He shrugged as his father's voice stomped through his brain, 'Acting isn't something you do for a profession. Acting is a hobby at best, a waste of time...' "I guess I'm just not sure that's really what I want anymore."

"Oh," Mrs. Allen said with a knowing nod. "Well, you know, there are other schools with excellent Theatre Arts programs."

"Yeah. I know."

"That is if you're still interested in pursuing acting."

He smiled slightly. "Who knows? Maybe I'll try my hand at rocket-science." When Mrs. Allen arched a skeptical eyebrow, Jaylon laughed. "I know stick with something you don't completely suck at."

"You know." Mrs. Allen slid her legs off the stage and swung them in front of her. "I think one of the most important decisions of your life is what you decide to do for your life's work. It's a decision a lot of people have made for them because they just follow the track they seem to be on at the time they graduate from high school.

"Then they get to college and sometimes they find out they made the wrong choice for themselves because they were listening to everybody else's idea of what they should do. Now you know I'm not going to tell you that you don't have talent on a stage because you do, but I'm also not going to tell you that that's the only career path you have open to you."

All he wanted to do was leave, forget life decisions, forget the future, forget everything, and just leave.

"No question money is a factor in making that decision, but so is doing something you love to do. Not something you like—something you love. Something that makes you feel alive. Something you could do 26 hours a day and never get tired of it. Regardless of what everybody else says—that's the thing you should pursue. Think about it, okay? And I'm here to talk if you need me."

"Thanks, Mrs. Allen," he said, truly feeling the appreciation although it only barely made it into his tone.

"Anytime." She stood on the stage. "Oh, what did you think of Hawk?"

"Hawk?"

She nodded at the script he'd just laid on the top of the other scripts. "From *Don't Listen*. He's a little like someone else I know." Her smile was teasing. "We'll see."

"Yeah," he said off-handedly as he backed away from the stage. "See you tomorrow."

"Take care, and think about what I said."

"As always," he said, and then he forced his feet to turn up the small incline and carry him to the back of the room. At the door he stopped just before he pushed out and looked back at the stage. *You need to be where you feel truly alive.*

With a half smile mixed generously with a small laugh, he pushed out into the hallway. Leaving acting, walking away and never coming back would be like driving a stake right through his heart, but fighting for that dream might smother the life right out of him as well, and in the end he would have the same thing anyway. Nothing.

No dream. No goal. And no one to care about it one way or the other.

It was a conundrum with no real answer anywhere in sight. What he really needed was Camille's Answer Wizard. For a single second he wondered if they made one for advanced life planning. Just type your question in, and bing out pops your answer. It would sure solve a lot of problems. With two books and the script on his hip, he left the school—destination: the only place on earth that still made some sense.

The script in hand and his head resting against the tree trunk, Jaylon watched the sun dip past the horizon beyond the trees. In ten minutes he would have to leave. His parents really didn't expect him home before then. In fact if he came home too early, someone was sure to ask why.

Why? As the sun disappeared in a fireball of orange and yellow, it was as good a question as any. Why had he felt the need to do that obnoxious person bit on Ariana yesterday? Why couldn't he stand up to his father? Why couldn't he just tell Ariana about his father's refusal to even consider Julliard?

Funny how every question came back to Ariana and what she thought about his life. That's what his whole life had been predicated on in the last few years—Ariana and what she thought. It was just easier that way. He could be her leading man. The strong but silent type, a half step behind her, always being careful not to step on her delicate train.

Ariana was high maintenance, but until yesterday he hadn't thought that was a particularly bad thing. It gave him something to do, a role to play. Servant to the queen. He closed his eyes to the sunset beyond. Now what was he? Ari's ex? That guy... what's his name... you know the one who was in all the plays with Ariana?

Dwelling in the pain wasn't making it go away, and it certainly wasn't making it any better. With a push, he regained his footing and stumbled once because his foot hadn't realized how long he'd sat there.

In the car he backed out without so much as one more glance at the fading sunset. It felt like he was leaving his dream behind, and somehow if he just didn't look, it was entirely possible that he could simply keep driving until the dream was no more than the tiniest of specks in the far, far distant past. If only it were that simple.

Chapter 11

For two weeks Camille had watched him, and although Jaylon was still as gorgeous as ever, he looked incredibly lonely, sad, and out-of-place. She wished Saturday had worked out better, but when her mother had announced an all-of-us shopping day, Daria simply could not be persuaded otherwise. As it turned out, it was an all-of-them shopping day—as it usually was.

Daria had come home with several new outfits, but Camille knew too much about the thin strand the family was holding on by, so she insisted she had plenty of clothes and needed nothing else. Besides, she knew the whole trip was just about assuaging her mother's guilt over not taking more interest in their lives. It never failed. Once or twice a year for a day or two they were suddenly the most important things in their mother's world. For the rest of the year, they were simply obstacles in her path.

With a shove Camille pushed those thoughts out of her mind as her attention caught on the black leather that had just brushed past her auditorium chair. She couldn't see his face or his eyes, but that wasn't necessary anymore. The sadness in the bend of his shoulders screeched across her heart, and she wished again that they could just talk. What she would say was a mystery, but anything was better than seeing him beaten to the ground.

"I even talked to her about it," Ariana's strained voice bounded through the crowd noise. "She is dead-set on choosing one of these stupid plays. They're all just so yesterday."

Wishing she wouldn't even as she did, Camille looked up and caught the arrow straight shoulders and razor thin waist as it moved past her. If she was just Ariana, she could walk up to Jaylon and... and what? The fact that she wasn't even in Ariana's hemisphere slammed that thought right out of Camille's mind.

"So, what's it going to be?" Nick asked as he took his seat next to Camille.

Off-handedly she pushed her glasses up and forced her attention back to the space surrounding her. "What's what going to be?"

"Your choice for the play?" he asked as though that question should be obvious.

"I kind of liked *Don't Listen to the Fates*. I think it would be fun to do."

Nick nodded. "Well, that's two votes." He expended a small amount of movement to get his books in order. "By the way, I've been meaning to ask you. Lexie's birthday is next week, have you gotten a date yet?"

By the way, Boris, have you set off the nuclear bomb yet? "Uh, no. I hadn't really thought about it." Unconsciously she pushed the edge of her glasses up. "Why?"

"Well, I could set you up if you'd like."

"A blind date?" Camille asked in horror. "No, I don't think so."

Mrs. Allen picked that moment to stride on to the stage.

"Okay, but you've got until Tuesday, and then I'll be forced to take matters into my own hands," Nick said far too seriously for Camille.

"I think we'll go ahead and get the vote out of the way," Mrs. Allen said from the stage. "We'll do this by secret ballot, and over the weekend I'll take the ballots and make my decision. Please take out a piece of paper, and write your choice on it."

It took only seconds for Camille to make her choice.

"Okay, now if everyone will please pass them to the center of the aisle," Mrs. Allen said when the noise level indicated that most choices had been made.

Instantly Camille took Nick's as she looked down to the other end of the row for the rest of the ballots.

"Jaylon, if you'll pick them up, please," Mrs. Allen said, and the ballots in Camille's hand threatened to scatter into the darkness at her feet.

Keeping her gaze glued to the far end of the auditorium on the ballots coming her way, she fought not to notice the black jacket approaching her row. However, the second he stepped next to her seat, she could feel the heat pouring off him. It seemed to rain down on her and flood through her neck and face until she was sure when the last ballot reached her that her whole body must be glowing bright red.

Quickly she stacked the votes together and fought to act natural as she turned to transfer them to him. But the second she looked up, all the battles ceased. He stood there, three feet above her, smiling softly, with not even a trace of sadness in his eyes.

With her heart in her throat, she laid the ballots into his out-stretched hand. Then in the last second before he turned back for the stage, one lid fell closed, and his smile brightened. And then he was gone. Camille closed her eyes as she slid down into her seat, letting the feelings inside her wash over her.

It was silly, stupid even. He probably winked at a lot of girls—all of them far more beautiful and sophisticated than she was. But for all the rationalizations of her brain, her heart simply wanted to live that one moment over and over again forever.

"I also want to remind you about the performance of *True North* tonight and tomorrow night at the Ashcroft," Mrs. Allen was saying from the stage, and although Camille knew she should be paying attention, that was the last thing any part of her wanted to do.

For the rest of the afternoon, she sailed on a cloud of Jaylon's smile and his eyes, looking through the dimness of the theatre right into her own. It crowded out everything else—even the fact that Nick and Lexie had made other plans for the evening. Ever-so-slowly she was losing her best friend. Ever-so-slowly their last year together was slipping away, and the only thing that could take her mind off of that sad fact was the few moments when she could look into Jaylon's eyes.

It wasn't a terrible thing that they had other plans anyway she thought as she pulled on the best dress she owned—the one with only two small darn marks at the hem. Nick would probably laugh at her if he knew she hadn't finished the *My Fair Lady* assignment. Carefully, she braided the two sides of her hair and then pulled them together at the nape of her neck.

Although it made no sense, she kind of liked the idea of going out to a play. It was better than sitting at home in front of the television all night feeling sorry for herself. One more check in the mirror, and she decided that was as good as she was going to get. She grabbed her notebook from the desk, gave a few final instructions to the babysitter and then said a quick good-bye to Daria before stepping out into the cold November air.

The Ashcroft Theatre was much smaller than the Mance Theatre, and Camille quietly chose a seat about seven rows back. She laid her coat on the back of her chair and settled in. With her notebook on her lap, she pulled her pen from her ear and then opened the playbill. "*True North*, a quasi-comedy about life." She laughed. "Huh. Sounds familiar."

Her attention slipped to the stage as the lights went down, and the curtain slowly slid to the sides to reveal wispy blue smoke pouring in from the edges of the stage. Through the blue smoke lit only with black light a lady in pink satin emerged from the back of the stage in all her glory.

In the darkness Camille squinted at the playbill, trying to figure out which character she was, but it was too dark to read, and Camille quickly gave up. The lady on stage looked every bit of ninety; however, she walked in a fluid, dance like fashion to the center of the stage, bringing her feather boa with her majestically.

"Life," the lady intoned. "It makes perfect nonsense while your living

it. Perfect nonsense. Take the first time Bobby Porter asked me for a date."
She lounged down onto a long couch dead center stage. "I was eight, and
there was only one thing I was certain of, and that was that all boys were
frog-holding, fist-fighting, dirty wastes of precious air."

The lights came up on the right side of the stage, revealing two small
children. The girl was dressed in a white and pink, lace and crinoline
number—the boy in dirty jeans and a slightly ripped yellow and brown plaid
shirt.

"I picked these for you special," the little boy said as he held out a
small handful of wilted wildflowers.

"Now what'd you go and do that for?" the little girl asked, crossing her
arms in front of her and turning her back to him. "Where'd you get 'em—
the meadow?"

Slowly the little boy's face fell as he shrank back. "I thought of you
when I saw 'em."

The little girl turned to the flowers disgustedly. "I hope I don't look
like that." Then with a smirk, she cocked her head. "Why don't you just take
your little flowers and go find some other girl to annoy?"

'Bratty,' Camille wrote in her notebook just as the bright light winked
off, once again revealing the lady in the cream lounge chair.

"Just like that," she said, arching her shoulders up. "That's what I said.
And it worked, too. Bobby went, and he gave those flowers to Betsy
Thompkins. 'Course she moved away when we were about 12, and I guess
that was the end of that."

Slowly she shook her head. "I always kind of wondered what would've
happened if I'd have taken his flowers. But like I said, life don't make no
sense—not a lick of it. And it don't get no better the older you get neither.
Just one long string of random moments going nowhere."

Her voice faded out, and she seemed to be lost in her own thoughts.
Then suddenly it was as though she had remembered that she hadn't been
speaking. "Bobby? Oh, yes. He asked me out again. I was 16 at the time,
and nothing was making any more sense.

"I told him that a hundred times, it don't make no sense, Bobby, but
Bobby never saw it that way."

Instantly bright lights illuminated the left side of the stage.

"I'm not joking, Ellie," a young boy said to a girl seated primly on an
ornately carved chair. "It's just ice cream. You don't even have to sit with
me if you don't want."

Camille laughed with the rest of the audience and made a note on her
paper.

"Bobby Porter, you don't have no business asking me out. Why your
daddy works down at the factory. What would that look like to everybody

else? It'd be a big step down for me. Although from your perspective I can see how it couldn't do nothing but help."

"Yep," the lady on the couch said as the bright lights snapped off, "that's what I said all right, Bobby Porter, it don't make no sense for me to go out with you. I wanted to go out with... now, what was that guy's name again? ... Hmm, completely slipped my mind now."

She thought for a moment more and continued. "I guess it don't make no difference now. But I'll tell you what that Bobby Porter, well, he was a persistent one if nothing else. He didn't take no for an answer unless the question was, aren't you ever going to give up?"

The lights snapped on to the right of the stage, and it was the same couple in slightly different clothes. Immediately the bridge of Camille's nose wrinkled in confusion, and she looked back over to the other side of the stage. How did they do that so fast? She shook her head to clear it of the confusion and refocused her mind on the on-going conversation to the right of the stage.

The boy stood in slightly ragged clothing, clutching his hat. "You don't want to go out with me? What are you too tired?"

"No," the girl said adamantly. Her arms were crossed firmly in front of her as though they were made of stone.

"No?" he asked, turning the hat in his hands. "Does that mean no you won't go out with me, or no, you're not tired?"

The girl unfurled her hands into the air as the audience laughed. Then she slammed her hands on her hips and stared at the boy. "You, Bobby Porter, are the most exasperating, irritating, and frustrating person in the whole world."

"And you, Ellie Jane are the most beautiful girl I've ever laid eyes on," he said without missing a beat.

"ARGH!" she screamed, throwing her hands in the air and stomping off the stage.

"Yep," the lady down front said as the backlights snapped off. "He was always like that."

Camille made a few notes and was suddenly glad she had come. A three-hour diversion from her life was exactly what she needed.

The lady was still sitting center stage on her lounge chair, but she wasn't sitting up straight anymore. Now she was lying back motionless. The only addition to the original set was a man sitting in a chair next to her, holding her hand.

"It's okay, Ellie," he said in a voice that yanked tears to Camille's lashes, her notes long-since forgotten. "I'll be here as long as you need me to be. I always have been, and I always will be because you, Ellie Jane, are my true north."

The lady seemed to hear that phrase, and she lifted her head. "Bobby? Is that you?"

"Yeah, Sweetness, it's me." He stroked her hand. "It's always been me, and it will always be me."

And with those words the curtains slid closed with four jerks. Along with the other theatregoers Camille's hands came together, first softly but gaining volume with each hit. The curtain came open again to reveal the actors taking their bows. It was too bad more people couldn't see that performance, Camille thought. The actors on stage continued to bow until finally the curtains swung closed, and the audience began their journey out.

Camille pushed the pen behind her ear and gathered her coat. It wasn't until she had stepped into the center aisle and glanced down the other side of seats that she stumbled into Jaylon's gaze looking right back at her. One glance and her face flushed as he smiled and offered a small wave.

"Hi," she said, trying to sound cheerful, but the syllable was drowned out by the noise of the departing theatregoers. Jaylon in a white T-shirt with an unbuttoned blue plaid shirt layered between it and his leather jacket made his way to her side.

"Well, fancy meeting you here," he said with a tinge of happiness lacing the statement. He ran a casual hand through his feathered locks to push them out of his eyes.

Camille was busy searching for something to look at other than the high cheekbones and the perfect smile. "Yeah, I didn't want to wait 'til the last minute to get in my last play."

Right next to her and with his elbow only a breath away, he walked with her up the aisle. "I hear you there. Knowing my luck I'd get sick for the last performance of *Man of La Mancha* or something."

She laughed as she felt his gaze slide over her face.

"So, you've got your two done then?" he asked.

Camille shrugged. "I will by Monday."

"Oh, yeah, right," he said, smiling sheepishly. He held the door to the lobby open on the push of the person ahead of them, and they stepped through it. "I'm surprised more people weren't here tonight."

"But the theatre was almost full," Camille said in confusion.

"No," he said, correcting himself with a small cough. "I meant people from drama class."

"Oh."

"I saw Mark earlier, but I think he cut out sometime in the middle of the second act."

Her eyebrows knitted together. "But then he missed Bobby at the end. Wasn't that kind of the point of the whole thing?"

Jaylon laughed. "Yeah, but let's not tell him that. Okay?"

Camille smiled at the teasing grin on his face. "That's cruel."

"It's not my fault. He should've stayed."

She shook her head and laughed.

"So, what are you up to now?" he asked, nonchalantly although the question threw her totally off-guard.

Quickly she looked at her watch. "I don't know. Going home to write my paper I guess."

"You've got all weekend to do that," he said, and she heard the edge of uncertainty in his voice. "How about we go over to Sal's and see what's going on over there?"

"Sal's?" The word snagged in her throat.

He smiled at her disarmingly, and there was a soft glint in his eyes. "Come on. I'll split some cheese fries with you."

For a moment her brain said she really should get home to take over for the babysitter, but with a quick glance at the wall clock, she knew she had some extra time. "Well, okay, but only for a little bit."

Jaylon couldn't believe his luck. Somehow he'd never even considered the possibility that she would be at this play. He opened his car door for her and watched her slip in as his heart did a small dance. Right or wrong, he was not going to let this golden opportunity get away from him. Quickly he slammed her door, ran around, crawled into his side, and put a CD into the player.

He glanced over at her but decided that was a recipe for having a wreck. "I missed you last weekend." From the side of his eye, he caught the questioning look she shot him. "At the center."

"Oh, yeah." She nodded slightly. "Mom decided we needed to do some bonding over a credit card and some clothes. Believe me, I would've preferred playing Dr. Mix-up."

Carefully he guided the car into traffic. "You and your mom don't get along?"

"It'd probably help if she knew I was around." The edge in her voice peeled in his ears as she looked down at her hands. "Or maybe if I just wasn't."

"Sounds serious."

Camille shrugged. "Once I got old enough to take care of myself, I kind of got replaced on her important things to care about list."

"What about your dad?" he asked, hoping that option evoked a more positive reaction.

However, Camille's face went hard as soon as the question was out of his mouth. "Which one do you mean?"

"I...I don't know." He glanced over at her. "How many are there?"

"Well, let's see," she said as the sarcasm dripped from the statement. "There's my dad, my original dad, but I haven't seen him in years. And there's Daria's dad, but he was only around long enough to get Mom pregnant, and then he skipped town. Then there was Leon Somebody. I don't remember him much, but he's in some pictures of when I was younger. Then there was some guy named Pete, but Mom found out he was married to someone else so she threw him out. And then there was Mr. Cordell, but he only lasted like six months or something."

"Jeez."

Camille snorted softly. "Yeah, you can say that again." She looked out the window, seeming to escape there. "It's okay. I guess I'm better off by myself anyway—well, me and Dar."

"You take good care of her, don't you?" Jaylon asked, wishing he could reach across the seat to her.

For a long moment she didn't say anything. Then she shook her head. "I try."

The car swung into Sal's parking lot, and Jaylon parked and then killed the engine. However, before he had a chance to make it to her door, she met him at the front of the car, and he purposely took up position behind her and followed her to the restaurant.

At the door he managed to reach around her and open it, and together they stepped into the warmth of Sal's Place. All the gazes turned to them as they made their way across the restaurant, and he felt each of them hit him like a punch. "How about over here?"

She didn't protest so he led her to one of the back booths. Not wanting to push his luck, he slid into the booth's opposite side and folded his hands on the table.

"You want anything other than cheese fries?"

Her gaze stayed firmly on the table. "I'm not really all that hungry."

"I'll tell you what. I'll get some, and you can eat whatever you want." He was only vaguely sure that she nodded, but he stood anyway. "I'll just go put in the order."

Wishing he couldn't feel all the gazes in the place following him, he sauntered to the counter and put in his order. As casually as he could remember how to be, he leaned on the counter and waited—not daring even a glance back into the restaurant.

"I'm telling you, Mrs. Allen is going to pull something else out at the last minute." Jaylon heard the voice behind him, and the feeling of wanting to be anywhere else dropped over him. "She cannot be seriously considering doing one of these plays. She just can't."

The clerk returned and pushed Jaylon's order across the counter before collecting his money. Taking in a long breath, Jaylon turned, and his gaze instantly caught on Ariana's. Her eyes went hard and then softened condescendingly.

"Jaylon," she said, glancing across at her table companion. "I didn't expect to see you here."

"Yeah," he said as he stepped over to the side of her table and found Keane looking up at him. In self-defense Jaylon turned a happy but mildly surprised look on his fellow thespian. "Don't have too much fun, you two. I've got to go, my order's getting cold."

"Oh, don't mind us. We wouldn't want to keep you," Ariana said, and the edge of her voice cut through his carefully constructed act.

Without bothering to reply, Jaylon stepped away from their table. He tried to get himself to feel even vaguely jealous as that's what a true ex would be feeling, but the only thing he could really feel was relief that he was walking away from Ari's table to Camille's.

"Sorry," he said as he slid the order onto the table between them. Smoothly he set her drink in front of her and unloaded the remainder of the tray. "Typical Friday night around here. It's nuts." He stacked his tray on another table and then slid back into the booth where he draped one arm over the empty seat next to him and reached for a fry with the other. "So, how'd you like the play?"

"Tonight's?" she asked, looking up like a frightened animal caught in a trap, and the smoothness seeped away from him.

Slowly he leaned forward, pulling his arm off the back of the booth and leaning it on the table. "Yeah. Have you decided what you're going to use to critique it?"

She sat for a small eternity without so much as reaching for a fry. "I thought it was pretty cool the way they kept switching sides of the stage so fast, and they looked so different every time. I can't figure out how they did that."

Jaylon smiled as he reached for another fry—the act of cool dropping away from him like a coat on a sweltering day. "It was the costumes. They were all made interchangeable. Add a vest, change a shirt, pin in some ribbons, take some out. The costume design people really did a good job."

He noticed Camille's shoulders relax slightly as she tentatively reached to the center of the table and took a fry.

"It was also kind of funny how she kept telling him to go away, and every time, there he was again," Camille said although she sounded anything but comfortable.

Finger-to-finger Jaylon spun a fry. "Yeah, but she was too full of herself for me."

Camille reached for another fry. "Yeah, but that was kind of the point.

Wasn't it?"

Jaylon's eyebrows arched as he shook his head. "That he could love someone so selfish?"

"No, that he loved her for who she was, and he didn't try to change her."

A peel of laughter jumped above the crowd noise, and Jaylon's gaze slid across the restaurant to the fall of black hair that was tossing side-to-side across the slender shoulders. Keane's slightly tanned face smiled as he watched his date. With a shake of his head, Jaylon looked back across the table at Camille in annoyance. "So that's what you think love is? Putting up with somebody even though they're self-centered and obnoxious?"

Slowly Camille's dark eyes melted into liquid just before her gaze fell so far down he could no longer see it. "No, but I think it does mean you don't hold every little fault against them, and you don't try to change them into what you want them to be."

"Huh," he snorted and bent his lips to the straw in his drink. However, for the brief second she glanced up at him, he caught the sadness behind her eyes. His anger at Ariana disappeared in the concern for Camille. Immediately his thoughts went to Nick, and Jaylon wondered if he was the cause of her sadness. "So, which play did you choose for the Spring Production anyway?"

In the span of a blink the sadness in her eyes vanished. "*Don't Listen to the Fates*."

"Really? I liked that one too."

"Yeah, it's kind of funny how they're all trying to improve their lives by trying to be somebody their not."

"You mean how they're trying to improve themselves by dating the right person."

She smiled as her head bobbed up and down. "I think too many people think that these days. If I could just go out with him, then I'd be someone."

"If I could just go out with her, my life would be perfect," he said, laying his hand on his heart dramatically.

Camille's face scrunched forward. "Good luck. Life isn't perfect no matter who you're with."

"Huh. That's the difference," Jaylon said, sitting up straight as the realization came over him.

"What difference?" Camille asked as she reached for one of the few remaining fries.

"Between *True North* and *Don't Listen*."

She took a small bite as seriousness washed over her features. "How do you mean?"

"I mean, Bobby loved her, and he wanted her to love him, but he didn't go all bending and contorting himself into something he wasn't to get her to love him."

"Huh," Camille said obviously impressed with his insight. "I never thought of it like that."

Jaylon gazed at her over the now empty basket. "Neither did I."

In the ensuing pause he watched her take a long drink, and his heart spun on the next question. He wanted to ask with every piece of his soul, but if her answer was no, he was afraid his whole world might crash down right at his feet.

Without warning she glanced up, and their gazes met. Hoping the smile that was in his heart was making it all the way to his face, he let his feelings have full rein. "So, are you coming to help out tomorrow?"

The question threw her gaze across the restaurant. "I don't know. I guess. I'll probably bring Dar anyway—as long as Mom doesn't rope us into something else."

His heart flipped over. "Oh, well, I thought we might try that mirror game from the first of drama with them."

Seriousness mixed with a large dose of horror descended onto her face. "In that case I'm definitely not coming."

He laughed at the scrunch on her face. "Oh, come on. You weren't that bad."

"Yeah, uh-huh, and the sky's not blue."

Of its own accord Jaylon's head shook. "Everybody has embarrassing moments."

"Not center stage they don't."

The smile softened right off of his face. "Well, most people don't have the guts to get up on center stage to begin with, so I think making a mistake up there is the supreme act of courage and grace."

"Grace?" Camille asked incredulously. "You haven't been watching me very closely. Have you?"

The last thing he wanted to do was to tell her just how closely he had been watching her. Unbidden his gaze fell to his watch. "Jeez, it's almost midnight. Where'd two hours go?"

"Midnight?" Camille scrambled for her belongings. "Oh, my gosh, I've got to get home."

"Oh." Jaylon stumbled up next to her. "I'm sorry. I didn't know you have a curfew."

"It's not curfew." Camille yanked her coat on. "The babysitter was supposed to be home an hour ago."

"Babysitter?" Jaylon asked in confusion as he followed her out of the restaurant, the gazes of curious on-lookers no longer even on his radar screen. "What babysitter?"

Quickly Camille pushed through the door and turned down the sidewalk in the opposite direction of his car.

"Hey." His hand reached out and arrested her flight. "The car's this way."

"But..." She looked over her shoulder at the bus stop bench.

"Come on," he said gently. "I can get you there in half the time."

For the longest moment of his life, he thought she might tell him she wanted nothing more than to get as far away from him as possible, but then fate smiled on him, and she turned her steps back up the sidewalk.

"Fine, but can we hurry?"

"You're wish is my command," he said, sweeping one hand in front of him.

"Forget the gallantry," she said as she grabbed his hand and pulled him down the sidewalk. "Just drive!"

He laughed as he stumbled after her ever-quickening steps to his car. With only one small stop on her side of the car, he ran around to his own side and fired up the engine. Smoothly he pulled out of the parking lot, and in seconds they were tracing their way through the city streets to her place.

"So, what's up with the babysitter anyway?" he asked.

"I just told her I would definitely be home before eleven."

Even as his hands guided the car through the streets, he looked over at her. "But why is that your job? Where's your mom?"

"Out."

"Out? Out where?"

"Who knows where," she said, and although it was clear that she wasn't happy about that fact, he barely heard the annoyance.

"You don't?"

"It's Friday night—I don't know. Bar? Date? Movies? Some guy's place?"

What was once mild worry suddenly felt like overwhelming concern. "She didn't tell you where she was going?"

"She never even came home." The hard edge of her voice cut his heart in two. "Believe me, it's pretty hard to keep up with someone who doesn't want you to."

"So you had to get a babysitter for Daria?"

Camille's laugh barely sounded on the air. "Pretty normal around my house."

Jaylon wanted to say that she shouldn't have to be a mother—she should just have to be a kid, but he knew that comment wouldn't help anything, so he kept it to himself. "Well, I'm sorry I kept you so long. If I would've known..."

She smiled at him across the seat. "Don't worry about it, okay? I really had fun." Then her smile melted into somberness. "The most fun I've had in a long time."

With every part of him he wanted to reach over the console to touch her and tell her that everything would be all right. But both hands stayed right where they were, clutching the steering wheel until they guided the car up to the curb in front of her apartment.

"Good luck with your paper," he said, fighting not to let his heart beat right out of his chest.

"You, too," she said with the faintest of smiles, and then before he had the chance to say another word, she jumped out of the car. "I'll see you tomorrow."

And with that she slammed the door. He watched her run up the walk and stand for only a single moment at the door as she unlocked it. Then she disappeared inside, and he was left watching nothing but a motionless door. For several seconds even that was enough. Slowly he let his head fall back against the headrest as he thought about her.

Even without her in the car, he felt her presence next to him. She was something special. She wasn't bent only on putting everyone else down in her race to make herself look superior. No, Camille Wright, although not a supermodel on the outside, was a girl with substance. She did the work and sought no applause or recognition from the outside world, and somewhere deep down, he knew she was the kind of girl he could fall for—hard.

With that thought tracing through his brain, he put the car in drive and pulled away from the curb. Although she was no longer in the car, in every way that counted she was still very much with him.

Chapter 12

Every piece of Camille's brain said to slow down. If she was just late enough for him to already be started, she could drop Daria off and then disappear. However, the only message getting to her body was "Let's go already!"

Even the wind whipping down the city streets couldn't deter her. It was one of those dreadful days when the high temperature was reached at midnight, and the only direction the mercury was going after that was down.

Hand in Daria's they ran all the way from the bus stop to the center and then had to collect themselves before they walked into the auditorium. Still questioning why she had thought it was so important to come, Camille shook the cold off as they stepped into the auditorium darkness, but instantly her breath caught.

On stage right, looking more handsome than any guy had a right to, Jaylon stood—his light blue shirt with the white collar and dark blue tie were offset by the dark suspenders running down either shoulder. Somehow her feet continued to move although she wasn't sure how.

"Daria!" Katelyn yelled excitedly from the stage, and in a breath Camille was caught in the depths of Jaylon's eyes.

He smiled as though she was the sunshine after a long, dark night. "Well, great. We've almost got everyone then."

Ripping her soul from his eyes, Camille knelt down next to Daria to help the little girl out of her coat. "Now you be good. Okay?"

Instantly fear replaced the excitement in the little girl's face. "You're not leaving. Are you?"

"Well,... I..." Camille's gaze traveled to the door, but she'd heard that crack in her own voice before, and as much as her brain told her to leave, her heart simply couldn't say the words. Finally she smiled as she looked at her sister. "No, of course not."

The excitement returned as Daria skipped away from her sister and up the stairs to the waiting children. With a reluctant sigh, Camille shrugged out of her own coat and followed her sister onto the stage. However, this time she was careful not to take the risk of looking at him again.

Once on stage Jaylon took over like he'd been waiting only for them. "Today we're going to try mirroring. You are going to get a partner and follow what they do." He looked around at the group of serious but slightly confused faces staring back at him. Then without warning he looked right at her. "Camille, why don't you help me show them?"

She wanted to tell him no, but with 18 pairs of expectant eyes looking up at her, that option evaporated. "O-kay." Carefully she stepped forward, and the moment her body came within sonar range of his, the memory that this was anything other than vitally important escaped from her mind.

"I'll go first," he said, looking right through her eyes into her heart, and she nodded unable to say anything.

Slowly he put both hands above his head, and almost without watching anything other than his eyes, she followed his movement. One arm came down and then out to the side, then the other arm came down in an all-out stretch. To one side and then the other his neck arched and then came back to the center. Without moving his feet, he twisted first one way and then the other, and her body followed his as though they were tied by some piece of magical rope.

Finally he came back to the center and smiled at her, and instantly her smile mirrored his. A brief second passed, and then he looked away from her back to the children. Her breath escaped in a whoosh as her eyes fell closed.

There was something about him that made everything else in the world cease to exist.

"Now, I want you all to get partners," he was saying, and Camille watched him. Even his back was good-looking. Strong and in control.

She forced her gaze past him to the children as they paired off. Each child had a mirror in a few seconds flat, and Jaylon turned back around to her.

"Camille and I will walk around and watch you. If you have trouble, just ask us. You may begin."

Although there were 18 children in the room, as they began, the only sound was the hum of the heaters.

"Very good, Daria," Jaylon said, walking slowly around the stage with his hands planted firmly behind his back. "Perfect, Jomei."

At first Camille felt totally ridiculous, but then it occurred to her that there was no one in the audience to watch her anyway, and besides she wasn't here for them, she was here for the kids. "Good job, Cory. Way to watch." She took several steps around the stage, liking the anonymity she finally felt up there. Yes, she was on the stage, but nobody was watching her. "Watch him carefully, Katelyn. There you go. That's better."

"Okay," Jaylon called after several minutes. "Let's switch leaders."

For a second the children broke concentration, and the hum was drowned out.

"Okay. Everybody ready?" he asked, and all 18 heads nodded. "Go."

The hum was back.

With supreme effort, Jaylon finished up with the parents picking up their children, and then bid them farewell as he strode to the corner of the theatre where Camille was helping Daria into her coat.

"Just let me get my coat," he said, sounding as though they had pre-arranged plans to leave together, although he of all people knew they didn't. A stolen moment here, a lucky break on stage to steal another there. That was all he could really hope for, and it would have to be enough although he wanted so, so much more. "Ready?"

Her answer came as more of an indifferent shrug, but he took what he could get and guided her out. "You hungry?"

"Hamburgers?" she asked.

"If you want," he said as though his life didn't hang on the balance of that offer.

"Sure why not?"

God Himself must have been smiling down on him. The bitter cold wind whipped around them as Jaylon shepherded them to his car. Quickly they piled in and headed for the restaurant.

"So, did you get your paper written?" she asked before he had a chance to find a similarly suitable topic.

"No, I figure I'd work on it this evening," he said, glancing at her as he pulled into traffic.

"Not going out tonight?" She cocked a teasing eyebrow at him.

He shrugged the question away. "My calendar kind of got freed up a couple weeks ago."

"Yeah," she said, and he heard the compassion in her voice. "I heard about that. You okay?"

It was strange. It had been almost two weeks, and she was the first person to ask if he was all right with the whole break-up thing. "Yeah. It's different though."

"I'll bet." She nodded, sympathy streaming through her eyes. "I can't imagine breaking up after going together as long as you two did."

"Since freshman year," he said, his voice near a whisper, and then a sigh escaped his throat. "But I think it was time."

"Oh, really? Why?"

The shrug crinkled his jacket. "I'm not the same person I was back then."

With a raise of her eyebrows, she nodded. "It's tough when somebody changes."

"Yeah, but it's even worse when somebody doesn't," he said before he could stop the words. He felt her next question forming between them, but thankfully they had arrived at the restaurant, and quickly he swung into a parking space. "This is it. You ready?"

"I guess," Camille said, thrown off-track by the sudden shift in conversation.

"I'll get Dar. You just get in." He looked at her and then back at Daria. "On three. Ready? One, two, three." One part of him followed Camille up and out of the car and then across the parking lot even as the majority of his brainpower was taken up by getting Daria out of the backseat and across the parking lot to the front door. "Man, it is freezing out there!"

He shook off the cold as Daria's hand left his to wrap itself in Camille's.

"Come on, let's find a table," Camille said, gently pulling Daria away from the door. The three of them tumbled into a booth and spent several minutes simply rubbing their hands together and soaking in the warmth surrounding them. "Man! Who forgot to shut off the air conditioners?"

"I don't know," he said with a laugh, "but I think they should be fired."

A shiver traveled right over Camille. "I'm just glad I don't live in Alaska."

"Here, here," Jaylon said, thawing out enough to remember how thankful he was to be here with her. "So, what do you want?"

"Hot chocolate." Camille blew into her rolled up hands as she studied the menu.

Jaylon laughed as the waitress appeared. They placed their order, and then the three of them were left alone. He knew it was silly, but as hard as he fought to keep his cool around her, it was always just a half-inch beyond his grasp. "You did good with the mirroring thing today. Thanks for helping me out."

"Yeah, right. Admit it. You're just happy I didn't fall on my face," Camille said teasingly.

Without thinking, Jaylon laughed at her forthrightness. "No, I was just happy you came." When she looked at him with confusion, he quickly added, "That way I didn't have to answer five million questions about where you where and why you weren't there."

The puzzled expression on her face only deepened. "Huh?"

He laughed again as he shifted in the booth. "Oh, the kids all wanted to know where Camille and Daria were last week. I thought I was going to have to post it on the ten o'clock news or something to get anything done."

"Oh," she said with a still-confused nod. "Well, we were glad we could help. Isn't that right, Dar?"

"Yeah," the little girl said, bouncing in her seat. "I liked playing mirroring."

"Here," Jaylon said as he lifted a hand to Daria. "Here's another one we do." He nodded at his hand, and carefully she put her hand next to his. "Now, watch my hand and go exactly where it goes."

As Camille watched, their hands began to move, but he never looked away from Daria's gaze.

"Good girl." Clockwise, counter-clockwise, up, down. They moved in perfect sync. Finally Jaylon smiled and pulled his hand back. "You're as good at that as your big sister is."

The waitress appeared at their table, three hot chocolates and hamburgers balanced carefully on her tray. She deposited the food and then left.

"So, you got big plans for Thanksgiving?" Jaylon asked before nonchalantly biting into his hamburger.

However, Camille had already taken a bite and was struggling to chew the bite before she answered. "Hmm." She held up a hand to him to indicate she had heard and would answer as soon as she could.

After a few more seconds of chewing, he took a small sip of cocoa. It didn't matter that there was no conversation. He just enjoyed the simple gift of watching her without cause to look away.

Finally, she swallowed and straightened. "I'm just going to make a little chicken or something. No big deal really."

"No family?" he asked as his eyebrows knit in the center of his forehead with concern.

"The less the better," Camille said with a touch of annoyance, and he remembered the litany of fathers. "How about you? Big family get-together?"

Unbidden his gaze fell to the table as his hand dropped the hamburger to his plate. "I'm sure Dad's folks will come, and Marianne will put on the house beautiful show for them, but it'll be just the five of us."

Camille's chewing on the other side of the table slowed. "Marianne?"

"Yeah." He batted the question away. "My stepmom."

"Oh."

He wanted to look at her, but his heart wouldn't let him. "My mom died when I was little, and Dad married Marianne a couple of years ago."

"Oh, I'm sorry," Camille said, and he could hear the sincerity.

"It's not a big deal." He shook his head to emphasize those words. "I barely even remember her."

"That must be hard—growing up without a mom."

"A lot like growing up without a dad," he said as his gaze snagged on hers, and a moment passed before either of them felt the need to look away. "How's that burger?"

She looked down at her almost gone burger and smiled. "Great."

When he left Camille and Daria off at their house, Jaylon's heart said it wouldn't be a crime to waggle an invitation in out of her; however, for once sanity won out. He bid them a hasty good-bye and watched long enough to make sure they got in all right, and then he spun the wheels and headed out to Hollybrook. There was guilt in his gut. It had been nearly three weeks since he'd made this trip, and that was far, far too long.

"Hey, Beautiful," he said as he folded himself down next to the lady sitting motionless and silent beside a menagerie of chirping birds. For a moment his thoughts slid to another lady sitting dead center stage on a chaise lounge chair, and he smiled. "How've you been?"

After a moment he pulled the little book out of his jacket pocket. "Look here what I brought you." He smiled for the old woman. It wasn't hard. He was just following the lead she had set down for him many years before.

"Okay, tell me you met Mr. Wonderful over the weekend," Nick said, sliding into the seat next to her on Monday afternoon.

Camille reached up and pushed her glasses up. "Tell me you've forgotten this whole stupid idea. I mean, listen, Nick. Come on. Wouldn't it be more romantic for you to just take Lex out yourself? You know—red roses, steak dinner, soft music, just the two of you."

Nick nodded. "Sounds great, except your friend doesn't want to celebrate without you."

Oh, now she wants to make a big deal out of being my friend.

"I'm really okay with it," Camille said, hoping he would decide she was serious. "Really I don't mind."

However, it was as though he was no longer listening to a word she said. "I was thinking I could always ask Mark. He seems like a nice enough guy."

"Now you're asking dates out for me?" she asked in panic. "How desperate does that make me look?"

Nick shrugged. "You tell me."

At that moment the black jacket caught her attention as it floated by her seat. Defiantly she turned her full attention on Nick if only not to have to look at it. "I'll get my own date, or I won't go."

"You will go because Lexie wants you to go, and the clock is ticking. If you don't get a date, I'll get one for you."

Mrs. Allen walked up onto the stage just as the bell rang. "First off, I need the critiques from anyone who attended a play over the weekend."

Camille was grateful when two other papers were passed down from the end. She added hers to the bottom of the stack stealthily and handed the stack to Tessa who was collecting them.

"That it?" Mrs. Allen asked, holding the papers in the air.

Unconsciously Camille nodded even as she relaxed, knowing that part of the class assignment was now finished.

"Okay," Mrs. Allen said obviously not happy with the number of papers turned in. "Some of you better get busy." With that she rolled the papers up in her hand and began class in earnest. "Now, I know you all are dying to know my decision about the play selection, so I won't put it off. We will be having auditions the Monday after Thanksgiving for the casting of *Don't Listen to the Fates*."

Moderate cheers crossed the audience as Camille smiled to herself. Well, the others would have a good play to produce anyway.

"This year we will be doing things a little differently," Mrs. Allen said, walking to the side of the stage to retrieve a handful of scripts and deposit the papers. "Instead of letting you sign up for the parts you want to audition for like last year, this year everyone will try out for all the parts—for a grade."

Soft groans echoed throughout the auditorium, accompanied by Camille's.

"You will audition one of four scenes," Mrs. Allen continued, "my choice."

She retraced her steps to the center of the stage. "Each of you will need to have a script anyway, so consider the script you receive today yours. You may mark it as you like—within reason of course." Bending down off the stage she handed the scripts to Keane and Jaylon to pass out to the others.

Thankfully, Camille noted that Jaylon would be staying on his side of the auditorium this time.

"Now as you all know the four main characters are not the only parts, but the other parts will be assigned based on your performance of the main parts."

Camille accepted the stack Keane handed her, took one, and passed them on to Nick.

"I will not forbid you to use your scripts in the auditions, but obviously it would be better for your audition and for your grade if you didn't. Yes, Mark, that means memorizing the part."

Another chorus of groans wafted across the auditorium.

"Try-outs will begin the Monday after Thanksgiving."

Barely listening to Mrs. Allen, Camille leafed through the script, wishing they could postpone the auditions until after Christmas break. Of course she wouldn't get a part, but even the thought of going through tryouts was enough to make her skin crawl.

"I thought today we could break up into partners and practice the passages we will use for auditions." Mrs. Allen quickly gave the instructions on how to locate the proper passages and then allowed the class to break up and work.

"What do you say?" Nick asked as Camille stayed firmly planted in her seat. "Partner?"

"Sure," she said with a small smile. She stood and followed him to the back as the remainder of the group scattered as well. Good. A nice, dark corner where nobody could hear her butcher the script. Perfect. "Which one do you want to start with?"

"Let's try page 20 first," he said as he sat down cross-legged on the carpet. Camille followed him, truly liking his choice of locations. "We can run through Dominique and Hawk's first fight."

"Okay," Camille said, knowing there was no way she would ever be able to pull off Dominique's haughty superiority even in practice.

"You first."

Camille swung her braid over her shoulder, pushed up her glasses, and settled in. "Oh, don't be so dramatic, Hawk. It's not like we were married or anything."

Remarkably Camille managed to avoid discussion of her non-existent date and most of the thoughts of the black jacket for the remainder of Monday. When she met Lexie at the cafeteria table Tuesday afternoon, she breathed a sigh of relief that for the moment anyway Nick was nowhere to be seen.

She waited a full three minutes before her curiosity got the best of her. "Where's Nick?"

"Sick," Lexie said over her cheese sandwich forlornly.

"Oh, really?" Camille asked, sorry for him but feeling her day brightening with the news. "What's wrong with him?"

"Stomach something. No big deal, but his mom thought he should stay home rather than making all the rest of us sick."

Camille considered this. It could be better, but it could be so, so much worse. He could be here hounding her about her non-date. "So I guess Friday's out then."

"Oh, no." Lexie shook her head. "He promised me he'd be well for Friday."

"Great." No part of Camille liked that news. "You know I was thinking, I bet the two of you would really rather be alone than to have me tagging along."

Lexie's face scrunched. "Don't you dare chicken out on me, Camille Wright. We've spent every one of my birthdays together since I was eight.

You can't bail on me now."

"I'm not bailing. I'll be here with you that whole day at school."

"That's not the same."

"Yeah, well, the last ten years you didn't have a boyfriend either, so it seems to me that a lot's not the same anymore." She had meant for the statement to be a joke, but once it was out, it sounded nothing like one.

Lexie's gaze never left the table as she continued to chew. "Does it really bother you how much time I spend with Nick?"

"No," Camille said defensively, and then she deflated. "Sometimes. I don't know. Nick's a great guy and everything. And we both knew things were going to change sooner or later. Hey, let's face it, next year we might not even live in the same state anymore."

The scowl on Lexie's face deepened. "Don't even say that!"

Camille shrugged. "We have to be realistic. It's a possibility."

After a long moment Lexie squared her shoulders. "Well, then that makes this year that much more important."

"Yeah," Camille said as her own shoulders fell. "I guess it does."

There was a long pause as the clinking of the cafeteria silverware filled the air between them.

"So, you'll find somebody then?" Lexie finally asked.

Camille exhaled, wishing her answer could be anything else. "Yeah, I'll find somebody."

If someone else commits you to something, you have the right to not follow through, but if you commit yourself to something, you are then obligated to make it happen. No matter what she did, she couldn't shake those thoughts. To Camille promises were something never to be taken lightly, and this one was no different. She had given her word, and like it or not, she now had to follow through on that word.

However, the second she had agreed, her body and spirit began conspiring to make every other part of her life fall apart. In the next three hours she managed to leave her Physics book in her locker, completely blank out on an English test, and fall down six stairs when she missed the first one. In the ungraceful trip to the bottom, she twisted her ankle, which reduced her to hobbling, pitiful wreck for the rest of the afternoon.

So much so that when Jaylon's voice broke through the crowd of students as she limped to the auditorium door, she couldn't even bring herself to care anymore.

"What did you do?" he asked as he surveyed her all the way down to her shoes.

"Oh, you know me. It's always something," she said as her annoyance with her whole miserable life bubbled to the top.

He pulled the door open and waited as she hobbled through. "No, seriously. What'd you do?"

"Grace here. I fell down some steps. Got my ankle good too."

"Are you okay?" he asked with growing concern as they made their way down the center aisle.

"Well, I might be if I could perform some kind of miracle and find some desperate soul who wouldn't freak out at the mere mention of going out with me on Friday." In the pain and frustration, the words were out of her mouth before they could be stopped, and in truth, she never even heard them.

At her row, she turned in, thankful only for the empty seat next to hers.

"Where's Nick?" Jaylon asked, looking back up the aisle.

"Sick," Camille said angrily as she threw her backpack to the floor and sat down in a heap.

"Oh," Jaylon said, and then he shifted his books to the other hip. "Then would you mind having some company?"

For the first time since she'd agreed to the Friday night double date nightmare, his question jolted her back to reality. With two blinks she took her first real look at him, and her brainwaves scrambled. "Oh, yeah. Sure. Of course."

The smile that always sent her heart pounding spread across his face as he slipped into the seat between her and the aisle. "Cool."

Fighting to keep herself from fidgeting, Camille pulled the pen from behind her ear and nailed her gaze to the stage where Mrs. Allen was already laying out the plan for the day.

"I had some questions yesterday after class about how I'm going to grade your auditions, so I thought we'd talk a little bit about that before we get started today. First of all, just getting or not getting a part will not necessarily earn you a good grade.

"The things I will be looking for as far as the grading is concerned are whether you understand the character's motivation and can convey that motivation in a meaningful way. Also, I will be looking for how you interact with another actor in a scene. And finally how well you can carry a performance off overall."

The black sleeve of Jaylon's jacket kept yanking Camille's gaze and thought pattern to it even as she tried to listen.

"Also, I'll be looking at whether or not you have the passages memorized. There are only four try-out parts for the girls and three for the boys, so memorizing them shouldn't tax your brains too much."

Maybe not, Camille thought, but sitting right next to Jaylon Quinn was completely overloading hers at the moment.

"Also for the next couple of days, I will let you use some class time to practice and memorize. You may work with a partner or on your own today, and I'll give you the whole period again. But don't squander this time because Thursday and Friday you'll only have half the class to practice, and next week I'm not promising anything."

Mrs. Allen stopped and thought for a moment, and then she dropped her hands. "Questions?"

No one raised a hand. In fact, no one even moved.

"Okay, then. Good luck," she said and then backed up before turning suddenly back. "Oh, wait. I have your papers from Monday for those of you who wrote them. They'll be up on stage. Okay, now you can get to work."

Camille watched Mrs. Allen lay the papers on the stage, wondering the whole time how many eons it would take her to make it all the way up there and back.

"You want me to get yours?" Jaylon asked, standing from his seat.

"Would you mind?" she asked, never quite looking all the way up.

"No problem."

When his presence moved away from her, Camille was convinced she must have fallen down Alice's rabbit hole. He wasn't really here. He hadn't really been sitting right next to her. No, if she just concentrated really, really hard she could make herself wake up from this dream, and she would no longer be in a parallel universe with a twisted ankle and Jaylon Quinn sitting with her. In fact, if she worked really hard, maybe she could make the whole, entire drama thing disappear for good. That would be a blessing.

"Good job," Jaylon said, reappearing next to her seat. "93." He flipped the paper onto her lap. "What'd you use to critique it anyway?"

"Oh, umm. How they used the lighting to emphasize the dimming of her mind," Camille said, looking over her paper. "What about you?"

Jaylon scrutinized his own paper like he was in a trance. "The costume design—like we talked about."

Her heart thudded forward as Camille nodded slightly. "Good choice."

"Yeah," he said, moving very slowly to put the paper into his book. Then he looked around the auditorium at the others who were already immersed in play practice. "So, umm. You want to run lines together?"

She looked up at him in wide-eyed fear. "Run lines?"

"You know. Practice, rehearse?"

"Oh, s-sure," she said, stumbling over the words. She was acting like an idiot, and she knew it. Forcing every scattering thought to stop and stand at attention, she pulled her script out of her backpack and stood. "Where to?"

Jaylon shrugged and pointed to the space at the back of the theatre where she and Nick had escaped the day before. "Back there?"

Gamely Camille followed him out of the row and into the aisle.

However, at each row she reached for the seat back to ease the strain on her ankle.

Three rows from the back, Jaylon looked at her and laughed softly. "Maybe we should've stayed where we were."

Despite all the pain shooting up her leg, Camille laughed as she turned and headed for the back corner. "Or maybe you should've chosen a non-wounded partner."

He laughed outright at that. "Too late now."

At her destination she carefully lowered herself to the floor and wrapped her legs together, wincing only once as she settled herself against one of the seatbacks, glad to no longer be moving.

"Better?" he asked with concern as he sat down facing her.

"I'll live."

He studied her for one more moment and then flipped open his script. "You got a preference about where we start?"

"Wherever you want," she said, knowing she was here to practice for him, not the other way around.

"Okay, how about Act Three Scene One. The park thing."

With a shove she pushed the meaning of that scene away from her and thumbed through the script to the page. "You're first."

As she watched him, Jaylon took a single deep breath closed his eyes and became Hawk Fletcher. In fact, when his eyes opened again, they seemed to no longer even be Jaylon's eyes. The transformation was so complete that Camille knew that simply reading the words on the page would not be enough effort on her part. Leaving out closing her eyes, which felt too weird, she followed his lead, relaxed her shoulders and imagined herself in a beautiful park on a spring day with the guy she had idolized for years sitting on a blanket right next to her—it wasn't too hard.

"So you've never wondered what you want to do with your life then?" Jaylon as Hawk asked.

"No." Camille shook her head to emphasize the point. "Mom used to take me to the office with her sometimes, and I'd watch her sitting there, taking orders from all these other people about when something was supposed to be done or how it was supposed to be done. I'd sit in that corner, and I'd be reading. But I wasn't really reading, I was watching. I was watching her—I was watching her lose who she was a little bit at a time.

"And then when I was older, I asked her once about why she didn't stand up to those people, and she said, 'Lauren, the only way to stand up to them is if you have more education than they do, and I just don't.'"

"But education's only a part of it," Hawk protested.

"Not according to my mom. To her, an education's everything. So I decided that I wasn't going to be the person on the outside, I was going to be on the inside of that office, and I'd never treat my workers the way they treated my mom."

"So, what then? You're going to be a banker? A lawyer? A doctor? What?"

"It doesn't matter. I'm going to be something. Something big. Something powerful. Something so important that people can't make me feel...like I'm not enough."

"Enough? How can you not be enough?"

Camille wasn't sure if it was her or Lauren talking at that moment. "You've seen me. The only time people even notice me is when I make a fool out of myself. All the other times it's like I'm just invisible."

"But you've always got your head in those books of yours. You don't even give people a chance to get to know you."

"Why should I? They're all a bunch of losers anyway."

"Whoa. That's pretty strong coming from somebody who's going to become some benevolent boss some day."

"Oh, I won't be like that then."

"Well, you're sure practicing pretty hard for the part right now."

In character Camille defiantly pulled her shoulders up a full foot. "Well, what about you, Mr. I've got it all figured out? I don't see you exactly banishing inferiority complexes in your fellow students."

He deflated only a touch. "That's not me though. That's just who I am at school."

"Well, you're practicing pretty hard for that part right now. Aren't you?"

Jaylon's break stretched on a little too long, and Camille looked up at him. The color of his face had drained out until it looked a sick ash color.

"Yeah," he finally said so softly she barely heard the word. "I guess I am."

She wanted to ask if he was all right. She wanted to, but she was afraid of the answer, and even more afraid that he might throw up all over her if he even tried to say something else.

"Pretty good," Jaylon said, breaking out of character with a snap.

Stunned, Camille couldn't decide what had just happened. Every part of him now sounded perfectly Jaylon, but only a few seconds ago, she could've sworn she'd heard his heart break.

"How about we try the one with Dominique and Ethan?" Jaylon asked, paging backward through the script.

"Oh, okay," Camille said, still stumbling to understand the last several moments.

"Well, well," Jaylon said, sliding into the part of slippery, slimy Ethan, "what have we here?"

"Hi, Ethan," Camille said, stretching for the sappy sweet voice of a girl trying too hard to impress; however, the right tone eluded her.

"Now here's a question," Jaylon said with no trouble getting into his part at all. "How is it that you know my name, but I don't know yours?"

Camille thought for a second that the stomach bug must've jumped the gap to her own throat as suddenly all she wanted to do was throw up. "Your reputation precedes you."

Jaylon's laugh sent shivers down her spine. "That's my kind of answer."

They had practiced all three boy-girl parts, and Camille was busy flipping through the script to the Dominique-Lauren discussion, which Jaylon had graciously agreed to read with her, when he suddenly threw a grenade right at her.

"So, what was it that you were saying about Friday night?" he asked as he searched for the audition section.

In mid-page-turn her hands stopped. "Huh?"

"Earlier. You said something about needing a date for Friday night. What's the problem? Nick going to be too sick to take you?"

"Huh?" she asked, getting even more confused.

Jaylon shrugged even as he continued his search. "I just figured you two must have some big shindig going on, and you're mad cause he's too sick to go."

In utter confusion, Camille struggled to figure out where this line of conversation had come from and where it was going. "Me and Nick?"

"Yeah. I mean you're going out and everything."

"Me and Nick?" she asked again, knowing she sounded utterly ridiculous. "We're not...umm, just a second, let me get this straight...you think that Nick and I are...dating?"

The last word sounded totally incredulous.

Jaylon's eyes narrowed as he looked at her, his script totally forgotten. "Yeah. I mean you're always together. You sit together and stuff."

"I sit by Elrad Hollister in Physics, but that doesn't mean I'm going out with the guy!"

Now it was Jaylon who was struggling. "But you always sit together, and you're partners for all the exercises, and you always leave together."

"That's cause he's the only one brave enough to practice with me!"

Silence fell over them as Jaylon began a frantic search through her eyes for how truthful she was actually being. "Are you telling me you never were going out with him?"

"No," she said emphatically. "In fact, he's going out with my best friend. In fact, he's the one making me so miserable right now—making me find a date for this weekend."

"What's up with this weekend anyway?"

"Oh, it's my best friend Lexie's birthday," Camille said, giving up all hopes of sounding anything even close to thrilled. "They want to double, and if I don't find someone, Nick's going to fix me up with *his* first choice."

"Who's that?" Jaylon asked as though he didn't want any part of hearing the answer.

"Mark," Camille said dramatically. "Or Oren somebody that Lexie made this face about." She squished her face together causing him to laugh out loud—a move that immediately made a pained look jump to her face. "Don't laugh. This is my life we're talking about."

Obviously fighting to squelch his laughter, Jaylon finally managed to level a serious face at her. "Well, if you're really that desperate, I could always go with you."

"You?" Camille asked, crashing back into whom she was talking to and what she was telling him. "Oh, no. I couldn't ask you to do that."

"Why not?"

"Be...because. I'm sure you've got a thousand things to do, and...and you don't want to waste your time..."

"First of all," he said as the laughter fell completely away from him, "I'm not doing anything else, and second of all, I'd love to go. That is, if you don't mind having me around."

Having him around? Having Jaylon Quinn around? No, she didn't mind at all although she had the distinct feeling that Alice's hole couldn't be too far behind her.

"Okay, then," she finally said as though they were signing a multi-million dollar deal. "That sounds great."

The bell picked that moment to ring, and he pushed up to his feet and then extended his hand to her. With a pull she righted herself and quickly let go of his hand. Feeling like every gaze in the place was locked on her, she made her way back to the center aisle as he followed her so closely she could actually feel him.

"I guess we can get together tomorrow or something so I can fill you in on where we're going, and times and all of that," she said, wishing she'd had more practice at this. More practice? *Any* practice at this.

"Okay. That sounds great," he said as they reached their seats and retrieved their belongings. "Oh, and what does your best friend like?"

"Like?"

"You know. Candy? Flowers?"

Camille laughed. "You better leave those for Nick, or you might be on more than a date."

He laughed. "Good point."

She limped with him to the back and out the door.

"So, I'll see you tomorrow then?" he asked at the intersection of hallways where their paths parted company.

"Yeah," she said, knowing full well in the bright light of the hallway that this must be a dream.

"I'll see you then," he said as that unnerving smile spread onto his face.

Unable to move she watched him turn and walk down the hallway, and then she shook her head in disbelief. It seemed that somebody had asked somebody out for Friday night, and although her sanity couldn't quite be sure, she had the vague suspicion that she had just gotten a date with Jaylon Quinn.

However, with no way of verifying that news flash, she forced her body to move in the other direction. Somehow she answered all of Lexie's questions about her ankle while simultaneously keeping mum about the drama class happenings. One part of her wanted to say something, to tell someone, to scream it to the world, but another part said that telling anyone might be just the thing to break the spell she had somehow fallen under.

And the last thing she wanted to do was to find out how this magic trick was done.

Wrapped tightly in his jacket, Jaylon sat on the south side of the tree letting it block as much of the chilled November wind as it could. Four feet from him the swing twisted in the intermittent gusts. In his hands the script lay rolled. Sitting here gave a whole new meaning to the term cold reading, but not even the bone-chilling air whipping around this spot could compete with the cold that had invaded his body when he'd read those words.

Unbidden his gaze fell on them again. "Well, you're practicing pretty hard for that part right now. Aren't you?" As memories of the countless people he had stepped on to become the Jaylon Quinn he was today tromped through his mind, he looked out across the gash in the earth to the sunset beyond. "Yeah, I guess I am."

Slowly his head shook just before it fell back onto the hard bark. As the tearing of his heart sounded in his ears, he glanced back at the house—now broken and abandoned. How many days had he spent here, and how many had he spent forgetting the lessons Grandma Lani had taught him?

In the confusion of his mind, he knew only one thing—that she wouldn't be proud of the man he was turning out to be. Camille's fragile features, tucked neatly behind a pair of wire-rimmed glasses floated into his mind, and he could see her even now reading the words that could just as well have been spoken about him—except he was the one on the inside of that office, watching his father as he ordered, commanded, and demanded his way over people.

"You have to be tough. Tough. You hear me?" his father had said on more than one occasion. "You have to put on your thick skin if you want to make it in this world." Jaylon could see his father sitting there on the edge of the bed, the darkness forming a background for his silhouette. "Crying won't make her come back, J. Look, I miss her too, but you don't see me blubbering like a little baby. Do you?"

A single tear slid down Jaylon's cheek as he watched the sky light up in a flare of color. If she just hadn't gotten sick. If his father had just found a way to make her better. If. If. If. A thousand ifs and still his father was right—none of them would ever bring her back.

The pain in his heart seized the breath from his lungs. In defiance he stood and swiped at the tears. Stupid. It was stupid to keep thinking about it. Stupid to cry now. No, now he needed to grow up already—like his father had said a thousand times.

It was just a script. Someone else's fantasy in someone else's head. It had nothing to do with him or his life. Nothing. If all he had to do was to remember that and the world could continue spinning just as it always had, then why was simply remembering that so unbelievably hard?

Camille stood in front of her mirror, script in hand. The drama book had suggested this practice routine, but it didn't seem to be helping much. "Hi, Ethan." She mumbled the next line to herself. "Oh, your reputation precedes you." Her gaze looked up into the mirror, but when she looked back down, she lost her place. "Of course, it's your kind of answer."

As her mind flew away from script, she wondered what idiot had come up with this idea. It wasn't working for her at all. "Ring? Oh, this ring? It's nothing... Really."

Giving up the mirror idea, she flopped backward on her bed. "Hi, Ethan."

Chapter 13

"I talked to Mark today," Nick said as he sat down at the cafeteria table Wednesday afternoon.

"Oh, yeah?" Camille asked, forking some meatloaf into her mouth. "About what?"

"About you," he said as though that should be obvious. "About Friday."

"Oh, yeah," Camille said as she wiped her mouth with her napkin. "I was going to talk to you about that."

"Cami," Lexie warned softly.

"No." Camille smiled at her friend in reassurance. "It's just I don't need you to find me a date anymore."

"You don't?" Nick asked uncertainly. "Why not?"

"I got my own."

Lexie's eyes widened. "You did?"

"Who?" Nick asked clearly suspecting some slight of hand trick.

"Jaylon," Camille said before she bit into her roll.

"Jaylon?" Nick asked in horror.

"Quinn?" Lexie asked, her eyes going even wider shock.

"Yep, Jaylon Quinn," Camille said with a defiant nod. "Aren't you proud of me?"

Nick looked at her for a long moment, and then a smile formed at the corners of his mouth. Like the sunshine following a rain, he laughed. "That's funny. That's a good one, Camille. You had me going there for a minute."

"I'm not kidding," Camille said as heat seeped up her cheeks. "I asked him, and he said he'd go."

"Jaylon?" Lexie asked, still stuck on the name. "Jaylon Quinn? *The* Jaylon Quinn?"

"Yes," Camille said in growing annoyance. "The Jaylon Quinn. What? Is that so hard to believe?"

Both friends looked like the answer to that question was a definite, positive, unequivocal yes, but neither had the chance to say that.

"Hi, guys," Jaylon said suddenly appearing at the end of their table, and all three gazes snapped to his face. "Mind if I join you?"

Lexie looked positively shell-shocked, and fear over what Nick might actually do if he got in close range of Jaylon jumped to Camille's mind, but those concerns were outweighed by the fact that Jaylon was standing there, looking utterly vulnerable and totally gorgeous.

"Have a seat," Camille said as though gorgeous, perfect guys routinely came up and asked to sit by her.

"Cool." Jaylon slid his tray onto the table next to Camille's and swung one leg over the bench seat. "So, Nick, you feeling better?"

"Oh, uh, yeah," Nick said, wholly unprepared for the question.

Jaylon nodded. "I'm glad." He looked down at his food and then back across the table. "And you must be Lexie."

When Jaylon extended his hand across the table, Camille thought Lexie might pass out right there. Finally though she accepted Jaylon's hand.

"So, you're the one with the birthday. Right?"

"Uh, yeah. Right," Lexie said, choking on every syllable.

"That's cool," Jaylon said with a smile. "The big one-eight. Huh?"

Lexie nodded as Jaylon turned his charm on Camille who was only moderately more prepared for this visit than her table companions.

"Did you work on the script last night?" he asked.

"Oh, yeah, a little. You?"

He picked up a forkful of lettuce. "Some. I'm just worried about how she's going to choose who we try out with. You know? The wrong partner could sink a whole audition."

"Maybe she'll let us rotate or something," Camille said, surprising no one more than herself. "I just wish I could memorize better. I mean give me some elements or formulas or something, and no problem, but this stuff is just so different."

"Not really. You just take it one chunk at a time—just like everything else."

"I don't know. I'm just glad I'm only going to have to memorize the try-out stuff."

"Why's that?" Jaylon asked, sounding genuinely confused.

"Why? Because I'm not going to get a part. That's why."

"How can you be so sure?"

Camille's gaze traveled across the table, and she found her two friends looking like a rapt audience. "Well, I'm not going to be there next semester for one thing."

"Oh, come on, you're not still thinking about dropping out. Are you?" Jaylon asked with some concern.

"No, I'm not only thinking about it. I'm doing it." She flipped the last of her roll back onto her tray. "Besides, Ariana will get Lauren, and Tessa or Jill will get Dominique."

"Tessa or Jill?" Jaylon asked as if that was a horrible idea.

"Ariana's a synch for the lead, and the only other major part is supporting." Camille shrugged. "Unless Mrs. Allen totally goes bonkers and names Tessa as Lauren or something." She waved her milk carton in the air. "Now, you know, I can see that working. Although Ariana would probably chew the curtains down if that happened."

At that moment her gaze crashed back to the table. Had she really just said that out loud? By the looks she was getting from across the table, it was apparent that she had. Sheepishly she set her milk down and gathered her sanity. "Sorry. I didn't mean it like that."

With a soft smile Jaylon ducked his head and then looked away. "No, you're right. Ari would probably freak."

The cafeteria sounds enveloped them as Camille struggled to find a new, less volatile topic. "So, Lex, have you decided where you want to go Friday?"

Still wide-eyed Lexie looked from Jaylon to Camille utterly speechless.

"I thought we might go out to eat somewhere and then go over to the observatory for their eight-thirty show," Nick supplied, looking at Lexie as though he wished that the opposite side of the table would be hit by a wayward asteroid.

"Oh?" Jaylon asked.

"But we don't have to," Lexie said quickly.

"No, that sounds great," Jaylon said, and Camille could've sworn his smile was genuine. "I've always wanted to see that. I've heard really great things about it."

"Yeah," Nick said with not one iota of enthusiasm.

Above them the bell sounded, and all four of them looked up at it like it was the first time they had ever heard it. Nick was the first to stand, followed closely by Jaylon who offered a hand to help Camille untangle herself from the table. However, his hand touching hers was making her brain do funny things so that she wasn't at all sure how much help he actually was.

She started for the tray depository feeling him following her, which sent her reasoning right out the window.

"I see your ankle is better," Jaylon said, appraising her.

"Oh, yeah, five ice packs will do wonders."

They stacked their trays along with the others.

Jaylon fanned his hand through his hair. "So, I guess I'll see you in drama?"

"Yeah," Camille said completely unsure of anything at the moment.

"Well, take care." He took three steps away from her and then turned back around with a wink. "And watch out for those stairs this time."

Stopping the smile that jumped to her face was impossible, and for one second too long she stood there. And then Jaylon disappeared into the crowd. The hard knock of a shoulder shoving its way past her startled her back to her senses enough to realize that Nick was no longer with their little group.

"Jeez," Camille said with annoyance. "Watch where you're going!"

But Nick just kept right on walking.

"What's his problem?" Camille asked Lexie.

"Forget about him. Let's talk about Jaylon Quinn," Lexie said, angry and curious at the same time as they headed out of the cafeteria. "How is it possible that you're friends with Jaylon Quinn, and this has never come up in conversation?"

At their lockers they traded out their books, and Camille made sure to grab her Physics book this time. "What's the big deal? So I know Jaylon Quinn."

"Hello! This is me you're talking to. Remember? Me. Lexie. Your we-tell-each-other-everything best friend."

Camille pushed through the crowd to catch up with Lexie who hadn't bothered to wait for her. "What's that supposed to mean?"

"It means I can't believe you never said a word to me about this, and now all of a sudden you've got a date with the most gorgeous guy in school, and he shows up at our table to chat? What? Did it never occur to you to say, 'Oh, yeah, by the way I got to talk to Jaylon Quinn today.'"

"We're just friends," Camille said as they neared their respective classrooms. "We're in drama together, and we happened to get to know each other. No big deal."

"Oh, really? Well, when you get finished justifying keeping this little, itty-bitty piece of news to yourself, let me know. Okay?"

In exasperation, Camille sighed. There was no point in arguing with Lexie when she got like this. Jaylon was just being nice. That's all. There was no big conspiracy to keep Lexie in the dark, and there was no good reason for her to be so mad. In fact, Camille was quite sure that Lexie left out quite a few details when they talked about Nick too. This was no different.

Anyway, none of that mattered. Lexie would get over it. Jaylon would get bored and go back to his super cool friends. And Camille would go back to her former existence—unnoticed and totally invisible. She just hoped that all happened sooner rather than later.

Sooner, however, came a lot sooner than she had expected. As usual when she got to drama, she huddled down into her seat, three rows back and hunched over her Physics book. Once Friday was over, and everyone came back to their senses again, this whole thing would just blow over.

Two seconds before she actually convinced herself of that, she heard Ariana's voice dancing down the aisle. Instinctively Camille shrank further in her seat and dug her way into her book.

"I was just thinking that we should get together and practice later—you know for old time's sake," Ariana was saying as she passed, and when Camille looked up, her heart plummeted. With one arm firmly tucked in Jaylon's, Ariana looked more like she was walking down the red carpet at the Oscar's rather than just showing up for drama class.

Everything inside her made Camille want to run, and her gaze did a passable job of it even without her feet. It wasn't until the bell rang that she realized Nick wasn't sitting beside her. Careful not to allow her gaze too much rein, she scanned the other students around her.

With only a cursory survey she located him, the next row up sitting next to Tony and obviously engrossed in some kind of intense conversation. Trying not to feel the hurt, she pushed up her glasses. Somehow she had managed to simultaneously alienate both Jaylon and Nick, and the worst part was she had no idea how she had accomplished that feat.

"Good afternoon," Mrs. Allen said, sounding far too chipper. "As promised I'm going to give you the last half of class to work on your scripts, but first, I want to explain how I'll be grading this last six weeks."

Camille shrank further in her seat. Invisibility had never looked so good.

When Mrs. Allen finally finished with grading procedures and an outline of the humiliation to come, she held up her hands. "Well, I guess that's it. If there are no questions, you can have the rest of the time to practice."

From the middle of the darkness around her Camille glanced around. Nick was talking with Melissa, Jennifer, and Tony, and it was abundantly clear to Camille that partnering with him today was out. She peered across the auditorium and watched as Ariana linked arms with Jaylon and led him up the stage steps. With a solid sigh Camille reached down and retrieved her script from her backpack.

"Hey, Camille," a soft voice from the darkness in front of her said.

She looked up and had never been so glad to see a friendly face. "Hey, Steph."

"You want to work together?" Stephanie, the dark-headed girl with pixy-like features, asked.

"Sure," Camille said. She looked around, and the only place not taken was the actual seats. "Have a seat."

Stephanie smiled gratefully and plopped down into the seat next to her. "Isn't this just the biggest pain in the world? I wish Allen would just let us sign up for the crew and be done with it."

"I hear you there," Camille said, relaxing instantly. "You're not excited about this audition either, huh?"

"No way. I didn't sign up for this class to get a part. I just wanted something to do besides schoolwork all the time."

That much Camille understood perfectly. "You want to start with the Dominique-Lauren thing?"

"Sounds good."

"I'll take Dominique. You take Lauren, and then we'll switch."

"Go for it."

Although Ariana was reading the same words Camille had read only the day before, somehow they sounded very different.

"It doesn't matter," Ariana said brusquely. "I'm going to be something. Something big. Something powerful. Something so important that people can't make me feel like I'm not enough."

"Enough?" Jaylon asked, feeling like he was just reading some words on a page. "How can you not be enough?"

"Oh, you've seen me," Ariana said, stretching the drama to its breaking point. "The only time people even notice me is when I make a fool out of myself. All the other times it's like I'm just invisible."

As his gaze searched out past the lights of the stage, he wished only that Ariana was invisible. Non-existent would be better. He shifted his body, trying to keep his mind on the script. "But you've always got your head in those books of yours. You don't even give people a chance to get to know you."

"Why should I?" Ariana scowled derisively. "They're all a bunch of losers anyway."

It was the first line he actually believed. "That's pretty strong coming from somebody who's going to become some benevolent boss some day."

Ariana looked down at her fingernails in bored frustration. "Oh, I won't be like that then."

"Well, you're sure practicing pretty hard for the part right now." The snort of contempt he exhaled with that line was no act. It wasn't how Hawk was supposed to deliver that line, but it was the way he, Jaylon, felt.

Ariana's scowl deepened. "Come on, J. We're supposed to be in love. Remember?"

When he looked at her, all he could think was, 'That will require the biggest acting job of my life.' "Yeah, I remember."

Trying not to search the crowd for either guy, Camille gathered her things and walked out with Stephanie. Although she was just a sophomore, Stephanie seemed to have her life together, which at the moment was far more than Camille could say for herself.

"I went to fashion camp over the summer, and we got to make our own gowns," Stephanie said as they walked out into the blinding light.

"You make your own clothes?" Camille asked genuinely impressed.

"Yeah, my mom taught me when I was like seven, and I've been designing and making stuff ever since." Stephanie put her hands out. "I made this shirt."

"You're kidding."

The shirt was a patchwork of several different fabrics, but in form, style, and proportion, it was perfect.

"That is so cool," Camille said. "You're going to have to show me some of your designs sometime."

Stephanie's excitement jumped to the surface. "I'd like that."

"Well, this is where I get off," Camille said. "I'll see you tomorrow."

Happily Stephanie smiled and nodded. "Take care."

Fully expecting another confrontation with Nick and Lexie, Camille strode to her locker; however, neither was anywhere in sight. She wasn't sure if that was a good sign or a bad one, but it was better not to think too much about it. Quickly she retrieved most of her books and slammed the door. "Give me books any day."

Pushing the depression away from her, she walked out into the bleak November afternoon and made her way to the bus stop. Strangely making friends was becoming rather easy these days, it was keeping those friends that was becoming cloyingly difficult.

At the bus stop, she leaned against the pole and re-examined the day. One moment she had a friend, the next she didn't. It was like there was some kind of revolving door on her life, and her friends just kept walking right through it.

Seeing no way to change that, she tightened her arms around her books. If she could just figure out what she was doing that was wrong, maybe life would quit spinning out of control.

"I'm sorry," someone suddenly said, leaning down into her space, and Camille jumped.

"Jaylon," she said, blinking, sure he was a mirage of some kind when she turned around. "What are you doing here?"

"I saw you standing over here." His gaze fell to the concrete between them. "I just wanted to come over and say I'm sorry about today."

"Sorry? Why?"

Through the fringe of his eyelashes, he looked at her. "I noticed Nick seemed kind of mad."

"Oh, you noticed that too, huh?" she asked with half a smirk.

"Yeah, and I thought maybe that was my fault."

Camille wasn't sure what to say. "He was just a little surprised."

"Looked like more than surprise to me."

She shrugged and bobbed her head. "Well, I think he would've rather picked my date for me."

Jaylon shifted his two books to the other hip. "Maybe it would've been okay if you'd chosen someone other than me."

Her heart wanted to argue, but her brain knew differently. "He just doesn't know you."

"Maybe he knows me better than you do."

Slowly her eyes narrowed with concern. "What does that mean?"

Sad understanding slipped into his eyes. "I just seem to bring out the worst in people."

"That's not true. The kids love you."

"They're different. They don't know what I'm really like."

As she looked into the vulnerability in his face, she smiled softly. "Or maybe they're the only ones you let see who you really are."

Liquid-softness fell over his eyes, and when he looked at her, there was a gratefulness in them she didn't remember having seen before. "So, you going home now?"

She nodded as the bus swooshed up to the curb, and the air brakes exhaled.

"What do you say I take you home?" Jaylon asked, and the vulnerability of his eyes jumped into his voice.

With only a single glance at the bus, Camille knew she couldn't leave him out in the cold like this. "Maybe we can run lines?"

His smile beamed at her from his eyes. "I'd like that."

Chapter 14

Camille wasn't at all sure where her sanity had disappeared to, but Jaylon had a way of making it vanish like a lady in a magic box.

"Make yourself comfortable," she said when they entered the apartment in tandem. "I've got to start some supper."

However, instead of sitting down on the couch like she'd expected, he followed her right into the kitchen where she dropped her books to the table.

"Jeez, big day in school?" he asked, surveying the stack.

She opened the refrigerator to examine the supper options. "I don't like to get behind."

"I can see that." He glanced around the apartment. "So, Dar's not home yet?"

Camille pulled out the chicken she had put there that morning. "It's Wednesday, so she won't be home 'til about six."

"Oh, what's Wednesday?"

"Mrs. Heirsh, the lady that brings her home, takes her own daughter to piano on Wednesdays, and rather than take her to piano, run Daria home, and try to be back in an hour, she just takes Dar with her."

"I bet that's fun to sit there for an hour."

Camille ripped the chicken package open. "Gives her time to get her homework done."

Jaylon stood looking at Camille's books as she clanked and clattered around the kitchen.

"What do you say we get started?" Camille asked as she began pulling the skin off the pieces of chicken and laying them in the baking dish.

"How are you going to read and cook at the same time?"

"Well, I worked on the Ethan-Dominique thing last night, so it would give me a chance to see how well I've got it down."

With an impressed nod, Jaylon pulled out his own script and rather than sitting at the table, he walked over to the cabinet and vaulted up onto it. "Let's see." He paged through his script until he came to the passage. "Well, well. What have we here?"

"Hi, Ethan," Camille said even as her fingers yanked the chicken skin free.

"Now here's a question," Jaylon said as he shifted on the counter. "How is it that you know my name, but I don't know yours?"

"Your reputation precedes you," she said with precisely the right words but missing the tone completely.

Jaylon stopped and looked at her for a long moment. "Do you know you sound like a piece of wood?"

"That wasn't the right line?" Camille asked, glancing over her shoulder.

"No, I mean, yeah. It was the right line, but that's not enough. You've got to feel the line. Be the character. Be Dominique."

Camille turned on him with a skeptical look. "I don't want to be Dominique."

"I know, but if you want a decent grade, you'd better find a way to want to be her."

With a frustrated sigh, Camille ripped the skin off of the last piece of chicken. Why wasn't it enough that she knew the words? What did he want? Sophia Loren?

"Let's try it again," Jaylon said. "And this time think about the most annoying, obnoxious, flirtatious girl you know. Then be her."

Camille tore the aluminum foil away from its box and wrapped it around the pan as her mind searched for a role model. Ariana. The one and only Ice Queen. "Okay."

"Well, well. What have we here?"

"Hi, Ethan," Camille said, reaching for the tone she had heard so many times in Ariana's voice.

"Now here's a question," Jaylon said, turning his body and script so he could watch her as she put the chicken in the oven. "How is it that you know my name, but I don't know yours?"

"Oh, your reputation precedes you," she said, and the heat and ice melted perfectly in the middle of her voice.

"That's my kind of answer."

Proud that she'd only missed two lines but worn out from stretching to hold on to Ariana's haughtiness, Camille finally decided to call an end to the practice session at 5:30. Daria would be home soon and so presumably would their mother, and Camille really didn't want them to come home and find her alone with Jaylon.

"That's it," she said, waving a white flag with her words as she laid her exhausted head on the table. "I'm shot."

"Well, I'm impressed." He folded his script up and then followed her up from the table, watching her pick up her books. "I bet you're the only one with that much memorized."

"Oh, yeah, right."

"I'm serious."

She dumped her books on the living room coffee table and straightened the ragged pillows on the couch to keep her hands busy. "But the words are just part of it. You know? I mean I don't know how you all do it."

"Do what?"

"Be someone else. Become someone else. To me, I know the words, but I'm still me. I'm not Dominique...or Lauren."

Jaylon laughed. "You just have to find the parts of them that are in you."

Camille leveled a skeptical gaze at him. "Me and Dominique? Uh-huh, yeah right."

"Haven't you ever wanted to be like her though? To be the center of attention, the one all the guys are after, and have your pick of any guy you wanted."

A slow heat crept up Camille's cheeks. "Hasn't everybody?"

"That's what I mean. You've seen them, and you've wondered what it would be like to be that person." He held up his script. "This is your chance. Find that part of yourself that would like to be them for a day, and then let it go."

Her face creased skeptically. "That's a lot harder than it sounds."

"Not once you figure out how."

At that moment she wished she could figure out how to do a lot of things—like how to stop thinking about him, and how to make sure her heart knew this was nothing more than a mirage that would disappear as quickly as it had come. "Well, I appreciate you coming and helping me. At least maybe now I won't totally bomb out."

Jaylon smiled and shook his head. "You've really got to work on that being humble thing. You know that?"

"Hey, you do what works."

The grin fell from his face. "Yeah, you do."

Camille's gaze traveled past his shoulder to the clock. 5:50. "Well, I'd better get the rest of dinner ready."

He stood for one more moment before nodding. "I had fun today—reading with you."

"Yeah, so did I."

They stood awkwardly for an interminable moment.

"Well, I'd better get," he finally said as he stepped to her door and then stopped and turned back to her. "Oh, I thought I'd tell you, if you want to take back your invitation for Friday, I'll understand."

That statement stopped Camille cold. "Take it back?"

His gaze dropped to the carpet, and even without looking in his eyes, Camille saw the vulnerability in them. "I don't want to mess up anything between you and your friends."

She wanted to reach out to him and pull him into her arms, but she just stood, firmly planted on the carpet. "Well, you're my friend too. So, I guess they're just going to have to deal with that. Now, aren't they?"

When he looked up, there was gratefulness written all over his face. "So we're still on then?"

"Yeah, we're still on."

Later alone in her room, she sat at her vanity table, gazing into the mirror. "Hi, Ethan." Lowering her lashes and head flirtatiously, she smiled. "Oh, your reputation precedes you."

The next morning as she struggled through her Economics test, Camille berated herself for spending so much time on drama the night before. She didn't want to get behind. What a joke. She stayed behind—perpetually.

By the time she finished the test, the bell for lunch had long since rung. Quickly she gathered her books and walked up to the desk to turn in her paper.

"Have some trouble?" Mr. Shelton asked.

"A little." Camille dropped her paper onto the stack and fled for the door. Taking the test was bad enough, taking a pop quiz about how bad the test was would be worse.

In the cafeteria she got her tray and walked uncertainly to the table occupied by Nick and Lexie. "Is there room here?"

They both looked up at her, and annoyance followed slowly by acquiescence gazed back at her. Lexie held a hand out to the other side of the table for Camille, who sat down and forked her food around the tray squares for several seconds.

Talking might not help, but not talking certainly wasn't doing much better.

"Look, I'm sorry I sprung the whole Jaylon thing on you guys yesterday," Camille said without ever looking up. "I guess I should've said something sooner. I just didn't know how. I mean I know how you feel about him." She looked at Nick. "And I wasn't sure how to tell you, or if you'd even want to know, which I guess you didn't."

"So you're really serious about this then?" Lexie asked still not wholly convinced. "You and Jaylon are really friends?"

"Yeah." Camille looked at her friend. "And it would really mean a lot to me if you guys would give him a chance." She looked back at Nick.

"He's really not as bad as you think he is."

Nick snorted softly.

"I'm serious," Camille said pleadingly. "He's really a nice guy."

"Look, Camille," Nick said with a sigh. "I know you think he's great guy and everything, but trust me, okay? He's not worth the DNA it took to make him."

"But you don't know him."

"No," Nick said, and harshness ripped through the word. "You don't know him. Believe me, the only person Jaylon Quinn cares about is Jaylon Quinn. If he has to use you for a step ladder to get what he wants, he will in a heartbeat and never so much as say thank you for your trouble."

Camille's face was set in a permanent frown. "He's not like that."

"Yes, he is."

"How do you know?" Camille challenged.

Nick shook his head. "Forget it. Okay. Just forget I said anything."

"No." She had come this far, and she wasn't about to back down now. "Either you tell me what is so unbelievably terrible about him, or I'm going to get up from this table and walk away right now." Her mind was made up, and when Nick made no move to explain himself, she laid her hands on either side of her tray. "Fine. If that's the way you want it."

When he looked up, there was fire in his eyes. Then his gaze slid over to Lexie, who looked like she might cry at any moment.

"Okay," he finally said. "If you want to know the truth, I'll tell you the truth."

Slowly Camille let go of her tray and told her brain to prepare for the worst.

Nick glanced at her. "I told you I'd had some parts in some community stuff?"

Camille nodded.

"Well, so did Jaylon," Nick said as bitterness dripped from his voice. "Every time I'd show up for an audition, he was there—all spit-shined and polished. And he was good, too. Real good. Used to make me sick."

So Nick was jealous, big deal. Everybody got jealous sometimes.

"He'd walk up to the center of the stage like he owned the whole blasted place. The judges, the casting directors—they all went ga-ga over him. The great Jaylon Quinn. He could do no wrong." The corners of Nick's mouth crushed themselves together. "I hated him.

"Then one summer we got cast in this play together. I guess that would've been right before freshman year. Anyway, my part only had like three lines, and his was like a hundred. Then just before the show started, he got an invitation to go to this acting camp in California or something like that. He was all excited about it. Kept telling everyone how cool it was that he was going to get to go to California. Hollywood here I come and all that."

Nick's jaw set. "I was just glad he was leaving. You know? That way the rest of us second class losers wouldn't have to hear about the great, almighty Jaylon Quinn and how wonderful he was." Softly Nick laughed as his fork spun circles on his plate. "The casting director was a wreck. Jay really left him in the lurch, but I'd been to every single practice. Every one. And I'd stand in for Jaylon when he didn't show up. But nobody noticed that—they were all just so happy when he was there, like he'd decided to grace everyone with his presence or something."

Nick shook his head at the thought. "But then Jaylon told them he was leaving, and they had to find somebody else, somebody to replace the great Jaylon Quinn. I mean two days before the performance really isn't the best time to try to find a replacement for something like that. They were even thinking about just canceling the show."

He picked up his head ever so slightly. "So, I went to the director and told him I could do it. At first he wasn't so keen on that idea, but then we did a run-through and I didn't screw anything up, so they figured they'd just found their solution, and everybody was all happy again. They were calling me their hero and saying they just didn't know what they would ever do without me."

Camille's gaze was locked on Nick, who never so much as glanced up from his tray. The hurt in his voice sent an ache right through her. Still, however, she held onto the hope that he was just making too much out of some petty little kid problem that ultimately meant nothing.

"Man, I was so excited. I called everyone I could think of. My grandparents even drove two hours to come for it. I practiced night and day for two solid days, and I had the part down. Then the night of the first performance, I walked into the dressing room, and there stood Jaylon and the director.

"'Oh, Nick,' the director said like we'd just been saved from certain death. 'Jaylon's decided to stay and finish the performances. Isn't that great?'"

"Ouch," Lexie said softly.

"Yeah, ouch." Nick glanced at her and then back to his tray. "'Tough luck.' That's what he told me, 'Tough luck, McGee.' Like that made everything all better. I know, it was four years ago, so get over it already. But I'm telling you he gets his kicks out of doing stuff like that. He'll get your hopes up, and then he'll yank the carpet right out from under you. Wham! And you never even see it coming."

Camille was struggling to get the Jaylon she knew to fit into the box Nick was painting, but try as she might, he just wouldn't fit. "Maybe he's changed."

"Nobody can change that much," Nick said, and then he looked at her. "Look, I know you think he's so wonderful and all, but trust me, he's not who you think he is. I guess what I'm saying is watch out. Okay? Don't get too close, and don't start thinking that you're anything other than some piece of furniture in his life that he can replace any time he decides to. That's just how he is."

Her gaze snagged on the hand across the room as it feathered through a fall of soft brown hair. Sitting by himself, Jaylon was reading something laying on the table, and she wondered for a moment what it was. When had he come in? Had he been here before she had arrived? Or did he see her sitting with her friends and decide to sit elsewhere?

Questions with no answers tumbled into her mind.

"Well, I guess we have a problem then," Camille said, still unwilling to turn her back on him. "I asked him out for Friday night, and I'm not going to tell him he can't go now. So, I guess either we go with you guys, or we go out by ourselves." She looked back at both friends. "It's your choice."

Lexie's face crumpled as she stood on the line Camille had just drawn. Fearfully, Lexie looked at Nick.

It was obvious that Nick wanted to tell Camille that Jaylon simply wasn't welcome, but then he caught Lexie's gaze, and he withered. "No, if you invited him, and you still want to bring him along, I guess that'll be okay. I'll just have to restrain myself from knocking his block off."

"I'd appreciate that," Camille said with only the slightest of laughs.

The next afternoon Camille sat in her seat in the auditorium. She and Nick had spent the class before basically strapped to one another's side. It was obvious that Nick was trying to protect her, and even more obvious that Jaylon understood exactly where he stood in Nick's eyes. What wasn't so obvious was how the two of them would react when they were forced into the same space for more than two seconds.

"Hey," Jaylon said, sitting down on his heels by her chair, startling her pencil into an arc across her paper. "Sorry."

"You know, you're really going to have to stop doing that," she said with a laugh.

He smiled and then grew serious again. "I was just wondering if we're still on for tonight."

"All systems are go," she lied brightly as she erased the errant line. "We'll be there to pick you up about six."

"Cool," Jaylon said, and then he glanced past her, and his face fell. "Well, I guess I'll see you then."

Gently he laid a hand on hers for one second, and then he stood, pulling her gaze up with him. She watched him as he strode down to the front and took his seat between two empty ones.

"Still under the influence, huh?" Nick asked with the resentment right under the surface.

She looked up at him, and her heart fell. "Yeah. I guess I am."

When they picked her up, Camille made sure that she sounded completely excited when she told Lexie Happy Birthday.

It was true, she was excited, but she was also so nervous that she thought she might very well be sick at any moment. In a not-too-comfortable silence, they rode to Jaylon's with Camille praying the whole way that both guys would behave themselves and not make her apologize to her best friend forever for ruining her 18th birthday.

Nick's car pulled up at the curb, and somehow Camille hadn't really realized it would be her job to go up to the door and get him. However, she quickly figured out that they couldn't very well sit out in front of his house and honk, so she pushed out and forced the strangling fear in her throat down.

That walk was the longest of her life. At the door, taking one more breath, she hit the doorbell. Anxiously she looked back at the car, going through a quick escape plan should the next moment be the disaster she was expecting. With a crack the door opened slightly, and then swung full open.

"Hi," Camille said to the stern-looking man with salt-and-peppered hair who stood on the other side of the threshold. "Umm, is Jaylon here?"

"Camille." Jaylon descended the staircase that led up from her view into obscurity above. "Sorry. I was running a little late."

"Oh, that's okay," Camille said with a cursory glance at the older man. "We're probably a little early."

Jaylon grabbed his jacket out of the closet and joined them at the door. "Oh, Dad, this is Camille Wright. Camille, this is my dad."

"It's nice to meet you." Mr. Quinn extended his hand without ever cracking so much as a smile.

She tried to make a smile form on her own face, but she was sure it looked far more like a grimace. "Nice to meet you."

For one long awkward moment they stood there, and then Jaylon looked at Camille, and she was sure it was a sigh she heard. "Well, we'd better get going."

"Yeah, they're waiting." She glanced out at the car—wholly unsure which place would be the most awkward.

"Twelve-thirty," Mr. Quinn said, and there was a slight edge to his voice.

Jaylon nodded. "We'll be here."

Quickly they ducked out and shut the door behind them. With only the walk down the sidewalk as their safety zone, instinctively they huddled closer together, bracing for the coming storm. At the car, he opened the back door, and she got in.

"Hi," he said by way of general greeting to the car's occupants.

"Hi," Lexie said, and silently Camille thanked her for at least trying to sound happy.

"Happy Birthday," Jaylon said as if that statement might get his head chopped off.

Nick pulled away from the curb without saying a word.

"Thanks," Lexie said, and Camille heard the awestruck tone of her voice, just as surely as Nick did.

"Well, how does it feel to be 18?"

"Good," Lexie said with a nod.

Car sounds overtook the conversation as Camille sat straight up wishing this didn't feel so much like getting her teeth pulled. "Tell him what you got, Lex."

"Oh, yeah. I got a CD player from Mom and Dad. It's a 60 changer," Lexie said, warming to the topic. "And Camille gave me this hair clip." She turned her head so he could see.

"Nice," Jaylon said.

"And Nick gave me this necklace." She tried to twist enough for Jaylon to see it, but she didn't quite make it far enough.

"I think you'll have to show me when we get there," Jaylon said with a laugh. "But I'm sure it's beautiful. Nick seems to have really good taste."

Lexie smiled brightly, and this time Camille was almost sure it wasn't a fake. "We were thinking we might go see the galaxy show at the Discovery Center after dinner. What do you think?"

"Sounds great to me," Jaylon said, and he settled back next to Camille.

As they sat around the table at the Italian restaurant, Camille couldn't decide who looked more uncomfortable—Jaylon or Nick. They were polite to a fault, but both of them looked like it was using every last brain cell to accomplish that.

"Hey, I heard the choir is going to D.C. in April," Jaylon said, and Camille was grateful for the effort.

"Yeah, but they're only taking half of us," Nick said. "I'm sure I won't even make the cut."

"Oh, why not?" Jaylon asked, looking genuinely surprised.

It was at that moment that Camille realized the dilemma Jaylon Quinn presented. He was such a good actor, it was impossible to know how much of his interest was sincere and how much was just a good show put on by someone who couldn't really care less.

"They're only taking four baritones. I'm number five."

"Oh. So, how do you get to be number four?"

"Impress Mr. Jacobs."

"Ah," Jaylon said, nodding as though he understood that perfectly.

"And that's a problem?" Camille asked, not sure of anything at the moment.

"Jacobs plays favorites," Jaylon said, filling in the gray areas. "If you're not one of them, tough luck."

The hairs on Camille's neck stood on end as she saw the look of revulsion slide across Nick's face.

"Yeah, tough luck," Nick said barely concealing the anger.

"You know though," Jaylon said slowly, "it'd be a shame to give up now and let Jacobs win. I've heard you—you're really good. I'm sure if you just put in a little more work..."

Nick shook his head. "No, I've already decided. I'm just going to concentrate on drama. That'll give me enough to do for the spring."

"Oh? What part do you want?" Jaylon asked obliviously, and alarm bells sounded in Camille's head.

"I'd really like to get Hawk." Nick shrugged. "But I'd settle for Ethan."

Jaylon nodded. "I can see you as Hawk before Ethan."

"Why?" Lexie asked as she twirled her spaghetti on her fork.

"Hawk's a nice guy," Jaylon explained as though that should be obvious. "Ethan's just a jerk."

"Yeah," Nick said with a small laugh, and Camille was thankful he didn't add what she knew he was thinking.

"How's that lasagna?" Camille asked Nick, grabbing the conversation steering wheel and turning it for all she was worth.

Nick looked down at his plate. "It's great. It's got some kind of seasoning on it. Kind of garlic or oregano. It's good."

Like a stone statue Camille sat in the theater style seat. The whole evening had been one continual headache after another, and the tension of trying to keep things light was beginning to pull every nerve she had to the surface.

On one side of her Jaylon sat up twice, shifted, and then settled in. On the other Lexie snuggled in to Nick with little trouble. Between them, Camille felt like she might be sick. It could be worse, she told herself. Nick and Jaylon could've started a food fight right in the middle of Orlando's. That thought made her laugh softly.

Jaylon turned his head to gaze at her. "What?"

"Nothing." The melancholy settled back over her.

"You know I was really worried about tonight," he said as he leaned in closer to her. Then in an inexplicable instant his hand bridged the gap between them and took hers gently. "But I'm glad I came."

"Me, too," Camille squeaked out just as the lights cut off, plunging them into total darkness. Her gasp was drowned out by a hundred others. Suddenly her heart took over her being as Jaylon's hand worked its way over hers. Fingers to palm he massaged the edge of her hand, and she had to fight to remember Nick's words. *Be careful. Don't let yourself get carried away. He's only in this for himself.*

At that moment the entire screen above them was suddenly covered in a blanket of light points. Thousands upon thousands of them, and the last shred of forced sanity in her brain was whisked away. In awe she gazed above her, trying to take it all in.

Then as though he'd practiced it a hundred thousand times, Jaylon pushed the armrest between them up, and his arm came around her shoulders. With her nerves right on the surface, she pushed her glasses up even as her head lay into soft crux under his collarbone.

It made no sense at all, but for that moment, she really didn't care what Nick or anyone else thought about them. In fact, she couldn't even bring herself to care that this fleeting moment would be gone in a blink, and Jaylon would go on with his life without her. No, for this one moment she just wanted to be here, with him, and forget everything else, and if it lasted forever, that would be all right too.

But on earth forever has a short life span, and this forever was no different. In what seemed like a blink, the lights snapped back on, and stiffly she untangled herself from his arms.

"That was awesome," Jaylon said, following her up to a sitting position still gazing up at the ceiling screen that had gone back to gray. "I'd give anything to know how they do that."

"It's fiber optics," Camille said as she stretched her neck so it could remember how to move. "They use a lamp power of 400 watts, but with the fiber optics they can project the stars at ten times the illuminance of a 4000 watt projector."

Jaylon stared at her perplexed. "How do you know that?"

Camille shrugged. "Science field trip. Fifth grade. That's when I decided I was going into Aerospace."

He smiled and lifted his chin back to the dome above them in understanding. "Well, I can see why you were inspired."

It was a good thing it was fifth grade and not now Camille thought. Now she could barely pay attention to anything other than keeping her breathing at a semi-normal rate.

"Hey, you two," Lexie said over Camille's head. "Was that some show or what?"

"Great," Jaylon said, reaching over and taking Camille's hand, which did nothing for her breathing situation. "Where to next?"

By the look in Lexie's eyes, Camille knew she hadn't missed the gesture.

"How about Slurpies all around?" Lexie asked with a wicked gleam in her eye.

"Slurpies?" Nick and Jaylon asked in incredulousness simultaneously.

Nick looked at them with uncertainty raining down his face. "In November?"

"Of course," Lexie said with a shrug, and then she looked at Camille who joined in with her laughter. "There's no line!"

Both guys looked at them like they had just lost their minds.

"Come on." Camille wrapped her arm around Jaylon's. "It's tradition."

Still with raised eyebrows, Jaylon nodded. "Tradition, huh? And who came up with this tradition?"

"Who do you think?" Camille asked, tilting her head demurely.

"Well, I think whoever came up with it should have her head examined," Jaylon said, but he couldn't contain the smile.

"Hey," Lexie said as they all exited the row. "Watch what you say about my friend."

"Yeah." Camille shouldered into Jaylon. "Watch what you say about me."

With a wink only she saw, he smiled. "I'll be careful. I promise."

Camille ducked her head as she followed her friends out.

"So, what, then Zazoo's?" Nick asked still looking somewhat mystified by the request.

"Zazoo's!" Camille and Lexie both said, dodging into each other and collapsing into giggles although each of them still held onto a guy's hand.

"Just don't let Lexie get too close to you," Camille warned, gazing at her friend with a teasing smirk.

"One time!" Lexie said in mock hurt. "One time and she'll never let me forget it."

"One time, yeah. And the next year, what happened?"

"Okay, one time, and then a small accident."

"Grape Slurpie on a new white shirt. That's a small accident?"

"I said I was sorry."

"Yeah, and that took that stain right out," Camille said with a serious nod. Then she ducked her head to address just Jaylon. "I'm telling you don't get too close to her."

"I'll take your advice, but I think our friend here may have some trouble with it," Jaylon said, grinning at Nick.

"Hey, what are you two whispering about?" Lexie asked, fighting to keep a frown on her face.

"Oh, nothing," Camille said, fighting the urge to skip to the car.

"Uh-huh." Lexie narrowed her eyes at them. "You just watch it, or I might have to wake you up."

Camille flung one hand in front of her face. "Oh, please, no. I'll be good." Then she leaned back to Jaylon and stage-whispered, "Whatever you do. Do not fall asleep with her around. Lexie's got a unique way of making sure you don't oversleep."

"Oh, yeah? What's that?" Jaylon asked, looking from one girl to the other obviously thinking the insane asylum might be a better destination for them.

"A baseball bat!" both of them said, falling into another round of giggles.

"What did you put in their dinner?" Jaylon asked Nick with concern.

"I don't know, but I'm beginning to think they're on something," Nick said.

"Yeah," Lexie said, giggling anew. "First we were on the car seat."

"And then we were on the restaurant seats!" Camille continued, following Lexie's lead.

"And then we were on the theater seats!" they both said, dissolving again into giggles.

The guys looked like they weren't quite sure what they had stumbled into. At the car Nick opened Lexie's door, and she unlocked the rest. Camille tumbled inside with Jaylon right behind her.

Nick started the car. "So you really want to go to the Zazoo's?"

"Zazoo's!" both girls said, and once again they collapsed into giggles.

It was after midnight when they made it back to Jaylon's door, and Camille had the feeling that she had never laughed so hard in her life. Her stomach and cheeks hurt, and every once in awhile another giggle would escape without warning.

"I had fun tonight," she said as they ambled up his walk.

"So did I," he said. "It was fun seeing you like that."

She looked at him puzzled. "Like what?"

"I don't know." At his front door he turned to her and ran his hands down her arms until at the bottom he grasped both hands in his. "Happy? Relaxed?"

"I'm relaxed," she said instantly defensive.

He laughed softly and then grew serious. "No, most of the time you're a kid trying to make everyone believe you're an adult."

The smile fell off of Camille's face as her head dropped forward. He waited a moment, but she couldn't bring herself to respond.

"Hey, I didn't mean to bring you down." He lifted her chin gently. "I just meant I'd like to see more of you like tonight."

She smiled, but it wasn't the unstoppable one she'd had before. "Thanks for coming."

"Thanks for asking." And then in a split second he leaned forward and brushed his lips over hers. "I'll see you tomorrow."

The touch of his lips reverberated through her, sending electric shock waves through her body all the way down to her toes. When she regained consciousness, she realized he was gone, and with great effort she forced her feet to turn and carry her back to the car.

"Home?" Nick asked when she got in the car.

She nodded unsure she had even moved. "Home."

Chapter 15

They spent Saturday miming with the kids and then took Daria to the hamburger joint for lunch. It was becoming so normal that Camille wasn't even surprised when he asked. In a strange way she seemed more alive with him around. The fear was still there, but it had been forced underground, and she had the vague feeling that if she could just keep it there, her life might actually get turned in the right direction.

Monday afternoon as she sat in the auditorium, she wasn't at all surprised when Jaylon stopped at her seat to say hi. However, when he asked to sit down with her, it took her a moment to decide he was serious.

"Sure."

He had just sat down when she heard the sound behind her.

She turned and found herself suddenly in the unenviable position of sitting between two adversaries. "Hey, Nick."

When Nick looked past her to Jaylon, she thought for a moment that he might simply turn around and leave.

"Did you recover from Slurpies in November?" she asked as the tension dropped over her again.

"Slurpies in November," Nick said, reluctantly taking the seat next to her without so much as a nod at Jaylon. "You two ought to have your heads examined."

"Hey, you were driving," she said. On her left Jaylon shifted in his seat, and she turned her attention to him. "So, one week to try-outs. You got the whole thing memorized yet?"

"I've been working on it," Jaylon said like a piece of wood.

"Yeah, I think I've decided to just play hooky on Monday," Camille said.

"There's a great plan," Nick said, and there was only harshness in the words. "Then Allen can flunk you, and you get to start over again."

Camille bit the edge of her bottom lip. "Oh, yeah. We wouldn't want that. Huh?" No one said anything, and she ducked her head over her physics homework. "No. We definitely wouldn't want that."

"That's the bell," Mrs. Allen said, striding onto stage as if on cue. "Get settled, please."

Slowly the noise level decreased to silence.

"A few minor details to get out of the way," Mrs. Allen said.

With her elbows glued to her sides lest she touch either guy, Camille sat, staring at Mrs. Allen and trying to make sense of what she was saying. Something about a play over Thanksgiving and running out of time. Then she said something, and suddenly everyone started moving again. Camille looked around, struggling to get her brain to work.

"Camille," Nick said, standing next to her seat, and when she looked up, she found herself in the middle of them, both of them staring down at her, and her with no idea what anyone had said.

With undisguised contempt Nick glanced at Jaylon. "You want to be my partner or not?"

Partner? Uh-oh. Camille glanced at Jaylon feeling the trap snap around her. "Umm, maybe we could ask Steph to join us."

"Steph?" Jaylon asked, but Camille didn't wait for him to put the pieces together. She didn't have time.

"Stephanie!" she called, jumping up from her seat. "Hey, why don't you come work with us?"

Surprise was the first thing to cross Stephanie's face, followed quickly by delight. When Stephanie made it abreast of them, Camille wrapped her arm through the smaller girl's with a veil of happiness draped firmly over the misgiving in her chest. "We need another girl, and you're the best Lauren around."

Stephanie smiled and allowed herself to be led to the back by Camille, who was followed closely by Jaylon and Nick. Knowing that if she had any hope of keeping the peace, she had to take the reins, Camille grabbed them with a vengeance.

"Steph, why don't you and Nick read the Lauren-Hawk part?" Camille asked as she folded her legs underneath her. "Then J. and I can take the Dominique-Hawk one."

"So you've never wondered what you want to do with your life then?" Nick asked, and Stephanie fell right into place as Lauren.

When the bell rang, Camille breathed a grateful sigh of relief. If it hadn't been for Stephanie, Camille was sure she would've been the punching dummy in the middle of two pugilists. The four of them walked to their seats and gathered their things.

"You read really well," Jaylon said to Stephanie, and he sounded like he meant it.

"Thanks," Stephanie said as a smile burst onto her face. Then she turned to Camille. "Well, I guess I'll see you tomorrow?"

"Yeah," Camille said from her position in between Jaylon and Nick even as she wished there was a way to simply disappear.

"See ya." With a wave, Stephanie sauntered up the aisle and disappeared through the door.

"She's nice," Nick said, startling Camille back from her escape plans.

"Yeah, she is." One guy on either side of her Camille stepped out of the row and made her way up the aisle. If she could just figure out a way to get them past this animosity, maybe this wouldn't be so difficult. "Boy, listening to you two, Mrs. Allen is going to have a tough time casting Hawk."

"I don't think Lauren is going to be a piece of cake to cast either," Jaylon said.

"Lauren?" Camille asked in surprise. "Ariana's got a lock on that part."

Nick shook his head as his arm pushed through the door to let the other two through. "I wouldn't be so sure of that."

"Trust me," Camille said. "The casting of Lauren won't even be a close race."

"Maybe, maybe not," Nick said.

"No, Nick. I think Camille has a point. Lauren's going to be easy to cast," Jaylon said.

Disgustedly Nick shrugged. "Whatever you say. You're the expert."

"Well, this is my turn," Jaylon said, stopping in the middle of the melee. "Take care you two."

"Yeah, you too," Camille said, and then she realized that Nick hadn't stopped with them. With a quick wave to Jaylon, she turned her steps down the hallway. "Hey, Nick, wait up!" Three long strides later she caught up with him. "Okay, I know this is a stretch, but could you at least not start World War III over this?"

"I was civil."

"Barely," she said. "Look, I know he's not your favorite person, and I can deal with that. But he is my friend, and I'd appreciate it if you'd at least try not to look like it's High Noon when he's around."

At their lockers, Camille opened hers with a bang.

"Trouble?" Lexie asked, raising her eyebrows.

"Jaylon," Nick said with a clinch of his jaw.

"Ah." Lexie nodded and then exhaled. "Is he really so terrible?"

"Yes," Nick said.

"No," Camille said at the same time.

Lexie looked from one to the other. "Fine. Then you're just going to have to agree to disagree about this and be done with it."

"Fine," Nick said angrily.

"Fine," Camille said as she slammed her locker closed and turned on her heel. "I've got to get home." And without waiting for a reply, she stomped out.

She could see being upset about the whole play thing. She really could, but she wasn't Nick. And he wasn't her. And no matter how hard she tried, she just couldn't make herself not trust Jaylon—or stop liking him.

At the bus stop, she leaned against the pole and tried to work through a solution to the whole mess, but all she found was more problems.

"Going my way?" Jaylon asked in her ear, and instantly Camille turned and smiled.

"You've got to quit doing that. You know?"

"I know." The gleam in his eyes said he had no intention of quitting. "But it's so much fun."

"For you maybe," she said, turning to face him.

"So, you want a ride or not?"

"What do you think?"

They had only been at her apartment a few minutes when Daria bounced in through the door.

"Hey, girlfriend," Camille said, greeting her sister. "How was school?"

"We made turkeys!" Daria said, and then she spied Jaylon who was sitting at the table.

"Hi, Dar," he said as if she might actually be mad he was there.

"Hi," she said softly as she cowered behind Camille.

He held a tentative hand out to the little girl. "Can I see your turkey?"

Slowly Daria set it on the table in front of him, and Jaylon fanned both hands through his hair as he laid his hands on the table before resting his chin on top of them. "Very, very nice. I think you could be an artist if the whole acting thing doesn't work out."

Daria giggled.

"You got homework?" Camille asked.

"A little," Daria said, scrunching her nose.

"Well, why don't you go get it done? Mom will be home in a little bit, and then we'll eat."

"Okay," Daria said and skipped off down the hallway.

Jaylon watched her go, and then he looked at Camille who had already resumed her position stirring supper. "You really are more like her mother."

Camille shrugged. "Somebody's got to." Feeling the statement encroaching a little too close to her core, she turned her attention to the script on the counter and leafed through it. "I really need to work on the Dominique-Lauren fight. I think I've got Lauren down pretty well, but Dominique is really giving me fits."

For a moment he looked like he might object, but then he picked up his script. "Go for it."

As he watched her, Jaylon couldn't help but notice how stilted she sounded as Dominique, and it occurred to him that what she had said the last time they were in this kitchen together was exactly right. She was nothing at all like Dominique—overbearing, self-centered, pushy, conceited. No, there wasn't even a smidgen of Dominique hiding anywhere in Camille.

He read Lauren's lines all the while wishing he could hear Camille read them. She was such a perfect Lauren, so natural in her love of books and her endearing awkwardness, but she was just as natural at the innate goodness that Lauren personified. Yes, Mrs. Allen had to be absolutely blind to pass over Camille for the part of Lauren.

"I hate to break this up," Camille said suddenly glancing at the clock over his head, "but I need to go check on Daria and her homework and finish supper before Mom gets home."

"Oh, no problem." Jaylon closed his script and stood from the table. "I guess I need to be getting home too."

A step at a time Camille followed him to the door. However, at the door his heart said he just didn't want to leave yet, and it turned him around and brought him with a bump right into her.

"Oh, sorry," she said, taking a surprised step backward.

His heart wanted to look at her, but his brain wouldn't let him for fear he might lose all semblance of cool right there. "I'll see you in school tomorrow?"

"Yeah," she said, but the syllable barely made it from her lips to his ears.

"Well, take care of yourself," he said, stalling for one more precious moment with her.

"You, too."

Then before he had time to question it, he leaned in and brushed her lips with his. It was a simple act that had hounded his mind ever since their first kiss on his doorstep, but the second his lips touched hers, the gesture was anything but simple. Stunned by the intensity that washed through him with that one simple touch, he pulled away from her and ran his fingers through his hair. "I'd better be going."

"Yeah."

With a single nod, he wrenched the doorknob and escaped outside. He didn't want to, but it was quickly becoming clear how close to the edge of sanity he was living these days. Camille Wright, with her glasses and books, made no sense in his life. And yet the more he was with her, the more it was beginning to feel like she was the only thing in his life that made any sense at all.

On a white, fluffy cloud of happiness Camille floated through classes on Tuesday and Wednesday. Even Nick and his never-ending abhorrence of Jaylon couldn't bring her down. Wednesday when she said good-bye to Jaylon in the middle of the bustling hallway, she wondered how she would ever last until Monday without seeing him again.

With the Thanksgiving holiday, the center would be closed for the weekend making even that prospect of seeing him disappear. So it was with a heavy heart that she said good-bye to him, promising even as she did so that she would practice over the break. Leaving him was like leaving a piece of her heart behind, and all day Thursday her thoughts kept bumping into him.

Thanksgiving with family. It sounded wonderful. In her world Thanksgiving was three people hovered over a small chicken, browned in the oven, some Stove Top Stuffing, and a couple of pathetic looking yams. It was supposed to be festive, but it wasn't.

Her family had never quite perfected the festive mood. There were always too many problems bearing down on them for that. After dinner, Camille escaped to her room under the pretext of working on college applications, but once there, she pulled out her script and flopped onto her bed.

If she could just get Dominique down...

Like sitting on a pincushion that had mistakenly been laid upside down, Jaylon sat at the dinner table. The spread was impressive even for Marianne, who of course hadn't lifted a finger in the preparation of the meal. In fact, House Beautiful could have walked in at that moment and start snapping pictures of the table, and it wouldn't have seemed at all strange.

"More turkey?" Marianne asked Jaylon's grandfather as she held up a slab with knife and fork.

"Certainly," Mr. Russell Quinn, Sr. said, offering his plate.

"It's all so wonderful, Marianne," Jaylon's grandmother said approvingly.

"Well, we're just so glad you all could make it," Marianne said with the fakest smile Jaylon had ever seen.

Burying his gaze deep in the middle of his turkey and gravy, he forked into it, wishing he could simply disappear.

"So, Jaylon, my boy, have you made the big decision yet?" his grandfather asked.

Jaylon dug deeper into his hole. "Umm, no. Not yet."

"Don't mumble," his father mumbled to him angrily. "You were raised better than that."

Reluctantly Jaylon looked up from his plate and cleared his throat. "Umm, no, Sir. I haven't made up my mind yet."

"He got an application to Duke yesterday," his father said, emphasizing the statement with a proud smile.

"Duke?" his grandfather said obviously impressed. "That's a good school. Good school, good grades, good job."

"That's what I keep telling him," his father said. "But you know kids today. They don't seem to see an opportunity when it walks up and knocks them over the head."

"Well, Russ," his grandfather said with a patronizing smile. "Now there are a lot of good schools out there. I'm sure Jaylon can find one he likes."

"What are you planning on studying?" his grandmother asked, completely oblivious to the fact that Jaylon was no longer a part of the conversation.

"I'm trying to talk him into marketing or finance," his father said. "Isn't that right, J?"

"Yeah," Jaylon said to his turkey.

"Jaylon Patrick," his father said sharply, causing every gaze in the room to snap to his face, and instantly he smiled at the rest of the table.

"Sorry," Jaylon said sullenly. "Umm, I haven't really decided what I'm going to study yet." He looked up at the gazes glued to him, and for one reckless second his heart took over for his brain. "I'd kind of thought about acting."

"Humph," his grandfather said, instantly dropping his gaze as he knifed into his turkey. "Actors are a dime a dozen, son, and most of them make about that much money at it too."

"Now, Russell, that's not true. Didn't you read what that Altman guy got for his last picture?" Jaylon's grandmother said.

"That's one in a million, Arlene. That's not reality," his grandfather said dismissively. Then he leveled his knife at Jaylon. "I say you should listen to your father. Marketing and finance are fine fields, and you wouldn't be scraping the bottom of the bucket to make ends meet either."

The fight and the recklessness beaten right out of him, Jaylon nodded as his head bent closer to the table. What he wanted mattered less than a squashed bug to these people, and that would never change.

"You really should listen to your grandfather. He knows of what he speaks," Jaylon's father said solidly. Then he looked to the far side of the table. "Could you pass me the yams?"

When the phone rang at one-thirty on Friday, Camille barely even heard it as she hunched over her Calculus. Another call for her mother. Another party. Another boyfriend. Another night for Camille to spend playing mommy—nothing new.

"Camille!" her mother called down the hall, startling her to her feet. "Phone!"

"Coming!" Without so much as a backward glance, she left her books, went down the hall, and into the kitchen. "Who is it?"

"Some boy." Her mother sat down at the table obviously having no intention of giving her oldest daughter privacy with this call.

Carefully Camille pulled the phone off the counter and cleared her throat. "Hello?"

"Hey," Jaylon said, and she couldn't stop the smile even as she turned to the counter.

"Hey."

"Happy Thanksgiving."

"Same to you."

"So, are you totally bored out of your mind yet?"

Camille sighed at the thought. "Getting there."

"So am I. You up for a little road trip?"

Concern and confusion draped over her. "Huh?"

"A road trip. You know. Get in the car and drive."

"Oh." Unconsciously her hand wrapped the phone cord around and around itself. "I don't know."

"Dar can come with us—if you're babysitting."

"It's not that." Camille glanced at her mother sitting at the table. "I've just got some homework I need to get done."

"Over the holidays?"

"I don't want to get behind."

"Well, you can bring your books if you want—if you need to study."

"In the car?"

"Or we could work on the script," he said hopefully, and then his side of the line went quiet. "I just thought it would be nice to get away for awhile."

"Yeah, I'd really like to," she said, her voice softening with each word. "But I don't think I'll be able to today, but thanks for asking."

"Sure." The line hummed between them. "Well, I guess I'd better go then."

"Okay." Her heart ached for making her say no. "I'll see you Monday?"

"Yeah, Monday."

"I'd better go. See ya later." And she signed off before she quietly replaced the phone on its base.

"Who was that?" her mother asked.

"A guy from school," Camille said with an off-handed shrug.

"Oh?" The interest in her mother's voice piqued. "What'd he want?"

"Not much." Camille reached into the cabinet and grabbed a glass. "He just thought I might want to go on a drive with him."

She felt her mother's gaze following her around the kitchen. "Why'd you turn him down?"

"I need to study."

Slowly her mother shook her head. "You and those books. They don't replace living you know?"

Camille filled her glass and replaced the water in the refrigerator. "I don't want to get behind."

"Behind? I'd think you'd be so far ahead by now that you could just quit studying for the rest of the year, and you'd still be ahead of everyone else."

Anger and frustration crashed over her. "How would you know? You're never around enough to notice."

The words knocked her mother back several inches, and for a long moment, she just sat, staring at her daughter. "I just hate for you to waste your whole senior year holed up in that room of yours. There's so much more to life."

Defiantly Camille raised her chin. "Like what? Guys? Parties? Dances?"

"Yeah," her mother said slowly.

"Well, maybe I want something different for my life. Maybe those things aren't as important to me as they are to..."

"Me?" her mother asked as her eyes softened. "Yes, Camille, I have a life, and I'm not going to apologize for that. But you deserve to have a life too."

"And Daria?" Camille asked as the anger jumped on her. "What does she deserve? Huh? To be left alone here for hours on end? Is that what she deserves, Mom?"

Her mother's gaze fell from Camille's face. "Look, I know I haven't always been the mother you wanted me to be, but I've done my best."

"Yeah? Well, your best isn't good enough." At that moment Camille's gaze snagged on Daria hovering in the doorway. Guilt layered on top of the guilt already in her heart, and seeing no way to say what she really wanted to, Camille stepped past her sister. "I've got studying to do."

She pushed the fearful sound of Daria's voice in the kitchen out of her head as she shut her door and sat down. The last thing she wanted to do was scare Daria. She, of all people, knew what it was like to hear people you loved fighting over you. But for some reason, when she was around her mother, she couldn't stop her words. It wasn't fair—being asked to be an adult when she had done nothing to ask for that mantle early.

Furiously she scribbled a formula on her notebook. What had Jaylon said about liking how she was when she had fun? Well, she did too. However, that wasn't real life. Not even close. Slurpies at midnight in November. That was for kids—for irresponsible, immature kids, and she had far too much to do to waste time being irresponsible and immature.

When the knock sounded on her door ten minutes later, she thought for a moment that she'd imagined it. Her pencil stopped in mid-formula, however, as she gazed at the door. Faintly it sounded again.

"Who is it?" she asked, not sure who would be worse—her mother or Daria.

"The Easter Bunny," the voice on the other side said, and she smiled despite the confusion that jumped to her mind.

She reached over and twisted the knob. "J?"

The door swung inward, and there, leaning on the doorframe was the black jacket, the dark hair, and the steel blue eyes, gazing down on her with a smile tucked firmly behind them.

"What are you doing here?" she asked as she sat back in her chair in astonishment.

"Well, I figured if I couldn't get Mohammed to the mountain, then I'd bring the mountain to Mohammed."

"Huh?"

He shrugged. "I figured if you were too busy to come with me, then I'd come sit with you."

Camille shook her head. "You must really be bored."

He laughed. "Totally. So, what do you say? You need some company?"

Her gaze fell to her books as the formulas swam before her eyes. "I don't know how much company I'll be."

"Well, anything's better than staring at my walls all afternoon." He straightened and took a hesitant step into her room. At her bed, he sat on the edge of it. "What are you studying?"

"Calculus."

He wrinkled his nose. "More math."

"As usual," she said with a laugh. She put her pencil back to the notebook, but Calculus had suddenly lost all of its allure. "So, how was your Thanksgiving?"

"Boring." He laid his chin on the corner of her chair, causing her thought processes to cease altogether. "How about yours?"

"About the same." She glanced over at him and laughed softly.

"What?"

"You must be really hard up to want to sit there and watch me do

Calculus."

"I figured if maybe I'd sit here long enough, you'd get tired of math and take me up on my offer."

"A drive?" she asked, returning her attention to her book in self-defense.

"It couldn't hurt to try."

Her pencil worked over the notebook. "Well, where would we go?"

"It's a secret."

Instantly wary she looked at him. "A secret? That's pretty broad."

He grinned at her. "Say you'll come, and you can find out."

She forced her pencil to continue for two more seconds, but when he didn't move, her brain frazzled. He couldn't really be serious about sitting here watching her all day. Could he?

"Your mom said it would be all right," he said, sensing he had a foothold.

"Oh, she did. Did she?" Camille asked, trying to be angry, but not quite making it.

"And she'll watch Dar, so we're free and clear."

Free and clear. For some inexplicable reason those words struck fear into her heart. "And what if I say no?"

"Then I sit here and watch you all afternoon."

With a sigh aiming for resignation, Camille looked at him. "You're not going to give this up. Are you?"

He raised both eyebrows at her. "Nope."

"Fine." She slammed her pencil to the desk. "Then I give up."

His smile lit his whole face. "Good. I was hoping you'd say that."

The side streets lined with houses flashed by the blue Camaro's windows until they gave way to open fields of pale yellow. All day long, all Jaylon could think about was getting away and coming here—with her. No one had to tell him, he knew she would understand. This place was so central to who he was and yet so secret that only he and a mind dimmed beyond recognition knew about it. It was the only place that his heart wanted to be anymore.

"When you said drive, you weren't kidding," Camille said, her gaze firmly planted outside.

"I hope you don't mind." He glanced over at her. "I just really didn't want to be alone."

Her gaze swung back into the car and settled on him. "Why not?"

"Oh, you know... life." He fought to get a relaxed smile on his face. "It's just been one of those days."

"Want to tell me about it?" she asked, reaching out to him with only her words, but he felt their gentle touch just the same.

He shook his head as the smile slid off his face. "It's a lot of things."

"Pick one."

He exhaled, wondering how ridiculous and insignificant his problems would seem next to hers. "I'm not going to apply to Julliard."

Instantly her eyebrows knitted together. "Why not?"

As though it meant nothing, he shrugged. "It's not worth it."

Gaping, she could hardly find the words. "Not worth it? But I thought it was your dream."

"Yeah, I thought so too." His hands guided the car around the final turn and up the driveway now overgrown except for the two tire tracks lining it.

Camille's gaze traveled from him out to the little farmhouse and the old tree beyond. "Where are we?"

Quickly, he shoved the car into park. "Come on."

With questioning eyes, she met him at the front of the car, and as though he was reaching for the last branch on his way down a mountainside, he grabbed for her hand. It felt right. As strange and unfathomable as that was, it just felt right.

Side by side they walked through the underbrush until he stopped at the tree and pulled her in to his chest.

"Jaylon, it's beautiful," she said, so softly he knew she felt the magic too.

The creek somewhere far below bubbled over the rocks on its way to forever as above them the wind brushed through the tree branches, which still clung to the last of their autumn clothes. Peace settled over him as his soul opened up. Without willing them to, his eyes fell closed and let the rest of his senses imprint this feeling on his memory instead.

Camille, small and soft, fit perfectly into the circle of his arms, and as he stood there wrapped around her, he wondered how he had ever thought he had truly lived before this moment. Words, pale and bleak, couldn't come close to describing the sensations unleashed by the feeling of her body next to his.

Gently his hands ran themselves over her arms even as he felt her head relax into the warmth of his chest. A single tear, unbidden, wound down his cheek, chilled by the soft wind wafting past him. If life could get anymore perfect than this, he certainly didn't know how.

Unconsciously his hand reached up and feathered his hair back from his eyes just before running itself deftly over his cheek. Crying. It was such a sissy thing to do. He would never have been caught dead with tears on his face in Ariana's presence or Seth's or anyone else's on the face of the earth.

He felt Camille's head lift, and when he looked down, he knew she had seen it. A soft smile formed in his heart. "So, what do you think?"

"I don't know what to think." She gazed up at him. "Why did you bring me here?"

The peace from moments before vanished, and nerves filled its space. "I've just always thought this was a really cool place. I thought you might think so too."

Her smile banished a measure of his nerves. "It's amazing." Once again, she laid her head into him and this time wrapped one arm around his waist. She stood, simply holding him for a long moment. "So, are you going to tell me or not?"

"Tell you what?"

"Why your dream isn't worth it."

He stood unspeaking, the words all jamming themselves into the same space in his brain, and somehow he hadn't even known they were there.

"You don't have to act like it doesn't matter," she said softly. "Because I know it does."

Slowly he shook his head, trying to clear it of his father's words and brush hers away simultaneously. "It was stupid to ever even think about going."

"Why?"

"Because I'm not good enough to get in there."

"How do you know?"

"Because." Anger flashed into his voice. "I look at Ari, and she's so intense about Julliard. It's like it's her destiny to go there and she'll die if she doesn't get to go. But it was never like that for me."

"Never?"

Confusion knotted across his forehead. "Not really. It was always more of her dream than mine."

Camille pulled back enough to look at him. "Then why does not going bother you so much?"

He couldn't meet her gaze as his fell to the grass at their feet. "Because I'm not just giving up on Julliard." Wordlessly she watched him, simply waiting for the rest of the story. He looked at her sadly. "My dad wants me to go to Duke."

Her gaze never wavered from his eyes. "And what do you want?"

With an angry yank, he pulled himself from her and leaned against the tree like a limp reed. "I don't know. What does it matter?"

"What does it matter?" she asked incredulously. "It matters for every conceivably important reason in the world."

"To who?" he asked, and the callousness bit into him. "Certainly not to my dad."

Her tone softened then. "Well, to me for one, but more importantly it matters to you."

"Oh, yeah? How do you know that?"

"Because your dreams are a part of you. That's how. They're a part of who you are—who you really are when nobody else is around. They aren't just a piece you can break off and set down and forget they ever existed. They're woven into you." She stepped behind him and placed her hand in the warm space over his heart. "They're woven into here."

Defiantly he tried to push the gentleness of her touch away from his heart. "But what if nobody else understands them? What if everybody else thinks I'm making a huge mistake?"

"Who's living this life you or them?"

He laughed softly at the import of that statement and shook his head. "You've got it all figured out. Don't you?"

"Me?" She let her hand drop as she stepped away from him toward the gash. "Yeah, right. I'm as lost as you are."

His gaze followed her the several paces she took away. "Well, you hide it pretty well."

Her arms wrapped around her chest. "I guess I've had a lot of practice." Then she turned on him, pinning him to the tree with one look. "But this isn't about me. It's about you and your decision or non-decision as it looks now. So, if Julliard is out, what then?"

He deflated further. "If I knew that, my life would be solved."

"Life doesn't get solved," she said with a laugh. "You get through every day just to get to the next day's problems. They don't just give up and go home you know."

He smiled at her hopefully. "Do you think maybe we could figure out a way to make them go home and not come back?"

"Julliard." Her gaze never softened. "If you're not applying there, then where?"

The smile faded. "I don't know."

"Duke?" she asked when he said no more.

The shake of his head preceded the syllable. "No."

"UCLA?"

Stunned that she had remembered that off-handed reference, he stopped. "Maybe."

"Maybe. Well, that's at least progress. Where else?"

"NYU," he said softly, giving voice for the first time to the thought that he'd only allowed himself to think in the middle of the night with the darkness surrounding him.

"NYU?" she asked, stopping her barrage of questions. "Really?"

He shrugged. "They've got a good drama school, and everything. But..."

"But what?" she asked, not letting him off the hook for even a second.

His head slowly moved back and forth. "My dad."

"Ah-ha." The confusion lifted from her face. "So it's not the school he's so worried about then."

Jaylon couldn't meet her gaze.

"Well, if drama isn't his idea of the perfect major, what is?"

Squirming just to say the word, he looked at her sheepishly. "Finance."

Her eyebrows shot up. "Finance? You?"

"Yes, me. Why? Is that so hard to believe?"

"Well, no," she said slowly, and then she looked right at him. "Well, yes. If you know anything about you, finance would be like last on the list— right behind chicken farming and calculus."

"That's pretty low," he said, fighting the smile.

She laughed. "Yeah, it is." Then she grew serious. "So, what then? Are you going to tell him you're going to live your own life, or are you going to let him live your life for you?"

Jaylon shrugged. "Do I have to answer that?"

"Yeah," she said softly. "I'm afraid you do."

As Jaylon lay between the sheets later, he thought about her words, and he knew she was right. If he followed the path his father had laid out for him, he would be miserable. He could take his dream and bury it beneath a mound of paperwork and expectations, and yet it would never really go away. It would always be right there with him.

In the darkness he laid his hand over his heart just as she had done, and the calmness of her presence fell over him. In a breath his decision was made. Whether it made any sense to his father or to anyone else, it was where he wanted his life to go. He sat up and snapped on the light.

Padding quietly across his room, he snapped on his computer and pulled up the application he had downloaded three months before.

"Your dreams are a part of you," she whispered from the depths of his heart. "They're a part of who you are—who you really are when nobody else is around."

With those words woven tightly into the fabric of his being, he laid his fingers to the keyboard, and for the first time he began putting his dreams down on paper for the rest of the world to see.

Chapter 16

The first impression Camille had of Jaylon when he took his seat next to hers on Monday afternoon was that he looked lighter somehow.

"Hey," she said. "How was the rest of your weekend?"

His smile was couched in undeniable happiness. "Great."

"Did you talk to your dad?"

"Not yet, but I sent this off." He flipped a set of stapled papers onto her lap.

Questioningly she picked them up, and understanding washed over her. "NYU."

He nodded. "Wish me luck."

"Luck," she said just as his gaze jumped over her head. She turned as Nick slid into the seat on the other side of her. "Well, look what the cat dragged in."

"You ready for this?" Nick asked, holding up the script, and immediately Camille wished he hadn't.

Out-of-control nerves attacked her. "As ready as I'll ever be I guess. You?"

Nick sighed. "I'm just ready to get it over with."

"Me, too," Jaylon said although Camille wasn't quite sure the conversation included him.

Furtively she handed the application back to Jaylon and sat up straighter when Mrs. Allen stepped onto the stage. Camille pushed her glasses up onto her nose, knowing there was no backing out now even though she was still looking for a last possible escape hatch.

"As you all know tryouts begin today." Mrs. Allen slid the chalkboard over to the center of the stage. "I've drawn up a preliminary schedule for the initial auditions. We'll start with each person trying out on one part for your grade, and then I'll have callbacks as I begin actually casting the parts. Questions?"

Camille sank in her chair, not buoyed one bit by the presence of the two experienced thespians on either side of her.

"We'll start with the Dominique-Lauren discussion," Mrs. Allen said, writing the topic on the board.

Praying that her name would not appear, Camille watched the chalkboard. Jennifer and Melissa. When Mrs. Allen turned, Camille let out a whoosh of air.

Jaylon leaned into her. "Saved."

Not thinking it was nearly as funny as he seemed to, she glowered at him. The two girls stepped onto stage looking as afraid as Camille knew she would eventually.

"Good luck," she whispered from her seat as, on stage, the fight started.

They made it through the fight, the scene with Hawk and Dominique, and one try-out featuring Ethan and Dominique before the bell rang. Camille stood even as Mrs. Allen continued to call out final instructions over the departing students.

"So, we're down to Ethan and Dominique and Hawk and Lauren," Jaylon said, looking over to Nick. "Which one do you want?"

"Lauren," Nick said, and although Camille knew he was seriously trying to be a pain, she laughed anyway.

"Now that I can see." She hugged her books and walked out between the two of them. "In neon lights, '*Don't Listen to the Fates*, featuring Nick McGee as Lauren.'"

"I don't know," Jaylon said jokingly. "He's good, but I still think that would be a stretch."

"Well, which one do you want?" Nick asked defensively as they reached the door.

"I'd like Hawk," Jaylon said honestly. "But I'm probably better for Ethan."

"Why's that?" Nick asked taken aback.

"Conceited, obnoxious, annoying?" Jaylon asked, looking at Nick. "You really have to ask?"

For a split second fear jumped into Camille's gut. *Please be nice, Nick. Please.*

"Well, you're not *that* bad," Nick said, and around the edges of the statement lurked a laugh.

"See," Jaylon said, looking at Camille with a nod. "Ethan."

She smiled at him and shook her head. "Just be glad you're going to get something. I'm just praying I don't get up there and choke." With one hand she reached up and clenched her throat as she made gagging sounds.

"Such great confidence she has," Jaylon said to Nick.

"Hey, if she gets on the stage, that's an accomplishment," Nick said.

The gagging noises stopped. "I'll have you know I have every one of these lines memorized, so there."

"Oh, yeah?" Nick asked teasingly. "Prove it."

For one blink she tried to make herself remember where she was, but then his challenge took over. "Mom used to take me to the office with her sometimes, and I'd watch her sitting there, taking orders from all these other people about when something was supposed to be done or how it was supposed to be done. I'd sit in that corner, and I'd be reading. But I wasn't really reading at all, I was watching. I was watching her—I was watching her lose who she was a little bit at a time.

"And then when I was older, I asked her once about why she didn't stand up to those people, and she said, 'Lauren, the only way to stand up to them is if you have more education than they do, and I just don't.'"

"But education's only a part of it," Jaylon said, falling right into the part even standing smack in the center of the hallway.

Camille shook her head. "Not according to my mom. To her, an education's everything. So I decided that I wasn't going to be the person on the outside, I was going to be on the inside of that office, and I'd never treat my workers the way they treated my mom."

"So, what then? You're going to be a banker? A lawyer? A doctor? What?"

"It doesn't matter. I'm going to be something. Something big. Something powerful. Something so important that people can't make me feel..." Suddenly Camille looked around and came back to reality even as her books crushed themselves against her. "...like I'm not enough."

Blinking back the shock, Nick gazed at her, his feet frozen to the spot. "That's amazing."

Without glancing at Jaylon, Camille shrugged. "It won't be tomorrow. I just wanted to prove to you I could do it."

"Well, you certainly did that," Nick said.

Jaylon stood for one more moment. "I'd better get."

"Take care," Nick said, waving slightly.

"I'll see you," Camille said, and fighting every conflicting emotion in her, she turned her steps down the hallway.

She felt Nick come abreast of her again.

"You've really been practicing then?"

"For the grade, nothing else."

"Well, if you do up there tomorrow what I just saw, you've got a lock on an A."

"Nick and Ariana," Mrs. Allen said, writing the two names on her chalkboard the next afternoon, and Camille felt the revulsion flow right off of Nick's left arm.

"Go get her, Tiger," Camille whispered to him, and then she moved her knees to let him out.

"This should be good," Jaylon said to her softly as Nick climbed the steps.

"No kidding." In her seat Camille folded her hands and prepared for the fireworks to start.

"Whenever you're ready," Mrs. Allen said, and then as though he had never so much as laid eyes on her before Nick sauntered up next to Ariana and surveyed her all the way to the floor.

"Well, well, what have we here?"

When Nick ambled back to their row, Jaylon held up his hand, and Nick slapped it even as he turned into the row.

"Great job," Camille said, wrapping her arm through Nick's excitedly.

"Eww!" Nick said, shaking all over, and Camille laughed.

"And now, reading for the parts of Hawk and Lauren," Mrs. Allen said on stage, "Jaylon and Camille."

Suddenly she couldn't breathe as all-out panic flooded her body. Nick looked at her and smiled. "Go get 'em, Tiger."

Not at all sure how, Camille stood, thankful only that if she fell, she could be reasonably sure that Jaylon would catch her or at least pick her up. At the steps, just before she made the decision to simply turn around and run, Jaylon took her hand and leaned in to her.

"We're just in your kitchen. It's no big deal. Just you and me." Shoulder to shoulder they climbed the steps. "In your kitchen. Just you and me."

Fighting to calm her racing pulse, Camille followed him to center stage, and he smiled at her as he let go of her hand and folded himself onto the floor.

"Just like my kitchen," she repeated to herself. "Just like my kitchen."

"So you've never wondered what you want to do with your life then?" Jaylon as Hawk asked, and when she looked into his eyes, all the fear left.

"No," she said solidly, and Lauren took over.

In a heartbeat she was back in her seat in the darkness, wondering if what she'd just experienced was a dream—a dream of the highest proportions.

"Way to go!" Nick said, lifting his hand into the air for her.

She barely managed to clutch onto it as she collapsed into her seat. "Ugh. Thank goodness that's over."

Her relief lasted only until the next time she was sitting between Nick and Jaylon on Wednesday afternoon.

"Today I'd like to do some call backs so that I can see how my character considerations interact together," Mrs. Allen said with a clipboard firmly in hand. "First, I'd like Jaylon and Ariana to do the Hawk-Dominique audition material."

Camille's gaze followed him up out of his seat and down the aisle, and she wondered with every step he took why in the world he would want to sit with her.

"This should be good," Nick said softly.

Calming herself down and closing her eyes, Camille willed peace into Jaylon's soul. "They're just lines, J. Remember that."

Flipping her hair over her shoulder, Ariana pranced past Jaylon up the steps and took her position on center stage. "Oh, don't be so dramatic, Hawk. It's not like we were married or anything. Besides people break up all the time. It's the other half of getting together."

"Maybe so," Hawk said as Jaylon anchored his hands on his hips angrily. "But I think you're enjoying this a little too much."

"I'm not enjoying anything. I just think it's time for us to see other people. That's all."

"Other people? And I'm sure you don't have anybody specific in mind."

"You don't have to get petty about it. I mean it's not like you're bad looking or anything. Surely there's somebody who wouldn't mind going out with you. Who knows you might even be doing someone a favor."

"Like I did you?" he asked, and the venom in the words was a little too real.

Ariana's face scrunched. "Date or don't date. Makes no difference to me."

Although there was no Lauren that walked by, Jaylon's gaze followed her past just the same. "It makes no difference, huh?"

"I couldn't care less," Ariana said with a shrug.

"Uh-huh," he said, nodding. "We'll see about that."

"What?"

Jaylon looked at Ariana with beaten down defiance. "I said it's been nice knowing you." He reached over and shook her hand. "I hope you and lover boy are very happy together." Dropping her hand like a guillotine, he stepped away from her. "Now, if you'll excuse me, I'll just be getting on with my own life."

"Very nice," Mrs. Allen said, clapping as she stepped back on stage. "Very nice."

Without a single backward glance at Ariana, Jaylon strode off stage.

"Ariana, if you'll stay up here, please." Mrs. Allen nodded at her. "And I'd like to have Camille come up."

Panic. Sheer, unmitigated, uncontrollable panic overtook every fiber in her body.

"That's you," Nick said at her side, but Camille just looked at him, blinking in wide-eyed fear.

At that moment Jaylon appeared at her other side and offered her a hand up. When she was on her feet, he pulled her to him for one moment. "Don't worry. She doesn't bite."

In a daze Camille approached the stage steps and put a hand on the wall to guide herself up them. On stage waiting like a barely leashed cougar stood Ariana, arms folded and looking totally aggravated. Camille swallowed hard, not at all sure Jaylon was telling the truth about the not biting thing. Somehow even breathing had gotten lost in the terror.

"I want the two of you to do the Dominique-Lauren section. Ariana you be Dominique. Camille, you be Lauren." Mrs. Allen stepped to the side of the stage. "Whenever you're ready."

"I don't know why you can't just be normal," Ariana said a little too realistically.

"Like you, I suppose," Camille shot back, surprising herself with her forcefulness.

"No, Lauren. I have no illusions that you could ever be like me. That would be asking the impossible, but would it kill you to take your nose out of a book for a change and act like a human being?"

"It's called getting an education, Dominique, and it wouldn't kill you to put your nose in a book once in awhile."

Disdain drained down Ariana's face. "Why would I want to do something like that?"

"To expand your horizons—past make-up and air-headed friends and boys."

"And that's what you're doing? Expanding your horizons?"

"Yes."

"Well, it looks to me like the only horizon you care about is school, and I don't mean the fun part of school either."

Camille stood for one minute, surveying but never really seeing Ariana. "And this is important now... why?"

"Because I have a reputation to uphold, and you are ruining it."

"Well, excuse me for being your sister. I'm sure whatever logic there is to the universe, it never meant to make such a horrid mistake."

"I'm sure," Ariana said, the contempt dripping from the words.

"Very nice," Mrs. Allen said with a clap. "Thank you both. Now, I would like to have Mark and Cathy run through the Hawk-Lauren exchange."

Regaining enough composure to follow Ariana off the stage, Camille made her way down the steps and up the center aisle and was glad for the black leather flag letting her know where her seat was.

She sat down and was immediately accosted by the hands of her two well-wishers.

"Way to go, Camille," Jaylon said, holding up a hand.

"Impressive," Nick said, holding his own up.

Not really sure of anything, she grabbed for both hands and took a deep breath before letting one of them go. Instinctively knowing she might slide right out of her chair if she dared to let all of her lifelines go, she gripped Jaylon's hand in a clench.

In a string of auditions most of the other students got their own turns on stage although Camille barely noticed. She was too busy replaying the feeling of gazing into an iceberg, knowing she was headed for a hit headlong.

When class broke with Mrs. Allen promising to make her final decision by Friday, Camille stood on wobbly legs and followed Jaylon into the aisle.

"Yeah, I'm sure Mrs. Allen was just being nice to her," Ariana said loudly enough for everyone to hear as she passed. "I mean Super-Freak auditioning with me? Who is she kidding anyway?"

Fighting to keep the shattering of her heart from being heard by everyone around her, Camille crushed her books to her chest and stepped past Jaylon. Without waiting for either guy, she pushed her feet ahead of her up the aisle, liking the growing darkness she encountered with every step.

"Camille," Jaylon said with worry lacing the plea, and then through the din she heard him hiss presumably to Nick, "I didn't do it."

She had no desire to turn around and make sure that was who the comment was aimed at, but when she reached the auditorium door, the lights on the other side made her want to be anywhere but right there.

"Camille." Jaylon's quickening steps carried him right to her side in the crowded hallway.

"I'm fine. I've just got a lot of stuff to do." Her steps never slowed as she pushed through students who were going in every direction around her. In a few heartbeats she realized he was no longer beside her, which to at least one part of her felt like a blessing. However, at her locker she couldn't exchange her books quickly enough to avoid Lexie or Nick.

"Ariana's a jerk, Camille," Nick said with that same pleading quality to his voice that Jaylon's had. "You did great."

"What's going on?" Lexie asked, the concern evident on her face and in her voice.

"Ariana," Nick said divisively. "Listen, Camille, she's just jealous of how well you did."

Camille slammed her locker, and then with the last rational piece left of her brain, she turned on Nick. "Yeah, and the sun now sets in the East." Not bothering to wait for his answer, she turned, and books in hand, stomped down the hallway and pushed out the door with a violent shove.

How stupid could she possibly be? So she had memorized a few lines. So she worked with Jaylon. So what? She was still Camille Wright, and no amount of rubbing elbows with celebrities would ever change that. Super-Freak. An apt description.

At the bus stop she pushed the edge of her glasses up with her shoulder and collapsed her body around her books. There was no use pretending she was something other than who she was—an inept, awkward, totally hopeless geek.

"Hey," Jaylon said, not wholly unexpectedly in her ear, but she never so much as moved to acknowledge his presence. "Need a ride?"

Gripping humiliation to her, she stood rock still, looking straight ahead lest he see the bleeding of her core in her eyes.

"Come on." Gently he put an arm around her shoulders and pulled her away from the pole.

Really she didn't want to go anywhere with him. Really she just wanted to stay by herself and sulk. Really, really she did.

Even in his car, she didn't release her clutch on her books. They were her only shield now, and she had no intention of letting them down. Wordlessly he started the car, and within minutes they were making their way through the streets in exactly the wrong direction.

"I thought we were going home," she said, bitterness biting through the words.

"We will...later."

In a pouting silence, she leaned back in her seat, determined to hold onto the anger and hurt no matter what he did. However, the farther out of the city they drove, the harder they became to hang on to.

When the car turned onto the tire tracks in the midst of a sea of yellow, she had to concentrate on the ache in her stomach not to notice the peace surrounding her. She wasn't going to give up her mortification so easily.

He got out of the car as soon as the motor died and came around to her side where he opened her door and offered her a hand up. "Come on."

Still clutching the books she stood from the car, and he looked at her and smiled. "I think we can leave these here."

Carefully he laid his hands on either side of her books and lifted them away from her. The instant they were gone, a chill settled over her, and she wrapped her arms around herself to deflect it.

"Come here." He put a hand at her waist and led her away from the car and over to the tree, which stood forlornly at the slope's edge. At the tree he folded himself into the protective hollow of its base and pulled her down with him.

Once down she fought to hold onto the anger even as he wrapped his arms around her and tugged her gently back against the solidity of his chest. If nothing else, it was warmer here, his jacket wrapping around her right along with his arms.

He didn't say anything. He didn't need to. His touch said everything words never could. That he was here for her. That he didn't believe anything anyone said about her, or even what she thought about herself. That with him, she was perfectly safe.

In the hollow of his arms, a decade's worth of humiliation and hurt flooded to the surface. The hurt she had held so closely to her for fear of anyone seeing how deeply wounded she was began to ache, and with that ache came the tears.

She didn't want to cry. She didn't want him, of all people to see them. To her they were a sign of weakness and vulnerability. And that, in her mind, was the epitome of foolishness—for if you let them see you vulnerable, that made their game of crushing you to the core that much more fun.

However, one by one the tears slid down her cheeks, stopped only when they dripped from her chin onto the leather below. At first she thought she could handle their hurtful words and stares of derision. If she just kept to herself, didn't get too close to them, they couldn't hurt her. And yet, they always found a way to slip past the guard who stood at the door of her heart.

They had gotten good at that—waiting until her guard was down to throw the nasty comments right at her core. It got to be a game—for them anyway. For her, it was always deadly serious because for her the pain didn't end when they walked away, it was locked into her heart. It became a part of her forever.

She hated them. But more, she hated herself for being someone who was so easily hurt, for being someone who invited their derision and contempt. That was the rub because not one of them could ever wound her the way she had wounded herself.

If in her heart she didn't believe their words, it would've been easy to deflect them. They would never have stood a chance. But she did believe them, and that made the ache sting that much more.

As she looked out across the peace of the little valley below her, the weight of her fight dropped away from her. Here there was no reason to fight anymore. Here all she had to do was feel, and to the depths of her being at that moment, she felt everything.

Hours, days, eternities could have passed without her really knowing it, but in the length of an indeterminate amount of time, her tears began to subside. Still his rock solid frame held hers. Still he was there, and no part of her could understand that.

"I'm such an idiot," she finally said even as she huddled into his jacket.

"No, you're not an idiot. You're human." His cheek rested on her hair as he hugged her tighter. "You had every right to be hurt."

She shrugged and sniffed. "I should be used to it by now."

"Nobody should have to get used to that."

"But it's not like I haven't heard it before."

"So? It doesn't matter how many times you shatter glass, if you hit it just right, it will still shatter a little more. There's no big mystery to that."

"I wish it didn't matter to me so much."

"What she said or what you feel?"

"Both."

His hug tightened as he breathed in. "Would that really make it better? I mean if she didn't say it, wouldn't you still believe it? And if you didn't feel anything, would that make her saying it all right?"

Camille thought about his questions, and as much as she wanted to say yes, she knew she couldn't.

"She only has power because you give it to her," he said gently. "You're easy prey, and she's a coward."

"Well, she's a pretty vociferous coward."

"She knows you won't fight back, and putting you down makes her look big to everyone else." His words sounded so convincing, and Camille didn't have strength left to argue. "It also makes everyone else afraid of her because if she can do that to you, then she can do it to them."

"But why do they listen? Why don't they stand up to her?"

"Why don't you?"

The question hit so central to the real problem that for a moment, Camille could find no words to answer. "Because maybe I think she's right."

"Ah," he said, nodding knowingly. "Well, until you unmask her for the fraud she is, she will continue to have that power over you."

Camille considered that a moment. "Do you believe her?"

"Makes no difference. You do."

"It makes a difference to me. Do you believe her?"

It took a long moment for him to answer. "No, I don't. But as long as you do, you give up your power to her."

"Then how do I stop believing her? How do I convince myself it's not true?"

He shifted slightly and took a long breath. "Remember the other day in the hall when you nailed Lauren's part without a blink?"

Slowly she nodded.

"That's how. One small step at a time, you stack up evidence that you are a good person, worthy of other people's admiration and approval."

She couldn't get close to how solid he sounded on the subject. "I am?"

"I don't know," he said softly. "Are you?"

Her gaze traveled out beyond the cliff to the other side. She could see the other side so clearly, but how could she get there? It seemed so far away—like an entirely different world.

"Look at all the things you do right now that you could be proud of," Jaylon said as his words blended harmoniously with the wind. "You take care of Daria, you handle classes that would send most people to the emergency room with brain bleed. You even took a class that seemed outside of your reach, and you're not only doing well in it, you're making the experience better for other people in the process."

"Oh, yeah?" Her finger made small circles on the leg of his jeans. "And who would that be?"

"Nick, for one. He's been in that class for four years now, and he's always hung out by himself—kept his distance from the rest of us like we had the plague."

"Well, he doesn't exactly think you all hung the moon like everyone else seems to."

"That's part of it," Jaylon acknowledged with a nod. "But it's more than that. He never really connected with anyone in class—until you."

With the tiniest of shoves, Camille pushed the compliment away from her.

"And then there's Stephanie. She's always so shy and quiet, I didn't even know what her voice sounded like until the other day."

"Steph's nice."

"Yeah, and I had no idea of that fact until you asked her to join us."

"Maybe you just weren't paying attention."

"Maybe not," he said softly, and she felt his chest rise and fall. "Which brings us to me. You know I've gone through my whole life thinking I was so much better than everyone else. I had money. They didn't. I had nice cars and nice clothes. They didn't. I had my life in order. They didn't. I thought those things made the way I treated everyone perfectly acceptable. The worst part is I never even questioned what I was doing until that night at *My Fair Lady*."

A smile seeped onto her face at the memory even as the questions slipped into her mind.

"I can't explain it really, but when I really started to get to know you, I realized what a jerk I was being." A muscle at a time he shifted underneath her. "I always thought I was something special, but putting everyone else down doesn't make you special—it just pulls everyone else down with you."

"But that's high school," she said with a dismissive shrug. "Everybody does it."

"That doesn't make it right, and it doesn't make doing it any less destructive. I've started watching, and you know what? I don't think most of us ever realize how destructive it really is."

"Yeah, but that's just the way it is. It's not like we can change it."

"Maybe not, but I can change me. I can change how I react to it. I can watch myself and make sure I'm not contributing to it."

"And you think that helps?"

"I know it does," he said with no question at all in his voice.

Slowly she arched her neck until she could look at his face. He looked down at her and smiled.

"How do you know?" she asked softly.

"Because." Gently he took her free hand and placed it into the warmth just under his jacket. "I feel it right here."

Chapter 17

Oblivious to the curious stares they received from their fellow students, Jaylon and Camille spent every free second together Thursday. At lunch she waved to him and invited him to their table, and although Nick had yet to give up his animosity, he at least had become cordial toward Jaylon.

During drama on Thursday, they sat together, a trio of friends, and remarkably the tensions had cooled. When they broke up into groups to work on set design concepts, Camille invited Stephanie over, not to save herself from certain disaster, but because she genuinely enjoyed spending time with the younger girl.

The script itself presented a particularly vexing problem—how to design sets that could serve diverse purposes simultaneously. How could a school hallway for instance be turned into a home dining room without the benefit of a curtain close? And how could a school dance be turned into outside without an eternity of resetting pieces?

Laughing and wholly unhesitant to make suggestions they worked together and finally came up with a plan that resembled something that might actually work. They had taken the first three acts and literally split the stage in half so that one part of it was taken up by the school hallway, and the other half was used by either the park or the home dining room or Lauren's bedroom.

Recalling the use of lighting at *True North,* Jaylon suggested darkening half to visibly force the audiences' attention to one side or the other. Building on that concept, Nick came up with a way to minimize the prop pieces so that a redesign could be accomplished with only one or two stagehands at most.

Stephanie and Camille took over the discussion when it shifted from set design to costume design, and with Stephanie firmly in charge, they mapped out a workable plan that would minimize the need for costume changes while maximizing the illusion that the audience was viewing a character on a different day.

By Friday when they all met in the third row, they each had their section of the plan in hand, and every member of their team had a piece of themselves represented in that plan. It was a combined work to be immensely proud of.

"Please pass your group projects to the front," Mrs. Allen said. "I will be going over your suggestions this weekend, and on Monday the stage manager's team can begin working on the set, props, and costumes."

After passing the reports to the front, they all sat back fully expecting the remainder of the period to be stress-free.

Once the reports were handed up to Mrs. Allen, she lifted them in the air. "This it?"

Nods moved across the auditorium like a wave.

"Great." Mrs. Allen laid the projects to the side and collected her clipboard. "And now, the moment you've all been waiting for."

Visibly Nick shifted at Camille's elbow, and she leaned over to him. "It's going to be good news, I promise."

He looked at her and smiled gratefully.

"We'll start at the bottom and work our way up the cast," Mrs. Allen said. The infamous clipboard was locked firmly in her grip. "First off, we've got Ethan's friends. In the part of Blake, Keane Dinsmore."

A mild celebration erupted at the base of the stage even as one-by-one Mrs. Allen continued to work her way up the list. "As Lauren's friend, Nicole...Stephanie Chamberlain."

"Yes," Nick said next to Camille as he reached over and gave an astonished Stephanie a quick hug. "Congrats, Steph."

Camille leaned over to wink at Stephanie. "Good job."

As each minor female part was given away, Camille's lungs increased their capacity until the part of Mrs. Waterford was doled out to Cathy. Sweet air flowed into Camille's lungs for the first time since August. All the minor parts were taken. She was off the hook—saved from the prospect of humiliating herself in front of an actual audience.

"And now the moment we've all been waiting for," Mrs. Allen said as though a drum roll might actually follow her words. "In the part of Ethan Drake—Nick McGee."

Instantly Camille turned to him excitedly. "Yes! Way to go, Nick!"

Nick's eyes widened to saucer-size. "Oh, my gosh. I don't believe it."

"Cool." Jaylon reached over to slap Nick's hand over Camille's head. "Good job, Nick."

"In the role of Dominique Waterford... Ariana Vandivere."

A screech that Camille wasn't quite sure was excitement sounded from the front row as students collapsed on the freshly named nominee with their congratulations.

"Oh, great," Nick said, the announcement not totally extinguishing the excited smile on his face, but still making it dim slightly.

"Don't worry." Camille leaned over to him. "She doesn't bite."

"Hawk Fletcher... Jaylon Quinn."

In half-a-heartbeat Camille spun to Jaylon with breathless excitement. "Yeah! Congratulations, J!"

"Thanks," he said happily accepting her hug.

"Good job," Nick said, and Camille could've sworn there was real admiration in his tone. "Congrats."

"You, too," Jaylon said with a nod and a quick handshake.

"And finally, in the role of Lauren Waterford... Camille Wright."

A gasp swept the audience even as every muscle in Camille's body screeched to a halt. Happy, excited waves of adulation crashed over her as she struggled to comprehend what had just occurred.

"Our set manager will be Kara, and her assistant will be Daniel," Mrs. Allen continued although Camille's ears were now ringing so loudly, she couldn't be sure anyone was saying anything.

"Way to go, girl," Nick said with a quick hug of her shoulders.

Stephanie swatted her on the knee, and when Camille looked over to her friend, Steph gave her a thumbs-up and a happy wink. Camille tried to smile, but even that was asking too much.

"Well, that's it for today," Mrs. Allen said. "We'll start fresh Monday. After school practices will begin the first of the year—Tuesdays and Thursdays, so clear your schedules. Congratulations to everyone. You all put in a lot of effort, and I know if everyone will continue to put in that much work, our Spring Production will be the best one we've ever had." She stopped for a moment and then smiled. "The rest of the day is yours."

Immediately Camille was showered with happy congratulations. Awkwardly she stood as what seemed like the whole class came to offer their best wishes. Knowing she would never be able to stand on her own, she held onto Jaylon's waist with a vise grip clutch.

Her only defense against the unbelievable news overtaking her was to focus her attention on everyone else.

"You'll be a great stage manager," she said as Kara shook her hand. She turned as someone tapped her arm with another congratulations. "Congrats yourself, Mark, or should I say Dad?"

The others who stopped by all looked surprised and pleased with the recognition she bestowed on them as though in the last five seconds what she thought of them suddenly mattered immensely.

Next to her, Jaylon was holding his own court of admirers. "Hey, best friend," he said to Tony who had snagged the role of Matt. The two of them shook hands presumably for the first time ever. "It'll be fun to work together."

"Yeah," Tony said, seemingly awestruck. "I can't believe I even got a part."

"What? After the audition you did with Steph, I'm surprised you didn't get Hawk."

Tony's face lit up. "It was all Stephanie. She was great." He looked down the row at Stephanie who smiled shyly, her cheeks turning crimson.

"Yes, she is," Jaylon said with a sincere nod, which caused Stephanie to blush even deeper.

The bell jangled, surprising Camille who couldn't have stopped herself from smiling if she had tried. Quickly she bent down to gather her books just as Tessa and a very angry Ariana pranced by.

"Dominique! I mean can you believe it?" Ariana asked with a dramatic sigh. "I've never been a supporting anything."

"Were truer words ever spoken?" Stephanie asked harshly, and Nick laughed.

However, Camille couldn't bring herself to straighten up. Ariana's tone of disgust was just too heavy, dragging her shoulders right into the ground.

Ariana tossed her hair. "Mark my words, she'll never make it to the Spring Production."

And then the voice traveled on.

"Come on," Jaylon said, trying to sound excited and happy, but not quite making it that far. "Let's go to Sal's to celebrate."

With great effort Camille stood, swinging her braid and her backpack up as she did. "I've got homework."

"I know," Jaylon said with a smirk as he took her hand. "You always have homework." He pulled her out into the center aisle as Nick and Stephanie followed, uncertain as to what to say to Camille.

"No, I really have homework," she said seriously. "And Daria's going to be home soon."

"So, we go home and get her," Jaylon said, unwilling to be deterred. "What do you guys say?"

"I say it sounds like fun," Nick said, and then he looked at Stephanie. "We'll go get Lexie and meet you guys there."

In the hallway, Camille tried once again to break away from him. "I've really got things to do."

"Yes, you do—like go out and have some fun for a change." His eyes gleamed at her wickedly. "And I'm not taking no for an answer."

That much was obvious. So with a heave of resignation, she let him put his hands on the wheels of her life and take her wherever he wanted to go.

The surprise on Daria's face that was still there when they made it to Sal's was matched only by Camille's wide-eyed disbelief. Of course, she had heard about Sal's and had even been to the restaurant the night after *True North*, but somehow she had never considered the possibility that half the students would be there after school.

"This place is a zoo," she said, holding onto Jaylon's hand on one side and Daria's on the other. Daria's for fear the child would get lost, Jaylon's for fear she would.

Sal's was wall-to-wall people, and the second they crossed into it, Camille felt every gaze turn toward them. Self-consciousness enveloped her, and she reached up and pushed her glasses up with her shoulder as she ducked behind Jaylon who pulled them through the crowd.

"Hey, guys," he said, stopping suddenly at a table, which caused Camille to bump right into him.

"Hi," Nick said, and Camille was thankful for the effort to sound happy he managed to put into his tone.

"Camille," Lexie said as though the sight of her best friend was wholly unexpected.

With her gaze practically glued to the floor, Camille slid into the chair Jaylon held out for her, and then she helped Daria into hers.

"Hi, Dar," Lexie said with a smile.

"Hi," the little girl said, and the overwhelmed pitch of the syllable said it all.

"What do you say, cheese fries and drinks all around?" Jaylon asked after he had seated himself and laid a casual arm across the back of Camille's chair.

"Sounds great," Nick said. "Let's go put in our order."

Without fanfare, the two guys stood and ambled through the crowd over to the counter. The second they were out of earshot, Lexie and Stephanie simultaneously leaned in to the table.

"Oh, my gosh," Lexie gushed. "Nick told me, Camille! You must be so excited."

"Yeah," Stephanie chimed in. "The lead, opposite Jaylon. Oh, I would die!"

Camille thought that was actually close to what she thought too. She shrugged and pushed up her glasses. "It's not that big a deal."

"Not that big a deal?" Lexie positively shrieked.

"Romantic scenes with Jaylon Quinn," Stephanie said dreamily. "I'd say that is a very big deal."

Camille's gaze traveled across the restaurant to the black leather jacket draped smoothly over the counter, and despite her best efforts, her heart swelled in her chest.

"Besides that," Lexie said with a smirk, "if I didn't know better, I'd say the stage isn't the only place you're becoming his leading lady."

Instantly, Camille felt the hot flush rise into her cheeks. "We're just friends."

"Uh-huh," Stephanie said, falling in line with Lexie easily. "I've seen the way he looks at you when we're practicing."

With annoyance Camille shrugged. "He's a good actor."

"I don't think he's acting," Stephanie said as her attention snagged on the returning food scouts. "You watch," she told Lexie with a nudge. "You'll see what I mean."

Something told Camille that Lexie didn't need the prompting. In the cafeteria Camille would catch Lexie gazing at Jaylon and then at her, and she knew her friend well enough to know that every one of those looks meant she had her own suspicions about how deep this friendship ran.

"Who's hungry?" Jaylon asked, setting three giant bowls of cheese fries into the center of the table.

"Me," Stephanie said, accepting the empty plate he handed her.

Camille didn't bother to look up, she had a good idea what her face looked like every time she caught a glimpse of Jaylon, and after the conversation seconds ago, she didn't want her friends to know how much she wanted them to be right.

Nick set a drink in front of her, but she barely even acknowledged the gesture. In a heartbeat Jaylon was again sitting by her, and this time she knew for a fact that all gazes were on them. She hated the limelight. She much preferred the anonymity of darkness.

"I think this calls for a toast." Jaylon lifted his glass. Instantly every other person at the table grabbed for theirs. Reluctantly Camille reached for hers only after she realized there was no getting out of it. "To Nick and Stephanie for great auditions and winning the parts that they did, and to Camille for getting Lauren. Here's to a fabulous Spring Production."

"Here, here," rang out around the table.

After only the smallest of sips Camille set her glass back on the table. She felt his arm on the back of her chair although it never so much as touched her. Sitting on the edge of her chair, she just managed to stay out of its electricity field. If she kept a low profile, maybe she could get out of this without too much collateral damage to herself. Unfortunately, after 45 minutes in the same position her back was killing her, and she wasn't sure if the queasiness in her stomach was from the fries or from the act she was fighting to put on.

"You know," she said when the fries were gone. "I really have to get home." She looked at her watch for emphasis.

"Yeah," Stephanie said, looking at her own watch. "So do I."

"Well," Nick said as he stood and helped Lexie get her coat on. "We'll have to do this again sometime."

"Yeah, we will," Jaylon said. He quickly shook Nick's hand and then barely managed to help Camille get into her coat before she pulled it on by herself.

The less he helped her, the better, she thought. Maybe then her heart wouldn't start depending on him to be there.

"It was fun," she said as a general statement to the assembled. "Be careful getting home." With a small push she guided Daria in front of her and out of the restaurant. But even being outside didn't make her feel less conspicuous. The gazes followed them everywhere.

Only when she'd gotten into his car and closed the door did the curious stares fall away from her. Jaylon climbed in on the other side and looked at her. "Home?"

Her gaze still downcast, she nodded. He was here, but it wouldn't last. And somehow she had to protect her heart from the inevitable. Sooner or later, he too would leave—just like all the rest of them had. Sooner or later this magic show would end, and she would be left with nothing. Sooner or later.

As he drove Jaylon tried to read her face. He knew that Ariana's comment had upset her, but her silence wasn't wholly about that. It had started the second Mrs. Allen had announced her name on stage. Not one second since that moment had she looked really happy about that fact. Not one.

Sure, she had accepted the congratulations of the others, but she always managed to deflect the adulation back on them. At Sal's, even with her friends, the people who had been her friends before Mrs. Allen's announcement, surrounding her, even then she didn't look happy. Scared and edgy was more like it.

He guided the car to a stop at her curb but didn't make it around to help her out before she already had Daria halfway out of the car.

"Thanks for the ride," she said without ever so much as looking at him.

"You're welcome." He followed her up the walk, stuffing his hands in his pockets. "So what are you doing tonight?"

"Studying." She tossed her braid over her shoulder as she unlocked her door and let Daria in.

Slipping in behind her, he sneaked into the apartment before she could slam the door in his face, which by the looks of things was exactly what she had planned.

"Go put your stuff in your room," she told Daria even as she slung her backpack to the table. "I'm going to start supper."

In the kitchen, leaning against the cabinet he watched her, simply trying to divine what was going through her mind. "I think Nick and Steph were excited."

"Yeah," she said as she fired up the oven.

He crossed his arms in front of him. "We've got a good cast to work with anyway."

"Yeah." She pulled a pizza out of the freezer and ripped the box open.

"I hope Mrs. Allen likes our set design. I think that could really be awesome."

"Yeah." With a clatter she pulled the pizza pan out of the drawer and dropped the frozen bread onto it. Then making as much noise as she could, she shoved it into the oven and slammed the door.

Every move she made pulled his head further to the side in concern until his ear was practically resting on his shoulder. "Mind telling me why you're so upset?"

She looked at him with genuine surprise. "I'm not upset." Then her gaze slid to the table and her books. "I've just got a lot to do."

In the split second before she stepped past him, his hand caught her arm. "Is it Ariana?"

Her flight stopped instantly even as her gaze dropped to their shoe tops. "No, I expected as much."

"She's wrong, you know." He tried to lean down enough to look into her eyes, but he had the sense that would require digging a hole in the floor. "But it's not all Ariana. Is it?"

Her gaze snapped to his and then fled to the cabinet edge.

"You want to tell me about it?"

"About what?" she asked, anger jumping to the surface. "About the fact that everyone knows I'm going to screw it all up? Or about the fact that I know I will?"

Calm washed through him as he looked at her. "You're not going to screw anything up."

Her jaw set in anger, but she said nothing.

"Do you know how I know that?"

Slowly she shook her head.

"Because I know you, and I know you don't do anything halfway. You will do everything in your power to make sure that play is the best one that's ever been performed. Besides you were by far the best Lauren that even got up there."

"Eight lines—wow," she said self-deprecatingly. "Lauren's got like 250 lines all together. I'll never be able to memorize that much."

"Sure you will. I'll help you."

She shrugged out of his grip and stalked over to the table. "I don't have time for this. I've got schoolwork and college applications to fill out, and scholarship applications to get out. I don't have time to waste on some dumb play. It's all such a waste of time anyway."

He wanted to say something to contradict that, but her statement hit him right in the soft spot his father's comments always did. Slowly he leaned back against the counter and crossed his arms to deflect the arrow that had already pierced right through his heart.

With her words still echoing between them, she looked over at him. "I'm sorry. I shouldn't have said that."

"Why not? It's what you believe, and for all we know it's probably true."

Her feet carried her over to the cabinet so that she was standing toe-to-toe with him. Gently she laid both hands on his crossed arms. "It's true for me. Okay? But I didn't mean it's a waste of time for everybody. I know it is important to you, and that's great. But...for me..."

His gaze caught hers then, and his heart started talking before his head could stop it. "I'm not asking for forever. Maybe you'll hate the whole thing, and you'll still want to quit, but can you at least give this a try? Just don't bow out now. Okay? I swear I'll help you as much as I can."

A snap at the door jerked both gazes to it, and instinctively he straightened as she stepped away from him. In the next second her mother was standing there, stunned into silence.

"Mom," Camille said, digging her hands into her pockets nervously.

"Hi," her mother said, looking back and forth between them. "I didn't know we were having company."

"Oh, yeah," Camille said. "Jaylon just brought us home. We went over to Sal's to celebrate."

"To celebrate what?"

It became clear in the next heartbeat that Camille wasn't going to make anything more than a few intelligible sounds, so Jaylon jumped in. "They gave out the parts for the school play today, and Camille and I both got one."

"Oh, really?" her mother's face turned to an incredulous smile. "That's wonderful."

"We were just working out our practice schedule," Jaylon continued quickly, lest Camille's mother put too many blocks together about him being here now.

"Well, don't mind me. I'm just going to go get comfortable. I guess supper's almost ready?"

Camille looked at the stove. "Five minutes."

"I'll just be three." And she disappeared down the hallway.

"So?" Jaylon asked when a door closed down the hall.

"So, what?"

"So, are you going to at least give this a try?" His gaze followed her over to the cabinet where she pulled some plates down. "Just don't say no,

Camille. Okay? Please."

With a sigh she looked at him in studied annoyance. "And you'll help me?"

"Every step of the way."

She stood for one more moment. "Fine. Then I won't say no."

Chapter 18

"Today and tomorrow we're going to do a simple read through for the cast," Mrs. Allen said on Monday afternoon. "As soon as the cast gets going, I want to meet with the crew over on this side. I'd like the cast to come up here, and take a seat on stage. Oh, and be sure to bring your script."

Together the four of them tromped up the stage steps and dropped to various places on the stage floor. Camille, ever conscious of each glance she and Jaylon got when they were together, made sure to put a full two feet between them. Getting too close while she read these lines out loud to a room full of people was dangerous enough, but with one sidelong glance at Ariana, she knew her best bet was to stay as far away from him as possible.

"Okay, Mark, you're first," Mrs. Allen said.

"My, my, Elaine, what are we celebrating?" Mark asked his stage wife. "You've got enough food here to feed half the country."

"Ned," Cathy, as Elaine, said slowly. "I think you'd better sit down. Dominique and Hawk have something to tell you."

"Oh, they do? Do they?"

"Daddy," Ariana said. "Hawk and I...are going steady."

A hush fell over the stage.

"Steady? That's not like...engaged. Is it?"

"Oh, Ned," Cathy said indignantly. "It's going steady. You remember that. He gave her his school ring."

"Well, of course he did," Mark said. "Well, let's see it." He took a moment to inspect the non-existent ring. "Well, Hawk, my boy, I always suspected we'd end up with you in the family. It looks like you're one step closer."

"Yes, Sir," Jaylon said, and Camille's heart jumped in her chest.

"Isn't it wonderful?" Cathy exclaimed. "I tell you it's fate. These two were meant to be from play school on. It's just so wonderful."

"Hrumph," Mark said impatiently. "You said that already."

"I know," Cathy said, and dreaminess took over her tone. "But it's just so true. The fates certainly knew what they were doing when they put these two together."

"Well," Mark said. "I suppose this is the kind of news that calls for a toast." He picked up a non-existent glass and held it aloft. Slowly Cathy, Ariana, and Jaylon followed suit. Then they all stopped and all four looked at Camille who in the script sat at the end of the table reading and totally oblivious to the previous discussion. "Uh-hmm. Lauren."

"Hmm?" she asked, still reading and not really paying attention.

"Would you like to join us?"

Camille looked up. "Oh, sorry." In the script she reached for her own glass, knocking it over and spilling it all over the table.

Ariana shrieked as if she'd just been drenched by real water, which of course, eventually she would be. "You stupid, clumsy little..."

"Dominique!" Mark and Cathy said simultaneously.

"You're always ruining everything! What did I do to be cursed with you?"

Although it was lines in a script she had read before, Camille cowered away from the furious barrage of insults Ariana continued to hurl at her.

"I'm sorry," she said more than once. "I didn't mean to."

"Lauren, you're excused," Mark said quickly cutting into Ariana's continued assault.

In her head, Camille saw herself slink around the dining table and run for her off-stage room even as Mark and Cathy tried to assuage their oldest daughter's tirade.

"Dominique, dear," Cathy said as her voice strained to remain calm. "Remember, we have guests."

"She should remember that," Ariana said bitterly.

"I'm sure it was an accident," Jaylon said, coming to a meager defense.

"She's an accident," Ariana said.

"Come on, dear," Cathy said. "Let's go get you cleaned up."

They didn't really leave, but Mark waited anyway. "So, you're going steady then?"

"Yes, Sir."

"Well, son, I wish you luck. You're going to need it."

A pause. "Very nice," Mrs. Allen said. "Very nice. You all continue with scene two. I'm just going to go down here to work with the stage crew."

Protectively Camille brought her knee up to her chest. She would need all the protection she could get from the next barrage and every one after that.

Never in her life had Camille been so happy to hear a bell. It had been nearly 45 minutes of non-stop insults hurled from Ariana the Almighty, who seemed to really be enjoying this. It wasn't at all difficult to cower and shy away from her—that's all Camille really wanted to do anyway.

"We'll start there tomorrow," Mrs. Allen called over the departing students.

Oh, joy. Camille slinked up the aisle and grabbed her books. Three months of this, and she might as well go crawl in a hole.

"You did good," Nick said with a nod as Camille yanked her books up from her seat.

"Yeah, I'm a regular Audrey Hepburn," Camille growled back, and both Nick and Jaylon arched eyebrows at each other.

"Hey, it could be worse," Nick said with a laugh. "She could've meant all that stuff."

"She didn't?" Camille asked furiously, and then she stepped out into the aisle without looking first. Instantly she was met by a five-ton wrecking ball striding up the aisle, and in a heartbeat she was on her knees with her books sprawled across the floor.

"You really should watch where you're going," Ariana said spitefully without ever so much as slowing down.

"Look who's talking," Jaylon shot back even as he bent down to help Camille. "You all right?"

On her hands and knees, Camille grabbed for her books. "Depends on what you mean by all right."

"Ignore her," Jaylon said as he handed her a book.

"Yeah, that should be real easy to do." Stiffly she stood. "I guess I'll see you all tomorrow for torture session day number two." And with that she turned on her heel and stomped out.

Fully expecting someone to follow her or call out to her, she tuned everything else out and simply walked as fast as she could. She didn't bother to stop at her locker or even to slow down before she hit the outside door. Who's stupid idea was this anyway? How had she let herself get talked into this? She should've just been smart and told them no—no, she wouldn't be in drama, she'd rather take her chances with the college application committee. No, she wouldn't be in the play. *Get someone else. Leave me alone.* That's what she should've said.

Jaylon was nice, sure, but he could find someone else to make doe eyes at him. That shouldn't be anything even resembling a problem. With quickening steps, she jumped on the bus and took her seat. What she needed was to get as far away from this mess as possible. Just get on the bus and keep riding. Who would miss her?

Ariana certainly wouldn't. Camille's ears burned with the thought of the brunette Attila the Hun. Ariana knew where Camille's place in life was, and it certainly wasn't on stage. Now, if she could just convince Mrs. Allen of that, maybe Mrs. Allen would let her off the hook. Reasonably she couldn't expect that, but still, in the back of her mind, she held onto that sliver of hope. Anything to keep from believing that she would actually have to live through this.

The rest of that week and most of the following did nothing to improve the situation. Focusing on everything other than drama, Camille managed to get through the other twenty-three hours of every day. However, it was the hour in the auditorium every day, being beaten down until she thought crawling on her belly might be a step up, that all hope of ever leading a normal life again crashed down around her.

Jaylon and Nick did everything they could to shield her from unnecessary taunts and insults, but on stage there was nothing they could do—except listen, and continue to assure her after it was over that nothing Ariana said was true. It was all a script.

She'd heard those words so many times, she wanted to scream. If it was just a script, then why did it feel so real? She wondered even as she stood on stage as Lauren if it was she who was Lauren, or Lauren who was she. A bumbling, mistake maker who nobody really wanted to be around and who Jaylon as Hawk only hooked up with to get back at her sister.

It all rang too true in Camille's heart. So much so that by the time finals rolled around and Christmas break was fast approaching, she was completely ready to give up.

Studying every waking moment and most sleeping moments as well wasn't helping. Sleep deprivation generally doesn't help the stability of one's mind and emotions, and Camille was no different. The day that school was to let out for the semester, she was so far behind, the prospect of the coming break was hardly a glimmer in the distance. She was a paper behind in English and faced two more tests that she had barely studied for. In an exhausted heap she fell into her seat at the cafeteria table, and without even looking at her food, she laid her head on the table.

"You look terrible," Lexie said with concern.

"Really?" Camille asked pathetically. "I look that good. Huh?"

Lexie laid her fork down. "Want to talk about it?"

For a moment Camille considered that proposition, and then she shook her head. "It won't do any good."

"Hallelujah!" Nick said, walking up and sliding his tray onto the table. "English is finished."

"How nice for you," Camille said, leveling a disgusted glance on him.

Nick's eyes narrowed as he sat down. "What's your problem?"

"Like you have to ask. Where've you been? Huh? Hiding under a rock the last two weeks?"

"Ari?" Nick asked with sympathy. "She's a witch, Camille. Deal with it, and get on with your life."

"Deal with it? Deal with it he says," Camille said in increasing hysteria. "That's easy for you to say, Mr. I've got women fawning all over me Ethan Drake. You don't have to hear her yelling at you for a solid hour every day."

Nick opened his mouth, but just before the words came out, Camille added, "And yes, she means it."

"You're making too much of this," he said with a shake of his head. "It's acting. You knew it was acting when you signed up for the class."

"You mean when I was signed up for the class," she said in annoyance. "Maybe I'll just quit."

"You can't quit," Nick said with instant concern.

"Come on, Camille. Look how far you've come," Lexie said just as her attention was yanked upward. "J."

Suddenly appearing at the end of the table, Jaylon stood there, looking like he might break into Nick's Hallelujah Chorus at any moment.

"Umm, Camille, can I talk to you?" he asked, shifting from foot-to-foot.

As she looked up from her cafeteria-table-pillow, her forehead wrinkled with concern. "Sure. What's up?"

"Not here," he said, and his voice barely contained his excitement.

"Not here?" she asked uncomprehendingly. "Where?"

In an instant he had her hand in his and he was pulling her away from the tables in a very un-Jaylon-like fashion. He didn't stop until they were out in the little courtyard, standing in foot-deep snow.

"Do you mind telling me what this is about?" Camille asked, her patience growing razor thin.

"This." He held up a piece of folded cream paper.

"What's that?" She took it from him and unfolded it carefully. Her gaze slid down the text of the letter. 'Please call to make an appointment to audition for the artistic review portion of your application which consists of presenting two contrasting monologues.' Her own problems escaped her memory. "NYU? Oh, Jaylon!" She jumped into his arms as his excitement poured into her. "Congratulations!"

"Mrs. Allen just gave it to me. I couldn't believe it. She wants me to make the appointment for over Christmas break so she can go with me."

Camille slid back to the snow with a crunch. "And so now what? This means you're in?"

"Well, no, not totally. But I'm one step closer." His eyes gleamed. "I just want to scream!"

She couldn't have wiped the smile off her face if she had wanted to. "I'm so proud of you." Then the unthinkable crossed her mind. "What's your dad going to say?"

Jaylon's excitement dimmed a full megawatt. "Probably that I can't go." His gaze caught hers. "But I'm going anyway. I don't care what he says. This is what I want, and I'm not taking no for an answer."

Hope rose in her heart as she hugged him once more. He deserved the chance to follow his dream, and standing there in the snow, it was possible to believe that he had more than just a chance.

When they finally came back down to earth, he looked at her and laughed. "I'm sorry. I bet you're starving."

"This was worth missing a little dried meatloaf."

He smiled, and the gleam had returned to his eyes.

His excitement hadn't dimmed by the time Jaylon slid into his seat next to hers in the auditorium and pointed to the writing on her paper. "What's that?"

"My final paper for English," she said, shaking her head in frustration. "Hudson wants it as soon as school's out, and it's giving me fits. Poetic sounding prose is not my forte."

"Mind if I take a look?" he asked as Nick entered the other end of the row.

"It's not very good."

"I'll be the judge of that." He took the notebook from her, easily recognizing the immaculate handwriting. She did everything to perfection.

'All that I can do is all that I must. For my dreams have been inscribed on my heart so deeply that they and me are now inseparable. As the stars are interwoven into the night sky, inextricably entwined, so my dreams are a part of me—no, they are me. I could no more set aside my dreams and walk away than a rose could set aside its scent and bloom without it. They and me are one.

'In the night before the light of my birth, my dreams were emblazoned into the fabric of that which would become my life. However, now, standing at the dawn of reaching for those dreams, unseen forces threaten to hurl them into the darkness of oblivion. For what? A few pennies? A few coins, which in the face of everything should mean nothing.

'Yet those few coins are beginning to mean everything to me. Everything. For like a gentle hand that at any moment could turn hostile and crush them before they are given their chance to shine, they hold the fragile porcelain of my dreams.

'In the absence of these precious pieces of metal, my dreams are as worthless as the dirt at my feet. Without them, the stars adorning the night sky could be nothing more than unattainable hallucinations in a mind that has held on too long to the belief that they are real and that they are reachable. If only… All that I can do is all that I must.'

"Camille," Jaylon breathed as he felt himself pulled into her world with a gentle, angelic hand.

"I know—awful," she said with a shake of her head. "Completely awful."

"All right, ladies and gentlemen," Mrs. Allen said from the stage, yanking his attention forward. "It's the moment you've all been waiting for. Please, spread out so we can get started."

In a daze Jaylon returned her notebook, but he never really saw it go. The words were still there, in front of him—emblazoned on his heart. He smiled at the reference as the memory of standing on a brush-covered embankment with her hand resting softly on his heart rushed over him. No, he thought with a smile. She never did anything halfway.

Just before he bent his head to start work on the final, he looked across to where she now sat four seats from him. Beauty didn't come close to describing her.

"So, what are you going to do with that paper?" Jaylon asked as he fought the mad crush of students to keep up with her in the hallway.

"I'm supposed to turn it in as soon as school's over." Camille looked at her watch. "Right now really. But what I really want to do is trash it."

"Listen, I know this is going to sound kind of strange," he said, thinking as fast as his feet were moving. "But do you think I could have a copy of it?"

Her steps slowed as she looked at him incredulously. "Of my paper?"

"Yeah, If you don't mind."

"I don't mind, but what in the world would you want it for? To line your birdcage?" She stopped at her locker, and although the bell had just rung releasing them for a full two weeks, when she finally got finished pulling books out, only two notebooks and her drama book were left in her locker.

He gazed at the stack of books in amazement.

"I know," she said with an irritated smirk.

He held up both hands. "Hey, I wasn't going to say anything."

"Sure you weren't." She nodded skeptically and then held up the notebook. "So, how are you going to copy this in the next two seconds?"

"Ever heard of Xerox?" he asked, and quickly he steered her into the school office.

As soon as he got home, Jaylon raced up to his room, closed the door behind him and stood in front of the mirror, the paper crushed firmly in his hand. "All that I can do is all that I must."

The words continued to echo through his mind even as he sat at his family's table three days later. This time the decorations were a thousand red bows tied in green holly, but beyond that it could very well have been the Thanksgiving dinner from what seemed like eons before.

Summoning his courage, Jaylon decided the time had come. "I'm going to New York on Friday."

Instantly all motion around the table stopped.

His father stared at him for a moment before continuing. "What for?"

"I have an audition with NYU," Jaylon said, pulling Camille's presence to him for strength.

The butter knife lifted from his father's roll. "An audition for what?"

"For drama school," Jaylon said. "They hold auditions to decide who they are going to accept."

"Do we have to do this now?" Marianne asked in instant despair.

Jaylon looked at her as calm decisiveness poured through him. It wasn't the time or the place, and yet he knew that if he went one more minute holding onto this secret, he would burst wide open. Calmly he looked back at his father. "I'm not asking for your blessing, but I'm going just the same."

"By yourself?"

"No, Mrs. Allen is going with me. We'll drive in on Friday, the audition's at 3. I've booked two hotel rooms for Friday night, and we'll be back sometime Saturday."

Even his father's eyes were hard. "And you think you can just up and leave like that without telling anybody?"

"I'm telling you now."

An uneasy silence settled over the table.

"Just like that?" his father finally asked.

Slowly Jaylon nodded. "Just like that."

When her mother called to her late Christmas Day, Camille was busy putting the finishing touches on her Princeton application. Rushing down the hallway, she grabbed the phone, praying it would be him.

"Hello," she said, anticipating the sound of his voice.

"Hey," he said softly. "You up for a little drive?"

A smile spread through her heart. "If you don't mind having some company."

As they drove, she snuck periodic glances at him. How luck had ever smiled on her so sweetly, she would never know.

"So have you worked on the script much?" she asked, and he looked over at her as though there were words perched on his tongue that might jump off at any moment.

Then just as quickly, he reverted his gaze back out the window. "No, you?"

"I thought I'd give it a few days rest. I'm kind of getting burnt out on it."

"Good plan," he said as his hands guided the car onto the snow-covered path. Only the tops of the yellow weeds formed little wisps of color in the blindingly white landscape. When the car was off, he sat for a minute just looking out at the lonely tree beyond. "I need to ask you something."

She didn't like the hesitant sound in his voice, and her gaze left the whiteness beyond to settle on him. His eyes fell closed, and in the next heartbeat he turned to her and took both of her hands in his.

"It's about your paper."

"My paper?" she asked, stumbling through his eyes. "What about my paper?"

His gaze fell from hers for a moment, and she watched his shoulders rise as the courage gathered in his face. When he looked back up, his steel-blue eyes pierced right through her. "I want to use it for one of my monologues."

"For one of your monologues?"

"For NYU."

The words crashed around her as she fought to make sense of them. "Why?"

Softening, his gaze pulled her into it. "Because it's so beautiful. Because I want something of you with me when I try out, and because it's the way I feel too."

Slowly she shook her head. "I don't understand."

His hands tightened on hers. "NYU is my dream—it has been for a long time. Getting up on that stage is my dream, but if I have to pay for it on my own..."

"If your dad doesn't come around."

He nodded, and in a breath his gaze caught hers. "Please."

Even if she had wanted to say no, fixed by the pleading in his eyes, yes was the only word her heart could find. "Of course you can use it."

A smile spread across his face even as she contemplated the question that would wipe it right back off again. "So, have you told your dad?"

Jaylon's face fell. "Yeah."

She couldn't tell at all from the syllable how that had gone. "And?"

"If there was a way he could stop me, he would. But I'm not 14 anymore. I can make my own decisions now."

"And he'll support you?"

"Probably not, but I can't worry about that right now. If I wait, I might miss my chance."

"So, you're really going through with this then?"

The smile seeped back into his eyes. "Yeah. Will you help me?"

She looked at him not sure what that meant. "Help you? How can I help you?"

"Just listen to me read. Give me your opinion. Help me memorize."

Her courage left for a fraction of a second, but when she looked into his eyes, it filled every inch of her being. "Yes, I'll help you."

Hours later when the sky had turned to a deep navy, they still sat, huddled together in the cold front seat of the blue car. In each other's arms, warmth surrounded them regardless of the frozen snow pack outside.

"All that I can do is all that I must," he whispered to the stars looking down on them. Gently he leaned down and kissed the top of her hair. "Thank you, Camille. This is the best Christmas gift ever."

The tightening of her arms around him, made any return comment unnecessary.

Five days later Camille wrapped her arms around herself as the chill of her bedroom seeped over her. The nerves took over as she sat down on the bed and huddled into the pillows. It was three o'clock. He was there now—at the audition. Closing her eyes she willed all the passion of her own soul into his. "No big deal, J. Do it just like under the stars. Just like under the stars. Okay? No big deal."

As he sat outside the room with Mrs. Allen at his side, Jaylon's nerves threatened to hijack his sanity. Searching for anything to keep from thinking about how much the next half hour could change his life, his mind went to Camille. She believed in him. She believed in his dreams. And if she believed, then he could too.

"Mr. Quinn," a stout, silver-haired lady said at the door. "They're ready for you."

On wobbly legs he stood, wondering exactly how he had arrived at this point.

Mrs. Allen smiled at him as she stood, making a final check of his appearance. "Take a deep breath. Think good thoughts. You'll do fine."

Good thoughts. Good thoughts. The phrase resonated through him. *Camille.* She was the best thought he could ever have. On the little stage with the spotlight on him, he took one more deep breath. "All that I can do is all that I must."

"So when will you find out?" Camille asked the second after Jaylon told her things had gone as well as he could have hoped for.

"I don't know. Sometime in March or early April."

She heard his sigh. "One step, J. One step at a time. That's all God asks you to do."

"I wish I was there with you."

"So do I," she said softly. "But tomorrow night. Okay?"

"You'll be all right with the kids tomorrow?" he asked. The one and only major snag in the whole plan besides being without her was missing a day at the center.

"You know me. I'll make it work somehow."

"I know you will." The line between them hummed. "I miss you."

"Just think tomorrow night, and it'll be here before you know it."

"Meet me under the stars?"

"It's a date."

And so they spent New Years Eve in a parked car under the stars—dreaming in each other's arms.

<u>Chapter 19</u>

As any student will tell you, Christmas Break is never long enough, and Camille's was no different. With books she had hardly opened tucked under her arm, she strode into school January 9th, wondering where two and a half weeks had disappeared.

The only thing she could clearly remember was the way the stars looked glowing outside his windshield.

"Well, she is alive," Lexie said, planting her hands on her hips.

"Ha. Ha," Camille said with a sneer.

Lexie leaned a shoulder against her locker and looked at her friend. "I take it your break was a good one."

"It was okay." One at a time Camille stowed her books into her locker.

"Okay? Your mom could hardly keep up with you."

"There's a switch."

"Every time I called she said you were out."

"Yeah."

"Where was out?"

The stars shone in her heart. "I was practicing."

"What? Your love scene?"

Flames danced up Camille's cheeks. She slammed her locker with a clang. "Very funny."

"I wasn't joking," Lexie said, turning to follow her friend down the hall. "So, how is Jaylon?"

Although she didn't want it to, the smile spread onto her face. "He's fine."

"I'll bet," Lexie said with more meaning behind the words than was on the surface. "What do you say we get together after school, and you can tell me all about it?"

"Oh, I can't. I'm meeting J. after school for practice."

"Tomorrow."

Camille shook her head. "After school practices start tomorrow." As they slid into their History seats, Camille caught the look of feeling left out

when it crossed her friend's face. "Maybe I can reschedule with J. tonight.
I'm sure he's got other things he needs to do anyway."

Gratefulness poured through Lexie's eyes. "I'd like that."

Jaylon's face fell when Camille told him, but he promised her he
understood. With one final squeeze of her hand, they parted in the center of
the hallway, and Camille went to find Lexie.

At their lockers she pulled hers open. "I'm all yours. What are we
doing?"

"Your place or mine?" Lexie asked.

"Better make it mine. Dar will be home before too long." Camille
traded out a few books and then closed her locker. They walked through the
doors and out into the cold. The snow was gone, but it had been replaced by
a bone-chilling wind. Squealing like out of control kindergarteners, they ran
for the bus stop and hopped from foot-to-foot until the bus arrived.

Lexie waited until they had a chance to thaw out before she broached
her first topic. "So, if Dar's going to be home, how were you and J. going to
practice?"

Camille shrugged. "He's been coming to my place when I've got Dar."

"And he doesn't mind that?"

"Are you kidding? Sometimes I think he comes to spend time with her
rather than with me."

"I doubt that."

"No," Camille said with a soft smile. "But they get along really well.
Dar likes him as much as I do."

"That's pretty obvious," Lexie said, gazing at her friend. "Not that I
blame you or anything."

"Of course not." The window tugged at Camille's gaze.

Lexie's gaze slipped across the expanse to her friend's face. "You've
changed."

It took a moment for Camille to answer. "You think so?"

"Yeah. You're less—I don't know—intense."

Camille laughed. "And that's a good thing?"

Lexie smiled at her. "Yeah, I think it is."

Arrival at their stop pushed the pause button on the conversation until
they were relocated in Camille's kitchen.

"You want some hot chocolate?" Camille asked.

"Sure," Lexie said as she leaned on the cabinet. "So, how's the play
going?"

"Ugh."

With a knit of her eyebrows, Lexie watched her. "That good, huh?"

"Worse," Camille said as she emptied the packets into the cups.

"What's so bad about it? I figured being the lead would be like super cool."

"Super horrible would be more like it."

Lexie waited with her face all scrunched together.

Finally Camille sighed. "I guess it wouldn't be so bad if Ariana wasn't in it."

"Because of Jaylon?"

Camille shook her head. "Because of me. She hates me. It's like her personal mission in life is to make sure I know how second rate I am."

"But you're not second rate."

Why was she forced to look at her inadequacies even with her best friend? "Come on, Lex. Let's not kid ourselves. We've never been on the top tier of the social ladder, and we never wanted to be either."

"On the outside," Lexie said as Camille set the cup in front of her.

"Huh?"

"Well, I don't know about you, but I've always watched all the first tier people, and I wanted to be just like them—have all the friends, go to all the best parties."

Slowly Camille shook her head as she sat down. "But you always made fun of them."

Lexie shrugged. "There was no reason not to. I mean it wasn't like I ever had a chance to become part of their group, so it was easier to make fun of them."

Camille sat in silence.

"You never wanted to be like them?" Lexie asked.

Just the thought made Camille sick. "No, I really didn't. I mean sure it would've been fun to go to a few parties, but I saw what it cost them to be popular, and I didn't want to have any part of that."

"What do you mean, what it cost them?" Lexie took a sip of her drink.

"You know, acting all superior all the time. Putting their noses in the air to look down at everybody else. That's not who I wanted to be."

"And now?"

Slowly Camille made circles with her finger on the table. "I still don't want to be like that, but..."

"Jaylon?"

Snapping up, her gaze defended him. "He's not like that."

However, Lexie never flinched. "But he was."

Camille couldn't argue. She'd seen it. Her gaze dropped. "She just makes me so mad sometimes. It's like I work my tail off, and no matter how well I do, she just drags me right back down again."

Putting one hand across to the other elbow, Lexie drilled her with her gaze. "Why do you let her?"

The shrug hurt. "What choice do I have?"

"Stand up for yourself. Make her back off."

It still felt absurd to her. "Now you sound like Jaylon."

Lexie laughed. "Well, that's one I never thought I'd hear. Okay, so, tell me for real. Are you two officially a couple or what?"

"I don't know." Camille sighed long and hard. "I really like him, you know. And when we're together, it's easy to think in terms of forever, but..."

"But?" Lexie coaxed when the sentence trailed off into oblivion.

"We're just so different. He's so into drama, and I'd rather have my fingernails pulled out with a tweezers. I love math, and he can't stand it. We're just so different."

"Those are just the surface things. You think I ever thought I'd be going with an artistic soul? Nick's kind of music is like opera and classical. Mine is more hard rock and head banging stuff. But underneath we're more alike than I can ever really believe. When I look at the future, it's hard to picture it without him. He understands me in a way no one ever has."

"And next year?" Camille asked, voicing the fear lurking under all her other protests.

Lexie was silent for a long moment. "I figure I'll worry about that when the time comes."

The door creaked, and one mitten at a time, Daria pushed her way into the room.

"Hey, Sweetheart," Camille said, going to help her get out of her clothes. "How was school?"

"Fun." Daria peeled out of her coat. "We got to make planets out of balls and walk around the sun."

"Wow. That does sound like fun. Why don't you go change your clothes, and I'll have some hot chocolate ready for you?"

"Okay." Daria skipped down the hallway.

"She's going to be lost without you next year," Lexie said softly.

That was another topic Camille didn't want to think about, so she changed the subject and kept the rest of the evening's topics well away from Jaylon, college, and next year. She didn't want to talk about that. It was just too depressing.

When Lexie left, Camille pulled the stack of scholarship applications from the top of her desk. One step at a time.

"Camille, honey, I can't hear you," Mrs. Allen called from her seat in the second row. "Remember use your diaphragm. Try it again."

With a single breath Camille looked down at her script again to get the right words in her head.

"English is driving me crazy," Jaylon said from his position next to her.

"I hate Macbeth."

"It's not hard once you figure out what they're saying," Camille said.

"That's the problem, I may never figure out what they're saying, and then I'm going to fail, and then I won't graduate."

"Don't you think you're stretching it a little there?"

"I just wish I could find somebody who could explain it so that I can understand it." He waited a beat. "You wouldn't consider helping me. Would you?"

"Me?"

"Yeah, you understand it, and I'm sure you could explain it better than Ms. Geoffery."

"I don't know," Camille said.

"Camille," Mrs. Allen called again. "I still can't hear you. Project, Dear. Think back row."

"I don't know," Camille shouted.

"No, I didn't mean to yell," Mrs. Allen said. "Project. Remember we worked on this at the beginning of the year."

"I've slept since then," Camille mumbled as she looked at her script.

"Start again at 'It's not hard once you figure out what they're saying.'"

With a low, frustrated growl Camille picked her script up and then laid it next to her side. "It's not hard once you figure out what they're saying."

"Better," Mrs. Allen said, although the fact that it wasn't as perfect as she wanted it to be came through loud and clear.

"That's the problem…"

"Want some company?" Jaylon asked as they exited the auditorium together after their first after school practice.

Camille squashed her books to her chest. "I've really got a lot to do. I've got a Calculus test tomorrow I haven't even looked at yet. I've got another stupid English paper due, and at some point I've got to get some of these scholarship applications done."

"Okay," he said with a nod. "Tomorrow then."

"Yeah, tomorrow." She went to her locker and traded out her books before stomping to the bus stop. Too much to do, and too many people wanting a piece of her time. She wasn't sure when that had happened, but suddenly her friends actually wanted to spend time with her. The problem was that now was a really bad time for them to decide that.

At the apartments, she went upstairs and retrieved Daria from her after school caretaker. It was almost six-thirty by the time she got home, and with no supper fixed and Daria in need of help with her homework, Camille realized that her own projects would have to wait.

When her mother got home, Camille called Daria for supper and ate at the speed of light.

"You're going to get sick if you eat that fast," her mother said.

"I've got stuff to do," Camille said between bites. "I didn't get half the stuff done I wanted to last night."

"Well, you really should slow down a little."

Slow down, it was a nice concept in theory. However, her reality had no space for theory. It barely had space for sleep. At three o'clock in the morning, she clicked off her light and gave up. She couldn't remember ever being so far behind. Everything was due two hours ago, and no matter how hard she worked, she couldn't seem to get caught up.

"What's that?" Jaylon asked, pointing to her notebook the next afternoon when he sat down next to her for drama.

"English," she said without ever looking up.

"Another paper?"

She just nodded and kept writing. The more she got done now, the less she would have to finish in the dead of the night.

"Afternoon," Nick said, sliding into his chair.

"Shh!" Camille warned viciously.

"English," Jaylon whispered over her head, and Nick nodded with raised eyebrows.

"There's the bell people," Mrs. Allen called, but Camille never stopped writing. "We're going to work on some blocking today to get some of the preliminaries worked out. I need all actors for Act One, Scene One to come on up."

Jaylon stood, but Camille's pen never quit.

He stopped and turned back for her. "Camille."

Still she wrote. Two more words. One more sentence. "What?"

"You coming?"

She looked up at him with bleary eyes, and then she heaved a sigh. She would get no more done now. "I guess so." Reluctantly she closed her notebook and followed him up the aisle and then the steps.

"Okay, you can tell from the script that this is a dinner table situation. I need five chairs. We're going to start over on stage left."

Camille glanced longingly out at her notebook sitting in the darkness. Why they needed her for this, she couldn't really tell. And worst of all, it was taking time away that she could only make up for when everyone else was long since asleep.

"Camille, you'll sit here," Mrs. Allen said, indicating the front chair.

There was no way out.

"How about a drive?" Jaylon asked when they were gathering their things after class.

Camille shook her head and could almost feel her tired brains rattling. "I've got stuff to do."

"You know if I didn't know better, I'd think you were ignoring me," he said, not altogether pleased.

Pleading exhaustion engulfed her. "I'm not ignoring you."

Jaylon sank into pleading of his own. "Then come with me. You can study out there. I promise. Besides it'll do you some good to get out of here and get some fresh air."

Camille considered the pros and cons of his offer, lining them up in her head. There were by far more cons, but the pro of having a few minutes alone with him, outweighed them all. "Okay."

"So what are you studying?" Jaylon asked as Camille sat in the moving car with her nose firmly planted in the book.

"Physics," she said without looking up.

He drove a little farther. "I don't know how you can read in the car. That would make me sick."

"Shhh!" she said, replicating her warning to Nick perfectly.

A hard ball formed in the pit of his stomach as he shifted his gaze back out to the road. If nothing else, they had always been able to talk, but now she seemed far more interested in her books than she was in him. Even when he was with Ariana, he wasn't always the focal point, but she usually remembered he was there too.

Carefully he guided the car into the yellow weeds before stopping and putting it into park. He killed the engine and sat for a full minute. "We're here."

"Just let me finish this," Camille said without ever looking up, and in fact, her head never moved. If the world exploded around her, he had the feeling that she wouldn't even know it. Boredom and frustration mingled in his chest as he gazed out to the tree beyond. Up and down his fingers tapped rapidly on the steering wheel.

"Shhh!" she said again, and this time there was more annoyance in the sound.

"Sorry," he whispered as anger scattered everything else in his chest. Spending time together had seemed like such a simple idea. Why was it beginning to feel like it involved calculations far beyond his grasp?

"Okay, that one's finished." Never releasing her book, she reached for the door handle and got out before he realized she was moving.

Quickly he followed her out, but even in the fresh air, she never looked at him. Instead she walked straight to the tree, sat down, and opened the book again. Fighting the anger, he picked a spot close to her and sat down.

228 ~ *Staci Stallings* ~

"You're in my light," she said.

"Sorry." He scooted a little further around the tree. "That better?"

"Much."

He looked out across the break in the earth, but the peace that view generally brought was nowhere to be found today. His fingers picked at the yellow grass as he leaned his head back against the tree and closed his eyes. The only sounds were the water, the tree, and the breeze brushing past.

It was strange, but those sounds were the most vivid of all his childhood. They, mixed generously with Grandma Lani's laugh, were what he remembered of this place, and now the only thing left of that memory was the underlying sounds. He thought about Grandma Lani—so patient, so kind. She understood about being a child.

A small laugh jumped to his mind as he recalled them standing on her front porch waving until his father was out of sight and then racing for the stash of ragged jeans and old T-shirts that she kept just for him. He had always felt the best in those clothes. He could run and climb and swing in those clothes. In those clothes he was free. Free to be a child. Free to be himself.

His father would never have understood—just like he didn't understand most things about his son. To his father he had always been a small trophy. An object to be polished and shown off, and then dismissed until the next time someone wanted to see him.

But to Grandma Lani, he was Jaylon. Boy, through and through. She understood that like no one else ever had. He opened his eyes and watched the swing that dangled from the branch above twisting in the breeze. On that swing he had learned to fly, learned how to let go of everything else and reach for life.

Somehow at that moment he needed to feel that acceptance again. Pushing up from the tree, he walked over to the swing and inspected the rope. Older but still sturdy. Checking the rope of the swing above him and the old branches, he sat down on the small piece of wood, and once he decided it was safe, he put his whole weight on it.

The air escaped his lungs when the old feelings began crashing in on him. Gently he laid his head against the scratchy rope and picked both feet up off the ground. For one moment in time he had flown. For one moment he had believed that anything was possible. And then reality.

Reality had a way of slapping you in the face just when you were perfectly at peace. Like this week with Camille. His gaze traveled over to her, still hunched over her Physics book. It was fun when he felt like he was the center of her world, when they were flying together. But he had to admit that her world didn't revolve around him. She had so many other things to contend with. So many other things that had nothing to do with him.

For many long moments he simply sat, watching her. Imprinting this picture onto his memory for the time when she, too, would no longer be here by his side. College, if not before, he would have to find a way to say good-bye to her just like...

Fighting that thought, he shook his head, stood, and walked back over to the tree—to her. Slowly he sat down next to her and gently wrapped his arms around her. If he could just hold onto her, maybe he could make her stay.

"What are you doing?" she asked in frustration as she squirmed to get loose from his grip.

He released her and sat back. "Nothing." He closed his eyes to stop the pain. It was inevitable. He would lose her too.

Then she looked over at him. "What's wrong?"

When he looked at her, he knew the pain was in his eyes as surely as it was in his heart. "I don't want to lose you."

She laughed softly. "You're not going to lose me."

He shook his head, berating himself for saying anything. She couldn't understand how important this was. Nobody could. Angrily he stood and walked over to the swing.

"Okay." She put her book down. Carefully she stood and dusted her jeans off. "Mind telling me what that statement was supposed to mean?"

The scratchy rope jabbed into his hand. "Nothing."

"Didn't sound like nothing to me."

"It's not important."

"Uh-huh." She shifted to the other foot. "Is this about my studying?"

"No. Yeah. Well, no."

She laughed softly. "That was as clear as mud."

One small inch at a time he turned, still hanging onto the swing rope, but he could only hold her gaze for seconds at a time. She was leaning against the tree with her arms crossed in front of her and a very concerned look was etched on her face.

"This used to be my grandma's place," he said quietly. Then his gaze slipped out across the gap in the earth. "We used to come out here all the time. It was like, out here, nothing bad could touch us. You know?"

She nodded but said nothing.

"I thought that's how it was always going to be," he said, and sadness seeped into the words. "But I guess things change." His gaze fell to the yellowed grass at his feet. "I don't want things to change."

For a long moment she stood there, against the tree just looking at him. In fact, he became a little unsure that she had even heard what he said. Then just before he decided she hadn't, she pushed away from the tree and stepped over to him.

"Do you want to swing?" she asked him.

He looked at her, and as dangerous as it felt, he knew he couldn't hide from her. "Yeah."

She smiled, nodded, and reached for the swing rope as he sat on the wood. Her hands grabbed his jacket, and gently she pulled him backward. Then in the next heartbeat he was flying through the air, out over the edge, until it was just him and the air again. On his return trip he felt her hands push his back, and peace broke through the pain.

"I feel like I'm five," she called as he sailed over the side again.

"So do I."

How many trips he made back and forth, he didn't know, but it was enough to begin believing that everything would be all right again. When she stopped pushing, Jaylon let the swing slowly come to a rest, and then he sat there for one more minute, just gazing out to the setting of the sun.

"What was she like?" Camille asked.

His attention snapped to her. "Who?"

"Your grandmother. She must've been pretty special."

"She was. But she's not gone—not really anyway."

Camille's head fell to the side in confusion.

"She lives at Hollybrook. Has for about six years now." He looked at Camille and smiled at the questions in her eyes. "She's got Alzheimer's."

Sadness fell over the confusion in her eyes. "Oh. I'm sorry."

"I know. She doesn't really know anybody anymore. She just kind of sits there and stares."

"Like *True North*."

He nodded. "I try to get over there as much as I can, but I don't think she knows I'm even there anymore."

"She might know more than you think."

Jaylon breathed that in. "That's why I keep going. I mean she was there for me when she didn't have to be."

"When your mom died."

Again he nodded. "I'm sure she was in as much pain as I was, but she never showed it. I'd come here, and we had so much fun together. It was magic."

Emotion crept into her voice. "That's why this place means so much to you."

"Uh-huh. It was always my escape. The one place I could go that made everything else make sense."

"Even after she wasn't here."

"Yeah. Even after she left." The squeezing pain in his chest wouldn't let him look at her, but he felt her move toward him just the same. When she stopped only a few inches from him, her hand reached over and laid itself on his shoulder.

"That's why you don't want me to leave."

His heart burst wide open when her arms came around him and pulled his head to her. He grabbed for her and clutched her waist. Like hanging onto the rope, he now felt like he would fall right through the earth if he ever let her go. "I don't want to lose you."

"I know," she said as she laid her cheek on the top of his head. "I know."

She was still covered up with work the next afternoon when she got to drama, but the expedition into the country had helped to clear away the simply urgent things to reveal the truly important things. And Jaylon was on the top of that list.

Today when he came in and sat down beside her, she took a moment to actually acknowledge him when he said hi.

"Hey," she said, gazing at him with a smile.

"More homework?" he asked, pointing at the scribbles in her notebook.

"As usual," she said with a shrug.

"Ready for another day in the salt mines?" Nick asked, sliding into his seat.

"And another and another," Camille said just as Mrs. Allen stepped onto the stage. Homework would have to wait. It was time to block.

Chapter 20

Three weeks later Camille was technically more than pleased with her progress. She knew practically every line, thanks to intensive memorizing drills spent with Jaylon coaching her the whole way. Her feet knew every block move in the whole script.

Stand, say the line, wait for the next line, take three steps, stop, say the next line, wait, turn. She had it down to a perfect science. The only problem was that drama had nothing to do with science. It was an anomaly that no matter how hard she tried, she simply could not grasp.

"You're too stiff, Camille," Mrs. Allen called from her seat in the audience during a Thursday after school practice at the beginning of February. "You look like a robot that needs grease. Loosen up."

Camille rolled her head over her shoulders and swung her arms in the air.

"Try it again."

"You act like you think you're better than me," Ariana said, crossing her arms in front of her.

"I'm not *acting* like anything," Camille said.

"Louder," Mrs. Allen called from the darkness.

"I'm not acting like anything," Camille repeated, desperately trying to get her voice to carry beyond the front of the stage. "Has it ever occurred to you that maybe I'm not even noticing you?"

"Well, you're certainly noticing Hawk."

"And that's a problem?"

"Louder."

"And that's a problem?"

"Stop," Mrs. Allen said in frustration as she stood and marched up the steps.

"Thank goodness," Ariana said under her breath as she stepped away from Camille, who looked at her in frustrated anger.

"Camille," Mrs. Allen said, walking right up to her, "you have to project your voice, Dear. Not yell. Project."

Camille nodded although how to accomplish that was still as much of a mystery as it had been back in August.

"Use your diaphragm," Mrs. Allen said, putting her hand in the center of Camille's stomach and pushing in. "Use your air to project your voice."

"Huh," Camille exhaled as Mrs. Allen pushed in again.

"Got it?"

Irritated, Camille nodded. Whether she had it or not didn't matter. What mattered was that she would never be able to do it.

"Try it again," Mrs. Allen said, backing away slightly.

"And that's a problem?" Camille asked and then looked at Mrs. Allen.

"Again."

"And that's a problem?"

With a sigh, Mrs. Allen shook her head and backed away. "Continue."

Derision glared at her from Ariana's eyes.

"And that's a problem?" Camille asked, pulling herself up to her full height and projecting as far as she could.

"Let me let you in on a little secret," Ariana said. "The only reason Hawk even knows you're alive is because he wants to get back at me."

"This may come as a shock to you, Dominique, but the world doesn't revolve around you."

"Stop," Mrs. Allen called again from the audience. "Stop. Stop. Stop."

In utter exasperation, Camille took a step backward and reached up to scratch her ear. She stood tapping her fingers against her leg as Mrs. Allen again climbed the steps.

"Ariana," Mrs. Allen said, obviously trying to contain her frustration, "why don't you call it a day? We'll start again tomorrow."

"Thank you," Ariana said, shooting an aggravated look at Camille.

Mrs. Allen waited until Ariana had vacated the stage and stepped through the exit before she turned to Camille. "Listen, Camille. I know you're trying, and I appreciate that, but it's February. We're supposed to go on in two months. Now, I don't want to sound the alarms, but if you can't get this..."

"But I'm doing my best," Camille said, and the prospect of having the role yanked from her suddenly felt like it would rip her heart in two.

"I know," Mrs. Allen said, nodding sadly. "I knew this was a long shot when I cast you."

"I'll get it," Camille said, the pleading sound peeling in her ears. "I'll work harder. I promise."

Mrs. Allen shook her head. "I can't afford to wait much longer. Someone will have to step in and learn Ariana's part."

The breath evaporated from Camille's lungs at the thought of Ariana and Jaylon starring together, practicing together, being together again.

"I swear," she said frantically. "I'll get it. Please, just give me a few more days. Please."

Mrs. Allen looked on the verge of simply saying no, but then with one more look at Camille, she exhaled. "All right. I'll give you until next Thursday, but it's got to be a whole lot better by then."

Camille nodded. "It will be. I swear."

The next morning Camille was up with the first beep of her alarm at five o'clock. She wasn't sure what time they actually unlocked the school, but she was determined to be there the second they did.

She threw on the first clothes she came to, grabbed her books and a banana from the refrigerator, and raced out into the chilly morning air. At the bus stop she hopped from foot to foot, saying her lines with each hop. Math was easy. Practice had never really been necessary for that, but this was something altogether different.

At school she sat down on the front steps and huddled next to the brick to get out of the wind. Even then, the lines were running through her head. "And that's a problem?" Pause. "This may come as a shock to you, Dominique..."

By the time the first janitor made it to the doors at 6:30, she was nearly a solid block of ice.

"Could you let me into the auditorium?" she asked him as she followed him through the front door. She saw the concerned look cross his face. "I'm the lead in the school play, and I really need to practice. Please." He still didn't look convinced, so she grabbed her script. "See, *Don't Listen to the Fates*. Lauren, that's my part."

She followed him down the hallway. "Please. I really, really need to practice, and Mrs. Allen won't be here for another hour. Please."

"All right," the old man finally relented. "But you behave yourself."

"Oh, I will," she said with a grateful nod.

With no one in the auditorium and only the normal lights on the stage, the place looked totally different. Camille laid her backpack on the top step and took a deep breath as she stepped to the center of the stage.

She rolled her head around her shoulders hearing the tendons creak on both sides. Letting every nerve in her body loosen, she swung her arms back and forth. With one more breath she pulled the words to her.

"This may come as a shock to you, Dominique." Her voice squeaked annoyingly, and she cleared her throat. "This may come as a shock to you, Dominique, but the whole world doesn't revolve around you."

Jaylon had completely exhausted his repertoire of children's games. He hadn't bargained on getting asked back for the spring semester, and although he was happy about that, he wasn't prepared for it. He had seen the rows upon rows of exercise books in Mrs. Allen's backstage office, and he was sure she would let him borrow a couple for a good cause.

With a yank he opened the auditorium door and stepped into the darkness on the other side. He hadn't expected the stage lights to be on or for anyone to even be in the room, but he realized in the next second that someone was on stage. Instantly his motion stopped as he looked to the stage.

"Not according to my mom," Camille was saying, her voice a mere whisper from where he stood.

His steps quieted as he shrank back to the edge of the auditorium.

"To her, an education's everything," Camille said, her voice straining. "So I decided that I wasn't going to be the person on the outside, I was going to be on the inside of that office, and I'd never treat my workers the way they treated my mom."

She waited a beat, and then two as his line traveled through his mind.

"It doesn't matter," she said, and his ears picked up the defiance. "I'm going to be something. Something big. Something powerful. Something so important that people can't make me feel...like I'm not enough."

Her head fell, and he saw the shake of her head. She closed her eyes and then opened them again. "Not according to my mom."

The scene repeated itself in front of his eyes. First once, then twice even as the questions ran through his head. Why was she here—before school in an empty auditorium? Running lines that she had long since memorized? It made no sense.

At that moment on stage Mrs. Allen walked out, and Jaylon froze.

"Camille, what are you doing here?"

"Oh." Camille turned in a breath. "Umm, I was just getting in a little extra practice."

"Well," Mrs. Allen said, softening, "I admire your spirit."

Quietly he backed to the door, opened it, and slipped out into the bright hallway even as his brain continued to run through the questions. Why did she think she needed extra practice? She was already practicing every waking hour the way it was. He wanted to ask her, but it was obvious that she didn't want anyone to know what she was doing.

All morning his brain worked on the problem. At lunch he sat beside her, and he could see the missed sleep in her eyes as she sat, reading her Economics book; however, their lunch companions didn't seem to notice anything out of the ordinary.

"So, what do you say?" Lexie asked as a general question to the table. "The movie starts at seven."

Jaylon noticed the sidelong glance Camille shot at him even as to all the outside world she continued to read.

"I've got homework," she said quietly as she reached for her milk carton.

"You've always got homework," Lexie said in frustration.

"I know," Camille said, and Jaylon could hear the tightrope her voice was walking on even as she glanced at him again. "But I'm kind of behind."

Lexie laughed softly. "Yeah, right."

"Actually I can't really go either," Jaylon said as his mind searched for a believable excuse. "I've got relatives coming in tonight. My dad kind of wants me to be there."

"Oh," Lexie said, and she looked like she might give voice to her annoyance. "Fine, then. Nick, would you like to go to the movies with me?"

"Sure," he said with a smile that barely masked his concern. "That sounds like fun."

Camille was still buried in her book when Jaylon got to the auditorium later that afternoon. Quietly he slipped into the seat next to her and settled in. Her attention from the material never wavered. When he noticed Nick enter from the other side, Jaylon put his finger to his lips without ever making a sound.

Nick nodded even as he took the seat next to hers. Jaylon couldn't help but watch her. Her intensity was fascinating.

"We'll go ahead and get started," Mrs. Allen said from the stage. "Umm, we'll take up where we left off yesterday with the Dominique-Lauren fight."

Camille never moved, so gently Jaylon nudged her with his elbow. "Cam, that's you."

"What?" she asked, looking at him with unseeing eyes.

He pointed to the stage. "That's you."

She looked up at the stage and then nodded as she closed her book. Her legs stood her up and walked her down the aisle as Jaylon watched her, and his own face contorted with concern.

As the two of them started on stage, Nick slid into the seat at Jaylon's elbow.

"What is up with her?" Nick asked.

Jaylon shook his head. "I don't know, but I'm worried."

"So am I," Nick said.

"Louder, Camille," Mrs. Allen said, and Jaylon noticed the frustration slide across her face.

"I'm not acting like anything," she said, and he winced at the pain in her voice.

Being on stage was putting yourself into a pressure cooker of emotions the way it was, and being yelled at by the director with everyone there to watch didn't help anything either. His attention honed in on her then. He could see it, the struggle to make everyone else happy. The fight to not mess anything up. His mind floated back to the tree as she scribbled furiously in her notebook and as she put it down to be with him. She was trying. There was no questioning that. But what was suddenly even more obvious was the fact that she felt she was failing.

"This may come as a shock to you, Dominique, but the whole world doesn't revolve around you."

As he watched her, his mind traced back through the time they had spent together, and the fact that her world revolved around everyone but her suddenly came into perfect focus. Daria, her mother, Lexie, Nick, even Jaylon himself. She was living her life for them. Even her studying seemed to be more about pleasing the teachers than it was about pleasing herself.

"Louder, Camille," Mrs. Allen said. "Louder."

His soul wound around the unshed tears in her voice.

"I don't have to stand here and take this," she said emphatically, the scripted line falling a little too close into reality.

"You mark my words," Ariana said harshly. "He'll dump you the second he no longer needs you to make a point."

All Jaylon wanted to do was wrap his arms around Camille at that moment and let her tears fall.

"Hey, I need to talk to Mrs. Allen a minute," Jaylon said to her when class was over. "Can you wait for me?"

Camille shrugged and sat down in the row, pulling a book to her lap even as she did.

"I'll see you guys Monday," Nick said, and Jaylon waved to him. Nick looked at Camille's head already bowed over the book. "Take care of her," Nick mouthed.

Jaylon nodded to him seriously and then bent down to her. "I'll just be a minute."

Camille nodded imperceptibly. With a sigh, he turned away and walked up the stage steps to the back of the stage where Mrs. Allen's office was tucked away. As he neared the office, however, he heard the voices and silenced his steps.

"I'm going to give her a few more days," Mrs. Allen said, "but I don't really think that's going to do too much good. I think we're going to have to be realistic. Ariana stepping in really won't be a big problem, but Tessa's going to need all the practice time she can get to make Dominique play right."

"It's too bad. Camille did such a good job at the audition," Kara said.

"Well, I think that was just a flash in the pan," Mrs. Allen said.

At the door to her office Jaylon reached up and knocked.

"Jaylon," Mrs. Allen said in surprise. "What's up?"

"I was just wondering if I could borrow one of your exercise books. I'm running out of material for the kids at the center."

"Oh, of course." Mrs. Allen stood and turned to her bookshelves as Jaylon and Kara exchanged polite nods.

"How's that going?" Mrs. Allen asked.

"Pretty well. The kids are great, and it's been great to have Camille there to help." The comment was an indirect plea on her part.

"Oh, I didn't know Camille was helping you," Mrs. Allen said in surprise.

"Yeah, her little sister's taking the class, so she stays and helps with what she can."

Mrs. Allen turned with three books in her hands. "Well, I'm glad to see her interest in drama isn't confined to our walls."

"Yeah," he said, accepting the books. "Thanks."

She nodded, and he turned to leave.

"Oh, by the way," he said, turning back. "I think Camille and I are going to work awhile out here. Is that all right?"

"Sure," Mrs. Allen said, and the smile on her face told him all he needed to know. By Monday, Camille would be out and Ariana would be in if he didn't do something to stop the switch right now.

"Thanks." He looked at Kara. "Take care."

And then he slipped out and back up onto the stage. Determination surged through him when he saw her still studying in the audience. She could do this. He knew she could. All he had to do was convince her of that fact.

"Making any headway?" he asked at her seat.

"Not enough." She shifted the book to the floor before standing to gather her things.

"Umm, listen." Jaylon looked back up through the stage curtains to Mrs. Allen's office. "I was wondering if you might want to get in a little extra practice."

"What's the use?" Camille asked dejectedly. "I could practice from now until forever, and I'm not going to get it."

He looked back at her, his brain stumbling through the ways to help. "You just need a little coaching. Someone to show you how."

She shook her head and reached for her backpack. "It's a waste of time."

He smiled softly, took her backpack from her and set it in the seat. "I'll be the judge of that. Come on. We've got work to do."

With reluctant steps she followed him out of the row and up the aisle. If he could just find a niche of hope in her performance, he was sure she would take hold of it and do everything she could to hold on.

"Now, first," he said when they were on stage. "This is not as hard as it looks. All it takes is a little practice. We'll start with the ABC's."

She looked at him like he was from Mars.

"Trust me." He took hold of her and turned her toward the audience. "Now put your feet a little wider apart. Get a good stance. There you go. Now I want you to say your ABC's loud so they can hear you down in the principal's office."

An annoyed look crossed her face, but she took a breath and started through the alphabet anyway. "A...B..."

Gently he put his hand under her ribcage. "Feel it in here."

"C...D...E..."

"Lower. Use your breath."

"F...G..."

"Not your chest. Think lower."

"H...I...J..."

"Good girl. Yeah, that's it."

"K...L...M..."

"Concentrate."

"N...O...P..."

"Push the air out."

"Q...R...S...T..."

"You've got it. Keep going."

"U...V...W...X...Y...Z."

"Fabulous." He leveled his gaze at her. "Did you feel the difference?"

She nodded.

"Then let's do it again. Close your eyes and feel where that air is coming from."

"A...B...C..."

The ABC's and numbers were going well, but she still wasn't sure she could translate that into the lines in the script. It was just too much to remember.

"How about we try something," Jaylon said with a gleam in his eyes that made Camille's fear shields fly up.

"What?"

"You'll see." He grabbed her hand and pulled her down the steps. When they were in the middle of the center aisle, he stood her on the side they usually sat on. "Stand here."

Then he let her go and crossed to the other side. "Ready?"

She nodded uncertainly, wondering what he had in mind this time.

"Surely you aren't going to listen to Dominique."

"Why not?" Camille asked, picking up her line effortlessly even as she laid her hand into the hollow under her ribs that his hand had vacated.

"Because you know how she is."

Concentrating on the air, Camille pushed the words ahead of it. "No. How is she?"

"Come on, Lauren. Be honest. Have you ever heard her say one good thing about anybody?"

"Hey, that's my sister you're talking about."

"And that includes you. If you're not beneficial to her, it doesn't matter who you are, she'll squash you like a bug." Jaylon held up his hand to stop the reading. "Back up."

Incomprehension struck her. "Huh?"

"Back up." He followed his own advice, stepping backward three seats into the row.

Not really sure what he was up to, Camille followed suit, and when she looked back across at him, he was already back in character.

"I thought you loved her," she said as the words came to her with barely a call.

"Yeah, I thought so too, but all either of us ever cared about was ourselves. We stayed together for the status that being together brought us."

"But everyone thought you were the perfect couple."

Jaylon held up his hand again and stepped back. Barely losing the conversation thread, Camille stepped back as well.

"We were never real," he said, his voice perfectly modulating for the increasing distance between them. "We were going through the motions, doing all the stuff we thought we were supposed to be doing."

"So how do I know that's not what you're doing now? Just going through the motions so it looks good to the outside world."

"Because I'm not."

"How can I know that?"

Still looking at her, Jaylon stepped three more seats back. Her heart couldn't look away from his eyes even as her feet carried her backward.

"How do *you* know?" he asked incredulously. "Well, how does it feel? Does it feel like I'm playing you?"

"I don't know," she said, and the breathing fell just below the surface of her thinking.

"Are you serious?" he asked, the hurt screaming across the growing chasm between them.

"You turned on a dime when Dominique dropped you, and you picked me up without so much as a single look backward. How do I know you won't drop me as soon as you get what you want?"

"And what do you think I want?"

Like dancers in the dark, they each took three more steps backward.

"You tell me," Camille challenged. "What do you want, Hawk? To show Dominique up? Is that what you want?"

Although barely above a whisper, his voice carried right to her with no problem. "No, Lauren. I want you."

Twenty-eight seats and an aisle separated them, but to Camille he was right in front of her. "Is that the truth, Hawk?"

"It's the truth. I promise you, it's the truth."

Camille felt like she'd just been snatched from the very jaws of death. She could do this, and now Mrs. Allen would have no choice but to let her keep the part.

"You want to do another one?" Jaylon asked from across the auditorium.

"Bring it on."

Chapter 21

The next afternoon after their hamburgers were gone, he had little trouble talking her into driving out to the country. They dropped Daria off and made sure their mother was home before they jumped in the car and left the city behind in the rearview mirror.

"So, how's school going?" Jaylon asked when the houses gave way to nature.

Camille laid her head back on the seat, exhausted beyond the breaking point. "Ugh. Too much to do. Not enough time to do it."

"Yeah, I've been noticing how much you've been studying lately."

"Oh, you've noticed that too huh?" Her gaze dropped to her fingers. "Studying's never really been a problem before..."

The sentence trailed off, and he looked over at her. "Before you had a life."

"Something like that." She looked out her window as barren trees flashed by. "At least with the books I've got a fighting chance."

"A fighting chance of what?"

"Of not messing something up." A sigh escaped before she could pull it back. "It just seems like everyone wants something from me, and I can't do enough to please anybody."

"Like me?"

The words ripped through her. "It's not that I don't want to spend time with you. But all the while I'm with you, I keep thinking about all the other stuff I need to be doing." She stopped and deflated. "That sounds awful."

Remarkably he didn't seem offended. "No, it doesn't."

But she was offended enough for both of them. "Yes, it does. If I was really serious about us, I would just forget about everything else."

"Hey, half of us is you," he said solidly, "and I don't want you to lose yourself just to be with me."

Why couldn't she just do it all? That would make things so much easier. "But everything else always seems so important. It's easy to keep pushing you aside. But then I think..."

There was the barest of pauses.

His glance was soft. "What about next year."

"Yeah," she said, deflating further. "What if I'm wasting my time with everything else instead of being with you."

The car crunched over the yellow grass. When he killed the engine, all sounds ceased, but Jaylon never moved.

"For a long time after she died I was angry at my mom," he finally said. "Sure I had memories of her, but I couldn't help but think she should've spent more time with me. She shouldn't have been running off on her errands all the time. And Dad made enough so she could've stayed home.

"It was a long time before I finally understood that I was a part of her life—not her whole life—a part. At first, that made me angry. I should've been everything to her. Then when I was about ten, I flat out told Grandma Lani that I hated my mother for leaving me like that.

"Grandma told me something that I don't think I ever understood until right now. She said, 'J., your mom loved you with all her heart, and she only wanted what was best for you. She would never have dreamed of keeping you right by her side forever because she knew you were meant to live.'"

Slowly he turned to Camille. "Just like you're meant to live. Yes, I want you by my side every second, but that's not what you're here for. You're here to live your life and to follow your dreams and to see where that takes you. I love you too much to deny you that."

Acceptance? Love? Life? Suddenly the car seemed suffocating and small. Camille reached for the door handle frantic for any escape route. In the cold air, she walked away from the car to the tree, pushing his words away from her with every step.

"What's wrong?" he asked when he caught up with her six feet from the drop-off.

"Nothing. I just needed a little air." *And to talk about something else,* she added silently. "So, has your dad come around about the whole NYU thing?"

She felt his concern for her melt away.

"No, he's pretty set that he doesn't want me to go, doesn't think it's a good idea, thinks I'm throwing my life away." Jaylon shrugged. "You get the idea."

"What if you get accepted? What then?"

"Then he'll yell, and I'll yell, and Marianne will say she has a headache and doesn't want to hear anymore. And then I'll leave, and probably never speak to them again. Unless..."

"Unless what?" Camille asked, hearing the break in his armor.

He didn't say anything for a long moment, and then he looked out to the other side. "Unless I give in and do it his way like I've always done."

Camille's eyes narrowed. "When did you give in?"

"A lot of times—especially when I was younger. I've gotten more stubborn with age."

She smiled. "That I know."

In the midst of his anger, Jaylon too smiled for one moment. Then he shook his head. "I just keep thinking about California. I missed my chance once—I don't want to miss it again."

"California? What was in California?"

"UCLA."

Camille shook her head in confusion. "Okay, I know you're smart and everything, but I really don't think UCLA would've accepted you until now."

"That's just it. They had accepted me—not for real school but for their summer drama program. I mean it was right there. I had the acceptance letter in my hand and everything. Three weeks in California with the best teachers UCLA had to offer. And then, I could've just written my ticket. Any school. Anywhere. I would've been set."

"Then, why didn't you go?"

Jaylon's head dropped as sadness washed through his face. "Dad said it was a big waste of time and that he didn't want to hear anymore about it."

"So you went back to be in the play here," Camille said, feeling the pieces fill in around her.

He nodded and then stopped as his eyebrows knitted in the center of his forehead. "How did you know about that?"

She considered begging off the question but decided that he deserved to know the truth. "Nick told me about it."

"Nick? Oh." Jaylon's gaze fell to the ground. "I guess I did a pretty good job of ruining things for him, too."

"Yeah. He thinks so anyway." Her gaze went to his face and held. "Why didn't you tell him—explain? Maybe he would've understood."

Jaylon shook his head. "I couldn't tell anybody. It hurt too much to even think about it, so I just put a big, happy face on and kept going."

"And your dad?"

"He thought I'd just forget about it after that, but I didn't. The next year I auditioned at the theatre again. With Dad away on business most of the time, I could pretty much sneak off when I needed to."

"Sneak off?"

He looked at her like he'd just been cornered. Then he sighed. "I guess it doesn't make any difference now, but Dad never knew about the plays. He would never have agreed to it, so I got really good at sneaking out. He never missed me when I was gone anyway."

"He wasn't worried about you?"

"As long as he thought I was in line with what he wanted, he never really bothered to check. It was easier not to tell him."

"But surely at some point that didn't work. Surely at some point he caught you."

"Oh, yeah. There were a lot of times he'd come home and want to have dinner together or I couldn't make it out before he roped me into something. But basically he lived his life, and I lived mine, and the less we actually got together, the better off we were."

"So, what happened when he caught you?"

Jaylon shrugged. "I'd just stay home for awhile. Make him happy with the whole being together thing, and then he'd get tired of it, and I was free to do whatever I wanted again."

"But what about the people in the play?"

"They always understood. I made it when I could. I always had my part down, so they never really missed me I guess. In fact, I don't think they ever really even noticed."

Camille could think of one person who noticed—intensely. "And when you got to high school?"

"I signed up for drama, so Dad really couldn't do much about that. I think he figured, 'Ah, let him go, he'll get tired of it.' That's why now is so bad. His plan didn't work, so he's mad at me for still liking drama and mad at himself for not finding a way to get it out of my head."

"And that's all right with him? Having a son he barely knows about to go off to college?"

"He doesn't say much anymore. If you ask me, he'll probably be happier when I'm gone and not around to make his life miserable anymore."

"Well, I know that feeling." Camille's train of thought crashed into her mother. "Besides that I won't be around to take care of Dar, I'm not sure Mom will even notice I'm gone next year."

"Who will take care of Dar?" Jaylon asked with instant concern.

The question dug into her. "Probably Dar. I hate it, but she'll have to muddle through just like I did."

Jaylon's head dropped to the side. "How many days did you spend at home alone?"

"Too many to count," Camille said with a laugh. "It was okay though. I read a lot and studied a lot. It was nice to have the apartment to myself."

"But didn't that get old? Being by yourself all the time?"

"I got really good at being alone."

His head bobbed up and down. "I think I'd go crazy if I didn't have a million people around me most of the time."

"And sometimes I think I'll go crazy with one other person around."

"Oh, yeah?" he asked teasingly. "You got anybody in mind when you say that?"

"Umm, no, nobody in particular," she said, smiling even as she shook her head.

Still, he studied her, cutting through her with his eyes like knives. "I don't believe you."

The need to find a shell wrapped over her. "Why not?"

"Because I've seen how you are."

Defiantly she lifted her chin. "Oh, yeah? How am I?"

"All huddled in your little cocoon, afraid to come out. Afraid you might actually have some fun if you let yourself go."

Surprised disbelief thundered through her heart. "Let myself go? I'm out here in the cold with you. What more do you want?"

"This." He lunged at her and caught both of her sides with his fingers.

It was like the hands thing. She knew he was coming before he ever moved, and she slipped away from him and took off running across the field. Then, when she whirled around and crouched low like a tiger that might pounce at any moment, he stopped. She pointed at him menacingly. "You just stay away from me."

His smile was at once teasing and mischievous. "Why? You scared of something?"

"No." She raised her finger higher in warning. "I just know how you are."

"Oh, yeah?" he asked, edging closer to her. "How am I?"

"Now, listen here. I did not come here to play touch football." She circled around him to the edge of the tree again.

"Well, what did you come out here to play?"

"That's not funny."

"It wasn't meant to be."

She leaned from one side of the tree to the other, trying to decide which way to run. "Behave yourself."

"Not possible."

"I've noticed." Picking the side of the tree closest to the slope to make her get away, she took off. However, like lightning he grabbed her and swung her into the air. "Hey, let me go."

"Why? You afraid to have a little fun?"

"I'm not afraid of anything," she said, pushing against him.

"Oh, no? How about the tickle monster."

"Ahh!" she yelled although no one was within a ten-mile earshot. "Stop it! Hey! I said, 'Stop it!' Ahh!"

His fingers managed to find every single vulnerable spot all up and down her ribcage as she collapsed into a helpless heap of giggles. Her feet found the ground but spun with no traction.

"Quit it!" Then as she fought to get away, she felt her foot meet up with something hard, and in a breath they were both falling. "Ahhh!"

The ground and his arm broke her fall as she landed only a half second before he fell on top of her. Stars danced through her head.

"Ugh. That'll teach you," she said, wishing she could sound angrier. Slowly she sat up and rubbed her head. "Oww."

"You think oww. I think my wrist is broken."

For one moment she looked with him in concern. "Really?"

He smiled with amusement. "No, but I made you look."

Defiance flashed through her. "Oh, yeah? Well, we'll just see who's ticklish." She pounced on him with claws out, and in seconds had him squirming to get free.

"Not fair! Hey, you! Quit it! Hey!" Rolling around in the grass, they tussled until they were both out of breath and laughing. Lying side by side, they gazed up at the powder blue sky, dotted in various patterns by white-blue clouds.

Her hand fell to the side and landed on his ribs. "You shouldn't do that."

"Me?"

"Yes, you," she said and picked her hand up to drop it on him again.

Gently he laid his hand on top of hers, and the warmth of it raced through her veins.

"See, that wasn't so bad, was it?" he asked.

"What falling? Or getting tickled to death?"

He rolled over and propped himself up on an elbow until he was leaning over her. "Having fun."

"No," she said softly. "That wasn't so bad." Her eyes fell closed as his lips dropped to hers, and suddenly the cold had no chance to get in. Lost in his kiss, she let herself stop thinking, stop analyzing, stop everything, and just live for one moment in time.

His lips left hers, but the warmth of them didn't. When she opened her eyes, he was looking right into her soul.

"I love you, you know that," he said softly.

With a hard, sharp snap, the spell broke. She pushed up and away from him.

"What? What'd I say?" he asked with concern when she managed to put several inches between them.

She sat, pulling breaths in, and trying to get all the words to line up in her head. She felt his fingers in her hair, pulling the grass free, and her hand reached up self-consciously. She probably looked frightful by now.

"I'm sorry," he said. "I didn't mean to upset you."

"You didn't upset me. I just really need to be getting home. That's all.

I've got to practice some more of that breathing stuff you taught me the other day." And breathing without him right next to her had to be a lot easier than this. Quickly she stood, but his hand caught hers before she took even a step.

"Can I help again?" he asked, and when she looked down at him, the vulnerability was shining in his eyes.

"How is it you always have a way to help me?"

"Because it wasn't so long ago that I was where you are, and it would've been nice to have someone to help me." He crawled to his knees. "What do you say? One more exercise."

What she really should've said was, "No, I should go home," but what she said was, "Okay, what do you got?"

Jaylon watched her on the other side of the slope. Even 30 yards away she was beautiful.

"Ready?" he called over the gapping hole between them.

"I'm ready," she said back.

"Hey, Lauren, whatcha doing?"

Camille cradled her make-believe book up next to her. "Studying."

"Whatcha studying?"

"Homework."

"Homework, huh? At lunch?"

"Is that a problem?"

"A problem, no, but wouldn't it be easier to study tonight at home?"

"Oh, I'll study then too, but I don't really have anything else to do right now. So..."

"Oh," he said taken aback slightly. "Well, what are you reading?"

"Macbeth."

"Macbeth? Wow. That must be fate. That's what we're reading, too." Then he stopped. "But isn't that senior year material?"

"Yeah, so?"

"So, you're not a senior."

"And your point is?"

"Well, you're not a senior and yet you're reading senior material, so unless you've just been accelerated two grades, you can't be studying."

Camille struck her best defensive pose. "I'm getting ahead."

"Two years ahead?"

"Yeah, two years ahead. Want to make something of it?"

"Oh, uh, no. But if you're not studying something for tomorrow and I'm free right now, I was wondering if you'd want to go grab a burger."

"A burger? With you?"

"Do you see anyone else standing here?"

"Unfortunately, no."

"Then what do you say?"

"About what?" Camille asked, bending her head as though she was reading again.

"About burgers."

"Oh, I can't."

"Why not?"

"Because, I'm studying."

A low laugh escaped from Jaylon as he felt the lights blink out on the stage around him. "You know," he called across the chasm. "This is a little too realistic!"

"Hey, this was your idea," she called back with a laugh.

"Then I must be insane," he said as the wind whisked his words away. "Want to try another one?"

"Go for it."

Monday afternoon, Camille decided that rather than waste precious time while she was on stage but not being used, it would be smart to bring her books along onto the stage. Mrs. Allen obviously had little confidence in the possibility that she would be the one to actually perform Lauren, as the teacher worked on every scene that didn't have her in it.

However, even with the book on her lap, it was difficult to keep her mind on her homework and off the fireworks on stage. Ariana and Jaylon were going at it—she accusing him of going after Lauren solely in response to being dumped; he accusing her of chasing after the most popular guy on campus heedless of the fact that she had promised to be his girlfriend only a week before.

When Nick made his grand entrance onto the stage, Camille couldn't help but laugh. Although inside, Camille knew that making doe-eyes at Nick was probably killing her, on the outside Ariana was putting on a very good show.

"Oh, Ethan, I was wondering where you went. I missed you so much."

"Yeah, holding her breath thinking you might not come back was about to kill her," Jaylon said in a nice stage whisper.

"I don't believe we've met," Nick said, extending the hand that wasn't around Ariana.

"Yeah, too bad I got cornered this time," Jaylon said. Then he extended his hand with an annoyed smile. "I'm sure Dominique has told you all about me."

Ariana's eyes shot knives at him as Jaylon smiled at her.

"Why would she do that?" Nick asked, looking down at her.

"Oh, you know," Ariana said quickly. "Old friends, old stories."

"Old loves," Jaylon said, and Nick's face contorted further. "Well, I'd better be going. Lauren and I are supposed to study later."

"Study?" Ariana asked with raised eyebrows.

"Yeah," Jaylon said with a wink. "You remember *studying*."

Ariana's face dropped the mask of complete bliss as Jaylon turned to leave.

"See ya later." Then he turned back to them. "Oh, and good luck, Ethan." Turning back to the audience as he left them behind, he added, "You're going to need it."

Although she had read the lines countless times, Camille laughed. She loved this script. The bell over her head rang, and she jumped. Her gaze fell to her book as she closed it. She hadn't gotten much done, but maybe she would have better luck tomorrow.

"You headed home?" Jaylon asked, offering her a hand up.

"Yeah." She reached down to get her things.

"You need a ride?" His hand came around her back protectively as he guided her down the steps.

"Is that an offer?" she asked, swinging her braid over her shoulder.

"It's an offer if you say yes, a beg if you say no."

"Then yes. I hate to see men beg."

Neither of them ever saw the glowering thespian they left behind.

The next afternoon facing four hours of practice that was sure not to include much of her, Camille hauled her books up to the stage and yanked one out. It didn't really matter which one. She was behind in most of them.

The only good thing that she could see was that Princeton would not get to see these grades before they sent out the acceptance letters—if hers was an acceptance letter. She hunkered down over her Chemistry book, looking forward to four nearly full hours of stuffing her head with formulas.

"Hey, Beautiful," Jaylon said, right in her ear before she even realized he was there. Her pencil point skipped across the page.

"You just love doing that don't you?" she asked in mock annoyance.

"Not half as much as you love me doing it." He leaned on the wall next to her. "So, what are we working on today? Atomic molecular astrophysics? Or no, no wait, modular thermalitical anomalectomy."

She laughed out loud. "You are crazy, you know that?"

"About you," he said so that only she heard, and he ducked his head to nuzzle the side of her neck.

"Hey!"

"That's the bell, people." Mrs. Allen strode onto the stage. "We'll start with the Dominique-Lauren fight so we'll need the card table and chairs out here."

"Duty calls," Camille said, closing her book and standing.

His smile followed her up. "Break a leg."

With a mock angry face, she gazed down on him. "You behave yourself."

He put his head to the side and looked up at her with puppy dog eyes. "Me? I always behave myself."

"Uh-huh. Yeah, right." She shook her head as she straightened her shirt, preparing for her turn in the spotlight. Just then Ariana sauntered by, and although she had the entire stage to walk on, she crashed right into Camille, knocking her back several steps.

"Hey, watch it," Camille said angrily.

"Why don't you watch it?" Ariana shot back.

With not-too-well disguised disgust, Camille finished the straighten job on her shirt and then pointed at Jaylon as though in added warning. Teasingly he winked at her, and she couldn't stop the smile. When she walked across the stage and sat down in the chair that for now would have to resemble a dining chair, she could feel Ariana's gaze, hot with anger descend on her.

"Okay, ladies," Mrs. Allen said as she stepped off the stage and took her seat in the audience. "Whenever you're ready."

"What're you doing?" Ariana asked, prancing into the room that comprised half of the stage.

"Studying," Camille said, and although her head was down, her voice had no problem carrying. "You should try it sometime."

Ariana crossed her arms. "You act like you think you're better than me."

"I'm not *acting* like anything," Camille said, and the irritation in her voice was no act. "Has it ever occurred to you that maybe I'm not even noticing you?"

"Well, you're certainly noticing Hawk."

Camille looked up at Ariana. "And that's a problem?"

Pure hatred rained down from Ariana's eyes. "Let me let you in on a little secret, sis. The only reason Hawk even knows you're alive is because he wants to get back at me."

Brashness drove through the middle of Camille's spirit. "You know, this may come as a shock to you, Dominique, but the world doesn't revolve around you."

"Ethan's does."

"Ethan's does. Yeah, right. Ethan's universe revolves around Ethan. I'm surprised he even notices anyone else is on the planet."

"Oh, wonderful. Now I'm getting advice from a two-year-old."

"Well." Camille stood and pulled her invisible books up with her. "This two-year-old has got a date for the Harvest Ball, which is a lot more than I can say for somebody else in the room."

With one step Camille suddenly stood toe-to-toe with Ariana.

"If you've got something to say, say it," Ariana said, looking down at her furiously.

"If Ethan is dumb enough to go out with you, he deserves what he gets." And with that Camille stomped off, stage left.

It wasn't until she was off the stage that she realized how quiet the auditorium was. Not a sound, not a movement anywhere. It suddenly occurred to her that even Mrs. Allen hadn't said a word the entire scene. That was definitely a first. Carefully Camille peaked out past the curtain just as Mrs. Allen made it to the stage.

"Very, very nice! Both of you." The enthusiasm intertwined every word. "That was so realistic."

A little too realistic for Camille's taste, but she was happy just the same.

"Let's move on to the next scene," Mrs. Allen said. "I need Nick and his cohorts on stage."

With a sigh of relief, Camille chose to walk around the back of the stage rather than across it to get to Jaylon. The less contact she had with the Ice Queen the better. At stage right, just at the top of the steps, she and Jaylon spent the rest of the afternoon thoroughly enjoying warning the other one not to get too far out of line.

In Camille's eyes it was the best practice ever.

Chapter 22

"So, you want some company later?" Camille asked Jaylon as they sat in their spot on the edge of the stage, waiting for the bell to ring.

"Oh, I can't today," he said.

"What, you get the starring role on Broadway or something?"

He shook his head. "No, yesterday was Grandma Lani's birthday. I really wanted to go over and see her."

"Oh," she said, silenced for only a second. Then she smiled. "Well, do you want some company?"

There really wasn't anything to be afraid of, but Camille clutched his hand anyway. She had heard about these places, of course, but she had never had an occasion to visit one. In fact, she didn't know all that many old people. Her mother's parents were both gone, and even when they were alive, she barely ever saw them.

Somehow this all felt as foreign as standing on the stage had that very first time.

"Well, hello, Mr. Gosa. How are you today?" Jaylon asked a hunched over old man who with the help of his walker was inching his way down the hall.

"Hrumph," the old man said.

"Yes, Sir. It is a nice day outside although they say it's supposed to get cold this weekend."

"Hrumph."

"Well, you have a nice day, too." As Camille watched in fascination, Jaylon laid a soft palm on the old man's shoulder. "I'd better go see Grandma Lani. She probably thinks I've forgotten about her."

"Hrumph."

"I'll see you later. You take care. You hear me?"

"Hrumph."

Cowering behind Jaylon and not letting his hand go for even an instant, Camille followed him down the corridor, deeper and deeper into the bright lights. When they turned the corner, the nurse looked up and smiled.

"She's in her room. Would you like me to help you?" the nurse asked without so much as a hello.

Jaylon nodded. "How's she doing?"

"She's been pretty listless lately. I think she missed her grandson."

They walked over to a door couched in the middle of several others.

"Elana," the nurse said with a small knock. "You've got company."

"Hey, Beautiful," Jaylon said, pulling Camille into the room. He let go of her hand long enough to lean down over the bed to give the white-haired, wrinkled old lady a kiss. "Happy Birthday."

The old woman's gaze surveyed him vacuously.

He stepped back to bring Camille to his side. "I brought somebody who wanted to see you."

Camille smiled although she couldn't at all be sure that's how it looked on the outside. "Hi."

Not once did the old woman's gaze register anything.

"I thought we might go over and see the birds today," Jaylon said as the nurse stepped to his side and they began the arduous task of transferring the woman from the bed to the wheelchair. "My special birthday treat."

Camille wished she didn't feel so utterly helpless, but she had no idea of where to even begin to help. Gently Jaylon sat the old woman into the wheelchair and made sure she was strapped in before he nodded in satisfaction.

"I promise I won't do any wheelies," he said, and for all the evidence that this should be a frightening, sad situation, he sounded absolutely ecstatic to be here.

As they walked down the hall, Camille wound her finger through his belt loop and listened as he kept up a non-stop conversation with the air in front of him.

"I bet these birds have been wondering where you got off to," he said. "They always sound so happy to see you. But I guess I can't really blame them. I'm always happy to see you, too."

They crossed over into a slightly darker room, and immediately Camille could hear the birds. When they rounded the next corner, it was easy to see why. What looked like a gazillion birds sat perched in a tree that stretched up into a glassed-in pentagon that soared far above them. Only the top of the cage was glass, however, the bottom was merely tightly knit wire stretched between two poles.

"Listen to them sing." Jaylon parked the chair a few feet from the cage. "Reminds me of the birds when we used to lay under the tree."

In an odd way Camille knew exactly what he was talking about. These birds did sound remarkably like the ones next to the slope. Jaylon pulled two chairs over from the wall and indicated that Camille was to sit in one. She did so, gingerly, not wanting to upset the lady who continued to stare at her with vacant eyes.

"Grandma, this is Camille." Jaylon reached over and took Camille's hand. "She's the one I've been telling you about."

Nothing from the eyes that continued to stare.

"I hope you don't mind, but we've been using your place as kind of our own practice stage. Camille's gotten the lead in the school play."

The eyes continued to stare.

"Yeah," Camille said, struggling to find her voice. "And Jaylon got Hawk. He's really good in that part. You should see him."

Jaylon's hand squeezed hers, swelling the courage in her chest.

"He's also applied to NYU," Camille said with a smile. "He tried out over Christmas, so I'm sure it's just a matter of time before he gets accepted."

Gratefully Jaylon smiled at her. "Camille's going to Princeton. She's going to study Aerospace Engineering." He looked back to the old woman. "Imagine that, me with a brainy woman. Who would've ever guessed? Huh?"

He sat for one moment and then seemed to realize something. "Oh, I brought you something you're going to love." He reached into his jacket and pulled out a small book. "Dickinson. I bought it just for you." Then with only one more glance at Camille, he opened the volume and began reading. "If you were coming in the fall, I'd brush the summer by..."

The eyes never registered anything even resembling recognition or understanding, but by the time they stood to depart, Camille honestly felt like she'd forged a connection with the woman. She was a link to Jaylon's past, and therefore, a link to Jaylon himself.

Never in all the world would any of their friends at school have guessed that the Jaylon Quinn they knew would sneak off to an old folks' home to read poetry to an old woman who would never so much as know who he was anymore. But from the Jaylon she was beginning to know, it fit perfectly.

She waited until they were back in the car and headed across town to her place before she broached the question that had been on her mind for months. "You never told me. How did your mom die?"

Jaylon looked over at her and then returned his gaze to the road. "Brain cancer."

Camille wanted to say something, but besides, "Sorry," she could find nothing.

"They found out in April, and three days after my birthday in August, she died. It was a really aggressive form, right on the brain stem. They did radiation and chemo, but I think all that accomplished was making her sick faster."

"How old were you?"

"Five. I turned six right before she died. Man, I still remember that party. She was so weak, she couldn't even sit up, but she wouldn't let them take her to the hospital. So she laid on her bed and sang happy birthday to me. That's one of the last things I remember about her."

His tone was the only thing that belayed the pain underneath the words. Softly Camille's gaze snagged on his silhouette.

"Dad's solution was just to stay at work. The more he worked, the less he thought about her...or me. I think it was easier for him not to think."

"But if he was working, who took care of...? Grandma Lani," she said as that piece clicked into place.

He nodded as his hands guided the car to her curb and went about the normal tasks of parking. "Marianne always says how nice she thinks it is that I still visit her, but I just think it's pay backs."

The noise around her ceased as Camille's hand went to his shoulder. "She's lucky to have you."

"No, I was lucky to have her," he said as a small tear slid down the side of his cheek.

"It's okay, you know," Camille said softly. "A few tears never hurt anybody."

When he looked at her, the anguish in his face said all that a million tears never could. "I miss them."

"I know." And then she folded him into her shoulder and held him as twelve years of unshed tears finally came to the surface. "I know."

"Camille," Mrs. Allen called from the foot of the stage two weeks later. "Honey, where did Lauren go? I think you lost her about three lines back."

"That wasn't the right line?" Camille asked, stepping back and scratching her ear.

"It was the right line, but it sounded like you were reading it right out of the script."

Although she wasn't quite sure that was a bad thing, Camille nodded.

"Try it again. Okay?"

"The Harvest Ball, wow," Stephanie said as they sat in Lauren's stage bedroom. "You must be in heaven."

"I just wish I could figure out why he asked me," Camille said as she sat, facing the audience that was supposed to be her mirror.

Stephanie's head fell to the side just as it always did. "Maybe he asked you because he likes you."

"Oh, yeah. And it had nothing to do with the fact that Dominique is my sister."

"Is it so hard to believe that he might actually like you?"

"Look at me. Who in their right mind would put the two of us together? Certainly not me."

"Camille," Mrs. Allen called. "You're doing it again. Don't just say the line. You have to feel the line, be the line. Okay? Try it again."

"Feel the line, be the line," Camille said, pulling herself up straighter. "Feel the line..."

"The Harvest Ball, wow."

When practice broke up, Mrs. Allen called Camille over to the side, and Camille reluctantly obeyed. This was not going to be fun.

"Camille, honey, I have to say, I can tell how hard you're working. I'm really impressed with the improvement in your projection."

"Thank you," Camille said, not at all sure the comment was a compliment.

"There's just one little thing. Umm, how do I put this? Sometimes you nail the lines so well, you blow me away, but sometimes you act like you're just a wooden puppet saying lines somebody else wrote. You're not feeling the part. It's all in your head. But acting doesn't come from your head, it comes from your heart."

I thought it came from your diaphragm.

"Work on it, okay?" Mrs. Allen said with a nod. "I trust you. You can get it. If you can make yourself believe you can get it, you'll be fine."

"I'll work on it," Camille said softly, and there was a beat of silence between them. Then Camille glanced over her shoulder. "Umm, is that all?"

Mrs. Allen waved her off, and Camille hurried to the edge of the stage to gather her books.

"What'd she want?" Jaylon asked, meeting her on the steps with concern.

"Oh, you know, I'm out of my league, and I should never gone out for drama in the first place." Camille swung her braid over her shoulder and stomped off the stage. "Same old thing."

"She said that?" he hissed, following her.

"No, but that's what she meant."

Depression hit Camille like a hard fist as she pushed out into the hallway. If she won the Nobel Prize, somebody would be there with the proof that she really hadn't deserved it. That was her life. Trying and trying, but never quite grasping that fabled golden ring.

"Is it the whole just saying the lines thing?" Jaylon asked, keeping up with her every step down the hallway even though she really wished he wouldn't.

Camille shrugged. "That's the point. Isn't it? Saying lines?"

"Well, kind of, but not really."

"Well, then enlighten me, Oh, Master of the Universe." She wrenched her locker door open. "What is the point of this?"

He regarded her for a moment and then plunged in. "You're not being Lauren. You're Camille acting like you're being Lauren."

"Yeah, so?"

"You can't do that. You have to *be* Lauren."

Confusion and fury crossed through her eyes.

He thought for another moment. "It's like learning Spanish. When you first start trying to learn it, you have to translate everything. Someone says something in Spanish, and you hear it in Spanish, but then in your head you have to translate what they said into English. Then you have to come up with something to say back in English, but before you can say it back, you have to translate it into Spanish."

Her look of annoyance deepened. For all she knew, he might be speaking Spanish right now for as much sense as all this was making to her.

"But then," he said as his face brightened, "somewhere in the middle of second year or so, someone says something in Spanish, and you reply in Spanish—no translating." He looked at her with understanding. "Right now, you're translating Lauren. Don't be you playing her—be her."

Be her. Two simple words. Five simple letters, and yet it was more difficult to accomplish than dissecting and explaining Einstein's Theory of Relativity.

In utter frustration, Camille stood in front of her mirror. *Be her. Be her. Be Lauren.* "I don't even know who Lauren is. Who is she?" Camille gazed into the mirror. "Who are you, Lauren?"

Then, as Camille stood there, looking into her own reflection, the eyes gazing back at her changed, and the words that began flowing from the middle of her seemed those of someone else entirely, and yet it was she who was speaking them.

"Nobody can ever love me for me," Lauren said softly. "I don't deserve something like that to happen, so the only explanation is that they have some ulterior motive—that liking me can get them something. Hawk is no different. He doesn't really love me. He can't love me because I don't love me.

"I look at me in the mirror, and I don't even know myself. I don't want to know myself. I want to bury my head in some book and stay there forever because books are safe. Hawk is not. Loving Hawk is not. Just like loving myself is not.

"It's safer to put a mask on and push the world away from me. It's safer than trying to believe that I could have something to contribute. Something good. Something no one else could ever give the world. That's why I hide. That's why."

The next moment and the next passed as Camille looked into Lauren's eyes, and for all the rationalizations of her mind, all Camille wanted to do was put her arms around the girl, and tell her that no matter how much sense it didn't make, Hawk really did love her.

"You are special," Camille said to her reflection, "and you are beautiful. Don't just listen to that. Believe it because it's true. You are worthy of love. Don't cheat yourself out of that because it's safe. It's not safe. It's lonely and it's painful, and you deserve better."

The veil lifted for a split second, and Camille was gazing into her own eyes again. An echo in her heart was the only thing that repeated: "You deserve better."

"Dominique, what's wrong?" Tessa asked as Ariana stomped onto the stage during the last non-dress rehearsal, and for a second, Camille wondered how she would ever pull that off in heels for the performance.

One thing, however, was more than clear, Ariana would have no trouble completely losing her composure.

"Ethan Drake is a jerk!" Ariana spat.

"What happened?" Tessa asked fearfully.

"Mindy Tarlington. Uck!" Ariana looked angrily at Tessa. "He was kissing Mindy Tarlington!"

"Oh, boy," Tessa said just as Nick rushed onto the stage.

"Dominique, hey. What'd you run off for?"

Dominique whirled on him. "I can't believe you can stand there and ask me that question."

Ethan stumbled for an apology. "What you saw...that wasn't me. I mean, yeah, it was me, but it wasn't what it looked like."

"Well, it looked like you were performing a tonsillectomy without the anesthetic!"

"But I didn't do anything. She slipped, and I was helping her up."

"How? With mouth-to-mouth?" Ariana looked at him with open contempt. "That's it. I've had enough."

"Enough?"

"Yes, enough. Enough of this! Enough of you! You're an egotistical, selfish, conceited, arrogant..."

"Hey," Nick said with a small, uncaring laugh. "Right back at you, Babe."

The rage boiling in Ariana's eyes was red hot. "That's it. Get out of my sight."

He stood for one more moment. "Gladly." Then he turned and caught Jill under his arm before he stomped off stage with Jill gazing at him in awestruck admiration.

"Don't let the door hit you on the way out," Ariana called as she planted her arms on her chest.

Tessa waited a full beat. "Don't worry about him, Dominique. You can do better."

But Ariana was already glaring at the happy couple, locked in each other's arms across the dance floor. "If you'll excuse me, I've got someone to speak with."

"Dominique," Tessa said, but it was obviously too late as Ariana was already halfway across the dance floor.

"So, Hawk," Ariana said, standing next to the swaying couple. "I can't believe you actually went through with this whole date thing."

Jaylon glanced up with a glare. "Leave us alone, Dominique." He lowered his head back to Camille's shoulder and commenced dancing.

Ariana shook her head slowly. "Lauren, Lauren, Lauren. Little baby sister. I never thought you could be so gullible."

Camille turned her head into his chest, trying to get away from Ariana's tirade.

"Let me guess," Ariana said as though she was Camille's best friend rather than her archenemy. "I bet he told you this was forever. I bet he told you it was fate. He used the same lines on me, you know."

"Dominique," Hawk said in warning.

"What? Are you afraid of what will happen if she knows the truth? If she knows that all you wanted was to make me mad."

"Dominique."

"I told you," Ariana said to Camille with a derisive snort. "I told you it was all a big game to him. He was never interested in you—he just used you to get back at me."

"I said, 'Leave us alone,'" Hawk said as his voice notched up a level.

"If you don't believe me, look at him," Ariana said. "Hawk never could lie with his eyes. You could always read him like an open book. Go on. Look at him, and ask him if I'm lying."

Heat poured through her as Camille's entire body filled with dread. She pulled away from Jaylon and looked at him, fighting the actual fear she could feel rising in her. "Is that true, Hawk?"

His gaze pleaded with her for forgiveness even as he trained it on hers. They stood, inches apart, locked in the direst of conversations.

"It is true," she said as her eyebrows narrowed. The next words were in her head, but it was impossible to get them out of her mouth. So, without the benefit of her parting lines, she broke away from him and ran off the stage.

"No, wait," he called, the second she left his grasp.

"Too bad," Ariana said when Camille was safely off stage.

Hawk turned to her with hate in his eyes. "How could I ever think I loved you?"

Ariana never flinched. "You're asking me?"

His jaw set as he glowered at her. Then he shook his head and turned. "Lauren, wait!"

Mrs. Allen stood from her seat in the audience. "Excellent. Very, very nice. Except, umm, Camille, Sweetheart, where were your last lines?"

Camille stepped out from backstage into the glaring lights. "I just thought it would be more effective if I just ran off."

"Yes, well, Dear. Those lines are the key to the next scene. They need to be there. In the future please remember to speak them before you run off. Other than that, very nice." She looked at her watch. "Well, gang, be ready, tomorrow we'll do our full dress rehearsal. Then we've got one more on Thursday. Friday it's for real."

Panic surged through Camille. Three days. Somehow it had seemed further away than that.

"You up for a little country drive?" Jaylon asked, sliding up next to her as the group broke for the evening.

Camille looked at him, and although she knew she should tell him no, not one part of her wanted to. Next week she would catch up. Next week she would worry about everything else. "Let's go."

Tiny buds sprouted right out of the tree limbs above them.

"I just love Spring," Jaylon said, breathing in as he held her. "I think they put the Spring Production in March just so you could feel like this."

"What? Panicked?" she asked only slightly teasing.

"Panicked?" He arched his head to look at her. "You've got Lauren down. Nobody could do it better."

"I don't know. That last scene...I'm not so sure about it."

"Why not?"

"Mrs. Allen wants this big production of how hurt Lauren is. I just don't think I can pull that off."

"Yeah, but you've nailed everything else, why would that be a problem?"

Camille sighed. "It's the whole, 'You lied to me' part. I mean, he lied to her, so what? It happens all the time. Get over it already."

With concern etching deeper onto his face, Jaylon arched his neck to get a better look at her. "You know I had that problem once. I couldn't let myself get angry. The director kept trying to explain it to me and explain it to me. But I just couldn't do it. So he sent me outside with this stick and I was supposed to hit it against the side of the building and say, 'I'm angry. I'm angry.'" Jaylon smiled at the skeptical look on her face. "I know it sounds stupid, but it worked."

She settled back against his chest as the birds chirped above them.

"Hey," he said slowly.

"No," she said instantly shaking her head.

"Why not? It might help, and it certainly couldn't hurt."

"Can't we just leave good enough alone?" she asked, wanting him to forget the whole stupid idea, but he was already up in search of a stick.

"Here we go." He walked back to her with what looked more like a whole tree limb.

"I don't want to do this."

"Of course you don't. Now, stand up."

In frustration she pushed up from the base of the tree.

"Here, now hold this." He forced the limb into her hand. "Now, hit the tree and say, 'You lied to me.'"

Like a wet noodle she tapped the side of the tree. "You lied to me."

"Oh, come on, you can do better than that. Hit it!"

"You lied to me," she said only slightly louder as the branch rapped against the tree.

"Harder."

"You lied to me." Her hand swung the branch, and it met the tree with a small thwack.

"Harder."

"You lied to me." The branch in her hands vibrated when it hit the tree causing shockwaves to race up her arm. "You lied to me!" She hit the tree again, and the stinging pain in her hand was matched only by that in her soul. The chains holding her true anger in check cracked. "You lied to me! You lied to me! You lied to me!"

With every utterance of the phrase she beat the tree harder until hysteria began to take over her being. "You lied to me! You lied! You lied! How could you lie like that? How could you just walk away like that? I trusted you!"

Sanity flew from her as her body was pulled backward away from her target, and yet she fought to batter it more, just as it had battered her. "You were never coming back! Never!"

"Camille. Camille," Jaylon's frantic voice broke through her sobs of grief and pain. "Camille."

Suddenly all the motion in her body ceased, and dull numbness enveloped her. She looked at Jaylon, but saw only the eyes from so long ago. "Why did you leave me?"

No words answered as Jaylon simply folded her into the warmth of his embrace and held her there as she cried. Tears upon tears upon tears, until she thought there could be no more, and still they formed, pushing up out of her heart in one long unstoppable march.

"Shh," Jaylon said, and she felt herself moving although she couldn't be sure how. Then she was sitting, encapsulated by him. Never speaking, he simple rocked her gently.

Slowly the pain numbed again, and her senses returned. She sniffed, fighting to corral the last of the tears.

"Who left you?" he asked in the air right next to her ear.

A shadow of a man's face floated into her mind. He was supposed to be someone she could trust, someone who would never let her down. He was her hero, and admitting that he'd lied meant admitting that he really wasn't coming back, that the hope would from this moment on be forever extinguished like a puff of flame on a dark, stormy night.

"It was a long time ago," she said as though that should erase the agony she had been in from that moment to this.

"Who was it?"

She buried her head, searching for the warmth of him, but all she could really feel was the cold ice of betrayal. "My dad." The pain and tears threatened again, but she beat them back as she had gotten so good at doing.

"How did he lie to you?"

"He told me he was coming back. He told me he loved me and that he would be back, but he wasn't coming back. He was leaving for good, and he knew it." She sniffed in defense of the small, frightened child looking pleadingly into her father's eyes.

His words brushed through the trees as his face hovered in front of her. "You be good for your mama, now. You hear? You work real hard in school, and you take good care of everything."

"I don't want you to go," the middle of her heart said.

"Come on, Baby. This isn't forever. I love you, and I'll be back. I promise."

Her heart crumpled over itself. "He lied to me, and he knew he was lying."

"People make mistakes," Jaylon breathed. "But holding on to those mistakes only hurts you. He took your childhood. Don't let him take the rest of your life too."

"But it hurts so bad."

"I know," he said as he rubbed the center of her back with the full weight of his palm. "I know."

Chapter 23

"Ten minutes to curtain," Kara called down the back stage corridor.

Both of Camille's palms went damp with the sweat pouring from them.

"Hold still," Misty said as she stood in front of the chair where Camille sat.

"I'm trying," Camille said even as her knee bounced up and down.

Misty backed up and looked at her sternly, the mascara brush held like a weapon. "If you don't hold still, you're going to look like a clown."

"We wouldn't want that. Now would we?" Ariana asked from behind them sarcastically as she stepped into the room.

"Oh, Ariana, stick a sock in it," Camille said furiously.

Ariana never moved. "Touchy. Touchy."

"Save it for the stage," Camille said, fighting to keep her eyes from blinking as Misty attacked again, and Ariana flounced out.

"Five minutes," Kara called into the room.

"Oh, no," Camille said in absolute horror.

"What?" Misty asked, stopping her work to stare at Camille.

"I've forgotten everything!"

Misty looked at her and laughed. "Actresses."

But Camille wasn't kidding.

When she took her seat at the table just down from Jaylon on the stage, Camille picked up her prop book and willed her mind to stay with her. Three hours and this would all be over. Well, at least this night would be over. There was always tomorrow night to have to deal with. Frantically, she readjusted her glasses in an all out attempt not to go stark-raving mad.

Just before the last of her sanity slipped through her grasp, she glanced down the table at Jaylon.

"And now, we present, *Don't Listen to the Fates*," Mrs. Allen said from the other side of the curtain, and then just before the lights collapsed the stage into darkness, Jaylon winked at her and smiled. The magic box of her heart opened, and her soul stepped out.

Even with her eyes closed, she felt the lights come up as a calm confidence she had never before experienced flooded through her. "You are worthy of love, Lauren," her head said softly. "Don't cheat yourself out of that because it's safe. It's not safe. It's lonely and it's painful, and you deserve better."

"My, my, Elaine, what are we celebrating?" Mark asked, and Camille felt Lauren take over.

"Woohoo!" Jaylon whooped as the curtain fell on their final curtain call of the evening. "We did it! Yes!"

Joyous cheers met his and rose above the stage. Camille was still in a state of shock. It was over. Their first performance was history, and she hadn't missed a single line, a single cue.

In her hands was a bouquet of roses, too numerous to count, and to unbelievable to comprehend.

"Good job, Camille." Nick stepped over to her and wrapped her in his embrace. "Man, you were amazing."

"Thanks," she said into his shirt.

"What do you say?" Jaylon called above the din. "Party at Sal's?"

More cheers erupted around them as Mrs. Allen stepped into the midst of the celebration. "Your attention, please."

The noise level plummeted.

"Very, very nice," Mrs. Allen said, and several of the actors hugged each other again. "But, we still have tomorrow night's performance. So, I want you all to go home and get a good night's sleep tonight."

Heads around the stage nodded although not one of them intended on sleeping anytime soon.

"Congratulations," Mrs. Allen said. "Oh, and I expect you all to be here tomorrow night at five p.m. sharp."

No one moved or said a thing until their teacher had again vacated the stage. Then it was like the earth coming back to life over the early morning dew. First one person moved, then another, then another until suddenly everyone was talking and laughing and congratulating each other again.

People Camille didn't even know were coming up to say how much they adored her performance. All she could do was smile and look over to Jaylon. Without him, she would've been out months ago—of that she had absolutely no doubt.

"Hey, Beautiful," Jaylon said, sliding up beside her and taking her hand in his between them many long minutes later as the crowd began to thin. "I've got to run home and change before we go. You want to come—or you could ride over with Nick and Lex."

Camille looked down at her attire—a bright pink, frilly lace and crinoline number the wardrobe department had thought was perfect. "Can I change first?"

When her gaze came up and met his, it was obvious he was trying not to laugh. "If I said, 'Please,' would I hurt your feelings?"

She laughed then. "No, hang on. I'll just be a minute."

Flowers in one hand and half her dress in the other, she shouldered her way back stage to where Misty was busy putting the make-up away for the night.

"Hey, could you help me with this?" Camille asked.

Misty smiled. "Sure thing."

In jeans and a T-shirt with the dress hung up, her make-up sand papered off, and her hair firmly back in a braid, Camille felt almost normal again. When she stepped back out onto the stage, no one seemed to even notice her.

"Ahh, the short life of fame," she mumbled.

"You ready?" Jaylon who had also changed into street clothes asked in her ear.

"Yeah."

"Let's get out of here."

To Camille this was just another ride in Jaylon's car, no big deal until they rounded the last curve and headed up the street for his house. At the curb, her nerves suddenly took over. "I think I'll just wait out here."

"Oh, come on," he said with a grin. "They won't bite."

However, Camille wasn't too sure about that. She clung to Jaylon's hand even as they stepped up the walk and into the foyer.

"Jaylon, is that you?" his father called from the back.

"Yeah," Jaylon called back, and before she could protest, he turned his steps and led her right into the den. "I'm just going to go change right quick."

In the old recliner his father, who was busy reading the paper, nodded. Then he looked up over the top of his reading glasses and saw Camille. "Oh, good evening."

"Hello," she said in fear as Jaylon pushed her in front of him.

"I'll just be a minute," he whispered in her ear, and then with a discreet peck on the cheek, he left her standing on the threshold of certain disaster.

"Please, have a seat," Mr. Quinn said, indicating the plaid couch to his right.

"Oh, of course, thank you," she said as she prayed her legs would hold her long enough to get her to her destination. Carefully she sat down.

"So, the performance went all right?" Mr. Quinn asked, and she could tell it was simply a feeble attempt at conversation.

"Yes, it went well, but I was kind of surprised you weren't there to see that for yourself." The words were out of her mouth before she knew they were in her head. Instantly fear struck her heart as she looked over at the man who was at least twice her size.

He lifted his paper a little higher. "I'm not really into all that theatre stuff."

"Oh, no. I didn't mean you were," she said, berating her tongue for its insistence that she say anything. "I just meant I thought you'd be more into your son than that."

The edge of his paper dropped, and he glared at her over his glasses. "That's a pretty strong statement."

"Why?" she asked as utter recklessness took over. "Because I said it out loud or because it's the truth?"

Annoyance with his current houseguest jumped to the surface as Mr. Quinn dropped the paper altogether. "Well, if you must know, I think this whole theatre business is a silly waste of time, and I can't understand why anyone would put so much time and effort into such a useless pursuit."

Although he was staring at her with knives, Camille couldn't help but laugh.

"What's so funny?" he asked as his eyes narrowed even further.

"Nothing. It's just that I used to think the same thing, but if there's one thing I've learned in the last seven months, it's that you don't have to understand somebody else to love them for who they are."

"Oh, really?"

"Besides," Camille said softening, "Jaylon doesn't need you to understand him or his dream. He just needs you to support him whether or not you understand what he's doing."

Mr. Quinn's face scrunched in annoyance. "How can I support him if he's throwing his life away?"

Camille sat for a long moment simply gazing at him as all the fear in her heart dispersed. "With all due respect, Mr. Quinn, aren't you throwing his life away right now?" She waited a moment for the rest of her courage to surface before she continued.

"You say you love him, but if you really love him, you have to love all the parts of him—even those you don't like very much, even the parts that don't make any sense to you. That's love. You can't pick and choose the parts of him you like or stick him into a box he hates and call that love. He's got the right to live his own life—to have his own dreams. If you reject his dream, then you reject him."

The older man sat in total silence when her words wound to a stop, and although she knew someone should say what she just had, she wasn't at all sure it should've been her.

A noise at the threshold startled both of them out of their thoughts.

"Hey," Jaylon said from the door softly. "You ready?"

"Yeah." She stood from the couch, and Mr. Quinn followed her up. She turned to him and smiled slightly as she reached out her hand to his. "Thank you for having me. I hope to see you again sometime."

Like a flower opening, Mr. Quinn smiled at her and shook her hand. "You can count on it."

"What was up with you and my dad?" Jaylon asked when they were alone for the first moment at the party. He had wanted to ask ever since he walked in the room, but his fear simply hadn't let him until now.

"We were just talking," Camille said with a shrug. "Getting to know each other."

Stephanie stepped up then as Jaylon nodded with no understanding whatsoever. Ariana had never said six words to his father, much less sat and talked with him. The prospect of the possible topics of conversation made the hairs on the back of his neck stand straight up on end.

"Steph wants to show me something," Camille said, breaking into his thoughts. "I'll be right back."

Again Jaylon nodded only vaguely aware of what she'd said this time, but before he had a chance to question it, they were gone.

"I finished it last night," Stephanie said as she hauled the carrying bag into the anteroom of Sal's. "I'm going to wear it for tomorrow night's cast party."

Dread raced through Camille with the mention of the party as her mind's eye scanned through her own closet. The final cast party was supposed to be semi-formal, which to her meant catastrophe.

Carefully Stephanie pulled the dress out of the bag. "What do you think?"

"Oh, Steph," Camille said as her breath was stolen right from her chest. "It's gorgeous!"

The light sea foam blue satin hung gracefully on the hanger. The top was held up with straps but was covered by a matching stole that when worn would bare the shoulders but look part of the bodice. The center of the stole was held together with a faux diamond pin that was eye-catching to say the least.

"You *made* this?" Camille asked incredulously as she fingered the soft satin.

"It took me two months—what with practices and all."

"When you said you sewed, I didn't think...wow."

Stephanie's smile spread across her whole face. "I wanted to show it to you."

"Why?" Camille asked, coming back from prom dress la-la land.

Slowly Stephanie shrugged. "I guess what you think means a lot to me." The younger girl's gaze tumbled to her shoes. "I never would've had the guts to get up there tonight if it wasn't for you."

Camille's eyes widened. "Why not?"

"You weren't a natural," Stephanie said with a single glance up, "but you didn't let that stop you. I figured if you could do it, so could I."

"Well," Camille said, reaching out and giving her friend a hug, "I'm glad you did. It was nice having a friend up there tonight."

Again Stephanie's smile spread across her face just as the party sounds brought them back into Sal's.

"Well, I'd better get this back out to the car before it gets messed up."

With one more nod Camille left her friend and wandered back into the party where Jaylon was standing, talking to Nick and Lexie. Quietly Camille stepped up and twisted her finger through Jaylon's belt loop.

"Hey." He wrapped his arm around her. "I was wondering where you went."

Before she could reply, a yawn wrenched her whole body. "Oh, sorry." She put her hand to her mouth. "It's been a long day." She shook the yawn off as Jaylon gazed at her with a laugh.

"Well, I'd better get our lead home. I'd hate to have to rely on Ari to get us through tomorrow night."

Nick laughed and then opened his arms for Camille one last time. "You did good, girl."

"Thanks," she said, and then she let him go to face Lexie whose eyes were shining in a way Camille had never seen them before.

"I hardly recognized you up there," Lexie said.

Camille's eyebrows went up. "Is that a good thing?"

"Yeah," Lexie said. "It's a very good thing."

At her door, Camille couldn't stop the yawns. "Oh, sorry."

Jaylon's eyes danced when he looked at her. "Tomorrow night we're going to party all night." He wrapped her in his arms and held her for a lingering moment. "But right now you better go get some sleep, or you might fall asleep during that fight scene with Dominique."

Camille smiled. "We wouldn't want that, now would we?"

Gently he pulled her back, and when his gaze touched hers, the moment froze between them. Waiting just one more second, he slowly leaned into her, and his lips brushed hers. Had it not been for his arms around her, Camille was quite sure she would've simply fallen through the earth. His lips, warm and soft on hers, unlocked the tiny magic box deep in her heart, and in the next instant its magic spread through her.

Still in a dream even when his lips were gone, Camille floated on the peace his presence gave her.

"You'll be at the center tomorrow?" he asked, the words barely finding the air between them.

She nodded, not even aware she was moving.

"I can't wait," he said as he pulled her to him once more.

Chapter 24

For most of the morning, Jaylon and Camille ran around acting like the little kids they were supposed to be taking care of. She knew it was silly, but she just couldn't help herself. Never in her life had she felt such happiness.

Spring was definitely in the air by the time they made it out to the country. With his hand in hers, they strolled from the car to the tree.

"You look happy," he said, gazing at her with a smile on his own face.

Her nostrils pulled in the glorious scent of new life all around her. "I am."

They walked several more steps. "So, have you heard from Princeton yet?"

She did a small twirl away from him. "Who cares? Isn't life wonderful?"

Barely keeping the laugh to himself, he looked at her in questioning concern. "It is?"

"Yes, and right now I don't want to think about Princeton or the play or homework or anything. I just want to be right here with you."

"Well, then you're in luck," he said, pulling her to his side even as they continued walking.

She gazed up at him. "Yes, I am."

The hug, which felt like the most natural action in the world, tightened in mid-step. Serenely she pulled in another breath. "You know this must be what heaven feels like."

After two more steps he pulled away from her. "No, do you want to know what heaven feels like?"

Her eyebrows shot up. "What do you have in mind?"

"Come here. I'll show you." Grabbing her hand, he led her around the tree to the swing on the other side.

"Oh, I don't know," she said, looking at it with instant concern.

"Come on. If it held me, it'll definitely hold you." When she looked at him, his eyes were smiling back at her. "One time."

Although it went against all of her better judgment, Camille allowed herself to be guided to the swing. His hand never left hers until she was safely seated, or as safely seated as one can be before she is sent flying over the edge of a 30-foot drop-off.

"You ready?" he asked, and inexplicably she nodded.

Her feet left the ground as she was pulled backward, and then with only the smallest of warnings his hold released, and in the next breath she was sailing over the valley below. Some form of a scream escaped her lungs, but in truth it had too much wonderment mixed with it to be a scream.

At the top of the other side of the pendulum her forward progress stopped, and she dropped back to the earth skimming back over the ground as it reached for her toes. His hands, strong and solid, met her on the other side and sent her once again flying over the edge.

The earth below rescinded its grip on her as body and soul she flew above it. In a completely detached way it was beautiful, like looking down from the perspective of angels. High above the valley, her progress paused and then pulled her back to the earth again. Floating, it was the best word she could use to describe the feeling.

Weightless floating, and as his hands sent her even further up into the air, she surrendered to that feeling—just let it take her. In a burst her soul released every concern she'd ever had, and for one precious moment there was nothing in the world but her and the air and life.

When arm-in-arm they walked up the stage steps at five, her feet still hadn't really touched ground again.

"I'll see you on stage," he said, brushing her cheek lightly with his lips.

"I can't wait," she whispered.

And then he left her to go to the guys' side of the dressing areas. One more breath to confirm this was the greatest day of her life, and Camille turned her own steps to the girls' side.

"How did this happen?" Mrs. Allen was practically yelling when Camille reached the dressing room.

"I don't know," Kara said frantically. "It was fine when I left it here last night. It was hanging right there."

Camille stepped into the small room, and all conversation ceased. She looked from Kara to Mrs. Allen and then her gaze dropped to Mrs. Allen's hands. Shards of pink, grimy and tattered, flowed down to the ground.

"My dress," Camille said in horror.

"I'm telling you I don't know how this could've happened," Kara said in all out panic. "Last night it was hanging right there, and when I got here today, it was laying on my desk...like this."

"Well, let's not panic." Mrs. Allen threw the dress to the floor in search of another idea. "Maybe we can put her in one of these other dresses."

"They're all taken," Kara said. "I only brought enough. I never thought we'd need more."

Mrs. Allen stared at the dresses angrily. "Well, then we'll just have to go get another one."

"In an hour?" Kara asked as Camille watched her fate being tugged between them.

"What happened?" Stephanie asked with concern as she stepped past Ariana, Tessa, and Misty who stood in the doorway.

"My dress got trashed." Camille turned and caught sight of the satisfaction on Ariana's face. Quickly Camille turned back to Mrs. Allen. "I've got my dress for the party in the car. Will that work?"

"Oh, yes, please, go get it," Mrs. Allen said.

"I'll be right back."

Camille raced to retrieve the keys from a very confused Jaylon. They didn't have time for explanations. They didn't have time for anything. In minutes she had the dress back in the dressing room. Feeling a surge of expectation fill the room, she pulled it out of the bag and held it up.

It had never been her dream dress. The fuchsia-purple was too gaudy, and the sleeves were off-set too far from the shoulders. It was obviously a knock-off that someone should've had the sense to bury long ago, but it was the best she had been able to come up with.

"It's...nice," Kara said as she examined the dress slowly. "But it's kind of...purple."

Mrs. Allen pushed her way back in the room and stopped with a look of horror on her face. "It's...nice."

"Umm," Stephanie said from the depths of everyone's denial that this dress could ever work. "I've got another idea."

"Let's hear it," Mrs. Allen said instantly.

"Anything," Kara said.

"I'll be right back." And before Camille could say anything, Stephanie was gone. Tension dropped over the room again as Camille quietly hung her dress on the rack.

"We'd better get started," Misty said to Camille with a sigh. "We're losing daylight."

Just then Stephanie ran back into the room, and Camille's world stopped when she saw the black bag. "Oh, Steph, no."

"Be quiet, I'm trying to make my grand entrance," Stephanie said. She hung the bag on the rack before slowly pulling the zipper down to reveal the soft sea foam satin. As she extracted the dress from its shell, gasps sounded throughout the room.

"Oh, it's gorgeous," Misty said in awe.

Camille smiled at Stephanie who stood there basking in the glow of her greatest creation. "She made it."

"No way!" Kara said as she reached out to gently touch the fabric.

"I was going to wear it for the cast party," Stephanie said, and then she looked at Camille, "but I'd be honored if you wore it for the play."

Tears welled up in Camille's eyes.

"Okay," Mrs. Allen said commandingly. "Everybody out. We've got a fitting to do."

Groans and moans erupted from every girl standing in the doorway.

"Don't grumble," Mrs. Allen said. "Get! Everyone should be in make-up already anyway."

The room emptied out, save for Camille and Stephanie.

"Call us when you get it on," Mrs. Allen said and quietly closed the door behind her.

"Let's get you in this thing," Stephanie said, but before she could so much as unzip the dress, Camille wrapped her arms around her friend.

"You're an angel. You know that?"

"Hey, right back at you, Babe," Steph said with a wink.

"How about I pick you up at seven?" Hawk asked as he stood stage right, swinging Lauren's hand.

"No," she said instantly. "Maybe we should just meet there. Dominique might freak if you show up at the house, and I don't want to cause any trouble."

Hawk nodded. "Okay. I'll see you there then."

"That's the music," Misty called into the backroom. "Come on, Camille."

From the depths of the dressing room, her hair wrapped in a French knot on her head, Camille stepped out, and the stole rested on her milk white shoulders as though she had stood in fittings for hours.

"How is it?" she asked Misty nervously.

"You look beautiful." Misty reached up and pulled Camille's glasses off and then nodded. "Perfect."

The dance music swelled around her as Camille closed her eyes to calm her racing heart. This was it. Two scenes and it would all be over. Slowly she turned, and guided only by the lights on the stage, she stepped through the curtain.

Measuring her steps to her appointed spot, she glided across the stage, hearing the audience's gasps even as she did.

"Lauren?" Hawk asked, suddenly appearing before her in a haze of blurriness.

"Hi," she said, forgetting for the moment that she was supposed to be projecting.

"You look... You look beautiful." It was the first time he'd stumbled over a line. "Would you like to dance?"

"I'd love to." She arched her wrists up to his neck as his hands went to her waist. They swayed three times, and then they were no longer acting. She laid her head onto his shoulder as they became one in the moment.

Lost in the safety of his arms, it was possible to believe that this was real. That he loved her, and she loved him, and that nothing could ever come between them again.

"Dominique, what's wrong?" Tessa asked from stage right, and instinctively Camille flinched.

"Ethan Drake is a jerk!"

"What happened?" Tessa asked as though she hadn't heard the next line a hundred thousand times.

"Mindy Tarlington. Uck!" Ariana glared at Tessa. "He was kissing Mindy Tarlington!"

"Oh, boy," Tessa said just as Nick ran onto the stage.

"Dominique, hey. What'd you run off for?"

She whirled on him. "I can't believe you can stand there and honestly ask me that question."

"What you saw...that wasn't me. I mean, yeah, that was me, but it wasn't what it looked like."

"Well, it looked like you were performing a tonsillectomy without the anesthetic!"

"But I didn't do anything. She slipped, and I was just helping her up."

"How? With mouth-to-mouth?"

Camille moved with Jaylon even as her blood froze in anticipation of the coming conflagration.

"That's it," Ariana screamed from across the stage. "I've had enough."

"Enough?" Nick asked incredulously.

"Yes, enough. Enough of this! Enough of you! You're an egotistical, selfish, conceited, arrogant..."

"Hey," Nick said calmly breaking into her litany. "Right back at you, Babe."

"That's it. Get out of my sight."

He stood for one more moment. Then he smiled at her, and Camille couldn't help but hear the satisfaction in his voice. "Gladly."

On his heel he turned, and Jill met him on his second step. He draped an arm around her, and together they made their exit.

"Don't let the door hit you on the way out," Ariana called angrily.

One beat and Tessa moved to Ariana. "Don't worry about him, Dominique. You can do better."

But Ariana was already staring past Tessa at Camille with a look she felt to her shoes. "If you'll excuse me, I've got someone to speak with."

"Dominique," Tessa said, but Ariana was already locked on her target.

"So, Hawk," Ariana said, stepping up to the swaying couple. "I can't believe you actually went through with this whole date thing."

Jaylon continued to dance. "Leave us alone, Dominique."

Ariana's voice dropped an octave. "Lauren, Lauren, Lauren. Little baby sister. I never thought you could be so gullible."

Camille's legs continued to move even as her soul cringed.

"Let me guess," Ariana said sweetly. "I bet he told you this was forever. I bet he told you it was fate."

Their dancing slowed as Camille's heart panged with the words. Still she kept dancing, fighting not to listen.

"Oh, yeah. He used the same lines on me. You know?"

Under her hands Camille felt Jaylon flinch.

"Dominique," he said in warning.

"What? Are you afraid of what will happen if she knows the truth? If she knows that all you wanted was to make me mad."

"Dominique." The name was sharp and hard.

"I told you," Ariana said to Camille with a knowing nod. "I told you it was all a big game to him. He was never interested in you—he just used you to get back at me."

Their dancing was now at a standstill.

Jaylon stepped between Ariana and Camille. "I said, 'Leave us alone.'"

"If you don't believe me, look at him," Ariana said to Camille as she looked at Jaylon with contempt. "Hawk never could lie with his eyes. You could always read him like an open book. Go on. Look at him, and ask him if I'm lying."

Camille gazed up at Jaylon's profile, and for half a second she thought he might not look down, but then his gaze turned to hers, and they were so close that the lack of glasses made no difference at all. He was there, in her line of sight, as clear as glass. "Is that true, Hawk?"

His gaze pleaded with her to understand, to not hate him, to not trash him over his stupidity. And inches apart, there was nowhere to run from the implications in his eyes.

"It is true," she said as her eyebrows narrowed. "You lied to me?" Her feet backed her away as his face blurred more from the tears than from anything. "I trusted you, and you lied to me!"

He reached out for her. "No, Lauren. Please..."

But she broke away from his grasp. "Don't touch me!" She looked from him to Ariana as blinding pain slashed through her. "Don't ever touch me again!"

And with that she ran off the stage.

"No, wait," Hawk called after her, but the stage sounds receded into the background the second Camille made it into the wings.

"Good job." Misty handed her glasses back. "Here let's mess up your hair a little."

One pin, two, and then wisps of hair cascaded down around her face. Misty tugged on the satin and ran a piece of wet cotton over Camille's bottom lashes to make her mascara run.

"Lauren, wait!" Jaylon called, racing off the stage into the wings as the curtains closed and stagehands rushed on to remove the dance props and set the lonely bench in the center of the stage.

Camille glanced at him over Misty's shoulder, but he, too, was busy coming undone.

"That's it," Kara called from the edge, and Misty stepped away from Camille. "Lights."

When the curtains slid open, pinpoints of light dotted the darkness, covering the back of the stage like stars. One beat, two, and then Kara swung her finger out to cue Camille.

Gathering all the pain she'd seen in his eyes when she ran away, Camille rushed in a disheveled mess onto the stage, looked back once, and collapsed into tears onto the bench.

"Lauren, please! Wait!" Jaylon called from off-stage, but she kept her face in her hands, sobbing as though her heart had just been broken in two.

Into the soft blue light, he stepped and caught sight of her crumpled on the bench. Like a magnet to its mate he walked across the stage, making hardly any sound as he did so, and every breath in the auditorium ceased. Softly he sat down next to her and put his hands on her shoulders. "I'm so sorry."

"How could you?" Camille asked through her tears as she wrenched herself out of his grasp and whirled around to face him. "I trusted you."

"I know." His eyes pleaded with her to give him another chance. "And I let you down. But you have to know, even though it started out as a lie, I really do care about you now."

"That's convenient." She stood and took a step away from him.

His gaze followed her across the stage. "It's not convenient. It's the way I feel."

"And what about the way I feel? Huh? I guess that's just a tiny little, insignificant detail."

She turned her back on him as she folded her arms across her chest. Still sniffling and crumpled, she went no further.

Slowly he stood and walked over to her. "You have to know I never meant to hurt you. I made a mistake. I admit that. But, please, don't throw us away because I was an idiot. Please, Lauren."

She considered his plea. "I just don't know how I can ever trust you again. You aren't who I thought you were."

He nodded as acceptance poured over his features. One centimeter at a time, he moved, turning away from her and walking all the way to the other side of the stage. Then just before he exited entirely, all motion stopped.

Across the stage, Camille felt him as he decided his next move. She felt the heat of his gaze burn through her back when he glanced back at her. She never lifted her head although she felt him turn and step back toward her. Closer and closer until he was barely an arm's length away.

"Hi," he said from behind her softly. "I'm Hawk. Hawk Fletcher."

With tear-stained eyes she looked over her shoulder at him.

"I don't believe we've met," he said, and when she didn't scream at him, he extended his hand in offering to hers.

She looked at his hand, and then she looked at him. Slowly her hand came up to meet his. It was like touching a live wire as the familiar electricity shot up her arm. "I'm Lauren. Lauren Waterford."

A smile overtook his face the moment her hand touched his.

Her eyes lowered teasingly although her words were deadly serious. "I guess you're going to say this must be fate."

He waited one beat, and then he smiled at her and shook his head. "Don't listen to the fates."

And with that, the curtains slid closed.

One second and then two, and then deafening applause erupted from the other side of the curtains. Jaylon looked at Camille, and in his eyes was pure excitement and joy. "You did it."

"No," she said softly. "We did it."

"Jaylon! Camille!" Kara called as the cast lined up on the stage.

Still holding hands and taking every opportunity to look at each other, they stepped to the center of the stage as the curtains slid open. Jaylon bowed as Camille curtsied, and as the applause continued, Jaylon swept his hand in front of him in deference to her. She bent again even as Jaylon let her hand go to applaud.

The curtains slid closed, and someone rushed onto the stage with a bouquet. For one second Camille wondered if they were the same ones from the night before, but she didn't have time to contemplate that question before the curtains slid open again.

Once more she curtsied, and then she looked at Jaylon, and simultaneously they stepped to the sides to applaud their supporting cast members who stepped forward as a group and took their bows. After a few more minutes the curtains slid closed again, and the applause from the outside died down even as the joy on stage rose.

"Camille," three girls said, rushing over to her. "You were great! That dress is so gorgeous! You look like a goddess. I thought I was going to cry when he walked back over to you. I bet you could've just died."

She never had to say a thing, she simply stood smiling and laughing at the excitement pouring out around her. In the next moment she caught sight of Lexie and stepped through the crowd to put her arms around her best friend.

"You are beautiful." Lexie hugged her friend. Then she pulled back to look at Camille. "And I don't just mean the dress."

One more quick hug, and Camille felt the small tug on the side of her dress. She looked down, and there, gazing up at her, stood Daria. Immediately Camille sat on her heels by her sister.

"You look like Cinderella," Daria said in fascination.

Camille straightened the little collar. "I feel like Cinderella." Like hugging her own little soul, she pulled Daria into her arms. "Thanks for coming, Dar."

When she stepped back, there were tears in the little girls' eyes. Camille wiped her own away and then stood and found herself face-to-face with her mother.

"You've grown up on me," her mother said, and there were tears behind the voice. She ran her hand over Camille's hair and cupped her daughter's face in her hands. "I'm so proud of you."

"Thanks." As Camille stepped into her mother's embrace, it was the first time she remembered ever feeling her acceptance. She pulled back and wiped more tears away. "Thanks for coming."

"I wouldn't have missed it."

At that moment Camille glanced past her mother, and shock gripped her. "Umm, will you excuse me?"

In a daze Camille crossed the stage, completely oblivious to the adulation raining down on her. Jaylon held his hand out for her, and she strode to his side.

"Somebody wants to talk to you," Jaylon said, standing solidly in front of a tall man as he pulled Camille to his side.

"Mr. Quinn," she said, and the shock was evident in her voice.

The silver-haired man with the strong face looked down at her. "I want to thank you, Camille. If it weren't for you, I would've missed this, and I would never have known how talented my son truly is. Thank you."

Camille smiled at him. "You're welcome. I'm glad you enjoyed it."

"Oh, I did, but I have to say I think you should consider following Jaylon to NYU. You two could take the theatre world by storm."

Camille laughed and shook her head. "I think I'll stick with calculus."

"Lucky calculus," Mr. Quinn said. He laughed and then looked back across the stage. "Well, I'd better let some of these other people talk to the stars. Congratulations. You were both wonderful."

"Thanks," they said simultaneously, and Jaylon's hand tightened on hers.

His father disappeared as the crowd collapsed onto them.

"You guys were great! That was so cool!"

"Huh-hmm!" Mrs. Allen said from the midst of the chaos. "May I just say I appreciate every minute you all put into this year's production. All that hard work paid off. Good job to everyone!"

A small cheer went up as Camille glanced across the stage and caught sight of Stephanie, the girl who had saved their entire evening.

"Come on," Camille said, pulling Jaylon through the noisy crowd. "Steph!"

With a whirl, Stephanie turned and Camille enveloped her into her arms. "Thank you so much! Man, I thought we were sunk."

"Thank *me*?" Stephanie asked excitedly. "Thank you! There was a production assistant from the Ashcroft here, and Mrs. Allen brought her up to meet me. I'm going to take my sketches and maybe get to design costumes for their Summer Production!"

"Oh, Steph!" Camille grabbed her friend and hugged her even tighter. "Congratulations!"

When Camille pulled back, she smiled at her friend. Then she looked down at the dress. "I'll just go get out of this so you can wear it for the party."

"No. Hey, it's yours," Stephanie said, shaking her head.

"Mine?"

"For tonight anyway. Maybe I'll get my chance to wear it someday— the prom or something. But for tonight, it's yours."

Camille's eyes fell closed as happiness flooded through her, and she hugged her friend once more. "Thank you."

At the cast party they made their entrance hand-in-hand, and Jaylon didn't even pause long enough for anyone to tell them congratulations. He'd had enough of that. All he wanted was to be with her, to be in her arms, and then to make this night last forever.

"Have I told you thank you?" she asked into his shirt as they began dancing, and he pulled back enough to look in her eyes.

"For what?"

"For not letting me quit. For not letting me give up on myself."

"I knew you could do it."

"Yeah, but I didn't."

He regarded her for a moment. "You know what I think?"

"What?"

"I think, you can do anything you set your mind to."

"Oh, yeah?" she asked as a glint flashed in her eyes. "Even this."

And without warning, she pulled his lips down to hers. Sweeter than fresh honey, her lips melted to his, and he held her—barely dancing except in his soul.

"Hey, hey, hey! Break it up, you two," Nick called as he and Lexie danced by.

Self-consciously their lips broke free, and they looked over at their friends with a laugh.

"You sure know how to ruin a good thing," Jaylon said playfully as Camille buried her head into his shoulder. "You know that?"

Nick pointed at Jaylon in warning. "Just keeping you honest."

"Well, that's good," Jaylon said as his heart erupted with joy, "because this is as honest as it gets."

And with that he stopped dancing, which immediately brought Camille's gaze to his. He closed his eyes, and when their lips met again, his soul had never been more honest.

<u>Epilogue</u>

"You up for a drive?" Jaylon asked over the phone lines three weeks later.

The night sky was already dotted with stars, but Camille didn't need even a second to think about it. "When can you be here?"

She walked next to him, huddling into him although the night was springtime warm.

"Did you hear about Ari?" Jaylon asked tentatively.

"No, what about her?" Camille asked in concern.

"Julliard turned her down." His words paused for two steps. "She's going to stay here and go to the community college next year."

Camille's heart fell for the death of a dream. "Couldn't she go to her second choice?"

"That was her second choice," he said just before they reached the tree.

"Oh," was all Camille could manage as she watched him sit down and then pull her down with him. Trusting him with her life, she leaned back into him and let the cares of the world evaporate around her.

"I've got some news," he said after a long pause.

"Oh, yeah? What's that?"

He shuffled underneath her and then held out a cream-colored envelope.

"NYU?" she asked, sitting up and taking the letter from him.

Off-handedly he shrugged. "I didn't want to open it until we were together."

Camille's heart laughed out loud as she looked from the letter to him. "I've got some news too."

"What's that?"

She reached into her pocket, pulled her own envelope out and held it up next to his for inspection.

"Princeton?"

"Yeah. I didn't want to open it until we were together." She waved the envelopes in front of him. "Which one do you want to open?"

He took a deep breath and then grabbed hers. "This one."

Excitement raced through her as she looked at him. "On three. Ready? One, two, three."

There was a flurry of torn paper, and then for a single moment they both sat, utterly motionless, reading.

"Dear Mr. Quinn," Camille read out loud as her excitement grew the further down she skimmed. "We are pleased to offer you admission into the New York University Theatre Arts Program for the Fall Semester..."

But he, too, was reading. "Dear Miss Wright: Based on your excellent academic record, Princeton would like to welcome you..."

For one split second they both stopped reading and looked at each other—stunned. In the next second the excitement broke between them, and they jumped into each other's arms.

"You made it!" they both yelled simultaneously. "You made it!"

"Oh my gosh, I don't believe it," she said, taking the letter he had been reading from his hand and skimming it quickly.

"You don't believe it? I don't believe it!" He took his own letter from her, and his gaze ran down it. "This is real. Oh my gosh! It's really happening. Ahh!"

She had never been so excited in her life, but then Camille looked at Jaylon, and the excitement drained away from her. "But you know what this means. Don't you?"

He stopped and looked at her, excitement still dancing in his eyes. "Yeah, it means our dreams are coming true."

"Well, yeah, but it also means..."

"What?" he asked, breaking her sentence in two. "That we aren't going to spend every future second together? That our paths aren't leading in the same direction? But we already knew that, didn't we?"

Her gaze pleaded with him to say that he wouldn't go, or that she shouldn't go or that their dreams weren't worth losing each other for; however, his gaze held nothing but calm acceptance. "But, J...."

Gently he wrapped his arms around her and tugged her back to him. "Nobody has forever, Camille. If you have one moment, you're luckier than most. We had one moment, and it was great. And who knows, maybe we'll have more. But you have to know I'll never regret the moment we had even if it doesn't last forever."

His grip tightened on her. "That's all we have anyway. This moment. You live this one, and you let the next one take care of itself. That's how it works." Tenderly he laid her into his arms. "And right now, this moment, the one thing I am sure of is that I love you, and for right now, for this moment, that's enough."

"It is?"

As he gazed down into her eyes, he nodded. "Yeah, it is." The stars glimmered above them as he pulled her to him. "I love you, Camille Wright. That's what I know. And that's all I need to know."

With his arms around her, Camille knew completely that wherever life took her from that point forward, she would remember this moment, being right here, under this tree, gazing up into his eyes right to the stars beyond. She would remember it because it was now woven into the fabric of her heart. "I love you, too, Jaylon Quinn."

One kiss and then she laid back into his chest. Gazing at the stars stretched out above them, they simply held each other and trusted that the future would take care of itself.

Coming 2008
Reunion

Jaylon and Camille fell in love in high school. But can that love survive miles, years, and dreams that have taken them where they never expected to go? **Reunion...** *Coming 2008*

~ The Dreams Series ~
by Staci Stallings

About the Author

A stay-at-home mom with a husband, three kids and a writing addiction on the side, Staci Stallings has four previous Inspirational Romance novels *The Long Way Home*, *Eternity*, *Cowboy*, and *Lucky* and one collection of short stories, *Reflections on Life* in print.

Stallings has also been a featured writer in the "From the Heart" series, in "Chicken Soup to Inspire the Body and Soul," "Soul Matters," "God's Way for Mothers" and in numerous inspirational, spiritual, and family-oriented ezines across the Internet. Although she lives in Amarillo, Texas, and her main career right now is her family, Staci touches many lives across the globe every week with her blog, "Homeward Bound" at http://stacistallings.blogspot.com/.

Read articles, e-books, and previews of Staci's books at:

http://www.stacistallings.com

You'll feel better for the experience!

Also Available from Staci Stallings

THE LONG WAY HOME

City-bred Jaxton Anderson thinks he knows more than the "country hicks" in Kansas ever will. However, one intriguing farm girl, Ami Martin, who is about as welcoming as the thorns on the rosebushes in her garden, and a grandfather Jaxton hasn't seen in years soon convince him that he doesn't have as much figured out as he thought. The harder Jaxton tries, the worse he makes things until a series of crises force him to reevaluate himself and the ideals he has always held to be important in this life.

Winner of the WordWeaving Award for Excellence

ETERNITY

Aaron Foster is in a bind. His fiancée has dumped him and moved out. Then to Aaron's horror, his new roommate, Drew Easton, unwittingly comes home with her. To save Drew's heart, Aaron conspires with his best friend, Harmony Jordan to break up Drew and Mandy by setting him up with Harmony. Unfortunately for Aaron, the plan works better than he could ever have imagined. Now with the tables turned, Aaron struggles with regret while remaining hopeful that somehow Harmony will come to want him as much as he now realizes he wants her.

REFLECTIONS ON LIFE

Fifty-two stories to encourage you on your journey. This book will compel you to look at each challenge in life as an opportunity to observe a miracle. It will encourage you to allow God to transform your ordinary life into an extraordinary one. It will remind you to reflect on your own life experiences and learn from them.

COWBOY

Cowboy is a grace-filled story about the power of giving everything to God and how a simple act of compassion can change lives forever. Emotional, soothing, and heart-wrenching, Cowboy is infused with the message that no matter who we are and no matter what life has thrown at us, we never have to walk alone.